SHERWOOD ANDERSON

MARCHING MEN

THE MAJOR FICTION OF SHERWOOD ANDERSON

Ray Lewis White, GENERAL EDITOR

A STORY TELLER'S STORY (1968)
TAR: A MIDWEST CHILDHOOD (1969)
MARCHING MEN (1972)

SHERWOOD ANDERSON

MARCHING MEN

A CRITICAL TEXT

Edited with an Introduction by
RAY LEWIS WHITE

CLEVELAND AND LONDON
THE PRESS OF CASE WESTERN RESERVE UNIVERSITY
1972

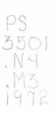
International Standard Book Number: 0–8295–216–5.
Library of Congress Catalogue Card Number: 73–149169

In honor of C. Hugh Holman

ACKNOWLEDGMENTS

THE Press of Case Western Reserve University and I are grateful for the goodwill and encouragement of the following individuals: Henry H. Adams, Illinois State University; Carlos Baker, Princeton University; James Ray Blackwelder, Western Illinois University; Richard R. Bone, Illinois State University; Matthew J. Bruccoli, University of South Carolina; Malcolm Cowley, The Viking Press; Lambert Davis, Director Emeritus, The University of North Carolina Press; Donald Gallup, The Beinecke Rare Book and Manuscript Library, Yale University; Milton Greenberg, Illinois State University.

C. Hugh Holman, University of North Carolina at Chapel Hill; Richard C. Johnson, The Newberry Library; Howard M. Jones, Harvard University; David Kesterson, North Texas State University; Matt. P. Lowman, The Newberry Library; Patricia Powell, Harold Ober Associates; H. B. Rouse, University of Arkansas; E. L. Rudolph, University of Arkansas; Mark Schorr, Harvard University; William A. Sutton, Ball State University; Lawrence Towner, Director, The Newberry Library; Ivan von Auw, Jr., Harold Ober Associates; James M. Wells, The Newberry Library.

We especially value the friendship of Mrs. Sherwood Anderson of Marion, Virginia, and the scholarly advice of Walter B. Rideout, University of Wisconsin.

Illinois State University   RLW

CONTENTS

INTRODUCTION

In his final memoirs, Sherwood Anderson wrote beautifully of the moment when, in a Chicago rooming house sometime in the winter of 1915–16, he created the first of his *Winesburg, Ohio* stories. Late in a winter afternoon, Anderson returned from his dreary work in an advertising office to sit at a desk in his small room that faced the Loop. There, his genius inspired to storytelling, he wrote "a story of another human, quite outside myself, truly told."

The story was one called "Hands." It was about a poor little man beaten, pounded, frightened by the world in which he lived into something oddly beautiful.

The story was written that night in one sitting. No word of it ever changed. I wrote the story and got up. I walked up and down in that little narrow room. Tears flowed from my eyes.

"It is solid," I said to myself. "It is like a rock. It is there. It is put down."

. . .

I am quite sure that on that night, when it happened in that room, when for the first time I dared whisper to myself, perhaps sobbing, that I had found it, my vocation, I knelt in the darkness and muttered words of gratitude to God.[1]

These ecstatic words do not exaggerate Sherwood Anderson's memory of an accomplishment of pure genius, for Anderson had been trying over at least a decade to use words tellingly, to recreate his own state of mind fictionally, and to perfect in prose stories of the tender, bittersweet lives surrounding him. *Marching Men*, the strangest of Sherwood Anderson's eight published novels, is a fascinating document from the author's

1. *Sherwood Anderson's Memoirs: A Critical Edition*, ed. Ray Lewis White (Chapel Hill: University of North Carolina Press, 1969), pp. 352–53.

years of apprenticeship to the craft of fiction, years of emo-
tional chaos and artistic striving that eventually led to the
masterwork of *Winesburg, Ohio*.

I.

The great legend about Sherwood Anderson remains his re-
jection of a career in business for a life devoted to literature.
After non-combat service in the Spanish-American War, Anderson pursued the American dream of success by attending
Wittenberg Academy for a high school education in 1899–1900,
after which he worked as an ambitious and clever advertising
copywriter in Chicago. In 1904 the young businessman continued taking the proper steps toward success: he married
Cornelia Lane, daughter of a modestly rich Toledo, Ohio,
manufacturer. In 1906 the Andersons moved to Cleveland,
where Sherwood managed a mail-order business. After a move
in 1907 to Elyria, Ohio, after the births of three children, and
after increasing tension over business difficulties, Anderson
walked away from his paint-distribution office, away from his
unsatisfactory family life, and wandered four days in a state
of amnesia.

Later Anderson was to explain this moment of total nervous
exhaustion, which came in November, 1912, as a crafty move
to escape business responsibilities; but the reality of an invol-
untary psychological rebellion is firmly established.[2]

Early in 1913, Anderson moved alone to Chicago and became involved with the literary renaissance ultimately crowned
by *Winesburg, Ohio* in 1919. Sherwood Anderson was thirty-
six when he left Ohio—a usually unpromising age at which
to embrace the literary life—but in 1913 he was not an inex-
perienced writer: in progression with his growing disillusion-
ment as a businessman, he was devoting more and more of
his energies to writing fiction—both as escape from and ther-
apy for the serious, unsolved problems of his middle years.

2. William Alfred Sutton, *Exit to Elsinore* (Muncie, Ind.: Ball State
University, 1967), fully discusses the breakdown and escape.

In the years from 1906 to 1913, Anderson suffered a growing psychological dysfunction as his life in business became far less important than his life with books: ". . . a curious sickness came. I had always been a passionate reader. It may be that I began to get, through my reading of the words of great men, a new conception of what a man's life might be." [3] The unhappy businessman tried filling his life with more office work, golfing, traveling, social and literary club meetings, and even physical dissipation. When such exterior interests provided no fulfillment, Anderson tried turning inward for resolution: he claimed as private an attic room in his house, ignored his family's demands for attention and affection, and moved from absorption in reading to release through writing—an event strikingly similar to his later creation of *Winesburg, Ohio:*

. . . one night I began to write. I wrote a little tale of something seen, or felt, something remembered out of my own experience of people.

The writing did something to me. Well, no doubt the tale I wrote that night was badly told. I can't remember.

What I do remember was a new feeling that came. In the act of writing the little tale about some other being I had for the time escaped from myself, had found something that gave me a new sense of reality, something I could not get from drinking, from going about with loose women.

. . .

I kept writing little tales of people. I put them through experiences I had myself been through and suddenly there came a new revelation.

It was this—that it is only by thinking hard of others that you can find out anything of self.[4]

Writing thus secretly, Anderson later claimed, he created at least five long books—four novels and a destroyed work on socialism. As two of the novel manuscripts—"Mary Cochran"

3. *Sherwood Anderson's Memoirs*, ed. White, p. 18.
4. *Sherwood Anderson's Memoirs*, ed. White, pp. 19–20.

and "Talbot Whittingham"—exist now only as fragments, and as no manuscript is known to survive for Anderson's first published novel, *Windy McPherson's Son* (1916), the genesis of the manuscript of *Marching Men* (which could have been written before *Windy McPherson's Son*) must exemplify Sherwood Anderson's early apprenticeship to creative writing.

Anderson was wrong in remembering his Ohio writing as done in secret, for even his business associates in Elyria knew of and worried about the businessman's literary penchant. Anderson's secretary in Elyria remembered his non-business activities on company time: "I typed his first two books—and corrected his spelling. . . . I typed up the manuscripts and got them ready for mailing. He'd send the manuscripts right from the office." [5] The town newspaper editor recalled: "He was busy with his writing during his stay in Elyria—working nights on his books and other expressions of his ideas concerning the lives of the common people with whom he mingled. . . . I had the privilege of reading his 'Marching Men' while it was in manuscript." [6]

One can assume that Anderson's secretary accurately remembered typing a complete copy of *Marching Men,* probably in 1911 or 1912. But the history of the *Marching Men* text does not end then, for Anderson took with him to Chicago in 1913 the manuscripts of the four Elyria novels. To chronicle the further development of the text of *Marching Men,* one must consult the writing of Harry Hansen, one of Anderson's literary friends in Chicago.

In *Midwest Portraits,* Hansen documents Sherwood Anderson's welcome into gatherings of the Chicago Renaissance group of literary and artistic bohemians:

Anderson wore his hair long and shaggy; his tie was often askew, his trousers bagged at the knees, he wore big, heavy shoes and his hands were large and clumsy; his face had in it powerful masses, rather than lines, but when he read it was with a voice that con-

5. Sutton, pp. 16–17.
6. Sutton, p. 17.

veyed gentleness and a great depth of sympathetic feeling. Often he read, with candles placed near him and half a dozen friends sitting back against the wall on the couch or grouped in various attitudes on the floor, parts of "Windy McPherson's Son" and "Marching Men," for it turned out that he had placed many thoughts on paper during the years when he was still living an orderly existence with little expectation that he was destined to be included among the influential writers of his generation.[7]

Through the advocacy of Floyd Dell and—indirectly—Theodore Dreiser, Anderson in 1916 signed a contract to publish three books with the New York office of John Lane, the British publisher. Lane published *Windy McPherson's Son* in 1916; then, according to Jefferson Jones, New York manager for the Lane company, " 'Marching Men' was published in the autumn [September] of 1917, in a first edition of 2,500 copies. . . . The London office of John Lane refused to issue an English edition. 'Marching Men' received scant attention. . . . The total sales reached 1,000 copies." [8]

Perhaps the advertising honesty of the John Lane Company kept sales low for *Marching Men,* for the book jacket proclaimed: "Not a war novel." Although *Marching Men* did have nothing to do with the World War in progress in 1917, the work was partly inspired by Anderson's experiences in the Spanish-American War. Having volunteered for adventure in 1898, Anderson trained in the South and served in Cuba after the fighting ended. A decade later Anderson's memory of military training generated the idea of the Marching Men:

With the permission of one of our lieutenants I had dropped out of the ranks. I had a stone in my shoe. . . .
"Duck into the woods. Get out of sight," he said and I ducked.

---

7. (New York: Harcourt, Brace [1923]), p. 112.
8. Hansen, pp. 121–22. The history of the text of *Marching Men* has been confused by an entry in the standard bibliography by Sheehy and Lohf (Los Gatos, Calif.: Talisman Press, 1960), p. 19. Item 5 lists a reprint in 1921 by the house of B. W. Huebsch in 264 pages, the 1917 printing by Lane having been in 314 pages. I have examined a copy of the 1921 reprint and find no alteration in its 314 pages.

I dare say he did not want other officers to see one of his men leave the ranks.

I was in the wood. I went in far enough not to be seen. I took the stone out of my shoe. I sat down under a tree.

This strange feeling had taken possession of me. I was there, an individual, a young man, half boy, sitting on the ground under a tree, but I was at the same time something else.

We had been marching for hours, I was not weary. It seemed to me, that day, that into my legs had come the strength of the legs of thirty thousand men.

I had become a giant.

I was, in myself, something huge, terrible and at the same time noble. I remember that I sat, for a long time, while the army passed, opening and closing my eyes.

Tears were running down my cheeks.

"I am myself and I am something else too," I whispered to myself.

I remember that later, when I got back to camp, I did not want to speak to others. I went into my tent and threw myself down on my cot. I did not want to eat. I was a man in love. I was in love with the thought of the possibilities of myself combined with others.[9]

Sherwood Anderson recalled having another experience which reinforced for him the theme of *Marching Men,* an episode from his days in Chicago after 1900:

It was a long time later. It was after the war. I was in Chicago and stood on the station of the elevated railroad. It was evening and people were pouring out of offices and stores. They came by thousands out of side streets and into the broad city street of faces. They were a broken mob. They did not keep step. There were thousands of individuals, lost like myself. As individuals they had no strength, no courage.[10]

Besides these two memories, Anderson used in *Marching Men* considerable other autobiographical material—mainly fictionalized adventures from his years in Chicago before the outbreak of the Spanish-American War and as an advertising solicitor and then copywriter there from 1900 to 1906. Among these

9. *Sherwood Anderson's Memoirs,* ed. White, pp. 185–86.
10. *Sherwood Anderson's Memoirs,* ed. White, p. 186.

experiences were his working in a warehouse, being robbed, going to night school, courting a rich girl, writing advertising copy, and loving a working girl. (All such autobiographical episodes—and others from Anderson's youth and his business years in Ohio—are documented as they occur in this text of *Marching Men.*)

II.

The manuscript of *Marching Men,* owned now by The New-berry Library of Chicago, is the only complete manuscript extant from Sherwood Anderson's days of apprenticeship to writing while operating his Ohio businesses from 1906 to 1913. Study of this manuscript corroborates generally the facts known about Anderson's composition of the novel.

The *Marching Men* manuscript consists of three hundred ninety-five pages of mixed typescript and holograph copy. There are two states of typewriter copy. The first, very neat typing from an elite-style machine, with usually standard spelling and punctuation, would seem to be the remnants of the earliest complete typescript of the novel, made by Anderson's secretary in Elyria, Ohio, before 1913. All of Book I and many passages thereafter in the manuscript of *Marching Men* exist in this elite-style copy.

However, not one page of the fragments from this earliest typescript of the novel remains unrevised. When Anderson retained complete pages of the early typescript in original sequence, as in Book I, he either wrote in (using both pencil and ink) copious revisions or corrections of transcription errors, or he pasted to the original transcript pages sheets of blank paper to provide additional space for revision and addition.

The second state of typewritten copy in the *Marching Men* manuscript—many passages of poorly typed, pica-style copy—is identical in its unprofessional format and rough mechanics to the thousands of other extant samples of Sherwood Anderson's own typing. Over one half of the *Marching Men* manuscript consists of both of these type styles—the professional copy and the author's own rough copy.

One can reconstruct with considerable assurance the author's preparation of the *Marching Men* manuscript for publication. Finding himself with a complete novel in the form copied by his secretary in Ohio before 1913, Anderson read parts of the typescript to friends in Chicago after 1913 or lent his typescript to them to read. Having received comment from these advisors or having independently decided on revision, Anderson wrote upon and around many pages of manuscript in original sequence. Other original pages he cut into passages to be discarded (now lost) or retained for revision. The retained original passages Anderson incorporated by pasting them onto sheets of new holograph copy. Often, however, the writer prepared revised copy or new material on his pica-style typewriter; these he incorporated by pasting them onto his new pages of holograph + original typescript. Sometimes it was necessary for Anderson to write an entirely new chapter. The following descriptions of the first chapters of the various books of the *Marching Men* manuscript will illustrate the generally mixed state of the manuscript:

Book I, Chapter I
Twelve pages, [1] unnumbered, 2–12 numbers typed; typescript with holograph revision in pencil and ink; on unruled white paper, 8½" × 11"; rough brown paper for additions pasted to right edges of pages 1, 3, 4, 9.

Book II, Chapter I
Nine pages, numbered 37–45 in pencil by author; typescript with holograph revision in pencil; on unruled white paper 8½" × 11"; rough brown paper for additions pasted to right edges of pages 37, 38, 39, 40, 42.

Book III, Chapter I
Six pages, numbered 1–6 in pencil by author; typescript inserts with holograph revision in pencil; on ruled brown paper, 8" × 11".

Book IV, Chapter I

Fifteen pages, numbered 1–3, 5–16 in pencil by author; author's draft in ink and pencil with revision and typescript inserts; on unruled brown paper, 9″ × 12″.

Book V, Chapter I

Nineteen pages, numbered 1–19 in pencil by author; author's draft in pencil with revision and typescript inserts, on unruled brown paper, 9″ × 12″.

Book VI, Chapter I

Eighteen pages, numbered 1–18 in pencil by author; author's draft in pencil with revision and typescript inserts; on unruled brown paper, 9″ × 12″.

Book VII, Chapter I

Sixteen pages, numbered 1–16 in pencil by author; author's draft in pencil with revision and typescript inserts; on unruled brown paper, 9″ × 12″.

Before having his new version of *Marching Men*—by now an already confusing patchwork of old and new typescript and holograph copy—retyped as a fair copy for printing, Sherwood Anderson allowed a further complication: some reader, not now identified, made several dozen changes in pencil in the manuscript. The alterations—an attempt to standardize Anderson's grammar, diction, and punctuation—were seldom rejected by the author, who accepted most of them into the new fair copy of his novel. The following examples demonstrate typical changes made by this unknown reader:

AUTHOR'S FORM	FOREIGN HAND
Standing before the counter	As he stood before the counter
he turned into the shop slamming the door	he turned into the shop and slammed the door
a fat man selling liquor	a fat man who sold liquor
He locked the door, putting the key	He locked it, and put the key

AUTHOR'S FORM	FOREIGN HAND
his voice rang resounding	his voice resounded
beginning to have also con- fidence in	beginning to have confidence also in
who hated McGregor	who hated him
young fellows	young men
waitresses who carries in the dinner	waitresses who serve them
the barber and the little mil- liner	the barber and a third one, frail and bloodless
placard on the bottle	label on the bottle
carefully guarded hord	carefully guarded hoard
Made bold by her own bold- ness	Made bold by her own timid- ity
planning an attack on her	planning a campaign against her
perhaps a woman	perhaps the yellow haired girl
file of boys in embarrassed silence	file of boys following in em- barrassed silence
he knew definitely	he was coming to know more and more definitely
an unthought of mystery	a meaningless mystery
that only look expensive	that merely look expensive
She put her hand	She put a trembling hand
wrote it down	wrote that music down

The clearest evidence of the whole complexity of the *Marching Men* manuscript would be a stylized "genetic" text of the
work. The changes shown in the following sample genetic
transcription of the first and last pages of the novel manuscript
(not including the forms in the 1917 printed novel) are not
at all atypical of the pervasive revisions toward the fair copy:

SAMPLE GENETIC TEXT

Key to Transcription

[revision begins
]   revision ends

SAMPLE GENETIC TEXT

Key to Transcription

+   addition
—   deletion
±   addition then deletion
*   *sic*
Italic foreign hand
/   manuscript line ends

[—It was Uncle Charlie Wheeler who gave a name to
Cracked McGregor's / tall son and fixed upon him the attention
of Coal Creek. *Standing* [±*As he stood* [—be— / fore the
counter in Nance McGregor's bake shop, Uncle Charlie [+Un-
cle Charlie Wheeler stamped on the steps before Nance
McGregors* bake shop on the Main Street of the town of Coal
Creek* Pennsylvania* and then went quickly inside. Something pleased Uncle Charlie and as he stood before the counter
in the shop he] laughed / and whistled softly. [—Turning to
[+With a] wink at the Reverend Minot Weeks who / stood
by the door leading to the street, he tapped with his knuckles
/ [—up]on the showcase. /

"It has," he said, waving attention to the boy, who was making a mess / [—at [+of] the effort to arrange Uncle 'Charlie's*
loaf into a neat package, "a / pretty name, a sweet name. They
call it Norman—Norman McGregor." /

Uncle Charlie laughed heartily and [+again] stamped with
his feet upon the floor. / Putting his finger to his forehead as
though in deep thought, he turned / to the minister. [+"I am
going to change all that*" he said. "Norman indeed! I shall
give him a name that [±shall [+will stick. Norman!] "Too soft
[— ! [+, [—T[+t]oo soft and delicate for Coal Creek, eh?" /
[—he said.] "It [—should [+shall] be christened. You and I
will be Adam and Eve in / the garden naming things. We'll
call it 'Beaut'* [—Beaut [+Our Beautiful One. Beaut] Mc-
Gregor." /

The Reverend Minot Weeks also laughed. He thrust four
fingers of each / hand into the pockets of his trousers, letting
the extended thumbs lie / along the swelling waist line. From
the front the thumbs looked like two / tiny boats on the horizon

of a troubled sea. They bobbed and jumped about / on the rolling, shaking paunch, appearing and disappearing as laughter shook / [—him. [+the minister.] /

The Reverend Minot Weeks went out at the door ahead of Uncle Charlie still / laughing. One guessed that he would go along the street from store to / store telling the tale [+of the christening] and laughing again. The tall boy could imagine the / details of the story. /

As for David he put / his hand on the sill of the / window and for just a / moment his body trembled / as with age and weariness. / "I wonder*" he muttered. "If / I had youth. Perhaps McGregor / knew he would fail and yet had / the courage of failure. I wonder if / both Margaret and myself lack the greater / courage, if that evening long ago / when I walked under the trees I / made a mistake. What if after / all [—this [+this] McGregor [—say [±saw [—both / roads and, then [+and his woman knew both roads.* What if they,] after looking deliberately / along the road toward beauty and / success, [—chose [+went], without regret, / [+along] the road to [—inevitable] failure."* /

The final stage in the development of the *Marching Men* manuscript is a fairly large group of changes made either by Sherwood Anderson in the lost fair copy of his novel or in his lost galley and page proofs, or by some editor for the John Lane Company at some point in the same materials. Adoption of the peculiarly British forms of the Lane company is obviously an editor's work; further changes toward standardizing Anderson's grammar, punctuation, diction, and general style are probably attributable to the Lane company. The following lists are representative of these revisions from penultimate manuscript to printed book:

MANUSCRIPT	1917 PRINTING
Uncle Charlie still laughing	Uncle Charlie, still laughing
as, with the loaf of bread under his arm, he	as with the loaf of bread under his arm he
so many and varied climates	so many varied climates

MANUSCRIPT	1917 PRINTING
colors	colours
one of our American cities	one of our cities
when men should march	when men would march
galvanized	galvanised
a "bit off his head."	"a bit off his head."
someone	some one
an eager, expectant air	an eager expectant air
scuffling	shuffling
broad and green	green and broad
wished to again hear	wished to hear
trouser pockets	trousers pockets
their narrow life	their narrow lives
a white thing shining	a white shining thing
McGregor arose and went	McGregor rose and went
troup of women dancers	troupe of women-dancers
defense	defence
all of that old misunderstood human sex love	all of the old perplexing human love
To his arm clung Edith.	Edith clung to his arm.
stone coping	stone curbing
impetus given to solidarity in the ranks of labor	impetus given to solidity in the ranks of labor
mechanic or a locomotive engineer	mechanic of a locomotive engineer
woman	women
A kind of shock	A shock
Poor and humble I should go	Poor and humble, I would go
the miners' houses	the miner's houses
social advance	social advancement
young fellows	young men
she was contented	she was content
her dresser	her desk
millions of other workers	millions of others workers
tussling	tusseling
after a while	after awhile
the practise of	the practice of
plow	plough

III.

The rationale for preparing critical texts of Sherwood Anderson's works is not simple. It is best understood in its contrast with the recent but already "classical" theory of bibliographical editing closely identified with the work of Fredson Bowers. Stated in very much simplified terms, the goal of such editing is the preparation of a critical text to be read as a "clean" text not modernized in either "accidentals" (spelling, capitalization, punctuation) or "substantives" (diction, words themselves, "meaning").[11] The copy-text for such an edition is the printed form of the work (normally the first printing) demonstrably closest to the author's final manuscript or typescript, assuming that the actual manuscript or typescript is not extant. Subsequent revisions definitely by the author are incorporated into the copy-text. All emendations in the copy-text are listed. The final result is a text that recovers the author's full intentions.

This procedure, admirably suited to the works of many authors, is not the most desirable approach to Sherwood Anderson's work, and the reason springs from Anderson's own attitude toward his writing. While he was an Ohio businessman writing fiction for self-therapy, Anderson fully realized his lack of formal education, his one-year high school curriculum at Wittenberg Academy having been patently "make-up" work. Knowing training in the accidentals of writing as well as in the rhetorical aspects of composition to be reputedly necessary for literary success, Anderson learned to apologize for his untutored prose. He learned to explain his irregular spelling, his often colloquial diction, and his sometimes ungrammatical if not illogical sentence construction as the expected product of a simple Midwestern "natural."

Having rationalized his composition difficulties, Sherwood Anderson continued all his life entrusting to his publishers

11. Bowers' theory is concisely expressed in "The Text of the Virginia Edition," in *The Works of Stephen Crane: I. Bowery Tales*, ed. Fredson Bowers (Charlottesville: University Press of Virginia, 1969), pp. xi–xxix.

final preparation of his writing, for to Anderson anyone formally educated obviously knew more about rhetoric and rules than he. The results are sad. Confronted with apparently formless sentences and wayward accidentals, professional editors rewrote, corrected, and standardized Anderson's writing. One would not exaggerate in speculating that almost no essay or book by Anderson was published as the author intended in his manuscripts. For this reason, the printed versions of Anderson's novels are not the most sound bases for critical editions. Instead, in distinction to Professor Bowers' theory of copy-text, one must return for authoritative readings of both accidentals and substantives to Anderson's manuscripts. Then the following procedures must be employed:

I. *Accidentals* The aim in editing Sherwood Anderson texts is not to provide a literal transcription of his manuscripts, for offering such a transcription would evade serious editorial responsibilities. Anderson's considering himself uneducated in the accidentals of composition does not belie his knowing how to present his material effectively—that is, as he wanted it read. When Anderson wrote *Marching Men* he was imitating whatever conventional novels he had read; his later, original style allowed him greater freedom in form and content. Thus, the *Marching Men* manuscript reveals Anderson's serious attempt to standardize his accidental forms. Further, his secretary in Ohio clearly corrected his punctuation as well as his spelling. The discarded original holograph passages of *Marching Men* being lost, one must accept the secretary's presumed corrections of Anderson's accidentals, incorporating into a critical text the author's paragraphing, punctuation, diction, word order, sentence divisions, and pet spellings. The extant holograph passages are incorporated without question.

However, one must in editing Anderson understand the need to supply a missing comma for a dependent clause or a phrase lacking one comma of a pair; one must leave Anderson his pet spellings (grey, theatre, practise) while standardizing his misspellings (from Book VII, Chapter II: occassional, fastinated, seperate, triumpth, hoards, significants, hidious, luducrous, disintrigate, disipline, wellfare, miniture, imagaination); one must decide that frequently occurring forms should coincide (hyphens in red-haired, black-bearded, capitals on Marching Men, Hell, West Side, Old Labor, Polish, State Street); and one must remove from the 1917 printed text the British house-forms of the Lane company, the emendations of the foreign hand, and editorial tampering with Anderson's word order and participials, awkward as they may originally be. The result is a text not identical to either a manuscript or a printed book, but rather a text faithful to Sherwood Anderson as understood by an experienced, sympathetic editor.

II. *Substantives* When the editor comes to substantive changes from the *Marching Men* manuscript to the printed text, he faces a more difficult task than in handling accidentals. If Anderson's fair copy, galley proofs, and page proofs were extant, one could presumably know whether variant substantives were the author's or the publisher's or the printer's work. The editor of *Marching Men* is not so fortunate, having only the penultimate manuscript and the printed text of the novel. Thus it would not be acceptable to reject substantive manuscript readings in favor of the printed forms, which *could* be the author's revisions. Nor can one fairly incorporate the printed forms and totally neglect the manuscript readings, which *might* be what Anderson intended. The following compromise procedure must be employed:

(1) Whenever substantives occur in the manuscript but not in the printed version, if the omitted forms smoothly fit into context, they are reprinted enclosed by brackets [ ]. If apparent revision makes such inclusion difficult, the original form is listed in the appended table of variants. When the table of variants includes a reading for which no signal at all occurs in the text, it is a reading that presumably was rejected by Anderson during revision of the typescript.

(2) Whenever forms appear in the book but not in the manuscript, such forms (unless accidental, as treated above) are incorporated into this text within brackets but marked with asterisks [*]. The appended table of variants lists manuscript

forms replaced by these revisions and thus impossible to include. Whenever a portion of the text is contained within [*] and no variant is given in the appended table, the bracketed reading represents pure addition in the published text of *Marching Men,* for which there is no parallel in the typescript.

The resulting text of *Marching Men* is thus a cautious reconstruction of Sherwood Anderson's valid manuscript readings along with clearly marked incorporation of major substantives from the printed version of the novel.

This text of *Marching Men* and a selection of Sherwood Anderson's earliest published essays and attempts at short fiction (from 1902 into 1914), reprinted below for the first time, make available documents of considerable importance to the reader interested in the transformation of a middle-aged Ohio businessman into the author of *Winesburg, Ohio.*

SHERWOOD ANDERSON

MARCHING MEN

MARCHING MEN

To American Workingmen

BOOK I

CHAPTER I

UNCLE Charlie Wheeler stamped on the steps before Nance McGregor's bake shop on the Main Street of the town of Coal Creek Pennsylvania and then went quickly inside. Something pleased [*him] and as he stood before the counter in the shop he laughed and whistled softly. With a wink at the Reverend Minot Weeks who stood by the door leading to the street, he tapped with his knuckles on the showcase.

"It has," he said, waving attention to the boy, who was making a mess of the effort to arrange Uncle Charlie's loaf into a neat package, "a pretty name[, a sweet name]. They call it Norman—Norman McGregor."

Uncle Charlie laughed heartily and again stamped [with his feet] upon the floor. Putting his finger to his forehead [*to suggest] deep thought, he turned to the minister. "I am going to change all that," he said. "Norman indeed! I shall give him a name that will stick. Norman! Too soft, too soft and delicate for Coal Creek, eh? It shall be [*re]christened. You and I will be Adam and Eve in the garden naming things. We'll call it 'Beaut.' Our Beautiful One. Beaut McGregor."

The Reverend Minot Weeks also laughed. He thrust four fingers of each hand into the pockets of his trousers, letting the extended thumbs lie along the swelling waist line. From the front the thumbs looked like two tiny boats on the horizon of a troubled sea. They bobbed and jumped about on the rolling, shaking paunch, appearing and disappearing as laughter shook [*him].

The Reverend Minot Weeks went out at the door ahead of Uncle Charlie still laughing. One [*fancied] that he would go along the street from store to store telling the tale of the christening and laughing again. The tall boy could imagine the details of the story.

It was an ill day for births in Coal Creek, even for the birth of one of Uncle Charlie's inspirations. Snow lay piled

along the sidewalks and in the gutters of Main Street, black
snow, sordid with the gathered grime of human endeavor that
went on day and night in the bowels of the hills. Through the
soiled snow walked miners, stumbling along silently and with
blackened faces. In their bare hands they carried dinner
pails.[1]

The McGregor boy, tall and awkward, and with a towering
nose, great hippopotamus-like mouth and fiery red hair,
followed Uncle Charlie, Republican politician, postmaster and
village wit, to the door and looked after him as, with the loaf
of bread under his arm, he hurried along the street. Behind
the politician went the minister still enjoying the scene in
the bakery. [*He] was preening himself on his nearness to
[the] life of the mining town. "Did not Christ himself laugh,
eat and drink with publicans and sinners?" he thought, as he
waddled through the snow.

The eyes of the McGregor boy, as they followed the two
departing figures and later as he stood in the door of the bake
shop watching the struggling miners, glistened with hatred. It
was the quality of intense hatred for his fellows in the black
hole between the Pennsylvania hills that marked the boy and
made him stand forth among his fellows.

In a country of so many [and] varied climates and occu-
pations as America, it is absurd to talk of an American type.
The country is like a vast, disorganized, undisciplined army,
leaderless, uninspired, going in route-step along the road, to
they know not what end. In the prairie towns of the West and
the river towns of the South from which have come so many
of our writing men, the citizens swagger through life. Drunken
old reprobates lie in the shade by the river's edge or wander
through the streets of a corn shipping village of a Saturday

1. Sherwood Anderson's description of Coal Creek is so unspecific
that it is unlikely the writer modeled his fictional town on any real
area; but for a possible influence on the imaginary Coal Creek see Anderson's description of his hobo trip about 1895 to Erie, Pennsylvania,
in Sherwood Anderson's Memoirs: A Critical Edition, ed. Ray Lewis
White (Chapel Hill: University of North Carolina Press, 1969), pp.
129–34.

evening with [a] grin on their faces.[2] Some touch of nature, a sweet undercurrent of life stays alive in them and is handed down to those who write of them, and the most worthless man that walks the streets of an Ohio or Iowa town may be the father of an epigram that colors all the life of the men about him. In a mining town or deep in the entrails of one of our [American] cities life is different. There the disorder and aimlessness of our American lives becomes a crime for which men pay heavily. Losing step with one another, men lose also a sense of their own individuality so that a thousand of them may be driven in a disorderly mass in at the door of a Chicago factory morning after morning, and year after year, with never an epigram from the lips of one of them.

In Coal Creek when men got drunk they staggered in silence through the street. Did one of them, in a moment of stupid animal sportiveness, execute a clumsy dance upon the barroom floor, his fellow laborers looked at him dumbly, or turning away left him to finish without witnesses his clumsy hilarity.

Standing in the doorway and looking up and down the bleak village street, some dim realization of the disorganized ineffectiveness of life as he knew it came into the mind of the McGregor boy. It seemed to him right and natural that he should hate men. With a sneer on his lips, he thought of Barney Butterlips, the town socialist, who was forever talking of a day coming when men should march shoulder to shoulder and life in Coal Creek, life everywhere, should cease being aimless and become definite and full of meaning.[3]

"They will never do [*that] and who wants them to,"

2. Anderson's major use of the southern river town occurs in his third novel, *Poor White* (New York: B. W. Huebsch, 1920) and in his only best-selling novel, *Dark Laughter* (New York: Boni and Liveright, 1925). See Robert L. Crist, "Sherwood Anderson's *Dark Laughter:* Sources, Composition and Reputation" (Ph.D. diss., University of Chicago, 1966).

3. The author's only period of intense political interest came in the 1930's, when he briefly favored socialism. For discussion of Anderson's political views, see James Schevill, *Sherwood Anderson: His Life and Work* (Denver: University of Denver Press, 1951), pp. 275–94; and G. Bert Carlson, Jr., "Sherwood Anderson's Political Mind: The Activist Years" (Ph.D. diss., University of Maryland, 1966).

mused the McGregor boy. A blast of wind bearing snow beat upon him and he turned into the shop slamming the door behind him. Another thought stirred in his head and brought a flush to his cheeks. He turned and stood in the silence of the empty shop shaking with emotion[s]. "If I could form the men of this place into an army I should lead them to the mouth of the old Shumway cut and push them in," he threatened, shaking his fist toward the door. "I should stand aside and see the whole town struggle and drown in the black water as untouched as though I watched the drowning of a litter of dirty little kittens."

The next morning when Beaut McGregor pushed his baker's cart along the street and began climbing the hill toward the miners' cottages, he went, not as Norman McGregor the town baker boy, only product of the loins of Cracked McGregor of Coal Creek, but as a personage; a being, the object of an art. [*The name given him by Uncle Charlie Wheeler had made him] a marked man. [*He was as] the hero of a popular romance, galvanized into life and striding in the flesh before the people. Men looked at him with new interest, inventorying anew the huge mouth and nose and the flaming hair. The bartender, sweeping the snow from before the door of the saloon, shouted at him. "Hey, Norman!" he called, "Sweet Norman! Norman is [such a pretty name,] too pretty [*a name]. Beaut is the name for you! Oh, you Beaut."

The tall boy pushed the cart silently along the street. Again he hated Coal Creek. He hated the bakery and the bakery cart. With a burning, satisfying hate he hated Uncle Charlie Wheeler and the Reverend Minot Weeks. "Fat old fools," he muttered, shaking the snow off his hat and pausing to breathe in the struggle up the hill. He had something new to hate. He hated his own name. It did sound ridiculous. He had thought before that there was something fancy and pretentious about it. It didn't fit a bakery cart boy. He wished it might have been plain John or Jim or Fred. A quiver of irritation at his mother passed through him. "She might have used more sense," he muttered.

And then the thought came to him that his father might have chosen the name.[4] That checked his flight toward universal hatred and he began pushing the cart forward again, a more genial current of thought running through his mind. The tall boy loved the memory of his father, "Cracked McGregor." "They called him 'Cracked' until that became his name," he thought. "Now they are at me." The thought renewed a feeling of fellowship, between himself and his dead father—it softened him. When he reached the first of the bleak miners' houses a smile played about the corners of his huge mouth.

In his day Cracked McGregor had not borne a good reputation in Coal Creek. He was a tall, silent man with something morose and dangerous about him. He inspired fear born of hatred. In the mines he worked silently and with fiery energy, hating his fellow miners among whom he was thought to be a "bit off his head." They it was who named him "Cracked" McGregor and they avoided him while subscribing to the common opinion that he was the best miner in the district. Like his fellow workers he occasionally got drunk. Going into the saloon where other men stood in groups buying drinks for each other he bought only for himself. Once a stranger, a fat man selling liquor for a wholesale house, approached and slapped him on the back. "Come, cheer up and have a drink with me," he said.

Cracked McGregor turned and knocked the stranger to the floor. When the fat man was down he kicked him and glared at the crowd in the room. Then he walked slowly out at the door staring around and hoping someone would interfere.

In his house also Cracked McGregor was silent. When he spoke at all he spoke kindly and looked into the eyes of his wife with an eager, expectant air. To his red-haired son he seemed to be forever pouring forth a kind of dumb affection.

---

4. Such emphasis on the father-son relationship and the meaning of names gives title and theme to Anderson's first published novel, *Windy McPherson's Son* (New York: John Lane, 1916; rev. ed., New York: B. W. Huebsch, 1922; Chicago: University of Chicago Press, 1965, Introduction by Wright Morris).

Taking the boy in his arms he sat for hours rocking back and forth [*and] saying nothing. When the boy was ill or troubled by strange dreams at night the feel of his father's arms about him quieted him. In his arms the boy went to sleep happily. In the mind of the father there was a single recurring thought, "We have but the one bairn, we'll not put him into the hole in the ground," he said, looking eagerly to the mother for [*approval].

Twice had Cracked McGregor walked with his son on a Sunday afternoon. Taking the lad by the hand the miner went up the face of the hill, past the last of the miners' houses, through the grove of pine trees at the summit and on over the hill into sight of a wide valley on the farther side. When he walked he twisted his head far to one side like one listening. A falling timber in the mines had given him a deformed shoulder and left a great scar on his face, partly covered by a red beard filled with coal dust. The blow that had deformed [*his] shoulder [*had] clouded his mind. He muttered as he walked along the road, talking to himself like an old man.[5]

The red-haired boy ran beside his father, happily. He did not see the smiles on the faces of the miners, who came down the hill and stopped to look [back] at the odd pair. The miners went on down the road to sit in front of the stores on Main Street, their day [*brightened] by the memory of the hurrying McGregors. They had a remark they tossed about. "Nance McGregor should not have looked at her man when she conceived," they said.

Up the face of the hill climbed the McGregors. In the mind of the boy a thousand questions wanted answering. Looking at the silent, gloomy face of his father, he choked back the questions rising in his throat, saving them for the quiet hour with his mother when Cracked McGregor was gone to the

5. Anderson's use of "grotesque" characters in *Marching Men* foreshadows his psychological technique in *Winesburg, Ohio* (New York: B. W. Huebsch, 1919). See David D. Anderson, "Sherwood Anderson's Idea of the Grotesque," *Ohioana*, VI (Spring, 1963), 12–13; and the critical essays in *Winesburg, Ohio: Text and Criticism*, ed. John H. Ferres (New York: Viking Press [1966]).

mine. He wanted to know of the boyhood of his father, of the
life in the mine, of the birds that flew overhead and why they
wheeled and flew in great ovals in the sky. He looked at the
fallen trees in the woods wondering what made them fall and
whether the others would presently fall in their turn.

Over the hill went the silent pair and through the pinewood
to an eminence half way down the farther side. When the boy
saw the valley lying so broad and green and fruitful at their
feet he thought it the most wonderful sight in the world. He
was not surprised that his father had brought him there. Sitting
on the ground he opened and closed his eyes, his soul stirred
by the beauty of the scene that lay before them.

On the hillside Cracked McGregor went through a kind of
ceremony. Sitting upon a log he made a telescope of his hands
and looked over the valley inch by inch like one seeking
something lost. For ten minutes he would look intently at a
clump of trees or a spot in the river running through the
valley, where it broadened and where the water, roughened by
the wind, glistened in the sun. A smile lurked in the corners of
his mouth. He rubbed his hands together. He muttered in-
coherent words and bits of sentences. Once he broke forth
into a low, droning song.

On the first morning when the boy sat on the hillside with
his father it was spring. The land was vividly green. Lambs
played in the fields. Birds sang their mating songs. In the air,
on the earth and in the water of the flowing river it was a
time of new life. Below the [wide,] flat valley of green fields
was patched and spotted with brown new-turned earth. The
cattle walking with bowed heads, eating the sweet grass, the
farm houses with red barns, the pungent smell of the new
ground, fired his mind and awoke the sleeping sense of beauty
in the boy. He sat upon the log drunk with happiness that the
world in which he lived could be so beautiful. In his bed
[*at] night he dreamed of the valley, confounding it with the
old Bible tale of the Garden of Eden told him by his mother.
He dreamed that he and his mother went over the hill and
down toward the valley but that his father, wearing a long,
white robe and with his red hair blowing in the wind, stood

upon the hillside, swinging a long sword blazing with fire, and drove them back.[6]

When the boy went again over the hill it was October and a cold wind blew down the hill into his face. In the woods golden brown leaves ran about like little frightened animals and golden-brown were the leaves on the trees about the farm houses, and golden-brown the corn standing shocked in the fields. The scene saddened the boy. A lump came into his throat. He wanted back the green, shining beauty of the spring. He wished to [again] hear the birds singing in the air and in the grass on the hillside.

Cracked McGregor was in another mood. He seemed more satisfied than on the first visit and ran up and down on the little eminence rubbing his hands together and on the legs of his trousers. Through the long afternoon, he sat on the log muttering and smiling.

On the road home through the darkened woods the restless, hurrying leaves frightened the boy so that, with his weariness from walking against the wind, his hunger from being all day without food, and with the cold nipping at his body, he began crying. The father took the boy in his arms and, holding him across his breast like a babe, went down the hill to their home.

It was on a Tuesday morning that Cracked McGregor died. His death fixed itself as something fine in the mind of the boy and the scene and the circumstance stayed with him through life, filling him with secret pride like a knowledge of good blood. "It means something that I am the son of such a man," he thought.

It was past ten in the morning when the cry of "Fire in the mine" ran up the hill to the houses of the miners. A panic

6. The writer's use of symbolic dreams in this novel may indicate an early knowledge (surely intuitive) of psychological theory. The standard discussion is Frederick J. Hoffman, *Freudianism and the Literary Mind*, rev. ed. (Baton Rouge: Louisiana State University Press, 1957), pp. 229–50; reprinted in *The Achievement of Sherwood Anderson: Essays in Criticism*, ed. Ray Lewis White (Chapel Hill: University of North Carolina Press, 1966), pp. 174–92.

seized the women. In their minds they saw the men hurrying down old cuts, crouching in hidden corridors, pursued by death. Cracked McGregor, one of the night shift, slept in his house. The boy's mother, throwing a shawl about her head, took his hand and ran down the hill to the mouth of the mine. Cold winds spitting snow blew in their faces. They ran along the tracks of the railroad, stumbling over the ties, and stood on the railroad embankment that overlooked the runway to the mine.

About the runway and along the embankment stood the silent miners, their hands in their trouser[*s] pockets, staring stolidly at the closed door of the mine. Among them was no impulse toward concerted action. Like animals at the door of a slaughter house they stood as though waiting their turn to be driven in at the door. An old crone with bent back and a huge stick in her hand went from one to another of the miners gesticulating and talking. "Get my boy—my Steve! Get him out of there!" she shouted, waving the stick about.

The door of the mine opened and three men came out, staggering as they pushed before them a small car that ran upon rails. On the car lay three other men, silent and motionless. A woman, thinly clad and with great cave-like hollows in her face, climbed the embankment and sat upon the ground below the boy and his mother. "The fire is in the old McCrary cut," she said, her voice quivering, a dumb, hopeless look in her eyes. "They can't get through to close the doors. My man Ike is in there." She put down her head and sat weeping. The boy knew the woman. She was a neighbor living in an unpainted house on the hillside. In the yard in front of her house a swarm of children played among the stones. Her husband, a great, hulking fellow, got drunk and, coming home, kicked his wife. The boy had heard her screaming at night.

Suddenly in the growing crowd of miners below the embankment Beaut McGregor saw his father moving restlessly about. On his head he had his cap with the miner's lamp lighted. He went from group to group among the people, his head hanging to one side[, listening]. The boy looked at him intently. He was reminded of the October day on the eminence overlooking the fruitful valley. Again he thought of his father as a man inspired, going through a kind of ceremony. The tall miner rubbed his hands up and down his legs. He peered into the faces of the silent men standing about. His lips moved and his red beard danced up and down.

As the boy looked a change came over the face of Cracked McGregor. He ran to the foot of the embankment looking up. In his eyes was the look of [*a] perplexed animal. The wife bent down and began to talk to the weeping woman on the ground, trying to comfort her. She did not see her husband and the boy and man stood in silence looking into each other's eyes.

Then the puzzled look went out of the father's face. He turned and running along with his head rolling about reached the closed door of the mine. A man, wearing a white collar and with a cigar stuck in the corner of his mouth, put out his hand. "Stop! Wait!" he shouted. Pushing the man aside with his powerful arm the runner pulled open the door of the mine and disappeared down the runway.

A hubbub arose. The man in the white collar took the cigar from his mouth and began swearing violently. The boy stood on the embankment and saw his mother running toward the runway of the mine. A miner, gripping her by the arm, led her back up the face of the embankment. In the crowd a woman's voice shouted, "It's Cracked McGregor gone to close the door to the McCrary cut!" The man with the white collar glared about, chewing the end of his cigar. "He's gone crazy," he shouted, closing again the door to the mine.

Cracked McGregor died in the mine, almost within reach of the door to the old cut where the fire burned. With him died all but five of the imprisoned miners. All day parties of men tried to get down into the mine. Below in the hidden passages under their own homes the scurrying miners died like rats in a burning barn, while their wives with shawls over their heads sat silently weeping on the railroad embankment. In the evening the boy and his mother went up the hill alone. From the houses scattered over the hill came the sound of women weeping.

For [*several] years after the mine disaster the McGregors, mother and son, lived in the house on the hillside. The woman went each morning to the offices of the mine where she washed windows and scrubbed floors. The position was a sort of recognition, on the part of the mine officials, of the heroism of Cracked McGregor.

Nance McGregor was a small, blue-eyed woman with a sharp nose. She wore glasses and had the name in Coal Creek of being quick and sharp. She did not stand by the fence talking with the wives of other miners but sat in her house sewing or reading aloud to her son. She subscribed for a magazine and had bound copies of it standing upon shelves in the room where she and the boy ate breakfast in the early morning. Before the death of her husband she had maintained a habit of silence in her house. After his death she expanded and, with her red-haired son, discussed freely every phase of their narrow life. As he grew older the boy began to believe that she, like the miners, had kept hidden under her silence a secret fear of his father. Certain things she said of her life encouraged the thought.

Norman McGregor grew into a tall, broad-shouldered boy with strong arms, flaming red hair and a habit of sudden and violent fits of temper. There was something about him that held the attention. As he grew older and was renamed by Uncle Charlie Wheeler he began going about looking for trouble. When [*the] boys called him "Beaut" [McGregor] he knocked them down. When men shouted the name after him on the street he followed them with black looks. It became a point of honor with him to resent the name. He connected it with the town's unfairness to Cracked McGregor.

In the house on the hillside the boy and his mother lived happily together. In the early morning they went down the hill and across the tracks to the offices of the mine. From the offices the boy went up the hill on the farther side of the valley and sat upon the school house steps or wandered in the streets waiting for the day in school to begin. In the evening mother and son sat upon the steps at the front of their home looking at the glare of the coke ovens on the sky and the lights of the

swiftly-running passenger trains, roaring, whistling and disappearing into the night.

Nance McGregor talked to her son of the big world outside
the valley. She told him of the cities [and of] the seas and
[of] [*the] strange lands and peoples beyond the seas. "We
have dug in[to] the ground like rats," she said, "I and my
people and your father and his people. With you it will be
different. You will get out of here to other places and other
work." She grew indignant thinking of the life in the town.
"We are stuck down here amid dirt, living in it, breathing it,"
she complained. "Sixty men died in that hole in the ground
and then the mine started again with new men. We stay here
year after year digging coal to burn in engines that take other
people across the seas and into the West."

When the son was a tall, strong boy of fourteen Nance
McGregor bought the bakery. To buy it she took the money
saved by Cracked McGregor. With it he had planned to buy
a farm in the valley beyond the hill. Dollar by dollar it had
been put away by the miner, dreaming of life in his own
fields.

In the bakery the boy worked, learning to make bread.
Kneading the dough his arms and hands grew as strong as a
bear's. He hated the work. He hated Coal Creek. He dreamed
of life in the city and of the part he should play there. Among
the young men he began to make, here and there, a friend.
Like his father he attracted attention. Women looked at him,
laughed at his big frame and strong homely features and
looked again. When they spoke to him in the bakery or on the
street he spoke back fearlessly, looking them in the eyes. Young
girls in the school walked home down the hill with other boys
and at night dreamed of Beaut McGregor. When someone
spoke ill of him they answered defending and praising him.
Like his father he was a marked man in the town of Coal Creek.

CHAPTER II

ONE Sunday afternoon three boys sat on a log on the side of the hill that looked down into Coal Creek. From where they sat they could see the workers of the night shift idling in the sun on Main Street. From the coke ovens a thin line of smoke rose into the sky. A freight train heavily loaded crept round the hill at the end of the valley. It was spring and over even that hive of black industry hung a faint promise of beauty. The boys talked of the life of people in their town and, as they talked, thought each of himself.

Although he had not been out of the valley and had grown strong and big there, Beaut McGregor knew something of the outside world. It isn't a time when men are shut off from their fellows. Newspapers and magazines have done their work too well. They reached even into the miner's cabin and the merchants along [the] Main Street of Coal Creek stood before their stores in the afternoon and talked of the doings of the world. Beaut McGregor knew that life in his town was exceptional, that not everywhere did men toil all day, black and grimy, underground, that not all women were pale, bloodless and bent. As he went about delivering bread he whistled a song, "Take Me Back to Broadway," he sang after the soubrette in a show that had once come to Coal Creek.[7]

Now sitting on the hillside he talked earnestly gesticulating with his hands. "I hate this town," he said, "the men here think they are confoundedly funny. They don't care for anything but making foolish jokes and getting drunk. I want to go away." His voice rose and hatred flamed up in him. "You wait," he boasted. "I'll make men stop being fools. I'll make children of them. I'll ——." Pausing, he looked at his two companions.

7. Anderson may refer anachronistically to the line "Give My Regards to Broadway" from George M. Cohan's *Little Johnny Jones* of 1904.

Beaut poked [at] the ground with a stick. The boy sitting beside him laughed. He was a short, well-dressed [*black-haired boy with] rings on his fingers [*who worked in the town pool room, racking the pool balls]. "I'd like to go where there are women with blood in them," he said.

Three women came up the hill toward them, a tall, pale, brown-haired woman of twenty-seven and two fairer, young girls. The black-haired boy straightened his tie and began thinking of a conversation he would start when the women reached him. Beaut [McGregor] and the other boy, a fat fellow, the son of a grocer, looked down the hill to the town over the heads of the newcomers and continued in their minds the thoughts that had made the conversation.

"Hello girls, come and sit here," shouted the black-haired boy, laughing and looking boldly into the eyes of the tall, pale woman. They stopped and the tall woman began stepping over the fallen logs, coming to them. The two young girls followed, laughing. They sat down on the log beside the boys, the tall, pale woman at the end beside red-haired McGregor. An embarrassed silence fell over the party. Both Beaut and the fat boy were disconcerted by this turn to their afternoon's outing. They wondered how it would [*turn] out.

The pale woman began talking in a low tone. "I want to get away from [*here]," she said, "I wish I could hear birds sing and see green things grow."

Beaut McGregor had an idea. "You come with me," he said. He got up and [*climbed] over the logs and the pale woman followed. The fat boy shouted at them, relieving his own embarrassment by trying to embarrass them. "Where are you going—you two?" he shouted.

Beaut said nothing. He stepped over the logs to the road and began climbing the hill, the tall woman walking beside him holding her skirts out of the deep dust of the road. Even on this, her Sunday gown, there was a faint black mark along the seams—the mark of Coal Creek.

As McGregor walked his embarrassment left him. He thought it fine that he should be thus alone with a woman. When she had tired from the climb he sat with her on a log beside the road and talked of the black-haired boy. "He has your ring on his finger," he said, looking at her and laughing.

She held her hand pressed tightly against her side and closed her eyes. "The climbing hurts me," she said.

Tenderness took hold of Beaut. When they went on again he walked behind her, his hand upon her back pushing her up the hill. The desire to tease her about the black-haired boy had passed. He wished he had said nothing [*about] the ring. He remembered the story the black-haired boy had told him of his conquest of the woman. "More than likely a mess of lies," he thought.

Over the crest of the hill they stopped and rested, leaning against a worn rail fence by the woods. Below them, in a wagon, a party of men went down the hill. The men sat upon boards laid across the box of a wagon and sang a song. One of them stood in the seat beside the driver and waved a bottle. He seemed to be making a speech. The others shouted and clapped their hands. The sounds came faint and sharp up the hill.

In the woods beside the fence rank grass grew. Hawks floated in the sky over the valley below. A squirrel, running along the fence, stopped and chattered at them. McGregor thought he had never had so delightful a companion. He got a feeling of complete, good fellowship and friendliness with this woman. Without knowing how the thing had been done he felt a [*certain] pride in it. "Don't mind what I said about the ring," he [*urged], "I was only trying to tease you."

The woman beside McGregor was the daughter of an undertaker who lived upstairs over his shop near the bakery. He had seen her in the evening standing in the stairway by the shop door. After the story told him by the black-haired boy [, who was the son of a cook in the hotel and worked in the pool room racking the balls,] he had been embarrassed about her. When he passed her, standing in the stairway, he went hurriedly along looking into the gutter.

They went down the hill and sat on the log upon the hill-side. A clump of elders had grown [up] about the log since his visits there with Cracked McGregor so that the place was

closed and shaded like a room. The woman took off her hat
and laid it beside her on the log. A faint color mounted to
her pale cheeks. A flash of anger gleamed in her eyes. "He
probably lied to you about me," she said. "I didn't give him
that ring to wear. I don't know why I gave it to him. He wanted
it. He asked me for it time and again. He said he wanted to
show it to his mother. And now he has shown it to you, and,
I suppose, told lies about me."

Beaut [McGregor] was annoyed and wished he hadn't
mentioned the ring. He felt that an unnecessary fuss was being
made about it. He did not believe that the black-haired boy
had lied but he did not think it mattered [to him].

He began talking of his father, boasting of him. His hatred
of the town blazed up[, absorbing him]. "They thought they
knew him down there," he said, "they laughed at him and
called him 'Cracked.' They thought his running into the mine
just a crazy notion like a horse that runs into a burning stable.
He was the best man in town. He was braver than any of
them. He went in there and died when he had almost money
enough saved to buy a farm over here." He pointed down the
valley.

Beaut began telling her of the visits to the hillside with his
father. He described the effect of the scene on himself when
he was a child. "I thought it was paradise," he said.

She put her hand on his arm and seemed to be soothing him
like a careful groom quieting an excitable horse. "Don't mind
them," she said, "you'll go away after a time and make a place
for yourself out in the world."

He wondered how she knew. A profound respect for her
came over him. "She is keen to guess that," he thought.

[*He] began talking of himself, boasting and throwing out
his chest. "I'd like to have the chance to show what I can do,"
he declared. A thought that had been [*in] his mind on the
winter day when Uncle Charlie Wheeler put the name of
Beaut upon him came back [into his mind] and he walked up
and down before the woman making grotesque motions with
his hands as Cracked McGregor had walked up and down
before him.

"I'll tell you what," he began and his voice was harsh. He had forgotten the presence of the woman and half forgotten what had been in his mind. He sputtered and glared over his shoulder up the hillside, struggling for words. "Oh, to Hell with men!" he burst [*forth]. "They are cattle, stupid cattle." A fire blazed up in his eyes and a confident ring came into his voice. "I'd like to get them together, all of them," he said, "I'd like to make them———." Words failed him and again he sat down on the log beside the woman. "Well I'd like to lead them to an old mine shaft and push them in," he concluded resentfully.

On the eminence sat Beaut and the tall woman and looked down into the valley. "I wonder why we don't go there [to live], mother and I," he said. "When I see it I'm filled with the notion. I think I want to be a farmer and work in the fields. Instead of that mother and I sit and plan of the city. I am going to be a lawyer. That's all we talk about. Then I come up here and it seems as though this is the place for me."

The tall woman laughed. "I can see you coming home at night from the fields," she said. "It might be to that white house there with the windmill. You would be a big man and would have dust in your red hair and perhaps a red beard growing on your chin. And a woman with a baby in her arms would come out of the kitchen door to stand leaning on the fence waiting for you. When you came up she would put her arm around your neck and kiss you on the lips. The beard would tickle her cheek. You should have a beard when you grow older. Your mouth is so big."

A strange new feeling shot through Beaut. He wondered why she had said that. He wanted to take hold of her hand and kiss her then and there. He got up and looked at the sun going down [in the West] behind the hill far away at the other end of the valley. "We had better be getting along back," he said.

The woman remained seated on the log. "Sit down," she said, "I'll tell you something—something [that] it's good for you to hear. You're so big and red you tempt a girl to bother you. First, though, you tell me why you go along the street looking into the gutter when I stand in the stairway in the evening."

Beaut sat down again upon the log thinking of what the black-haired boy had told him of her. "Then it was true—what he said about you?" he asked.

"No! No!" she cried, jumping up in her turn and beginning to pin on her hat. "Let's be going."

Beaut sat stolidly on the log. "What's the use bothering each other?" he said. "Let's sit here until the sun goes down. We can get home before dark."

They sat down and she began talking, boasting of herself as he had boasted of his father.

"I'm too old for that, boy," she said, "I'm older than you by a good many years. I know what boys talk about and what they say about women. I do pretty well. I don't have anyone to talk to except father and he sits all evening reading a paper and going to sleep in his chair. If I let boys come and sit with me in the evening or stand with me in the stairway talking it is because I'm lonesome. There isn't a man in town I would marry—not one."

The speech sounded discordant and harsh to Beaut. He wished his father were there rubbing his hands together and muttering rather than this pale woman who stirred him up and then talked harshly like the women at the back doors in Coal Creek. He thought again as he had thought before that he preferred the black-faced miners drunk and silent to their pale, talking wives. On an impulse he told her that, saying it crudely so that it hurt.

Their companionship was spoiled. They got up and began climbing the hill, going toward home. Again she put her hand to her side and again he wished to put his hand at her back and push her up the hill. Instead he walked beside her in silence, again hating the town.

Half way down the hill the tall woman stopped by the roadside. Darkness was coming on and the glow of the coke ovens lighted the sky. "One living up here and never going down there might think it rather grand and big," he said. Again the hatred came. "They might think the men who live down there knew something instead of being just a lot of cattle."

A smile came into the face of the tall woman and a gentler look stole into her eyes. "We get at one another," she said, "we can't let one another alone. I wish we hadn't quarreled. We might be friends if we tried. You have got something in you. You attract women. I've heard others say that. Your father was that way. Most of the women [*here] would rather have been the wife of Cracked McGregor, ugly as he was, than to have stayed with their own husbands. I heard my mother say that to father when they lay quarreling in bed at night and I lay listening." [8]

The boy was overcome with the thought of a woman talking to him so frankly. He looked at her and said what was in his mind. "I don't like the women," he said, "but I liked you, seeing you stand in the stairway and thinking [maybe] you had been [*doing as you pleased]. I thought maybe you amounted to something. I don't know why you should be bothered by what I think. I don't know why any woman should be bothered by what any man thinks. I should think you would go right on doing what you want to do, like mother and me about my being a lawyer."

He sat on a log beside the road near where he had met her, watching her go down the hill. "I'm quite a fellow to have talked to her all afternoon like that," he thought and pride in his growing manhood crept over him.

---

8. In *Sherwood Anderson's Memoirs,* ed. White, p. 81, the author recounts his mother's similar response to a derogatory comment about her husband: "Once I heard her speaking to a woman in our street. It may be that woman had dared to sympathize with her. 'Oh,' she said, 'it's all right. Don't you worry. He isn't ever dull like most of the men in this street. Life is never dull when my man is about.'"

CHAPTER III

THE town of Coal Creek was hideous. People from prosperous towns and cities of the middle west, from Ohio, Illinois and Iowa, going east to New York or Philadelphia, looked out [*of] the car window[s] and seeing the poor little houses scattered along the hillside thought of books they had read of life in hovels in the old world. In chair-cars men and women leaned back and closed their eyes. They yawned and wished the journey would come to an end. If they thought of the town at all they regretted it mildly and passed it off as a necessity of modern life.

The houses on the hillside and the stores along Main Street belonged to the mining company. In its turn the mining company belonged to the officials of the railroad. The manager of the mine had a brother who was division superintendent. It was the mine manager who had stood by the door of the mine when Cracked McGregor went to his death. He lived in a city some thirty miles away going there in the evening on the train. With him went the clerks and even the stenographer[*s] from the offices of the mine. After five o'clock in the afternoon no white collars were to be seen upon the streets of Coal Creek.

In the town men lived like brutes. Dumb with toil they drank greedily in the saloon on Main Street and went home to beat their wives. Among them a constant low muttering went on. Feeling the injustice of their lot they could not voice it logically. When they thought of the men who owned the mine they swore dumbly, using vile oaths even in their thoughts. Occasionally a strike broke out and Barney Butterlips, a thin little man with a cork leg, stood on a box and made speeches regarding the coming brotherhood of man. Once a troop of cavalry was unloaded from the cars and, with a battery, paraded the main street. The battery was made up of several men in brown uniforms. They set up a Gatling gun at the end of the street and the strike subsided.

An Italian, living in a house on the hillside, cultivated a garden. His place was the one beauty spot in the valley. With a wheelbarrow he brought earth from the woods [*at] the top of the hill. On Sunday [mornings] he could be seen going back and forth whistling merrily. In the winter he sat in his house making a drawing on a bit of paper. In the spring he took the drawing and, by it, planted his garden utilizing every inch of his ground. When a strike came on he was told by the mine manager to go [*on] back to work or move out of his house.[9] He thought of the garden and the work he had done and went back to his routine of work in the mine. While he worked the [striking] miners marched up the hill and destroyed the garden. The next day the Italian also joined the [*striking miners].

In a little [old] one-room shack on the hill lived an old woman. She lived alone and was vilely dirty. In her house she had old broken chairs and tables, picked up about town, and piled in such profusion that she could scarcely move about. On warm days she sat in the sun before the shack chewing on a stick that had been dipped in tobacco. Miners coming up the hill dumped bits of bread and meat-ends out of their dinner pails into a box nailed to a tree by the road. These the old woman collected and ate. When the soldiers came to town she walked along the street jeering at them. "Pretty boys! Scabs! Dudes! Drygoods clerks!" she called after them, walking by the tails of their horses. A young man with glasses on his nose [*who was] mounted on a grey horse turned and called to his comrades, "Let her alone—it's old Mother Misery herself."

When the tall, red-haired boy looked at the workers and at the old woman who followed the soldiers he did not sympa-

9. This episode is probably based on one of Anderson's neighbors during his business career in Elyria, Ohio—an Italian and his garden remembered in *Sherwood Anderson's Memoirs*, ed. White, pp. 254, 258, 262–63, 265–67, 269, 271.

thize with them. He hated them. In a way he sympathized
with the soldiers. His blood was stirred by the sight of them
marching shoulder to shoulder. He thought there was order and
decency in the rank of uniformed men moving silently and
quickly along and [*he] half wished they would destroy the
town. When the strikers made a wreck of the garden of the
Italian[s] he was deeply touched and walked up and down
in the room before his mother proclaiming himself. "I should
have killed them had it been my garden," he said. "I should
not have left one of them alive." In his heart, he, like Cracked
McGregor, nursed his hatred of the miners and of the town.
"The place is one to get out of," he said. "If a man doesn't
like it here, let him get up and leave." He remembered his
father working and saving for the farm in the valley. "They
thought him cracked but he knew more than they. They would
not have dared touch a garden he had planted."

In the heart of the miner's son strange, half formed thoughts
began to find lodging[*s]. Remembering in his dreams at
night the moving columns of men in their uniforms he read
new meaning into the scraps of history picked up in the school
and the movements of men in old history began to have significance for him.[10] On a summer afternoon as he loitered before the town's hotel, beneath which was the saloon and
billiard room where the black-haired boy worked, he overheard
two men talking of the [in]significance of men [and the significance of the man].

One of the men was an itinerant oculist who came to the
mining town once a month to fit and sell spectacles. When
the oculist had sold several pairs of spectacles he got drunk,
sometimes staying drunk for a week. When he was drunk he

10. Anderson is remembering his own experiences (non-combat) as
a soldier in the Spanish-American War. The standard discussion is William Alfred Sutton, "Sherwood Anderson: The Spanish-American War
Year," *Northwest Ohio Quarterly*, XX (January, 1948), 20–36. For the
author's memories of his war service, see *A Story Teller's Story: A Critical Text*, ed. Ray Lewis White (Cleveland: Press of Case Western Reserve University, 1968), pp. 167, 199–208; and *Sherwood Anderson's
Memoirs*, ed. White, pp. 16–17, 45, 165–98, 255.

spoke French and Italian and sometime[*s] stood in the bar-room before the miners quoting the poems of Dante. His clothes were greasy from long wear and he had a huge nose streaked with red and purple veins. Because of his learning in the languages and his quoting of poems the miners thought the oculist infinitely wise. To them it seemed that one with such a mind must have almost unearthly knowledge concerning the eyes and the fitting of glasses and they wore with pride the cheap, ill-fitting things [that] he thrust [*up]on them.

Occasionally, as though making a concession to his patrons, the oculist spent an evening among them. [*Once] after re-citing one of the sonnets of Shakespeare he put a hand [up]on the bar and, rocking gently back and forth, sang, in a drink-broken voice, a[n Irish] ballad beginning "The Harp that once through Tara's Halls, The Soul of Music Shed." [11] After the song he put his head down upon the bar and wept while the miners looked on [*touched] with sympathy.

On the summer afternoon, when Beaut McGregor listened, the oculist was engaged in a violent quarrel with another man, drunk like himself. The second man was a slender, dandified [*fellow] of middle age who sold shoes for a Philadelphia jobbing house. He sat in a chair tilted against the hotel and tried to read aloud from a book. When he had got fairly launched in a long paragraph the oculist interrupted. Stagger-ing up and down [upon] the narrow board walk before the hotel the old drunkard raved and swore. He seemed beside himself with wrath.

"I am sick of such slobbering philosophy," he declared. "Even the reading of it makes you drool at the mouth. You

11. The Irish poet Thomas Moore (1779–1852) wrote "The Harp That Once Through Tara's Halls" in 1834:

> The harp that once through Tara's halls
>   The soul of music shed,
> Now hangs as mute on Tara's walls
>   As if that soul were fled.—
> So sleeps the pride of former days,
>   So glory's thrill is o'er,
> And hearts that once beat high for praise
>   Now feel that pulse no more!

do not say the words sharply and they can't be said sharply.
I am a strong man myself."

Spreading his legs wide apart and blowing up his cheeks,
the oculist beat [with his hand] upon his breast. With a wave
of his hand he dismissed the man in the chair.

"You but slobber and make a foul noise," he declared. "I
know your kind. I spit upon you. The Congress at Washington
is full of such fellows as is also the House of Commons in
England. In France they were once in charge. They ran things
in France until the coming of a man such as myself. They were
lost in the shadow of the great Napoleon." [12]

The oculist, as though dismissing the dandified man from
his mind, turned to address Beaut [McGregor]. He [*talked
in French] and the man in the chair fell into a troubled sleep.
"I am like Napoleon," [*the drunkard declared], breaking
again into English, and tears began to show in his eyes. "I
take the money of these miners and I give them nothing. The
spectacles I sell to their wives for five dollars cost me but
fifteen cents. I ride over these brutes as Napoleon rode over
Europe. There would be order and purpose in me were I not
a fool. I am like Napoleon in that I have utter contempt for
men."

Again and again the words of the drunkard came back into
the mind of [*the] McGregor boy influencing his thoughts.
Grasping nothing of the philosophy back of the man's words
his imagination was yet touched by the drunkard's tale of the
great Frenchman babbled into his ears, and it in some way
seemed to give point to his hatred of the disorganized ineffectiveness of the life about him.

After Nance McGregor opened the bakery another strike
came to disturb the prosperity of the business. Again the
miners walked idly through the streets. Into the bakery they

12. Anderson later recalls being obsessed with Napoleon in the same
period that he began *Marching Men*. See *Sherwood Anderson's Memoirs*,
ed. White, pp. 9, 187, 199, 200, 252, 260, 544.

came, getting bread and telling Nance to write the debt
down against them. Beaut McGregor was disturbed. He saw
the money of his father being spent for flour which, when
baked into loaves, went out of the shop under the arms of
[*the] miners who shuffled as they walked. One night a man,
whose name appeared on their books, followed by a long
record of charged loaves, came reeling past the bakery.
McGregor went to his mother and protested. "They have
money to get drunk," he said, "let them pay for their loaves."

Nance McGregor went on trusting the miners. She thought
of the women and children in the houses on the hill. When
she heard of the plans of the mining company to evict the
miners from their [*houses], she shuddered. "I was the wife
of a miner and I'll stick to them," she thought.

One day the mine manager came into the bakery. He leaned
over the showcase talking to Nance [McGregor]. The son
went and stood by his mother's side listening. "It has got to
be stopped," the manager was saying, "I will not see you ruin
yourself for these cattle. I want you to close this place till the
strike is over. If you won't close it, I will. The building belongs
to us. They didn't appreciate what your husband did and why
should you ruin yourself for them?"

The woman looked at him and answered in a low tone full
of resolution, "They thought he was crazy and he was," she
said, "but what made him so? The rotten timbers in the
mine[s] that broke and crushed him. You, and not they, are
responsible for my man and what he was."

Beaut McGregor interrupted. "Well, I think he is right,"
he declared, leaning over the counter beside his mother and
looking into her face. "The miners don't want better things
for their families, they want more money to get drunk. We will
close the doors here. We'll put no more money into bread to
go into their gullets. They hated father and he hated them and
now I hate them also."

Beaut walked around the end of the counter and went with
the mine manager to the door. He locked the door, putting the
key into his pocket. Then he walked to the rear of the bake

shop where his mother sat on a box weeping. "It's time a man took charge here," he said.

Nance McGregor and her son sat in the bakery looking at each other. Miners, coming along the street, tried the door and went away grumbling. Word ran from lip to lip up the hillside. "The mine manager has closed Nance McGregor's shop," said the women leaning over back fences. Children sprawling on the floors of the houses put up their heads and howled. Their lives were a succession of new terrors. When a day passed that a new terror did not shake them they went to bed happy. When the miner and his woman stood by the door talking in low tones they cried, expecting to be put to bed hungry. When guarded talk did not go on by the door the miner came home drunk and beat the mother and the children lay in beds along the wall trembling with fright.

Late that night a party of miners came to the door of the bakery and beat upon it with their fists. "Open up here!" they shouted. Beaut [McGregor] came out of the rooms above the bakery and stood in the empty shop. [Above,] his mother sat in a chair [*in her room] trembling. He went to the door and, unlocking it, stepped out. The miners stood in groups on the wooden sidewalk and in the mud of the road. Among them stood the old crone who had walked [*beside] the horses shouting at the soldiers. A miner with a black beard came and stood before the boy. Waving his hand at the crowd he said, "We have come to open the bakery. Some of us have no ovens in our stoves. You give us the key and we will open the place. We'll break in the door if you don't want to do that. The company can't blame you if we do it by force. You can keep account of what we take. Then when the strike is settled we will pay you."

A flame shot [up] into the eyes of the boy. He walked down the steps and stood among the miners. Thrusting his hands into his pockets he peered into their faces. When he spoke his voice rang resounding through the street, "You jeered at my father, Cracked McGregor, when he went into the mine for you. You laughed at him because he saved his money and didn't spend it buying you drinks. Now you come here to get bread

his money bought and you do not pay [for it]. Then you get
drunk and go reeling past this very door. Now let me tell you
something." He thrust his hands into the air and shouted. "The
mine manager didn't close this place. I closed it. You jeered at
Cracked McGregor, a better man than any of you. You've had
fun with me—laughing at me. Now I jeer at you." He ran up
the steps and, unlocking the door, stood in the doorway. "Pay
the money you owe this bakery and there will be bread for sale
here," he called, going in and locking the door.

The miners walked off up the street. The boy stood within
the bakery his hands trembling. "I've told them something,"
he thought, "I've shown them they can't make a fool of me."
He went up the stairway to the rooms above. By the window
his mother sat, her head in her hands, looking down into the
street. He sat in a chair thinking of the situation. "They will be
back here and smash the place like they tore up that garden,"
he said.

The next evening Beaut [McGregor] sat in the darkness on
the steps before the bakery. In his hand[*s] he held a hammer.
A dull hatred of the town and of the miners burned in his
brain. "I'll make it hot for some of them if they come here," he
thought. He hoped they would come. As he looked at the
hammer in his hand a phrase from the lips of the drunken old
oculist, babbling of Napoleon, came into his mind. He began
to think that he also must be like the figure of which the
drunkard had talked. He remembered a story the oculist had
told [him] of a fight in the streets of the European city and
muttered, waving the hammer about. Upstairs his mother sat
by the window, [with] her head in her hands. From the saloon
down the street a light gleamed out on the wet sidewalk. The
tall pale woman who had gone with him to the eminence overlooking the valley came down the stairway from above the
undertaker's shop. She ran along the sidewalk. On her head she
wore a shawl and as she ran she clutched it with her hand.
The other hand she held against her side.

When the woman reached the boy [*who sat in silence]
before the bakery she put her hands on his shoulders and
[, looking into his face,] plead with him. "Come away," she said,

"get your mother and come to our place. They are going to smash you up here. You'll get hurt."

Beaut arose and pushed her away. Her coming had given him new courage. His heart jumped at the thought of her interest[s] in him and he wished that the miners might come so [*that] he could fight them before her. "I wish I could live among people as decent as she," he thought.

A train stopped at the [*station] down the street. There came the sound of tramping of men and quick, sharp commands. A stream of men poured out of the saloon onto the sidewalk. Down the street came a file of soldiers, [*with] guns swung across their shoulders. Again Beaut [McGregor] was thrilled by the sight of trained, orderly men moving along shoulder to shoulder. In the presence of these men the disorganized miners seemed pitifully weak and insignificant. The girl, pulling the shawl about her head, ran up the street [*to disappear] into the stairway. The boy, unlocking the door, went upstairs and to bed.

After the strike Nance McGregor, owning nothing but unpaid accounts, was unable to open the bakery. A small man with a white mustache who chewed tobacco came from the mill and took the unused flour, shipping it away. The boy and his mother continued living above the bakery store room. Again she went in the morning to wash [*the] windows and scrub [*the] floors in the offices of the mine. Her red-haired son stood upon the street or sat in the pool room talking to the black-haired boy. "Next week I will be going to the city and will begin making something of myself," he said. When the time came to go he waited, idling in the streets. Once when a miner jeered at him for his idleness he knocked him into the gutter. The miners, who hated him for his speech on the steps, admired him for his strength and brute courage.

CHAPTER IV

In a cellar-like house, driven like a stake into the hillside above Coal Creek, lived Kate Hartnet with her son Mike. Her man had died with the others during the fire in the mine. Her son, like Beaut McGregor, did not work in the mine. He hurried through Main Street or went half running among the trees on the hills. Miners, seeing him hurry along with white intense face, shook their heads. "He's cracked," they said. "He'll hurt someone yet."

Beaut [McGregor] saw Mike hurrying about the streets. Once encountering him in the pine woods above the town he walked with him trying to get him to talk. In his pockets Mike carried books and pamphlets. He set traps in the woods and brought home rabbits and squirrels. [Also] he got together collections of birds' eggs which he sold to women in the trains that stopped at Coal Creek. When he caught birds he stuffed them, put beads in their eyesockets and sold them also. He proclaimed himself an anarchist and, like Cracked McGregor, muttered to himself as he hurried along.

One day Beaut came upon Mike Hartnet reading a book as he sat on a log overlooking the town. A [kind of] shock ran through McGregor when he looked over the shoulder of the man and saw what book he read. "It's strange," he thought, "that this fellow should stick to the same book that fat old Weeks makes his living by."

Beaut sat on the log beside Hartnet and watched him. The reading man looked up and nodded nervously [*then] slid along the log to the farther end. Beaut laughed. He looked down at the town and then at the frightened, nervous, book-reading man on the log. An inspiration came to him.

"If you had the power, Mike, what would you do to Coal Creek?" he asked.

The nervous man jumped [up] and tears came into his eyes. He stood before the log and spread out his hands. "I

should go among men like Christ," he cried, pitching his voice
forward like one addressing an audience. "Poor and humble I
should go teaching them of love." Spreading out his hand[*s]
like one pronouncing a benediction, he shouted, "Oh men of
Coal Creek, I would teach you love and the destruction of
evil."

Beaut jumped up from the log and strode before the trembling figure. He was strangely moved. Grasping the man he
thrust him back upon the log. His own voice rolled down the
hillside in a great roaring laugh. "Men of Coal Creek," he
shouted, mimicking the earnestness of Hartnet, "listen to the
voice of McGregor. I hate you. I hate you because you jeered
at my father and at me and because you cheated my mother,
Nance McGregor. I hate you because you are weak and disorganized like [frightened] cattle. I should like to come among
you teaching the power of force. I should like to slay you one
by one, not with weapons but with my naked fists. If they have
made you work like rats buried in a hole, they are right. It is
man's right to do what he can. Get up and fight. Fight and I
will get on the other side and you can fight me. I will help drive
you back into your holes."

Beaut ceased speaking and jumping over the logs ran down
the road. Among the first of the miners' houses he stopped
and laughed awkwardly. "I am cracked also," he thought—
"shouting at emptiness on a hillside." He went on [*in a reflective mood], wondering what power had taken hold of him.
"I would like a fight—a fight against odds," he thought. "I'll
stir things up when I am a lawyer in the city."

Mike Hartnet came running down the road at the heels of
McGregor. "Don't tell," he plead trembling. "Don't tell about
me in [*the] town. They will laugh and call names after me.
I want to be let alone."

Beaut [McGregor], shaking himself loose from the detaining
hand, went on down the hill. When he had passed out of sight
of Hartnet, he sat down on the ground. For an hour he
[*looked] at the town [*in the valley and thought] of himself. He was half proud, half ashamed of the thing that had
happened.

In the blue eyes of [Beaut] McGregor anger flashed quick and sudden. Upon the streets of Coal Creek he walked, swinging along, his great body inspiring fear. His mother, grown grave and silent, worked in the offices of the mines. Again she had a habit of silence in her own home and looked at her son, half fearing him. All day she worked in the mine offices and in the evening sat silently in a chair on the porch before her house and looked down into Main Street.

Beaut McGregor did nothing. He sat [in chairs] in the dingy little pool room talking with the black-haired boy [who wore rings on his fingers,] or walked over the hills swinging a stick in his hand and thinking of the city to which he would presently go to start his career. As he walked in the streets women stopped to look [back] at him, thinking of the beauty and strength of his maturing body. The miners passed him in silence, hating him and dreading his wrath. Walking among the hills he thought much of himself. "I'm capable of anything," he thought, lifting his head and looking at the towering hills, "I wonder why I stay on here."

When he was eighteen, Beaut's mother fell ill. All day she lay on her back in bed in the room above the empty bakery. Beaut shook himself out of his waking stupor and went about seeking work. He hadn't felt that he was indolent. He had been waiting. Now he bestirred himself. "I'll not go into the mines," he said, "nothing shall get me down there."

He got work in a livery stable, cleaning and feeding the horses. His mother got out of bed and began again going to the mine offices. Having started to work, Beaut stayed on thinking it but a way station to the position he would one day achieve in the city.[13]

In the stable worked two young boys, sons of coal miners. They drove traveling men from the trains to farming towns in valleys back among the hills. In the evening with Beaut

13. The present livery-stable episode is autobiographical, as retold in *Sherwood Anderson's Memoirs*, ed. White, pp. xxvi, 110–14, 115. See also Linda Carol Traynham, " 'The Chosen of His Race': The Horse as Symbol in Sherwood Anderson's Fiction" (M.A. thesis, University of South Carolina, 1966).

McGregor they sat on a bench before the barn shouting at people going past the stable up the hill.

The livery stable in Coal Creek was owned by a hunchback named Weller who lived in the city and went home at night. During the day he sat about the stable talking to red-haired McGregor. "You're a big beast," he said laughing. "You talk about going away to the city and making something of yourself and still you stay on here doing nothing. You want to quit [*this] talking about being a lawyer and become a prize fighter. Law is a place for brains not muscles." He walked through the stables leaning his head to one side and looking up at the big fellow brushing the horses. McGregor watched him and grinned. "I'll show you," he said.

The hunchback was pleased when he [had] strutted before McGregor. He had heard men talk of the strength and the evil temper of his stableman and it pleased him to have so fierce a fellow cleaning the horses. At night in the city he sat under the lamp with his wife and boasted. "I make him step about," he said.

In the stable the hunchback kept at the heels of McGregor. "And there's something else," he said, putting his hand[s] in his pockets and raising himself on his toes. "You look out for that undertaker's daughter. She wants you. If she gets you there'll be no law study but a place in the mine[*s] for you. You let her alone and begin taking care of your mother."

Beaut [McGregor] went on cleaning [*the] horses and thinking of what the hunchback had said. He thought there was sense to it. He also was afraid of the tall, pale girl. Sometimes when he looked at her a pain shot through him and a combination of fear and desire gripped him. He walked away from it and went free as he [walked away and] went free from the life in the darkness down in the mine. "He [*has] a kind of genius [*for] keeping away from the things he [*don't] like," said the liveryman, talking to Uncle Charlie Wheeler in the sun before the door of the post office.

One afternoon the two boys who worked in the livery stable with McGregor got him drunk. The affair was a rude joke, elaborately planned. The hunchback had stayed in the city for the day and no traveling men got off the trains to be driven over the hills. In the afternoon hay, brought over the hill from the fruitful valley, was being put into the loft of the barn and, between loads, McGregor and the two boys sat on the bench by the stable door. The two boys went to the saloon and brought back beer, paying for it from a fund kept for that purpose. The fund was the result of a system worked out by the two drivers. When a passenger gave one of them a coin at the end of a day of driving he put it into the common fund. When the fund had grown to some size the two went to the saloon and stood before the bar drinking until it was spent, coming back to sleep off their stupor on the hay in the barn. After a prosperous week the hunchback occasionally gave them a dollar to go into the fund.

Of the beer McGregor drank but one foaming glass. For all his idling about Coal Creek he had never before tasted beer and it was strong and bitter in his mouth. He threw up his head and gulped it, turning and walking toward the rear of the stable to conceal the tears that the taste of the stuff had forced into his eyes.

The two drivers sat on the bench and laughed. The drink they had given Beaut was a horrible mess concocted by the laughing bartender at their suggestion. "We'll get the big fellow drunk and hear him roar," the bartender had said.

Walking toward the back of the stable a convulsive nausea seized Beaut. He stumbled, and, pitching forward, cut his face on the floor [of the stable]. Then he rolled over on his back and groaned. A little stream of blood ran down his cheek.

The two boys jumped up from the bench and ran toward him. They stood looking at his pale lips. Fear seized them. They tried to lift him but he fell from their arms and lay again on the stable floor, white and motionless. Filled with fright they ran from the stable and through Main Street. "We must get a doctor," they said, hurrying along. "He's mighty sick—that fellow."

In the doorway leading to the rooms over the undertaker's shop stood the tall, pale girl. One of the running boys stopped and addressed her. "Your redhead," he shouted, "is blind drunk lying on the stable floor. He has cut his head and is bleeding."

The tall girl ran down the street to the offices of the mine. With Nance McGregor she hurried to the stable. The store-keepers along Main Street looking out [*of] their doors saw the two women, pale and with set faces, half carrying the huge form of Beaut McGregor along the street and in at the door of the bakery.

At eight o'clock that evening Beaut McGregor, his legs still unsteady, his face white, climbed aboard a passenger train and passed out of the life of Coal Creek. On the seat beside him a bag contained all his clothes. In his pocket lay a ticket to Chicago and eighty-five dollars, the last of Cracked Mc-Gregor's savings. He looked out of the car window at the little woman, thin and worn, standing alone on the station platform and a great wave of anger passed through him. "I'll show them," he muttered. The woman, looking at him, forced a smile to her lips. The train began to move into the West. Beaut [McGregor], looking at his mother and at the deserted streets of Coal Creek, put his head down upon his hands and in the crowded car, before the gaping people, wept with joy that he had seen the last of [his] youth. He looked back at Coal Creek full of hate. Like Nero he might have wished that all of the people of [*the] town had but one head so that he might have cut it off with one sweep of a sword or knocked it into the gutter with one swinging blow.

BOOK II

CHAPTER I

It was late in the summer of 1893 when McGregor came to Chicago; an ill time for boy or man in that city. The big exposition of the year before had brought multiplied thousands of restless laborers into the city and its leading citizens, who had clamored for the exposition and had loudly talked of the great growth that was to come, did not know [*what to do with] the growth now that it had come. The depression that followed on the heels of the great show and the financial [*panic] that ran over the country in that year had set thousands of hungry men to wait dumbly on park benches, poring over want advertisements in the daily papers and looking vacantly at the lake, or had driven them to tramp aimlessly through the streets filled with forebodings.[1]

In time of plenty a great American city like Chicago goes on showing a more or less cheerful face to the world while in nooks and crannies, down side streets and alleys, poverty and misery sit haunched up in little ill-smelling rooms breeding vice [and waiting]. In times of depression these creatures crawl forth and, joined by thousands of the unemployed, tramp the streets through the long nights, or sleep upon benches in the parks. In the alleyways off Madison Street on the West Side and off State Street, on the South Side, eager women driven by want sold their bodies to passersby for twenty-five cents. An advertisement in the newspapers of one unfilled job brought a thousand men to block the streets at daylight before a factory door. In the crowd[*s] men swore and knocked each other about. Workingmen, driven to desperation, went forth into quiet streets and, knocking over citizens,

1. Sherwood Anderson was not in Chicago during the Columbian Exposition of 1893. Anderson first came to Chicago in 1896 or 1897 after his mother's death in 1895. For his account of this time in Chicago, see *A Story Teller's Story*, ed. White, pp. 166 ff.; and *Sherwood Anderson's Memoirs*, ed. White, pp. xxvii, 15–16, 145–65, 175, 288–89, 315.

took their money and watches and ran trembling into the darkness. A girl of Twenty-fourth Street[, held up on the street,] was kicked and knocked into the gutter because [*when attacked by thieves] she had but thirty-five cents in her purse. A professor of [*the University of Chicago], addressing his class, said that, having looked into the hungry distorted faces of five hundred men, clamoring for a position as dishwasher in a cheap restaurant, he was ready to pronounce all claims to social advance[*ment] in America a figment in the brains of optimistic fools. A tall, awkward man walking up State Street threw a stone through the window of a store. A policeman hustled him through the crowd. "You'll get a workhouse sentence for this," he said.

"You fool, that's what I want. I want to make property, that won't employ me, feed me," said the tall, gaunt man who, trained in the cleaner and more wholesome poverty of the frontier, might have been a Lincoln, suffering for mankind.[2]

Into this maelstrom of misery and grim, desperate want walked Beaut McGregor of Coal Creek—huge, [*graceless] of body, indolent of mind, untrained, uneducated, hating the world. Within two days he had snatched, before the very eyes of that hungry, marching army, three prizes, three places where a man might, by working all day, get clothes to wear upon his back and food to put into his stomach.

In a way McGregor had already sensed something the realization of which will go far toward making any man a strong figure in the world. He was not to be [*bullied] with words. Orators might have preached to him all day about the progress of mankind in America, flags might have be[*en] flapped and newspapers might have dinned the wonders of

2. Anderson writes of Lincoln in "Father Abraham," *The Sherwood Anderson Reader*, ed. Paul Rosenfeld (Boston: Houghton Mifflin, 1947), pp. 530–602; *A Story Teller's Story*, ed. White, pp. 24, 31–32, 61, 148, 159, 176, 179, 202; *Tar: A Midwest Childhood, A Critical Text*, ed. Ray Lewis White (Cleveland: Press of Case Western Reserve University, 1969), pp. 20, 21, 24, 26, 107; and *Sherwood Anderson's Memoirs*, ed. White, pp. 11, 186, 342, 478, 499. See David D. Anderson, "Sherwood Anderson's Use of the Lincoln Theme," *Lincoln Herald*, LXIV (Spring, 1962), 28–32.

his country into his brain. He would only have shaken his big head. He did not yet know the whole story of how men, coming out of Europe and given millions of square miles of black fertile land, mines and forests, have failed in the challenge given them by fate and have produced out of the stately order of nature only the sordid disorder of man. McGregor did not know the fullness of the tragic story of his race. He only knew that the men he had seen were, for the most part, pigmies. On the train, coming to Chicago, a change had come over him. The hatred of Coal Creek that burned in him had set fire to something else. He sat, looking out of the car window at the stations running past during the night and the following day at the cornfields of Indiana, making his plans. In Chicago he meant to do something. Coming from a community where no man arose above a condition of silent, brute labor, he meant to step up into the light of power. Filled with hatred and contempt of mankind, he meant that mankind should serve him. Raised among men who were but men, he meant to be a master.

And his equipment [to get what he wanted] was better than he knew. In a disorderly, haphazard world hatred is as [*effective] an impulse to drive men forward to success as love and high hope. It is a world old impulse, sleeping in the heart of man since the day of Cain. In a way it rings true and strong above the hideous jangle of modern life. Inspiring fear, it usurps power.

McGregor was without fear. He had not yet met his master and looked with contempt upon the men and women he had known. Without knowing it, he had, besides a huge body, hard as adamant, a clear and lucid brain. The fact that he hated Coal Creek and thought it horrible proved his keenness. It was horrible. Well might Chicago have trembled and rich men, strolling in the evening along Michigan Boulevard, have looked fearfully about as this huge, red fellow, carrying the cheap handbag and staring with his blue eyes at [the great buildings and] the restless, moving [meaningless] mobs of people, walked for the first time through its streets. In his very frame there was the possibility of something, a blow, a shock, a thrust out of the lean soul of strength into the jelly-like fleshiness of weakness.

In the world of men nothing is so rare as a knowledge of men. Christ himself found the merchants hawking their wares even on the floor of the temple and in his naive youth was stirred to wrath and drove them through the door like flies. And history has represented him in turn as a man of peace so that after these centuries the temples are again supported by the hawking of wares and his fine boyish wrath is forgotten. In France, after the great revolution and the babbling of many voices, talking of the brotherhood of man, it wanted but a short and very determined man, with an instinctive knowledge of drums, of cannons and of stirring words, to send the same babblers screaming across open spaces, stumbling through ditches and pitching headlong into the arms of death. In the interest of one who believed not at all in the brotherhood of man they, who had wept at the mention of the word brotherhood, died fighting brothers.

In the heart of all men lies sleeping the love of order. How to achieve order out of our strange jumble of forms, out of democracies and monarchies, dreams and endeavors is the riddle of the Universe and the thing that in the artist is called the passion for form and for which he also will laugh in the face of death is in all men. By grasping that fact Caesar, Alexander, Napoleon and our own Grant have made heroes of the dullest clods that walk, and not a man of all the thousands who marched with Sherman to the sea but lived the rest of his life with a something sweeter, braver and finer sleeping in his soul than will ever be produced by [*the] reformer[s] scolding of brotherhood from a soap box. The long march, the burning of the throat and the stinging of the dust in the nostrils, the touch of shoulder against shoulder, the quick bond of a common, unquestioned, instinctive passion that bursts in the orgasm of battle, the forgetting of words and the doing of the thing, be it winning battles or destroying ugliness, the passionate massing of men for accomplishment—these are the signs, if they ever awake in our land, by which you may know you have come to the days of the making of men.

In Chicago in [*1893] and in the men who went aimlessly seeking work in the streets of Chicago in that year there were none of these signs. Like the coal mining town from which Beaut McGregor had come the city lay sprawling and ineffective before him, a tawdry, disorderly dwelling for millions of men, built[, amid a great clutter of sentimental words about greatness,] not for the making of men but for the making of millions by a few odd meat packers and drygoods merchants.

With a slight lifting of his great shoulders McGregor sensed these things although he could not have expressed his sense of them and the hatred and contempt of men born of his youth in the mining town was rekindled by the sight of city men wandering, afraid and bewildered, through the streets of their own city.

Knowing nothing of the customs of the unemployed McGregor did not walk [in] the streets looking for signs marked "Men Wanted." He did not [*sit on park benches studying] [the] want advertisements [in daily papers—] the want advertisements that so often prove[*d] but bait put out by suave men up dirty stairways to glean the last few pennies from pockets of the needy. Going along the street he swung his great body [boldly] through [*the] doorways leading to the offices of factories. When some pert young man tried to stop him he did not say words but drew back his fist threateningly and, glowering, walked in. The young men at the doors of factories looked at his blue eyes and [after looking] let him pass unchallenged.

In the afternoon of his first day of seeking, Beaut got a place in an apple warehouse on the North Side, the third place offered him during the day and the one that he accepted.[3] The chance came to him through an exhibition of strength. Two men, old and bent, struggled to get a barrel of apples from the sidewalk up to a platform that ran waist high along the front of the warehouse. The barrel had rolled to the side-

3. The author is using for background his own experiences as a Chicago warehouse worker as described in *A Story Teller's Story*, ed. White, pp. 100–104, 139–40, 148, 150–52; and *Sherwood Anderson's Memoirs*, ed. White, pp. xxvii, 15–16, 145, 146, 157, 165 ff.

walk from a truck standing in the gutter. The driver of the truck stood with his hands on his hips laughing. A [tall] German with blond hair stood upon the platform swearing in broken English. McGregor stood upon the sidewalk looking at the two men who [*were struggling] with the barrel. A feeling of immense contempt for their feebleness shone in his eyes. Pushing them aside he grasped the barrel and, with a great heave, sent it up onto the platform and spinning through an open doorway into the receiving room of the warehouse. The two workmen stood on the sidewalk smiling sheepishly. Across the street a group of city firemen, lounging in the sun before an engine house, clapped their hands. The truck driver turned and [*prepared] to send another barrel along the plank extending from the truck across the sidewalk to the warehouse platform. At a window in the upper part of the warehouse a grey head protruded and a sharp voice called down to the tall German[, standing on the platform]. "Hey, Frank, hire that 'husky' and let about six of the 'dead ones' you've got around here go home."

McGregor jumped upon the platform and walked in at the warehouse door. The German followed, inventorying the size of the red-haired giant with something like disapproval. His look seemed to say, "I like strong fellows but you are too strong." He took the discomfiture of the two feeble workmen on the sidewalk as in some way reflecting upon himself. The two men stood in the receiving room looking at each other. A bystander might have thought them preparing to fight.

And then a freight elevator came slowly down from the upper part of the warehouse and from it jumped a small, grey-haired man with a yard stick in his hand. He had [*a sharp, restless eye] and a short, stubby grey beard. Striking the floor with a bound he began talking. "We pay two dollars for nine hours' work here—begin at seven, quit at five. Will you come?" Without waiting for an answer he turned to the German. "Tell those two old 'rummies' to get their time and get out of here," he said turning again and looking expectantly at McGregor.

McGregor liked the quick little man and grinned with approval of his decisiveness. He nodded his assent to the proposal and, looking at the German, laughed. The little man

disappeared through a door leading to an office and McGregor
walked out into the street. At a corner he turned and saw the
German standing on the platform before the warehouse looking after him. "He is wondering whether or not he can whip
me," thought McGregor.

In the apple warehouse McGregor worked for three years,
rising during his second year to be foreman and replacing the
tall German. The German expected trouble with McGregor
and was determined to make short work of him. He had been
offended by the action of the grey-haired superintendent in
hiring the man and felt that a prerogative belonging to himself had been ignored. All day he followed McGregor with his
eyes, trying to calculate the strength and courage in the huge
body. He knew that hundreds of hungry men walked the
streets and in the end decided that the need of work, if not
the spirit of the man, would make him submissive. During
the second week he put the question that burned in his brain
to [*the] test. He followed McGregor into a dimly-lighted
upper room where barrels of apples, piled to the ceiling, left
only narrow ways for passage. Standing in the semi-darkness
he shouted, calling the man who worked among the apple
barrels a foul name, "I won't have you loafing in there you
red-haired bastard," he shouted.

McGregor said nothing. He was not offended by the vileness
of the name the German had called him and took it merely as
a challenge, [*that] he had been expect[*ing] and [*that]
he meant to accept. With a grim smile on his lips he walked
toward the German and when but one apple barrel lay between them [he] reached across and dragged the foreman,
sputtering and swearing, down the passageway to a window
at the end of the room. By the window he stopped and, putting
his [great] hand to the throat of the struggling man, began
choking him into submission. Blows fell on his face and body.
Struggling [*terribly] the German kicked McGregor's legs
with desperate energy. Although his ears rang with the
hammer-like blows, that fell about his neck and cheeks,
McGregor stood silent under the storm. His blue eyes gleamed
with hatred. The muscles of his [*great] arms danced in the

light from the window. As he looked into the protruding eyes
of the writhing German he thought of fat Reverend Minot
Weeks [*of] Coal Creek and added an extra twitch to the
flesh between his finger[*s]. When a gesture of submission
came from the man against the wall he stepped back and let
go his grip. The German dropped to the floor. Standing over
him McGregor delivered his ultimatum. "You report this or
try to get me fired and I'll kill you outright," he said. "I'm
going to stay here, on this job, until I get ready to leave it.
You can tell me what to do and how to do it but when you
speak to me again say 'McGregor'—Mr. McGregor that's my
name."

The German got to his feet and began walking down [*the]
passageway between the rows of piled barrels. As he went he
helped himself along with his hands. McGregor went back to
work. After the retreating form of the German he shouted,
"Get a new place when you can, Dutch. I'll be taking this job
away from you when I'm ready for it." [4]

That evening as McGregor walked to the car he saw the
little grey-haired superintendent standing waiting for him [on
a corner] before a saloon. The man made a sign and McGregor
walked across and stood beside him. They went together
into the saloon and stood leaning against the bar looking at
each other. A smile played about the lips of the little man.
"What have you been doing to Frank?" he asked.

McGregor turned to the bartender who stood waiting
before [*him]. He thought that the superintendent intended
to try to patronize him by buying him a drink and he did not
like the thought. "What will you have? I'll take a cigar for
mine," he said quickly, defeating the superintendent's plan by
being the first to speak. When the bartender brought the
cigars McGregor paid for them and walked out at the door.
He felt like one playing a game. "If Frank meant to bully me
into submission this man also means something."

On the sidewalk before the saloon McGregor stopped. "Look

4. Anderson later wrote humorously of his boxing attempts in *A Story
Teller's Story*, ed. White, pp. 150–53, 160–61; and in *Tar*, ed. White,
pp. 198–99.

here," he said, turning and facing the superintendent, "I am after Frank's place. I am going to learn the business as fast as I can. I won't put it up to you to fire him. When I get ready for the place he won't be there."

A light flashed into the eyes of the little man. He held the cigar McGregor had paid for as though about to throw it into the street. "How far do you think you can go with your big fists?" he asked, his voice rising.

McGregor smiled. He thought he had earned another victory and lighting his cigar held the burning match before the little man. "Brains are intended to help fists," he said, "I've got both."

The superintendent looked at the burning match and at the cigar between his fingers. "If I don't, which will you use on me?" he asked.

McGregor threw the match into the street. "Aw! don't bother asking," he said, [*holding] out another match.

McGregor and the superintendent walked along the street. "I'd like to fire you, but I won't. Someday you'll run that warehouse like a clock," [*said the superintendent.]

McGregor sat in the street car and thought of his day. It had been, he felt, a day of two battles. First the direct brutal battle of fists in the passageway and then this other battle with the superintendent. He thought he had won both fights. Of the fight with the tall German he thought little. He had expected to win that. [*The other was different.] The superintendent he [*felt had wanted] to patronize him, patting him on the back and buying him drinks. Instead he had patronized the superintendent. A battle had gone on in the brains of the two men and he had won. He had met a new kind of man, one who did not live by the raw strength of his muscles, and he had given a good account of himself. The conviction that he had, besides a good pair of fists, a good brain swept in on him, glorifying him. He thought of the sentence, "Brains are intended to help fists," and wondered how he had happened to think of it.

CHAPTER II

THE street in which McGregor lived in Chicago was called Wycliff Place after a family of that name that had once owned the land thereabout. The street was complete in its hideousness. Nothing more unlovely could be imagined. Given a free hand, an indiscriminate lot of badly trained carpenters and brick layers had builded houses beside the cobblestone road that touched the fantastic in their unsightliness and inconvenience.

The great West Side of Chicago has hundreds of such streets and the coal mining town out of which [our] McGregor [*had come] was more inspiring as a place in which to live. As an unemployed young man, not much given to [*chance] companionship[*s], Beaut had spent many long evenings wandering [*alone] on the hillsides above his home town. There was a kind of dreadful loveliness about the place at night. The long black valley with its dense shroud of smoke that rose and fell and formed itself into fantastic shapes in the moonlight, the poor little houses clinging to the hillside, the occasional cry of a woman being beaten by a drunken husband, the glare of the coke fires and the rumble of coal cars being pushed along [*the] railroad tracks, all of these made a grim and rather inspiring impression on the young man's mind so that although he hated the mines and the miners he sometimes paused in his night wandering[*s] and stood with his great shoulders lifted, breathing deeply and feeling things he had no words in him to express.

In Wycliff Place McGregor got no such reactions. Foul dust filled the air. All day the street rumbled and roared under the wheels of trucks and light, hurrying delivery wagons. Soot from [*the] factory chimneys was caught up by the wind and having been mixed with powdered horse manure from the roadway flew into the eyes and the nostrils of pedestrians. Always a babble of voices went on. At a corner saloon teamsters stopped to have their drinking cans filled with beer and stood about swearing and shouting. In the evening women and children went back and forth from their houses carrying beer in pitchers from the same saloon. Dogs howled and fought, drunken men reeled along the sidewalk and the women of the town appeared in their cheap finery and paraded before the idlers about the saloon door.

The woman who rented the room to McGregor boasted to him of Wycliff blood. It was that, she told him, that had brought her to Chicago from her home at Cairo, Illinois. "The place was left to me and not knowing what else to do with it I came here to live," she said. She explained to him that the Wycliffs had been people of note in the early history of Chicago. The huge old house with the cracked stone steps and the ROOMS [*TO] RENT sign in the window had [*once] been their family seat.

The history of this woman was characteristic of the miss-fire quality of much of American life. She was at bottom a wholesome creature who should have lived in a neat frame house in a village and tended a garden. On Sunday she should have dressed herself with care and gone off to sit in a country church with her hands crossed and her soul at rest.

The thought of owning a house in the city had however paralyzed her brain. The house itself was worth a certain number of thousands of dollars and her mind could not rise above that fact, so her good broad face had become grimy with city dirt and her body weary from the endless toil of caring for roomers. On summer evenings she sat on the steps before her house clad in some bit of Wycliff finery taken from a trunk in the attic and when a lodger came out at the door she looked at him and said wistfully, "On such a night as this you could hear the whistles on the river steamers in Cairo." [5]

5. In the manuscript of *Marching Men*, the paragraphs that follow are rearranged thus:
"In the little court . . ."
"McGregor seldom saw . . ."
"McGregor lived in . . ."
"In this room sat . . ."

McGregor lived in a small room at the end of a hall on the second floor of the Wycliff house. The windows of the room looked down into a dirty little court almost surrounded by brick warehouses. The room was furnished with a bed, a chair that was always threatening to come to pieces and [*a] desk with weak carved legs.

In this room sat McGregor night after night striving to realize his Coal Creek dream of training his mind and making himself of some account in the world. From seven thirty until nine thirty he sat at a desk in a night school.[6] From ten until midnight he read in his room. He did not think of his surroundings, of the vast disorder of life about him, but tried with all his strength to bring something like order and purpose into his own mind and his own life.

In the little court under the window lay heaps of discarded newspaper tossed about by the wind. There in the heart of the city, walled in by the brick warehouse[s] and half concealed under piles of chair legs, cans and broken bottles, lay two logs, in their time, no doubt, a part of the grove that once lay about the house. The neighborhood had passed so rapidly from country estate to homes and from homes to rented [*lodgings] and huge brick warehouses that the marks of the lumberman's axe still showed in the butts of the logs.

McGregor seldom saw the little court except when its ugliness was refined and glossed over by darkness or by the moonlight. On hot evenings he laid down his book and, leaning far out of the window, rubbed his eyes and watched the discarded newspapers, worried by the whirlpools of wind in the court, run here and there, dashing against the warehouse walls and vainly trying to escape over the roof. The sight fascinated him and brought a thought into his mind. He began to think that the lives of most of the people about him were much like the dirty newspaper[s] harried by [*adverse winds] and surrounded by ugly walls of facts. The thought drove him

6. In the fall of 1897 Anderson studied a business course at the Lewis Institute in Chicago. See *Sherwood Anderson's Memoirs,* ed. White, pp. xxvi, 16, 169–70, 288.

from the window to renewed effort among his books. "I'll show them. I'll do something here, anyway," he growled.

One living in the house with McGregor during those first years in the city might have thought his life stupid and commonplace, but to him it did not seem so. It was for the miner's son a time of sudden and tremendous growth. Filled with confidence in the strength and quickness of his body he was beginning to have also confidence in the vigor and clearness of his brain. In the warehouse he went about with eyes and ears open, devising in his mind new methods of moving goods, watching the men at work, marking the shirkers, preparing to pounce upon the tall German's place as foreman.

The superintendent of the warehouse, not understanding the turn of the talk with McGregor on the sidewalk before the saloon, decided to like him and laughed when they met in the warehouse. The tall German maintained a policy of sullen silence, going to laborious lengths to avoid addressing him.

In his room at night McGregor began to read law, reading each page over and over and thinking of what he had read through the next day as he rolled and piled apple barrels in the passages in the warehouse.

McGregor had an aptitude and an appetite for facts. He read law as another and gentler nature might have read poetry or old legends. What he read at night he remembered and thought about during the day. He had no dream of the glories of the law. The fact that these rules laid down by men to govern their social organization were the result of ages of striving toward perfection did not greatly interest him and he only thought of them as weapons with which to attack and defend in the battle of brains he meant presently to fight. His mind gloated in anticipation of the battle.

CHAPTER III

AND then a new element asserted itself in the life of Mc-
Gregor. One of the hundreds of disintegrating forces that attack strong natures, striving to scatter their force in the back
currents of life, attacked him. His big body began to feel with
enervating persistency the call of sex.[7]

In the house in Wycliff Place McGregor passed as a mystery. By keeping silence he won a reputation for wisdom. The
clerks in the hall bedrooms thought him a scientist. The woman
from Cairo thought him a theological student. Down the hall a
pretty girl with large black eyes, who worked in a department
store down town, dreamed of him at night. When in the evening he banged his door to his room and strode down the hallway going to the night school she sat in a chair by the open
door of her room. When he passed she raised her eyes looking
at him boldly. When he returned she was again by the door
and again she looked boldly at him.

In his room, after the meetings with the black-eyed girl,
McGregor found difficulty in keeping his mind on the reading.
He felt as he had felt with the pale girl on the hillside beyond
Coal Creek. With her, as with the [*pale] girl, he felt the
need of defending himself. He began to make it a practice to
hurry [*along] past her door.

The girl in the [little] hall bedroom thought constantly of
McGregor. When he had gone to night school another young
man of the house who wore a Panama hat came from the floor
above and, putting his hands on the door frames of her room,
stood looking at her and talking. In his lips he held a cigarette
which, when he talked, hung limply from the corner of his
mouth.

7. The corresponding autobiographical accounts for this period in
Sherwood Anderson's life are in *Sherwood Anderson's Memoirs*, ed.
White, pp. 146–49, 157–64, 201–10, 230–34, 263–65, 269–71, 294–303.

This young man [*and] the black-eyed girl kept up a continuous stream of comments on the doings of red-haired McGregor. Begun by the young man, who hated McGregor because of his silence, the subject was kept alive by the girl who wanted to talk of McGregor.

On Saturday nights the young man and the girl sometimes went together to the theatre. One night in the summer when they had returned to the front of the house the girl stopped. "Let's see what the big redhead is doing," she said.

Going around the block they stole in the darkness down an alleyway and stood in the little dirty court looking up at McGregor who, with his feet in the window and a lamp burning at his shoulder, sat in his room reading.

When they returned to the front of the house the black-eyed girl kissed the young man, closing her eyes and thinking of McGregor. In her room later she lay abed [day-]dreaming. She imagined herself assaulted by the young man, who had crept into her room, and that McGregor had come roaring down the hall to snatch him away and fling him outside the door.

At the end of the hallway near the stairway leading to the street lived a barber. He had deserted a wife and four children in a town in Ohio and to prevent recognition had grown a black beard.[8] Between this man and McGregor a companionship had sprung up and they went together on Sunday mornings to walk in the park. The black-bearded man called himself Frank Turner.

Frank Turner had a passion. Through the evenings and on Sunday afternoons he sat in his room making violins. He worked with a knife, glue, pieces of glass and sand paper and spent his earnings for ingredients for the making of varnishes. When he got hold of a piece of wood that seemed an answer to his prayers he took it to McGregor's room and, holding it up to

8. As Anderson revised *Marching Men* after leaving his business in Ohio early in 1913, this passage could be the author's dramatization of his own actions in separating from his wife and three children after a nervous breakdown late in 1912. The best account of Anderson's famous "escape" from business into art is William Alfred Sutton, *Exit to Elsinore* (Muncie, Ind.: Ball State University, 1967).

the light, talked of what he would do with it. Sometimes he brought a violin and, sitting in the open window, tested the quality of its tone. One evening he took an hour of McGregor's time talking of the varnish of Cremona and reading to him from a worn little book [*concerning] the old Italian masters of violin making.

On a bench in the park sat Turner, the maker of violins, the man who dreamed of the rediscovery of the varnish of Cremona, talking to McGregor, son of the Pennsylvania miner.

It was [on] a Sunday afternoon and the park was vibrant with life. All day the street cars had been unloading Chicagoans at the park entrance. They came in pairs and in parties, young fellows with their sweethearts and fathers with families at their heels. Now at the end of the day they continued to come, a steady stream of humanity flowing along the gravel walk past the bench where the two men sat in talk. Through the stream and crossing it went another stream homeward bound. Babies cried. Fathers called to the children at play on the grass. Cars, coming to the park filled, went away filled.

McGregor looked about him thinking of himself and of the restless moving people. In him there was none of that vague fear of the multitude[s] common to many solitary souls. His contempt of men and of the lives lived by men reinforced his native boldness. The odd little rounding of the shoulders of even the athletic young men made him straighten with pride his own shoulders and, fat and lean, tall and short, he thought of all men as [things blown here and there in a disorderly world or as] counters in some vast game[*s] at which he was presently to be a master player.

The passion for form, that strange intuitive power that many men have felt and none but the masters of human life have understood, had begun to awaken in him. Already he had begun to sense out the fact that for him [the study of] law was but an incident in some vast design [which he meant to try to understand] and he was altogether untouched by the desire for getting on in the world, by the greedy little snatching at trifles, that was the whole purpose of the lives of [*so many of]

the people about him. When somewhere in the park a band
began to play he nodded his head [*up and down] and ran
his hand nervously up and down the legs of his trousers. Into
his mind came the desire to boast to the barber [sitting beside
him], telling of the things he meant to do in the world, but he
put the desire away. Instead he sat silently blinking his eyes
and wondering at the persistent air of ineffectiveness in the
people who passed. When a band, playing march music and
followed by some fifty men wearing white plumes in their hats
and walking with self-conscious awkwardness went by, he was
startled. [With a jump of his heart he remembered the soldiers
who had marched in the streets of Coal Creek and how the
swing of their bodies had thrilled him.] Among the people he
thought there was a change. Something like a running shadow
passed over them. The babbling of voices ceased and like himself the people began to nod their heads. A thought, gigantic
in its simplicity, began to come into his mind, but [it] was
wiped out immediately by his impatience with the marchers.
A madness to spring up and run among them knocking them
about and making them march with the power that comes of
abandonment almost lifted him from the bench. His mouth
twitched and his fingers ached for action.

In and out among the trees and on the green spaces moved
the people. Along the shores of a pond sat men and women eating the evening meal from baskets or from white cloths spread
on the grass. They laughed and shouted at each other and at
the children, calling them back from the gravel driveways filled
with moving carriages. Beaut saw a girl throw an egg shell hitting a young fellow between the eyes and then run laughing
away along the shore of the pond. Under a tree a woman
nursed a babe, covering her breasts with a shawl, so that just
the black head of the babe showed. Its tiny hand clutched at
the mouth of the woman. In an open space in the shadow of
a building the young men played baseball, the shouts of the
spectators rising above the murmur of [*the] voices of [the]
people on the gravel walk.

A thought came into McGregor's mind that he wanted to discuss with the older man. He was moved by the sight of women about and shook himself like one awakening from a dream. Then he began looking at the ground and kicking up the gravel with his foot. "Look here," he said, turning to the barber, "what is a man to do about [*women], about getting what he wants from the women?"

The barber seemed to understand. "It has come to that then?" he asked looking up quickly. He lighted a pipe and sat looking at the people. It was then he told McGregor of the wife and four children in the Ohio town, describing the little brick house and the garden and the coop for chickens at the back like one who lingers over a place dear to his fancy. Something old and weary was in his voice as he finished.

"It wasn't a matter for me to decide," he said. "I came away because I couldn't do anything else. I'm not excusing myself, I'm just telling you. There was something messy and disorderly about it all, about my life with her and with them. I couldn't stand it. I felt myself [going down,] being submerged by something. I wanted to be orderly and to work, you see. I couldn't let violin making alone. Lord, how I tried—tried bluffing myself about it—calling it a fad."

The barber looked nervously at McGregor reassuring himself of his interest. "I owned a shop on the main street of our town. [*Back of it was] a blacksmith shop. During the day I stood by the chair in my shop talking, to men being shaved, about the love of women and a man's duty to his family. Summer afternoons I went and sat on a keg in the blacksmith shop talking of the same thing with the smith but all that did [*me] no good.

"When I let myself go I dreamed, not of my duty to my family, but of working undisturbed as I do now here in the city, in the evenings in my room and on Sundays."

A sharpness came into the voice of the speaker. He turned to McGregor and talked vigorously like one making a defense. "My woman was a good enough sort," he said. "I suppose loving is an art like writing a book or drawing pictures or making violins. People try to do it and don't succeed. In the end we threw the job up and just lived together like most people do. Our lives got mussy and meaningless. That's how it was.

"Before she married me my wife had been a stenographer in a factory that made tin cans. She liked that work. She could make her fingers dance along the keys. When she read a book at home she didn't think the writer amounted to much if he made mistakes about punctuation. Her boss was so proud of her that he would brag of her work to visitors and [*sometimes would] go off fishing leaving the running of the business in her hands.

"I don't know why she married me. She was happier there and she is happier back there now. We got to walking together on Sunday evenings and standing under the trees on side streets kissing and looking at each other. We talked about a lot of things. We seemed to need each other. Then we got married and started living together.

"It didn't work out. After we had been married a few years things changed. I don't know why. I thought I was the same as I had been and I think she was. We used to sit around quarreling about it, each blaming the other. Anyway we didn't get along.

"We would sit on the little front porch of our house in the evening, she bragging of the work she had done in the can factory [office before she married me] and I dreaming of quietude and a chance to work on the violin[*s]. I thought I knew a way to increase the quality and beauty of tone and I had that idea about varnish I have talked to you about. I even dreamed of doing things those old fellows of Cremona didn't do.

"When she had been talking of her work in the office for maybe a half hour she would look up and find that I hadn't been listening. We would quarrel. We even quarreled before the children after they came. Once she said she didn't see how it would matter if no violins had ever been made and that night I dreamed of choking her in bed. I woke up and lay there beside her thinking of it with something like real satisfaction in just the thought that one long hard grip of my fingers would get her out of my way for good.

"We didn't always feel that way. Every little while a change would come over us both and we would begin to take an interest in each other. I would be proud of the work she had done in the factory [office] and would brag of it to men coming into the shop. In the evening she would be sympathetic about the violins, putting the baby to bed and letting me alone at my work in the kitchen.

"Then we would begin sitting [together] in the darkness in the house holding each other's hands. We would forgive things that had been said, and play a sort of game, chasing each other about the room in the darkness, knocking against [*the] chairs and laughing. Then we would begin to look at each other and kiss. Presently there would be another baby." [9]

The barber threw up his hands with a gesture of impatience. His voice lost its softer, reminiscent quality. "Such times didn't last," he said. "On the whole it was no life to live. I came away. The children are in a state institution and she has gone back to her work in the office. The town hates me. They have made a [kind of] heroine of her. I'm here talking to you with these whiskers on my face so that people from my town wouldn't know me if they came along. I'm a barber and I would shave them off fast enough if it wasn't for that."

A woman walking past looked back at McGregor. In her eyes lurked a [kind of] invitation. It reminded him of something in the eyes of the pale daughter of the undertaker of Coal Creek. An uneasy tremor ran through him. "What do you [*do] about women now?" he asked.

The voice of the smaller man [*a]rose harsh and excited in the evening air. "I get the feeling taken out of me as a man would have a tooth fixed," he said. "I pay money for the ser-vice[s] and keep my mind on what I want to do. There are plenty of women for that, women who are good only for that. When I first came here I used to wander about at night, want-ing to go to my room and work but with my mind and my will paralyzed by that feeling. I don't do that now and I won't again. What I do many men do—good men—men who do good

9. Anderson later described having witnessed such a scene as a paper boy in *Tar*, ed. White, pp. 146–48; and in *Sherwood Anderson's Memoirs*, ed. White, pp. 89–90.

work. What's the use thinking about it when you only run
against a stone wall and get hurt?"

The black-bearded man arose, thrust his hands into his
trouser[*s] pockets and looked about him. Then he sat down
again [heavily]. He seemed to be filled with suppressed excitement. "There is a big hidden something going on in modern
life," he said, talking rapidly and excitedly. "It used to touch
only the men higher up, now it reaches down to men like me—
barbers and workingmen. Men know about it but don't talk
and don't dare think. Their women have changed. Women used
to be willing to do anything for men, just be slaves to them.
The best men don't ask that now and don't want [*that]."

He jumped to his feet standing over McGregor. "Men don't
understand what's going on and don't care," he said, "they are
too busy getting things done or going to ball games or quarreling about politics.

"And what do they know about it if they are fools enough to
think? They get thrown into false notions. They see about them
a lot of fine, purposeful women, maybe caring for their children, and they blame themselves for their vices and are
ashamed. Then they turn to the other women anyway, shut-
ting their eyes and going ahead. They pay for what they want
as they would pay for a dinner, thinking no more of the
women who serve them than they do of the waitresses who
carry in the dinner in the restaurants. They refuse to think of
the new kind of women that [*is] growing up. They know that,
if they get sentimental about them, they'll [soon] get into
trouble or get new tests put to them, be disturbed, you see, and
spoil their work or their peace of mind. They don't want to get
into trouble or be disturbed. They want to get a better job or
enjoy a ball game or build a bridge or write a book. They think
that a man who gets sentimental about any woman is a fool
and of course he is." [10]

10. For Anderson's later treatment of the feminist theme, see his *Perhaps Women* (New York: Horace Liveright, 1931); and Edward Francis
Carr, "Sherwood Anderson: Champion of Women" (M.A. thesis, University of Pittsburgh, 1946).

"Do you mean that all of them do that?" asked McGregor. He wasn't upset by what had been said. It struck him as being true. For himself he was afraid of [*women]. It seemed to him that a road was being built by his companion along which he might travel with safety. He wanted the man to go on talking. Into his brain flashed the thought that, if he had the thing to do over, there would have been a different ending to the afternoon spent with the pale girl on the hillside.

The barber sat down [again] upon the bench. The flush went out of his cheek[*s]. "Well, I have done pretty well myself," he said, "but then you know I make violins and don't [often] think of women. I have been in Chicago two years and I have spent just eleven dollars. I would like to know what the average man spends. I wish some fellow would get the facts and publish them. It would make people sit up. There must be millions spent here every year.

"You see, I'm not very strong and I stand all day [long] on my feet in the barber shop." He looked at McGregor and laughed. "The black-eyed girl in the hall is after you," he said. "You had better look out. You let her alone. Stick to your law book[*s]. You're not like me. You are big and red and strong. Eleven dollars won't pay your way here in Chicago for no two years."

McGregor looked again at the people moving toward the park entrance in the gathering darkness. He thought it wonderful that a brain could think a thing out so clearly and words express thoughts so lucidly. His eagerness to follow the passing girls with his eyes was gone. He was interested in the older man's viewpoint. "And what about children?" he asked.

The older man sat sideways on the bench. There was a troubled look in his eyes and a suppressed, eager quality in his voice. "I'm going to tell you about that," he said, "I don't want to keep back anything.

"Look here!" he demanded, sliding along the bench toward McGregor and emphasizing his points, by slapping one hand down upon the other. "Ain't all children my children?" He paused, trying to gather his scattered thoughts into words. When McGregor started to speak he put up his hand as though

to ward off a new thought or another question. "I'm not trying
to dodge," he said, "I'm trying to get thoughts that have been
in my head day after day in shape to tell. I haven't tried to express them before. I know men and women cling to their children. It's the only thing they have left of the dream they
had before they married. I felt that way. It held me for a long
time. It would be holding me now only that the violins pulled
so hard at me."

He threw up his hand impatiently. "You see I had to find an
answer. I couldn't think of being a skunk—running away—
and I couldn't stay. I wasn't intended to stay. Some men are
intended to work and take care of children and serve women
perhaps but others have to keep trying for a vague something
all their lives—like me trying for a tone on a violin. If they
don't get it, it doesn't matter, they have to keep trying.

"My wife used to say I'd get tired of it. No woman ever
really understands a man caring for anything except herself. I
knocked that out of her."

The little man looked up at McGregor. "Do you think I'm a
skunk?" he asked.

McGregor looked at him gravely. "I don't know," he said.
"Go on and tell me about the children."

"I said they were the last things to cling to. They are. We
used to have religion. But that's pretty well gone now—the old
kind. Now men think about children, I mean a certain kind of
men—the ones that have work they want to get on with—children and work are the only things that kind care about. If
they have a sentiment about women, it's only about their own
—the one they have in the house with them. They want to keep
that one finer than they are themselves. So they work the[ir]
other feeling[s] out on the paid women.

"Women fuss about men loving children. Much they care. It's
only a plan for demanding adulation for themselves that they
don't earn. Once when I first came to the city I took a place as
servant in a wealthy family. I wanted to stay under cover until
my beard grew. Women used to come there to receptions, and
to meetings in the afternoon, to talk about reforms they were
interested in—— Bah! They work and scheme trying to get at

men. They are at it all their lives, flattering, diverting us, giving us false ideas, pretending to be weak and uncertain when they are strong and determined. They have no mercy. They wage war on us, trying to make us slaves. They want to take us captive home to their houses, as Caesar took captives home to Rome.

"You look here!" He jumped to his feet again, shaking his fingers at McGregor. "You just try something. You try being open and frank and square with a woman—any woman—as you would with a man. Let her live her own life, and ask her to let you live yours. You try it. She won't. She will die first." [11]

He sat down again upon the bench, and shook his head back and forth. "Lord, how I wish I could talk!" he said. "I'm making a muddle of this, and I wanted to tell you. Oh, how I wanted to tell you! [I want to keep you out of making a muddle of your life with women.] It's part of my idea that a man should tell a boy all he knows. We've got to quit lying to them."

McGregor looked at the ground. He was profoundly and deeply moved and interested, as he had never before been moved by anything but hate.

Two women coming along the gravel walk stopped under a tree, and looked back. The barber smiled, and raised his hat. When they smiled back at him, he rose and started toward them. "Come on, boy [, let's get them]," he whispered behind his hand to McGregor.

When McGregor looked up, the scene before his eyes infuriated him. The smiling barber with his hat in his hand, the two women waiting under the tree, the look of half guilty innocence on the faces of all of them, stirred a blind fury in his brain. He sprang forward, clutching the shoulder of Turner with his hand. Whirling him about, he threw him to his hands and knees. "Get out of here, you females!" he roared at the women, who ran off in terror down the walk.

The barber sat again upon the bench beside McGregor. He

11. Such a statement became Sherwood Anderson's complaint against his second wife, Tennessee Mitchell, whom he married in 1916. See William Alfred Sutton, "Sherwood Anderson's Second Wife," *Ball State University Forum,* VII (Spring, 1966), 39–46.

rubbed his hands together, brushing the bits of gravel out of the flesh. "What's got wrong with you?" he asked.

McGregor hesitated. He wondered how he should tell what was in his mind. "Everything in its place," he said finally, "I wanted to go on with our talk."

Lights flashed out of the darkness of the park. The two men sat on the bench, thinking each his own thoughts.

[Finally the barber spoke.] "I want to take some work out of the clamps tonight," [*the barber] said, looking at his watch.

Together the two men walked along the street. "Look here," said McGregor. "I didn't mean to hurt you. Those two women, coming up and interfering with what we were working out, made me furious."

[The barber began again on the same subject.] "Women always interfere," [*said the barber]. "They raise hell with men." His mind ran out and began to play with the world old problem of the sexes. "If a lot of women fall in the fight with us men, and become our slaves—serving us, as the paid women do—need they fuss about it? Let them be game and try to help work it out as men have been game and have worked and thought through ages of [*perplexity] and defeat."

The barber stopped on the street corner to fill and light his pipe. "Women can change everything when they want to," he said, looking at McGregor and letting the match burn out in his fingers. "They can have [suffrage and] motherhood pensions and [real independence and] [*room to work out their own problem in the world or] anything else that they really want. They can stand up face to face with men [if they will]. They don't want to. They want to enslave us with their faces and their bodies. They want to carry on the old, old weary fight." He tapped McGregor on the arm. "If a few of us —wanting with all our might to get something done—beat them at their own game don't we deserve the victory?" he asked.

"But I sometimes think I would like a woman to live with, you know, just to sit and talk with me," said McGregor.

The barber laughed. Puffing at his pipe he walked down the street. "To be sure! To be sure!" he said. "I would. Any man

would. I like to sit in the room for a spell in the evening talking
to you, but I would hate to give up violin making and be bound
all my life to serve you and your purposes just the same."

In the hallway of their own house the barber spoke to Mc-
Gregor as he looked down the hallway to where the door of
the black-eyed girl's room had just crept open. "You let women
alone," he said, "when you feel you can't stay away from them
any longer you come and talk it over with me."

McGregor nodded and went along the hallway to his own
room. In the darkness he stood by the window and looked
down into the court. The feeling of hidden power, the ability to
[a]rise above the mess into which modern life had sunk, that
had come to him in the park returned and he walked nervously
about. When finally he sat down upon a chair and leaning forward put his head in his hands he [was very grateful for the
adventure with the barber. He] felt like one who has started
on a long journey through a strange and dangerous country
and who has unexpectedly come upon a friend going the same
way.

CHAPTER IV

THE people of Chicago go home from their work at evening. Drifting they go, in droves, hurrying along. It is a startling thing to look closely at them. The people have bad mouths. Their mouths are slack and the jaws do not hang right. The mouths are like the shoes they wear. The shoes have become run down at the corners from too much pounding on [*the] hard pavements and the mouths have become crooked from too much weariness of soul.

Something is wrong with modern American life and we Americans do not want to look at it. We much prefer to call ourselves a great people and let it go at that.

It is evening and the people of Chicago go home from work. Clatter, clatter, clatter go the [run down] heels on the hard pavements, jaws wag, the wind blows and dirt drifts and sifts through the masses of the people. Everyone has dirty ears. The stench in the street cars is horrible. The antiquated bridges over the rivers are packed with people. The suburban trains going away south and west are cheaply constructed and dangerous. A people, calling itself great and living in a city, also called great, go to their houses a mere disorderly mass of humans cheaply equipped. Everything is cheap. When the people get [*home] to their houses they sit [*on] cheap chairs before cheap tables and eat cheap food. They have given their lives for cheap things. The poorest peasant of one of the old [*countries] is surrounded by more beauty. His very equipment for living has more solidity.[12]

The modern man is satisfied with what is cheap and unlovely because he expects to rise in the world. He has given his life to that dreary dream and he is teaching his children to fol-

12. For a discussion of Anderson's life-long regret at the passing of craftsmanship, see Thomas Reed West, *Flesh of Steel: Literature and the Machine in American Culture* (Nashville: Vanderbilt University Press, 1967), pp. 21–34.

low the same dream. McGregor was touched by it. Being confused [*by] the matter of sex he had listened to the advice of
the barber and meant to settle things in the cheap way. One
evening a month after the talk in the park he hurried along
Lake Street on the West Side with that end in view. It was near
eight o'clock and growing dark and McGregor should have
been at the night school. Instead he walked along the street
looking at the ill-kept frame houses. A fever burned in his
blood. An impulse, for the moment stronger than the impulse
that kept him at work over books night after night there in the
big disorderly city, and as yet stronger than any new impulse
toward a vigorous, compelling march through life, had hold of
him. His eyes stared into [*the] windows. He hurried along,
filled with a lust that stultified his brain and [his] will. A
woman sitting at the window of a little frame house smiled and
beckoned to him.[13]

McGregor walked along the path leading to the little frame
house. The path ran through a squalid yard. It was a foul place
like the court under his window behind the house in Wycliff
Place. Here also, discolored [news]papers, worried by the
wind, ran about in crazy circles. McGregor's heart pounded
and his mouth felt dry and unpleasant. He wondered what he
should say and how he should say it when he came into the
presence of the woman. He wished there were someone
[about] to be hit with his fist. He didn't want to make love, he
wanted relief. He should have much preferred a fight.

The veins in McGregor's neck began to swell and as he stood
in the darkness before the door of the house he swore. [Then]
he stared up and down the street but the sky, the sight of
which might have helped him, was hidden from view by the
structure of an elevated railroad. [And so,] pushing open
the door of the house he stepped in. In the dim light he could
see nothing but a form sprang out of the darkness and a pair of
powerful arms pinned his hands to his side[*s]. McGregor

13. In his later autobiographical account of this incident, the author
behaves much less heroically. See *Sherwood Anderson's Memoirs*, ed.
White, pp. 163–64.

looked quickly about. A man, huge as himself, held him tightly against the door. He had one glass eye and a stubby black beard and in the half light looked sinister and dangerous. The hand of the woman, who had beckoned to him from the window, fumbled in McGregor's pockets and came out clutching a little roll of money. Her face, set now and ugly like the man's, looked up at him from under the arms of her ally.

In a moment McGregor's heart stopped pounding and the dry, unpleasant taste went out of his mouth. He felt relieved and glad at this sudden turn to the affair.

With a quick upward snap of his knees into the stomach of the man who [*had] held him, McGregor freed himself. A swinging blow to the neck sent his assailant groaning to the floor. McGregor sprang across the room. In the corner by the bed he caught the woman. Clutching her by the hair he whirled her about. "Hand over that money. [Give it back to me. Do you hear?]" he said fiercely.

The woman put up her hands, pleading with him. The grip of his hand[*s] in her hair brought the tears to her eyes. She thrust the roll of bills into his hands and [*waited], trembling, thinking he intended to kill her.

A new feeling swept over McGregor. The thought of having come into the house at the invitation of this woman was revolting to him. He wondered how he could have been such a beast. As he stood in the dim light thinking of this and looking at the woman he became lost in thought and wondered why the idea given him by the barber [and] that had seemed so clear and sensible now seemed so foolish. His eyes stared at the woman, as his mind returned to the black-bearded barber talking on the park bench, and he was seized with a blind fury, a fury not directed at the people in the foul little room but at himself and his own blindness. Again a great hatred of the disorder of life took hold of him and as though all of the disorderly people of the world were personified in her he swore and shook the woman as a dog might have shaken a foul rag.

"Sneak! Dodger! Mussy fool[s]!" he muttered, thinking of himself as a giant attacked by some nauseous beast. The woman screamed with terror. Seeing the look on her assailant's face and mistaking the meaning of his words, she trembled and thought again of death. Reaching under the pillow on the bed she got another roll of bills and thrust that also into McGregor's hands. "Please go," she plead. "We were mistaken. We thought you were someone else."

McGregor strode to the door, past the man on the floor who groaned and rolled about. He walked around the corner to Madison Street and boarded a car for the night school. Sitting in the car he counted the money in the roll thrust into his hand by the kneeling woman and laughed so that the people in the car looked [around] at him in amazement. "Turner has spent eleven dollars among them in two years and I have got twenty-seven dollars in one night," he thought. [Presently] he jumped off the car and walked along under the street lights striving to think things out. "I can't depend on anyone," he muttered. "I have to make my own way. The barber is as confused as the rest of them and he doesn't know it. There is a way out of the confusion and I'm going to find it but I will have to do it alone. I can't take anyone's word for anything."

CHAPTER V

THE matter of McGregor's attitude toward women and the call of sex was not, of course, settled by the fight in the house in Lake Street. He was a man who, even in the days of his great crudeness, appealed strongly to the mating instinct in women and more than once his purpose was to be shaken and his mind disturbed by the forms, the faces and the eyes of women.

McGregor thought he had settled the matter. He forgot the black-eyed girl in the hallway and thought only of advancement in the warehouse and of study in his room at night. Now and then he took an evening off and went for a walk through the streets or in one of the parks.

In the streets of Chicago, under the night lights, among the restless moving people, he was a figure to be remembered. Sometimes he did not see the people at all but went swinging along in the same spirit in which he had walked in the Pennsylvania hills. Some elusive quality in life that seemed to be forever out of reach he was trying to get hold of. He didn't want to be a lawyer or a warehouse man. What did he want? Along the street he went trying to make up his mind and because his was not a gentle nature his perplexity drove him to anger and he swore.

Up and down Madison Street he went striding along [with his fists closed and] his lips muttering words. In a corner saloon someone played a piano. Groups of girls passed laughing and talking. He came to the bridge that led over the river into the loop district and then turned restlessly back. On the sidewalks along Canal Street he saw strong-bodied men loitering before cheap lodging houses. Their clothing was filthy with long wear and there was no light of determination in their faces. In the little fine interstices of the cloth of which their clothes were made was gathered the filth of the city in which they lived and in the stuff of their natures the filth and disorder of modern civilization had also found lodging.

On walked McGregor looking at man-made things and the flame of anger within burned stronger and stronger. He saw the drifting clouds of people of all nations that wander at night in Halstead Street and, turning into a side street, saw also the Italians, Poles and Russians that at evening gather on the sidewalks before tenements in that district.

The desire in McGregor for some kind of activity became a madness. His body shook with the strength of his desire to end the vast disorder of life. With all [of] the ardor of youth he wanted to see if, with the strength of his arm, he could shake mankind out of its sloth. A drunken man passed and following him came a large man with a pipe in his mouth. The large man did not walk with any suggestion of power in his legs. He shambled along. He was like a huge child, with fat cheeks and great [heavy] untrained body, a child without muscles and hardness, clinging to the skirts of life.

McGregor could not bear the sight of the big ungainly figure. The man seemed to personify all of the things against which his soul was in revolt and [so, stopping,] he stood crouched, a ferocious light burning in his eyes.

Into the gutter rolled the [large] man stunned by the force of the blow dealt him by the miner's son. He crawled on his hands and knees crying for help. His pipe had rolled away into the darkness.

McGregor stood on the sidewalk and waited. A crowd of men, standing before a tenement house, started to run toward him. Again he crouched. He prayed that they would come on, [*and] let him fight them also. In anticipation of a great struggle joy shone in his eyes and his muscles twitched.

And then the man in the gutter got to his feet and ran away. The men, who had started running toward him, stopped and turned back. McGregor walked on, his heart heavy with the sense of defeat. He was a little sorry for the man he had struck and who had made so ridiculous a figure crawling about on his hands and knees and he was more perplexed than ever.

. . . .

McGregor tried again to solve the problem of women. He had been much pleased by the outcome of the affair in the little frame house and the next day bought law books with the twenty-seven dollars thrust into his hand by the frightened woman. Later he stood in his room stretching his great body, like a lion returning from the kill, and thought of the little black-bearded barber in the room at the end of the hall stooping over his violin, his mind busy with the attempt to justify himself because he would not face one of life's problems. The feeling of resentment against the man had gone. He thought of the course laid out for himself by that philosopher and laughed. "There is something about it to avoid, like giving yourself up to digging in the dirt under the ground," he told himself.

McGregor's second adventure began on a Saturday night and again he let himself be led into it by the barber. The night was hot and the younger man sat in his room filled with a desire to go forth and explore the city. The quiet of the house, the distant rumble of street cars, the sound of a band playing far down the street disturbed and diverted his mind. He wished that he might take a stick in his hands and, going forth, prowl among the hills as he had gone on such nights in his youth in the Pennsylvania town.

The door to his room opened and the barber came in. In his hand he held two tickets. He sat on the window sill to explain.

"There is a dance in a hall on Monroe Street," said the barber excitedly. "I have two tickets here. A politician sold them to the boss in the shop where I work." The barber threw back his head and laughed. To his mind there was something delicious in the thought of the boss barber being forced by the politician[*s] to buy dance tickets. "They cost two dollars each," he cried and shook with laughter. "You should have seen my boss squirm. He didn't want the tickets but was afraid not to take them. The politician could make trouble for him and he knew it. You see we make a hand book on the races in the shop and that is against the law. The politician could make trouble for us. The boss paid out the [*four] dollars swearing under his breath and when the politician had gone out he

threw them at me. 'There, take them,' he shouted, 'I don't want
the rotten things. Is a man a horse trough at which every
beast can stop to drink?' "

McGregor and the barber sat in the room laughing at the
boss barber who had smilingly bought the tickets while con-
sumed with inward wrath. The barber [*urged] McGregor to
go with him to the dance. "We will make a night of it," he said.
"We will see women there—two that I know. They live upstairs over a grocery store. I have been with them. They will
open your eyes. They are a kind of women you haven't known
—bold and clever and good fellows too." [14]

McGregor got up and [*pulled] his shirt over his head. A
wave of feverish excitement ran over his body. "We'll see about
this," he said, "we'll see if this is another wrong trail you are
starting me on. You go to your room and get ready. I'm going
to fix myself up."

In the dance hall McGregor sat on a seat by the wall with
one of the two women lauded by the barber and the little
milliner. To him the adventure had been [*a] failure. The
swing of the dance music struck no answering chord in him. He
saw the couples on the floor, clasped in each other's arms,
writhing and turning, swaying back and forth, looking into
each other's eyes, and turned aside wishing himself back in his
room among the law books.

The barber talked to two of the women, bantering them. Mc-
Gregor thought the conversation inane and trivial. It skirted
the edge of things and ran off into vague references to other
times and adventures of which he knew nothing.

The barber danced away with one of the women. She was
tall and the head of the barber barely passed her shoulder. His
black beard shone against her white dress. The two women
sitting beside him talked and McGregor gathered that the frail
woman was a maker of hats. Something about her attracted
him and he leaned against the wall looking at her, not hearing
the talk.

14. In his *Memoirs*, ed. White, pp. 157–63, Anderson writes of an
affair with a "woman over the store."

A youth came up and took the other woman away. From across the hall the barber beckoned to him.

A thought flashed into his mind. This woman beside him was frail and thin and bloodless like the women of Coal Creek. A feeling of intimacy with her came over him. He felt as he had felt concerning the tall pale girl of Coal Creek when they together had climbed the hill to the eminence that looked down into the valley of farms.

CHAPTER VI

EDITH CARSON, the milliner whom fate had thrown into the company of McGregor, was a frail woman of thirty-four and lived alone in two rooms at the back of her millinery store. Her life was almost devoid of color. On Sunday morning she wrote a long letter to her family on an Indiana farm and then, putting on a hat from among the samples in the show case along the wall, [she] went to church, sitting by herself, in the same seat, Sunday after Sunday, and afterward remembering nothing of the sermon.

On Sunday afternoon[s] Edith went by street car to a park and walked alone under the trees. If it threatened rain she sat in the larger of the two rooms back of the shop sewing at new dresses for herself or for a sister who had married a blacksmith in the Indiana town and who had four children.

Edith had soft, mouse-colored hair and grey eyes with small brown spots on the iris. She was so [*slender] that she wore pads about her body under her dress to fill it out. In her youth she had had a sweetheart—a fat, round-cheeked boy who lived on the next farm. Once they had gone together to the fair at the county seat and, coming home in the buggy at night, he had put his arm about her and kissed her. "You ain't very big," he said.

Edith sent to a mail order house in Chicago and bought the padding which she wore under her dress. With it came an oil which she rubbed on herself. The placard on the bottle spoke of the contents with great respect, calling it a wonderful developer. The heavy pads wore raw places on her side against which her clothes rubbed. She bore the pain with grim stoicism, remembering what the fat boy had said.

After Edith came to Chicago and opened [*a] shop of her own, she had a letter from her former admirer. "It pleases me to think that the same wind that blows over me blows also over you," it said. After that one letter she did not hear from him again. He had the phrase out of a book he had read and had written the letter to Edith that he might use it. After the letter had gone he thought of her frail figure and repented of the impulse that had tricked him into writing. Half in alarm he began courting and soon married another girl.

Sometimes, on her rare visits home, Edith had seen her former lover driving along the road. The sister who had married the blacksmith said that he was stingy, that his wife had nothing to wear but a cheap calico dress and that, on Saturday, he drove off to town alone, leaving her to milk the cows and feed the pigs and horses.[15] Once he encountered Edith on the road and tried to get her into the wagon to ride with him. Although she had walked along the road ignoring him she took the letter about the wind, that blew over them both, out of a drawer on spring evenings, or after a walk in the park, and read it over. After she had read it she sat in the darkness at the front of the store looking through the screen door at people in the street and wondering what life would mean to her if she had a man on whom she could bestow her love. In her heart she believed that, unlike the wife of the fat youth, she would have borne children.

In Chicago Edith Carson had made money. She had a genius for economy in the management of her business. In six years she had cleared a large debt from the shop and had a comfortable balance in the bank. Girls who worked in factories or in stores came and left most of their meager surplus in her shop and other girls who didn't work came in, throwing dollars about and talking about "gentlemen friends." Edith hated the bargaining but attended to it with shrewdness and with a

15. The same motif became Anderson's famous short story, "Death in the Woods," *American Mercury*, IX (September, 1926), 7–13; *Death in the Woods and Other Stories* (New York: Liveright, 1933), pp. 3–24. See Sister M. Joselyn, "Some Artistic Dimensions of Sherwood Anderson's 'Death in the Woods,'" *Studies in Short Fiction*, IV (Spring, 1967), 252–59; and Mary Rohrberger, "The Man, the Boy, and the Myth: Sherwood Anderson's 'Death in the Woods,'" *Midcontinent American Studies Journal*, III (Fall, 1962), 48–54.

quiet, disarming little smile on her face. What she liked was to sit quietly, in the room, and trim hats. When the business grew she had a woman to tend [*the] shop and a girl to sit beside her and help with the hats. She had a friend, the wife of a motorman on the street car line, who sometimes came to see her in the evening. The friend was a plump little woman, dissatisfied with her marriage, and [*she] got Edith to make her several new hats a year for which she paid nothing.

Edith went to the dance at which she met McGregor with the motorman's wife and a girl who lived upstairs over a bakery next door to [*the] shop. The dance was held in a hall over a saloon and was given for the benefit of a political organization in which the baker was a leader. The wife of the baker came in and sold Edith two tickets, one for herself and one for the wife of the motorman who happened to be sitting with her at the time.

That evening, after the motorman's wife had gone home, Edith decided to go to the dance and [coming to] the decision was something like an adventure in itself. The night was hot and sultry, lightning flashed in the sky, and clouds of dust swept down the street. Edith sat in the darkness behind the bolted screen door looking at the people who hurried homeward down the street and a wave of revolt at the narrowness and emptiness of her life ran through her. Tears sprang to her eyes. She closed the shop door and, going into the room at the back, lighted the gas and stood looking at herself in the [*mirror]. "I'll go to the dance," she thought. "Perhaps I shall get a man. If he won't marry me he can have what he wants of me anyway."

In the dance hall Edith sat demurely by the wall near a window and watched the couples whirling [*about] on the floor. Through an open door she could see couples sitting in another room [*around] tables and drinking beer. A tall young man in white trousers and white slippers went about on the dance floor, smiling and bowing to the women. Once he started across the [dance] floor toward Edith and her heart beat rapidly but, just when she thought he intended speaking to her and to the motorman's wife, he turned and went to another part of the room. Edith followed him with her eyes, admiring his white trousers and his shining white teeth.

The wife of the motorman went away with a small, straight man with a grey mustache whom Edith thought had unpleasant eyes and two girls came and sat beside her. They were customers of her store and lived together in a flat over a grocery on Monroe Street. Edith had heard the girl, who sat in the workroom with her, speak slightingly of them. The three sat together along the wall talking of hats.

And then across the floor of the dance hall came two men, a huge red-haired fellow and a little man with a black beard. The two women hailed them, and the five sat together making a party by the wall, the little man keeping up a running stream of comments about the people on the floor with Edith's two companions. A dance struck up and, taking one of the women, the black-bearded man danced away. Edith and the other woman again [*talked] of hats. The huge fellow beside her said nothing but followed the women about the dance hall with his eyes. Edith thought she had never seen so homely a fellow.

At the end of the dance the black-bearded man went through the door into the room filled with little tables and made a sign to the red-haired man to follow. A boyish looking fellow appeared and went away with the other woman and Edith sat alone on the bench by the wall beside McGregor.

[McGregor began to talk.] "This place doesn't interest me," [*said McGregor quickly]. "I don't like to sit watching people hop about on their toes. If you want to come with me, we'll get out of here and go to some place where we can [*talk and] get acquainted."

The little milliner walked across the floor on the arm of McGregor her heart jumping with excitement. "I've got a man," she thought exulting. That the man had deliberately chosen her, she knew. She had heard the introductions, and the bantering talk of the black-bearded man; and [she] had noted the indifference of the big man to the other women.

Edith looked at her companion's huge frame and forgot his homeliness. Into her mind came a picture of the fat boy, grown into a man, driving down the road in the wagon, and leeringly asking her to ride with him. A flood of anger at the memory of the look of greedy assurance, in his eyes, came over her. "This one could knock him over a six-rail fence," she thought.

"Where are we going now?" she asked.

McGregor looked down at her. "To some place where we can talk," he said. "I was sick of this place. You ought to know where we are going. I'm going with you. You aren't going with me."

McGregor wished he were in Coal Creek. He felt he should like to take this woman over the hill and sit [beside her] on the log, talking of his father.

As they walked along Monroe Street Edith thought of the resolution she had made standing before the [*mirror] in her room at the back of the shop on the evening when she had decided to [*come] to the dance. She wondered if the great adventure was about to come to her and her hand trembled on McGregor's arm. A hot wave of hope and fear [*shot] through her.

At the door of the millinery shop, she fumbled with uncertain hands, unlocking the door. A delicious feeling shook her. She felt like a bride, glad, and yet ashamed and afraid.

In the room at the back of the shop the tall man lighted the gas, and pulling off his overcoat threw it on the couch at the side of the room. He was not in the least excited and with a steady hand lighted the fire in the little stove. Then looking up he asked Edith if he might smoke. He had the air of a man come home to his own house and the woman sat on the edge of her chair, unpinning her hat, and waiting hopefully to see what course the night's adventure would take.

For two hours McGregor sat in the rocking chair in Edith Carson's room, talking of Coal Creek and of his life in Chicago. He talked freely, letting himself go as a man might in talking to one of his own people after a long absence. His attitude, and the quiet ring in his voice, confused and puzzled Edith. She had expected something quite different.

Going [in]to the little room at the side, she brought forth a teakettle and prepared to make tea. The big man still sat in her chair smoking and talking. A delightful feeling of safety and coziness crept over her. She thought her room beautiful but mingled with her satisfaction was a faint grey streak of fear. "Of course he won't [ever] come back again," she thought.

CHAPTER VII

In the year following the beginning of his acquaintanceship with Edith Carson McGregor continued to work hard and steadily in the warehouse and with his books at night. He was promoted to be foreman, replacing the German, and he thought he had made progress with his studies. When he did not go to the night school he went to Edith [*Carson's] place and sat reading a book and smoking his pipe by a little table in the back room.

About the room and in and out of her shop moved Edith going softly and quietly. A light began to come into her eyes and color into her cheeks. She did not talk but new and daring thoughts visited her mind and a thrill of reawakened life ran through her body. With gentle insistence she did not let her dreams express themselves in words and almost hoped that she might be able to go on forever thus, having this strong man come into her presence and sit absorbed in his own affairs within the walls of her house. Sometimes she wanted him to talk and wished that she had the power to lead him into the telling of little facts of his life. She wanted to be told of his mother and father, of his boyhood in the Pennsylvania town, of his dreams and his desires but for the most part she was content[ed] to wait and only hoped that nothing would happen to bring an end to her waiting.

McGregor began to read books of history and became absorbed in the figures of certain men, all soldiers and leaders of soldiers, who stalked across the pages wherein was written the story of man's life. The figures of Sherman, Grant, Lee, Jackson, Alexander, Caesar, Napoleon and Wellington seemed to him to stand starkly up among the other figures in the books and going to the public library at the noon hour he got books concerning these men and for a time lost interest in the study of law and devoted himself to contemplation of the breakers of [the] laws.[16]

There was something beautiful about McGregor in those days. He was as virginal and pure as a chunk of the hard black coal out of the hills of his own state and like the coal ready to burn himself out into power. Nature had been kind to him. He had the gift of silence and of isolation. All about him were other men, perhaps as strong physically as himself and with better trained minds, who were being destroyed and he was not being destroyed. For the others life let itself run out in the endless doing of little tasks, the thinking of little thoughts and the saying of groups of words over and over, endlessly, like parrots that sit in cages and earn their bread by screaming two or three sentences to passersby.

It is a terrible thing to speculate on how man has been defeated by his ability to say words. The brown bear in the forest has no such power and the lack of it has enabled him to retain a kind of nobility of bearing sadly lacking in [*us]. On and on through life we go, socialists, dreamers, makers of laws, sellers of goods and believers in suffrage for women, and we [*continuously] say words, worn-out words, crooked words, words without power or pregnancy in them.

The matter is one to be thought of seriously by youths and maidens inclined to garrulousness. Those who have the habit of it will never change. The gods, who lean over the rim of the world laughing at us, have marked them for their barrenness.

And yet the word must run on. McGregor, the silent, wanted his word. He wanted his true note as an individual to ring out above the hubbub of voices and then he wanted to use the strength and the virility within himself to carry his word far. What he did not want was that his mouth become foul and his brain become numb with the saying of the words and the thinking of the thoughts of other men and that he in his turn

16. For Anderson's discussions of his early reading, see *A Story Teller's Story*, ed. White, pp. 115–18, 121, 164–68, 172, 184–85, 220; *Tar*, ed. White, p. 44; and *Sherwood Anderson's Memoirs*, ed. White, pp. 18, 19, 70, 103, 248, 256–57, 268, 336, 338.

become a mere toiling, food-consuming, chattering puppet to the gods.

For a long time the miner's son wondered what power lay in the men whose figures stood up so boldly in the pages of the books he read. He tried to think the matter out as he sat in Edith's room or walked by himself through the streets. In the warehouse he looked with new curiosity at the men who worked in the great rooms piling and unpiling apple barrels and the boxes of eggs and fruit. When he came into one of the rooms the men, who had been standing in groups idly talking of their own affairs, began to run busily about. They no longer chattered but as long as he remained worked desperately furtively watching as he stood staring at them.

McGregor wondered. He tried to fathom the mystery of the power that made them willing to work until their bodies were bent and stooped, that made them unashamed to be afraid and that left them in the end mere slaves to words and formulas.

The perplexed young man, watching the men in the warehouse, began to think that the passion for reproduction might have something to do with the matter. Perhaps his constant association with Edith awakened the thought. His own loins were heavy with the seeds of children and only his absorption in the thought of finding himself kept him from devoting himself to the feeding of his lusts. One day he had a talk concerning the matter with a man at the warehouse. The talk came about in this way.

In the warehouse the men came in at the door in the morning drifting in [one by one] like flies that wander in at [*the] open window[*s] on a summer day. With downcast eyes they shuffled across [*the] long floor white with lime. Morning after morning they came in at the door and went silently to their places looking at the floor and scowling. A slender bright-eyed young man, who acted as shipping clerk during the day, sat in a little coop and to him the men as they passed called out their numbers. From time to time the shipping clerk, who was an Irishman, tried to joke with one of them, tapping sharply upon his desk with a pencil as though to compel attention. "They are no good," he said to himself, when, in response to his sallies, they only smiled vaguely. "Although they get but a dollar and a half a day they are overpaid." Like McGregor he had nothing but contempt for the men whose numbers he put in the book. Their stupidity he took as a compliment to himself. "We are the kind who get things done," he thought, putting the pencil back of his ear and closing the book. In his mind the futile pride of the middle-class man flamed up. In his contempt for the workers he forgot also to have contempt for himself.

One morning McGregor and the shipping clerk stood upon a board platform facing the street and the shipping clerk talked of parentage. "The wives of the workers here have children as cattle have calves," said the Irishman. Moved by some hidden sentiment within himself he added heartily, "Oh well, what's a man for? It's nice to see kids around the house. I've got four kids myself. You should see them play about in the garden at my place in Oak Park when I come home in the evening."

McGregor thought of Edith Carson and a faint hunger began to grow within him. A desire that was later to come near [*to] upsetting the purpose of his life began to make itself felt. With a growl he fought against the desire and confused the Irishman by making an attack upon him. "Well how are you any better?" he asked bluntly. "Do you think your children any more important than their[*s]? You may have a better mind but their bodies are better and your mind hasn't made you a very striking figure as far as I can see."

Turning away from the Irishman who had begun to sputter with wrath McGregor went up an elevator to a distant part of the building thinking of the Irishman's words. From time to time he spoke sharply to a workman who loitered in one of the passages between the piles of boxes and barrels. Under his hand the work in the warehouse had begun to take on order and the little grey-haired superintendent who had employed him rubbed his hands with delight.

In a corner by a window stood McGregor wondering why he also did not want to [*devote his life to being] the father of children. In the dim light, across the face of the window, a fat old spider crawled slowly. In the hideous body of the insect there was something that suggested to the mind of the struggling thinker the sloth of the world. Vaguely his mind groped about trying to get hold of words and ideas to express what was in his brain. "Ugly crawling things that look at the floor," he muttered. "If they have children it is without order or orderly [*purpose]. It is an accident like the accident[s] of the fly that falls into the net built by [*the] insect here. The coming of the children is like the coming of the flies, [*it] feeds a kind of cowardice in men. In the children men hope vainly to see done what they have not the courage to try doing."

With an oath McGregor smashed with his heavy leather glove the fat thing wandering aimlessly across the light. "I must not be confused by little things. There is still going on the attempt to force me into the hole in the ground. There is a hole here in which men live and work just as there is in the mining town from which I came."

Hurrying out of his room that evening McGregor went to see Edith. He wanted to look at her and to think. In the little room at the back he sat for an hour trying to read a book and then for the first time shared his thoughts with her. "I am trying to discover why men are of so little importance," he said suddenly. "Are they mere tools for women? Tell me that. Tell me what women think and what they want?"

Without waiting for an answer he turned again to the reading of the book. "Oh well," he added, "it [*doesn't] need to bother me. I won't let any woman lead me into being a reproductive tool for her."

Edith was alarmed. She took McGregor's outburst as a declaration of war against herself and her influence and her hands began to tremble. Then a new thought came to her. "He needs money to get on in the world," she told herself and a little thrill of joy ran through her as she thought of her own carefully guarded hoard. She wondered how she could offer it to him so that there would be no danger of a refusal.

"You are all right," said McGregor preparing to depart. "You don't interfere with a man's thoughts."

Edith blushed and like the workmen in the warehouse looked at the floor. Something in his words startled her and when he was gone she went to her dresser and, taking out her bank-book, turned its pages with new pleasure. Without hesitation she, who indulged herself in nothing, would have given all to McGregor.

And out into the street went the man thinking of his own affairs. He dismissed from his mind the thought[*s] of women and children and began again to think of the stirring figures of history that had made so strong an appeal to him. As he passed over one of the bridges he stopped and stood leaning over the rail looking at the black water below.[17] "Why has thought never succeeded in replacing action[s]?" he asked himself. "Why are the men who write books in some way less full of meaning than the men who do things?"

McGregor was staggered by the thought that had come to him and wondered if he had started on a wrong trail by coming to the city and trying to educate himself. For an hour he stood in the darkness trying to think things out. It began to rain but he did not mind. Into his brain began to creep a dream of a vast order coming out of disorder. He was like one standing in the presence of some gigantic machine with many intricate parts that had begun to run crazily each [*part] without regard to the purpose of the whole. "There is danger in thinking too [eh]?" he muttered vaguely. "Everywhere there is danger, in labor, in love and in thinking. What shall I do with myself?"

McGregor turned about and threw up his hands. A new thought swept like a broad path of light across the darkness of his mind. He began to see that the soldiers who had led thousands of men into battle[s] had appealed to him because in the working out of their purposes they had used human lives with the recklessness of gods. They had found the

17. In his *Memoirs*, ed. White, pp. 315, 355, Sherwood Anderson fondly recalls his attraction to the Chicago River bridges.

courage to do that and their courage was magnificent. Away down deep in the hearts of [*men] lay sleeping a love of order and they had taken hold of that love. If they had used it badly did that matter? Had they not pointed [out] the way?

Back into McGregor's mind came a night scene in his home town. Vividly he saw in fancy the poor unkempt little street facing the railroad tracks and the group[*s] of striking miners huddled in the light before the door of a saloon while in the road a body of soldiers marched past, their uniforms looking grey and their faces grim in the uncertain light. "They marched," whispered McGregor. "That's what made them seem so powerful. They were just ordinary men but they went swinging along, all as one man. Something in that fact ennobled them. That is what Grant knew and what Caesar knew. That is what made Grant and Caesar seem so big. They knew and they were not afraid to use their knowledge. Perhaps they didn't bother to think how it would all come out. They hoped for another kind of man to do the thinking. Perhaps they did not think of anything at all but just went ahead and tried to do [*each his] own part.

"I will do my part here," shouted McGregor. "I will find the way." His body shook and his voice roared along the foot path of the bridge. Men stopped to look back at the big shouting figure. Two women walking past screamed and ran into the roadway. McGregor walked rapidly away toward his own room and his books. He did not know how he would be able to use the new impulse that had come to him but as he swung [his body] along through dark streets and past [long] rows of dark buildings he thought again of the great machine running crazily and without purpose and was glad he was not a part of it. "I will keep myself to myself and be ready for what happens," he said, burning with new courage.

BOOK III

CHAPTER I

WHEN McGregor had secured the place in the apple ware-house and went home to the house in Wycliff Place with his first week's pay, twelve dollars, in his pocket he thought of his mother, Nance McGregor, working in the mine offices in the Pennsylvania town, and, folding a five dollar bill, sent it to her in a letter. "I will begin to take care of her now," he thought and with the rough sense of equity in such matters, common [*to] laboring people, had no intention of giving himself airs. "She has fed me now I will begin to feed her," he told himself.

The five dollars came back. "Keep it. I don't want your money," the mother wrote. "If you have money left after your expenses are paid begin to fix yourself up. Better get a new pair of shoes or a hat. Don't try to take care of me. I won't have it. I want you to look out for yourself. Dress well and hold up your head, that's all I ask. In the city clothes mean a good deal. In the long run it will mean more to me to see you be a real man than to be a good son."

Sitting in her rooms over the vacant bake shop in Coal Creek Nance began to get new satisfaction out of the contemplation of herself as a woman with a son in the city. In the evening she sat thinking of him moving along the crowded thorough-fare[*s] among [the] men and women and her bent little old figure straightened with pride. When a letter came telling of his work in the night school her heart jumped and she wrote a long letter filled with talk of Garfield and Grant, and of Lincoln lying by the burning pine knot reading his books. It seemed to her unbelievably romantic that her son should someday be a lawyer and stand up in a crowded court room speaking thoughts out of his brain to other men. She thought that if this great, red-haired boy, who at home had been so unmanageable and so quick with his fists, was to end by being a man of books and of brains, then she and her man, Cracked McGregor, had not lived in vain. A sweet new sense

of peace came to her. She forgot her own years of toil and
gradually her mind went back to the silent boy sitting on the
steps with her before her house, in the year after her husband's
death, while she talked to him of the world, and thus she
thought of him, a quiet, eager boy, going about bravely there
in the distant city.

Death caught Nance McGregor off her guard. After one of
her long days of toil in the mine office she awoke to find him
sitting grim and expectant beside her bed. For years she, in
common with most of the women of the coal town, had been
afflicted with what is called "trouble with the heart." Now and
then she had "bad spells." On this spring evening she got into
bed and, sitting propped among the pillows, fought out her
fight alone like a worn-out animal that has crept into a hole in
the woods.

In the middle of the night the conviction came to her that
she would die. Death seemed moving about in the room,
[*and] waiting for her. In the street two drunken men stood
talking, their voices, concerned with their own human affairs,
coming in through the window and making life seem very
near and dear to the dying woman. "I've been everywhere,"
said one of the men. "I've been in towns and cities I don't even
remember the names of. You ask Alex Fielder who keeps a
saloon in Denver. Ask him if Gus Lamont has been there."

The other man laughed. "You've been in Jake's drinking too
much beer," he [*jeered].

Nance heard the two men stumble off down the street, the
traveler protesting against the unbelief of his friend. It seemed
to her that life with all of its color, sound and meaning was
running away from her presence. The exhaust of the engine
over at the mine rang in her ears. She thought of the mine as
a great monster, lying asleep below [*the] ground, its huge
nose stuck into the air, its mouth open to eat men. In the
darkness of the room her coat, flung over the back of a chair,
took the shape and outline of a face, huge and grotesque,
staring silently past her into the sky.

Nance McGregor gasped and struggled for breath. She
clutched the bedclothes with her hands and fought grimly and

silently. She did not think of the place to which she might go
after death. She was trying hard not to go there. It had been
her habit of life to fight not to dream dreams.

Nance [McGregor] thought of her father, drunk and throwing his money about in the old days before her marriage, of
the walks she, as a young girl, had taken with her lover on
Sunday afternoons, and of the times when they had gone
together to sit on the hillside overlooking the farming country.
As in a vision the dying woman saw the broad fertile land
spread out before her and blamed herself that she had not
done more toward helping her man in the fulfillment of the
plans she and he had made to go there and live. Then she
thought of the night when her boy came and of how, when
they went to bring her man from the mine, they found him
apparently dead under the fallen timbers so that she thought
life and death had visited her, hand in hand, in one night.

Nance sat up stiffly in bed. She thought she heard the sound
of heavy feet on the stairs [and she forgot that her boy no
longer lived in her house]. "That will be Beaut coming up from
the shop," she muttered and fell back upon the pillow dead.

CHAPTER II

BEAUT McGREGOR went home to Pennsylvania to bury his mother and on a summer afternoon walked again on the streets of his native town. From the [*station] he went at once to the empty bake shop, above which he had lived with his mother, but he did not stay there. For a moment he stood, bag in hand, listening to the voices of the miners' wives in the room above and then put the bag behind an empty box and hurried away. The voices of women broke the stillness of the room in which he stood. Their thin sharpness hurt something within him and he could not bear the thought of the equally thin sharp silence he knew would fall upon the women who were attending his mother's body in [*the] room above when he came into the presence of the dead.

Along [the] Main Street [of Coal Creek] he went to a hardware store and from there went to the mine office. Then with a pick and shovel on his shoulder he began to climb the hill up which he had walked with his father when he was a lad. On the train, homeward bound, an idea had come to him. "I will bury her among the bushes on the hillside that looks down into the fruitful valley," he told himself. The details of a religious discussion between two laborers that had gone on one day during the noon hour at the warehouse had come into his mind and as the train ran eastward he, for the first time, found himself speculating on the possibility of a life after death. Then he brushed the thought[*s] aside. "Anyway if Cracked McGregor does come back it is there you'll find him, sitting on the log on the hillside," he thought.

With the tools on his shoulder McGregor climbed the long hillside road, now deep with black dust. He was going to dig the grave for the burial of Nance McGregor. He did not glare at the miners who passed swinging their dinner pails as [*they] had done in the old days, but looked at the ground and thought of the dead woman and a little wondered what place a woman [*would] yet come to occupy in his own life. On the hillside the wind blew sharply and the great boy, just emerging into manhood, worked vigorously making the dirt fly. When the hole had grown deep he stopped and looked to where, in the valley below, a man who was hoeing corn shouted to a woman who stood on the porch of a farm house. Two cows, standing by a fence in a field, lifted up their heads and bawled lustily. "It is the place for the dead to lie," whispered McGregor. "When my own time comes I shall be brought up here." An idea came to him. "I will have father's body moved," he told himself. "When I have made some money I will have that done. Here we shall all lie in the end, all of us McGregors."

The thought that had come to McGregor pleased him and he was pleased also with himself for thinking the thought. The male in him made him throw back his shoulders. "We are two of a feather, father and me," he muttered, "two of a feather and mother has not understood either of us. Perhaps no woman was ever intended to understand us."

Jumping out of the hole he strode over the crest of the hill and began the descent toward the town. It was [now] late afternoon and the sun had gone down behind clouds. "I wonder if I understand myself, if anyone understands," he thought, going swiftly along with the tools clanking on his shoulder.

McGregor did not want to go back to the town and to the dead woman [staring at the ceiling] in the little room. He thought of the miners' wives—attendants to the dead—who would sit with crossed hands looking at him and turned out of the road to sit on the fallen log where once on a Sunday afternoon he had sat with the black-haired boy who worked in the pool room and where the daughter of the undertaker had come to sit beside him.

And then up the long hill came the woman herself. As she drew near he recognized her tall figure and for some reason a lump came into his throat. She had seen him depart from the town with the pick and shovel on his shoulder and, after waiting what she thought an interval long enough to still the tongues of gossip, had followed. "I wanted to talk with you," she said climbing over logs and coming to sit beside him.

For a long time the man and woman sat in silence staring at the town in the valley below. McGregor thought she had grown more pale than ever and looked at her sharply. His mind, more accustomed to look critically at [*women] than had been the mind of the boy who had once sat talking to her on the same log, began to inventory her body. "She is already becoming stooped," he thought. "I would not want to make love to her now."

Along the log toward him moved the undertaker's daughter and with a swift impulse toward boldness slipped a thin hand into his. She began talking of the dead woman lying in the upstairs room in the town. "We have been friends since you went away," she explained. "She liked to talk of you and I liked that also."

Made bold by her own boldness the woman hurried on. "I do not want you to misunderstand me," she said. "I know I can't get you. I'm not thinking of that."

She began to talk of her own affairs and of the dreariness of life with her father but McGregor's mind could not center itself on her talk. When they started down the hill he had the impulse to take her in[to] his arms and carry her as Cracked McGregor had once carried him but was so embarrassed that he did not offer to help her. He thought that for the first time someone from his native town had come close to him and [*he] watched her stooped figure with an odd new feeling of tenderness. "I won't be alive long, maybe not a year. I've got the consumption," she whispered softly as he left her at the entrance to the hallway leading up to her home and McGregor was so stirred by her words that he turned back and spent another hour wandering alone on the hillside before he went to see the body of his mother.

In the room above the bakery McGregor sat at an open window looking down into the dimly lighted street. In a corner of the room lay his mother in a coffin and two miners'

wives sat in the darkness behind him. All were silent and
embarrassed.

McGregor leaned out of the window and watched a group
of miners who gathered at a corner. He thought of the undertaker's daughter, now nearing death, and wondered why she
had suddenly come so close to him. "It is not because she is a
woman, I know that," he told himself and tried to dismiss the
matter from his mind by watching the people in the street
below.

In the mining town a meeting was being held. A box lay at
the edge of the sidewalk and upon [*it] climbed that same
young Hartnet who had once talked to McGregor and who
made his living by gathering birds' eggs and trapping squirrels
in the hills. He was frightened and talked rapidly. Presently
he introduced a large man with a flat nose who, when he had
in turn climbed upon the box, began to tell stories and anec-
dotes designed to make the miners laugh.

McGregor listened. He wished the undertaker's daughter
were there, sitting in the darkened room beside him. He
thought he should like to tell her of his life in the city and of
how disorganized and ineffective all [of] modern life seemed
to him. Sadness invaded his mind and he thought of his dead
mother and of how this other woman would presently die.
"It is just as well. Perhaps there is no other way, no orderly
march toward an orderly end. Perhaps one has to die and
return to nature to achieve that," he whispered to himself.

In the street below the man upon the box who was a traveling
socialist orator began to talk of the coming social revolution.
As he talked it seemed to McGregor that his jaw had become
loose from much wagging and that his whole body was loosely
put together and without force. The speaker danced up and
down on the box and his arms flapped about and these also
seemed loose, not a part of the body. "Vote with us and the
thing is done," he shouted. "Are you going to let a few men
run things forever? Here you live like beasts paying tribute to
your masters. Arouse [*yourselves]. Join us in the struggle.
You [*yourselves] can be master[*s] if you [*will] only
think so."

"You will have to do something more than think," roared McGregor, leaning far out at the window. Again, as always when he had heard men saying words, he was blind with anger. Sharply he remembered the walks he had sometimes taken at night in the city streets and the air of disorderly ineffectiveness all about him. And here in the mining town it was the same. On every side of him appeared blank empty faces and loose, badly knit [together] bodies. "Mankind should be like a great fist ready to smash and to strike. It should be ready to knock down what stands in its way," he cried astonishing the crowd in the street and frightening into something like hysterics the two women who sat with him beside the dead woman in the darkened room.

CHAPTER III

THE funeral of Nance McGregor was an event in Coal Creek. In the minds of the miners she stood for something. Fearing and hating the husband and the tall big-fisted son, they had yet a tenderness for the mother and wife. "She lost her money handing us out bread," they said, pounding on the bar in the saloon. Word ran about among them and they returned again and again to the subject. The fact that she had lost her man twice, once in the mine when the timber fell and clouded his brain and then later when his body lay black and distorted near the door to the McCrary cut, after the dreadful time of the fire in the mine, was perhaps forgotten but the fact that she had once kept a store and that she had lost her money serving them was not forgotten.

On the day of the funeral the miners came up out of the mine and stood in groups in the open street and in the vacant bake shop. The men of the night shift had their faces washed and had put white paper collars about their necks. The man who owned the saloon locked the front door and, putting the keys into his pocket, stood on the sidewalk looking silently at the windows of Nance McGregor's rooms. Out along the runway from the mines came other miners—men of the day shift. Setting their dinner pails on the stone along the front of the saloon and crossing the railroad they kneeled and washed their blackened faces in the red stream flowing at the foot of the embankment. The voice of the preacher—a slender, wasp-like young man with black hair and dark shadows under his eyes—floated out to the listening men. A train of loaded coke cars rumbled past along the back of the stores.

McGregor sat at the head of the coffin dressed in a [*new] black suit. He stared at the wall back of the head of the preacher—not hearing—thinking his own thoughts.

Back of McGregor sat the undertaker's pale daughter. She leaned forward until she touched the back of the chair in front [of her] and sat with her face buried in a white handkerchief. Her weeping cut across the voice of the preacher in the closely crowded little room filled with miners' wives and in the midst of his prayer for the dead she was taken with a violent fit of coughing and had to get up and hurry out of the room.

After the services in the rooms above the bake shop a procession formed on Main Street. Like awkward boys the miners fell into groups and walked along behind the black hearse and the carriage in which sat the dead woman's son [*with] the minister. The men kept looking at each other and smiling sheepishly. There had been no arrangement to follow the body to its grave and when they thought of the son and the attitude he had always maintained toward them they wondered whether or not he wanted them to follow.

And McGregor was unconscious of all this. He sat in the carriage beside the minister and with unseeing eyes stared over the heads of the horses. He was thinking of his life in the city and of what he should do there in the future, of Edith Carson sitting in the cheap dance hall[s] and of the evenings he had [later] spent with her, of the barber on the park bench talking of women and of his life with his mother when he was a boy in the mining town.

As the carriage climbed slowly up the hill followed by the miners McGregor began to love his mother. For the first time he realized that her life was full of meaning and that in her woman's way she had been quite as heroic in her years of patient toil as had been her man Cracked McGregor when he ran to his death in the burning mine. McGregor's hands began to tremble and his shoulders straightened. He became conscious of the men, the dumb, blackened children of toil dragging their weary legs up the hill.

For what? McGregor stood up in the carriage and turning about looked at the men. Then he fell upon his knees on the carriage seat and watched them eagerly his soul crying out to something he thought must be hidden away among the black mass of them, something that was the keynote of their lives, something for which he hadn't looked and in which he had not believed.

McGregor, kneeling in the open carriage at the top of the hill and watching the marching men slowly toiling upward, had of a sudden one of those strange awakenings that are the reward of [the] stoutness in stout souls. A strong wind lifted the smoke from the coke ovens and blew it up the face of the hill on the farther side of the valley and the wind seemed to have lifted also some [*of the] haze that had covered his eyes. At the foot of the hill along the railroad he could see the little stream—one of the blood red streams of the mine country—and the dull red houses of the miners. The red of the coke ovens, the red sun setting behind [*the] hills to the west, and, last of all, the [blood] red stream, flowing like a river of blood down through the valley, made a scene that burned itself into the brain of the miner's son. A lump came into his throat and for a moment he tried vainly to get back his old satisfying hate of the town and the miners but it would not come. Long he looked down the hill to where the miners of the night shift marched up the hill after the carriage and the slowly moving hearse. It seemed to him that they, like himself, were marching up out of the smoke and the little squalid houses, away from the shores of the blood red river into something new. What? McGregor shook his head slowly like an animal in pain. He wanted something for himself, for all these men. It seemed to him that he would gladly lie dead like Nance McGregor to know the secret of that want.

And then as though in answer to the cry out of his heart the file of marching men fell into step. An instantaneous impulse seemed to run through the ranks of stooped, toiling figures. Perhaps they also, looking backward, had caught the magnificence of the picture scrawled across the landscape in black and red and had been moved by it so that their shoulders straightened and the long subdued song of life began to sing in their bodies. With a swing the marching men fell into step. Into the mind of McGregor flashed a thought of another day when he had stood upon this same hill with the half crazed man who stuffed birds and sat upon [*a] log by the roadside reading the Bible and [*how he] had hated these men because they did not march with orderly precision like the sol-

diers who came to subdue them. In a flash he knew that he who
had hated the miners hated them no more. With Napoleonic in-
sight he read a lesson into the accident of the men's falling into
step behind his carriage. A big, grim thought flashed into his
brain. "Someday a man will come who will swing all of the
workers of the world into step like that," he thought. "He
will make them conquer, not one another, but the terrifying
disorder of life. If their lives have been wrecked by disorder
it is not their fault. They have been betrayed by the ambitions
of their leaders; all men have betrayed them." McGregor
thought that his mind swept down over the men, that the
impulses of his mind like living things ran among them, crying
to them, touching them, caressing them. Love invaded his
spirit and made his body tingle. He thought of the workers in
the Chicago warehouse and of the millions of other workers
who, in that great city, in all cities, everywhere, went at the
end of the day shuffling off along the streets to their houses
carrying with them no song, no hope, nothing but a few paltry
dollars with which to buy food and keep the endless hurtful
scheme of things alive. "There is a curse on my country," he
cried. "Everyone has come here for gain, to grow rich, to
achieve. Suppose they should begin to want to live here.
Suppose they should quit thinking of gain, leaders and
followers of leaders. They are children suppose like children
they should begin to play a bigger game. Suppose they could
just learn to march, nothing else. Suppose they should begin
to do with their bodies what their minds are not strong enough
to do—to just learn the one simple thing, to march, whenever
two or four or a thousand of them got together to march."

McGregor's thoughts moved him so that he wanted to yell.
Instead his face grew stern and he [*tried] to command
himself. "No, wait," he whispered. "Train yourself. Here is
something to give point to your life. Be patient and wait."
Again his thoughts swept away, running down to the advancing men. Tears came into his eyes. "Men have taught
them that big lesson only when they wanted [them] to kill.
This must be different. Someone must teach them the big
lesson just for their own sakes, that they also may know. They

must march fear and disorder and purposelessness away. That must come first."

McGregor turned and compelled himself to sit quietly beside the minister in the carriage. He became bitter against the leaders of men, the figures in old history that had once loomed so big in his mind.

"They have half taught them the secret only to betray them," he muttered. "The men of books and of brains have done the same. That loose-jawed fellow in the street last night—there must be thousands of such, talking until their jaws hang loose like worn-out gates. Words mean nothing but when a man marches with a thousand other men and is not doing it for the glory of some king then it will mean something. He will know then that he is a part of something real. He will catch the rhythm of the mass and glory in the fact that he is a part of the mass and that the mass has meaning. He will begin to feel great and powerful." McGregor smiled grimly. "That is what the great leaders of armies have known," he whispered. "And they have sold men out. They have used that knowledge to subdue men, to make them serve their own little ends."

McGregor continued to look back at the men and in an odd sort of way to wonder at himself and the thought that had come to him. "It can be done," he presently said aloud. "It will be done by someone sometime. Why not by me?"

They buried Nance McGregor in the deep hole dug by her son, before the log on the hillside. On the morning of his arrival he had secured permission of the mining company who owned the land to make this the burial place of the McGregors.

When the service over the grave was finished he looked about him at the miners, standing uncovered along the hill and in the road leading down into the valley, and felt that he should like to tell them what was in his mind. He had an impulse to jump upon the log, beside the grave, and, in the presence of the green fields his father loved and across the grave of Nance McGregor, shout to them saying, "Your cause shall be my cause. My brain and strength shall be yours.

Your enemies I shall smite with my naked fist," [but] instead he walked rapidly past them and, topping the hill, went down toward the town into the gathering night.

McGregor could not sleep on that last night he was ever to spend in Coal Creek. When darkness came he went along the street and stood at the foot of the stairs leading [up] to the home of the undertaker's daughter. The emotions that had swept over him during the afternoon had subdued his spirit and he wanted to be with someone who would also be subdued and quiet. When the woman did not come down the stairs to stand in the hallway as she had done in his boyhood he went up and knocked [*at] her door. Together they went along Main Street and [*climbed] the hill.

The undertaker's daughter walked with difficulty and was compelled to stop and sit upon a stone by the roadside. When she attempted to rise McGregor gathered her into his arms and when she protested patted her thin shoulder with his big hand and whispered to her. "Be quiet," he said. "Do not talk about anything. Just be quiet."

The nights in the hills above mining towns are magnificent. The long valleys, cut and slashed by the railroads and made ugly by the squalid little houses of the miners, are half lost in the soft blackness. Out of the darkness sounds emerge. Coal cars creak and protest as they are pushed along rails. Voices cry out. With a long reverberating rattle one of the mine cars dumps its load down a metal chute into a car standing on the railroad tracks. In the winter little fires are started along the tracks by the workmen who are employed about the tipple and on summer nights the moon comes out and touches with wild beauty the banks of black smoke that drift upward[s] from the long rows of coke ovens.

With the sick woman in his arms McGregor sat in silence on the hillside above Coal Creek letting new thoughts and new impulses play with his spirit. The love for the figure of his mother that had come to him during the afternoon returned and he took the woman of the mine country into his arms and held her closely against his breast.

The struggling man in the hills of his own country, who was trying to clear his soul of the hatred of men bred in him by the disorder of life, lifted his head and pressed the body of the undertaker's daughter hard against his own body. The woman, understanding his mood, picked with her thin fingers at his coat and wished she might die there in the darkness in the arms of the man she loved. When he became conscious of her presence and relaxed the grip of his arms about her shoulders she lay still and waited for him to forget again and again to press her tightly and let her feel in her worn-out body his massive strength and virility.

"It is a job. It is something big I can try to do," he whispered to himself and in fancy saw the great disorderly city on the western plains rocked by the swing and [the] rhythm of men, aroused and awakening with their bodies a song of new life.

BOOK IV

CHAPTER I

CHICAGO is a vast city and millions of people live within the limits of its influence. It stands at the heart of America almost within sound of the creaking green leaves of the corn in the vast corn fields of the Mississippi Valley. It is inhabited by hordes of men of all nations who have come across the seas or out of western corn shipping towns to make their fortunes. On all sides men are busy making fortunes.

In little Polish villages the word has been whispered about, "In America one gets much money," and adventurous souls have set forth only to land at last, a little perplexed and disconcerted, in narrow, ill-smelling rooms in Halstead Street in Chicago.

In American villages the [same] tale has been told. Here it has not been whispered but shouted. Magazines and newspapers have done the job. The word regarding the making of money runs over the land like a wind among the corn. The young men listen and run away to Chicago. They have vigor and youth but in them has been builded no dream, no tradition of devotion to anything but gain.

Chicago is one vast gulf of disorder. Here is the passion for gain, the very spirit of the bourgeoisie gone drunk with desire. The result is something terrible. Chicago is leaderless, purposeless, slovenly, down at the heels.

And back of Chicago lie the long corn fields that are not disorderly. There is hope in the corn. Spring comes and the corn is green. It shoots up out of the black land and stands up in orderly rows. The corn grows and thinks of nothing but growth. Fruition comes to the corn and it is cut down and disappears. Barns are filled to bursting with the yellow fruit of the corn.

And Chicago has forgotten the lesson of the corn. All men

have forgotten. It has never been told to the young men who
come out of the corn fields to live in the city.[1]

Once and once only in modern times the soul of America
was stirred. The Civil War swept like a purifying fire through
the land. Men marched together and knew the feel of shoulder
to shoulder action. Brown, stout, bearded figures returned,
after the war, to the villages. The beginning of a literature of
strength and virility arose.

And then the time of sorrow and of stirring effort passed
and prosperity returned. Only the aged are now cemented
together by the sorrow of that time and there has been no
new national sorrow.

It is a summer evening in America and the citizens sit in
their houses after the effort of the day. They talk of the
children in school or of the new difficulty of meeting the high
prices of food stuff. In cities the band[*s] play in the park[s].
In villages the lights go out and one hears the sound of hurrying horses on distant roads.

A thoughtful man walking in the streets of Chicago, on
such an evening, sees women in white shirt waists and men
with cigars in their mouths sitting on the porches of the
houses. The man is from Ohio. He owns a factory in one of the
large industrial towns there and has come to the city to sell
his product.[2] He is a man of the better sort, quiet, efficient,
kindly. In his own community everyone respects him and he
respects himself. Now he walks giving himself over to thoughts.
He passes a house set [back] among trees where a man cuts
grass by the streaming light from a window. The song of the
lawn mower stirs the walker. He idles along the street, looking
in through [*the] windows at prints upon the walls. A white-
clad woman sits playing [*on] a piano. "Life is good," he
says, lighting a cigar, "it climbs on and up toward a kind of
universal fairness."

1. Besides his lyrical use of Midwestern cornfields in *Mid-American
Chants* (New York: John Lane, 1918), Anderson exploited the subject
in his *Memoirs*, ed. White, pp. 46, 47, 48–51, 247, 486–87.

2. Anderson may be giving a self-portrait here, as the circumstances
of this manufacturer from Ohio resemble those of the author in Cleveland and Elyria, Ohio, during the early writing on *Marching Men*.

And then in the light from a street lamp the walker sees a man staggering along the sidewalk, muttering and helping himself with his hands upon a wall. The sight does not greatly disturb the pleasant, satisfying thoughts that stir in his mind. He has eaten a good dinner at the hotel. He knows that drunken men are often but gay money-spending dogs who, tomorrow morning, will settle down to their work feeling secretly better for the night of wine and song.

My thoughtful man is an American with the disease of comfort and prosperity in his blood. He strolls [slowly] along and turns a corner. He is satisfied with the cigar he smokes and, he decides, satisfied with the age in which he lives. "Agitators may howl," he says, "but on the whole life is good, and, as for me, I am going to spend my life attending to the business [*in] hand."

The walker has turned a corner into a side street. Two men emerge from the door of a saloon and stand upon the sidewalk under a light. They wave their arms up and down. Suddenly one of them springs forward and, with a quick forward thrust of his body and the flash of a clenched fist in the lamplight, knocks his companion into the gutter. [The physical ugliness of the city asserts itself.] Down the street he sees rows of tall, smoke-begrimed brick buildings hanging black and ominous against the sky. At the end of a street a huge mechanical apparatus lifts cars of coal and dumps them roaring and rattling into the bowels of a ship that lies tied in the river.

[*The walker throws his cigar away and looks about. A man walks before him] in the silent street. He sees the man raise his fist to the sky and notes with a shock the movement of the lips and the hugeness and ugliness of the face [*in] the lamplight.

Again he goes on, hurrying now, around another corner into a street filled with pawn shops, clothing stores and the clamor of voices. In his mind floats a picture. He sees two boys, clad in white rompers, feeding clover to a tame rabbit in a suburban back lawn and wishes he were at home in his own place. In his fancy [*the] two sons are walking under apple trees, laughing and tussling for a great bundle of newly pulled, sweet smelling clover.[3] The strange looking red man with the huge face [*he has seen in the street] is looking at the two children over a garden wall. There is a threat in the look and the threat alarms him. Into his mind comes the notion that the man looking over the wall wants to destroy the future of his children.

The night advances. Down a stairway beside a clothing store comes a woman clad in a black dress and with gleaming white teeth. She makes a peculiar little jerking movement with her head to the walker. A patrol wagon with clanging bells rushes through the street, two blue-clad policemen sitting stiffly in the seat. A boy—he can't be above six—runs along the street, pushing soiled newspapers under the noses of idlers on the corners; his shrill, childish voice rises above the din of the trolley cars and the clanging notes of the patrol wagon.[4]

The walker throws his cigar into the gutter and, climbing the steps of a street car, goes back to his hotel. His fine, reflective mood is gone. He half wishes [*that] something lovely [*might] come into American life but the wish does not persist. He is only irritated and feels that a pleasant evening has been in some way spoiled. He is wondering if he will be successful in the business that brought him to the city. As he turns out the light in his room and, putting his head upon the pillow, listens to the noises of the city, merged now into a quiet, droning roar, he thinks of the brick factory on the banks of the river in Ohio. As he falls into sleep the face of the red-haired man lowers at him from the factory door.

When McGregor returned to the city after the burial of his mother he began at once to try to put his idea of the marching

3. Such a pastoral episode, perhaps based on the experience of Anderson's small children in Ohio, is the basis for the writer's first published short story, "The Rabbit-pen," *Harper's Magazine*, CXXIX (July, 1914), 207–10. See Ray Lewis White, "A Critical Analysis [of Sherwood Anderson's First Published Story]," *Readers and Writers*, I (April, 1968), 32–33, 36.

4. Again Anderson remembers his own boyhood job as newsboy, described in *Tar*, ed. White, pp. 142, 145, 147–48, 154, 156, 157, 161, 162, 168, 176–80, 188–95, 200, 201, 213; and in *Sherwood Anderson's Memoirs*, ed. White, pp. 27, 28, 57–62, 67, 93–94, 101, 183–84.

men into form. For a long time he did not know how to begin. The idea was vague and shadowy. It belonged to the nights in the hills [*of his own country] and seemed a little absurd when he tried to think of it in the daylight of North State Street in Chicago.

McGregor felt that he had to prepare himself. He believed that he could study books and learn much from men's ideas, expressed in books, without being overwhelmed by their thoughts. He became a student and quit the place in the apple warehouse to the secret relief of the little bright-eyed superintendent, who had never been able to get himself up to the point of raging at this big red fellow as he had raged at the German before McGregor's time. The warehouse man felt that [*during the meeting] on the corner before the saloon [*on the day McGregor began to work for him something had happened. The miner's son] had unmanned him. "A man ought to be boss in his own place," he [*sometimes] muttered to himself, walking in the passageways among rows of piled apple barrels in the upper part of the warehouse [and] wondering why the presence of McGregor irritated him.

From six o'clock in the evening until two in the morning McGregor now worked as night cashier in a restaurant on South State Street below Van Buren and from two until seven in the morning he slept in a room whose windows looked down into Michigan Boulevard. On Thursday he was free, his place being taken for the evening by the man who owned the restaurant, a small, excitable Irishman by the name of Tom O'Toole [who had a gift for picturesque profanity].[5]

McGregor got his chance to become a student through the bank account belonging to Edith Carson. The opportunity arose in this way. On a summer evening after his return from Pennsylvania he sat with her in the darkened store back of the closed screen door. McGregor was morose and silent. On the evening before he had tried to talk to several men at the warehouse about the Marching Men and they had not understood.

5. As there is no record of Anderson's working in a restaurant, he may here fictionalize an experience of his young brother Earl, described in *Sherwood Anderson's Memoirs*, ed. White, pp. 309–10.

He blamed his inability with words and sat in the half darkness with his face in his hands looking up the street, saying nothing and thinking bitter thoughts.

The idea that had come [*to] him made him half drunk with its possibilities and he knew that he must not let it make him drunk. He wanted to begin forcing men to do the simple thing full of meaning rather than the disorganized, ineffective things and he had an ever present inclination to arise, to stretch himself, to run into the streets and with his great arms see if he could not sweep the people before him, starting them on the long, purposeful march that was to be the beginning of the rebirth of the world, filling with meaning the lives of men. Then when he had walked the fever out of his blood and had frightened the people in the streets by the grim look in his face he tried to school himself to sit quietly waiting.

The woman sitting beside him in a low rocking chair began trying to tell him of something that had been in her mind. Her heart jumped and she talked slowly, pausing between sentences, to conceal the trembling of her voice. "Would it help [*you] in what you want to do if you could quit [working] at the warehouse and spend your days in study?" she asked.

McGregor looked at her and nodded his head absent-mindedly. He thought of the nights in his room when the hard, heavy work of the day in the warehouse seemed to have benumbed his brain.

"Besides the business here I have seventeen hundred dollars in the savings bank," said Edith, turning aside to conceal the eager, hopeful look in her eyes. "I want to invest it. I don't want it lying there doing nothing. I want you to take it and make a lawyer of yourself."

Edith sat rigid in her chair waiting for his answer. She felt that she had put him to a test. In her mind was a new hope. "If he takes it he won't be walking out at the door some night and never coming back."

McGregor tried to think. He had not tried to explain to her his new notion of life and did not know how to begin.

"After all why not stick to my plan and be a lawyer?" he

asked himself. "That might open the door. I'll do that," he said aloud to the woman. "Both you and mother have talked of it so I will give it a trial. Yes I'll take the money." Again he looked at her, sitting before him, flushed and eager, and was touched by her devotion as he had been touched by the devotion of the undertaker's daughter in Coal Creek. "I don't mind being under obligations to you," he said, "I don't know anyone else I would take it from."

In the street later the troubled man walked about trying to make new plans for the accomplishment of his purpose. He was annoyed by what he thought to be the dulness of his own brain and [*he] thrust his fist up into the air to look at it in the lamplight. "I'll get ready to use that intelligently," he thought, "a man wants trained brains backed [*up] by a big fist in the struggle I am going into."

It was then that the man from Ohio walked past, with his hands in his pockets, and attracted his attention. To McGregor's nostrils came the odor of rich, fragrant tobacco. He turned and stood, staring at the intruder on his thoughts. "That's what I'm going to fight," he growled, "the comfortable, well-to-do acceptance of a disorderly world, the smug men who see nothing wrong with a world like this. I should like to frighten them so that they [would] throw their cigars away and run about like ants when you kick over ant hills in the field[s]."

CHAPTER II

McGREGOR began to attend some classes at Chicago University and walked about among the massive building[*s], erected, for the most part, through the bounty of one of his country's [*leading] business men, wondering why the great center of learning seemed so little a part of the city. To him the University seemed something entirely apart, not in tune with its surrounding. It was like an expensive ornament worn on the soiled hand of a street urchin. He did not stay there long.[6]

One day he got into disfavor with the professor in one of the classes. He sat in a room among other students his mind busy with thoughts of the future and of how he [*might] get his movement of the marching men under way. In a chair beside him sat a large girl with blue eyes and hair like yellow wheat. She like McGregor was unconscious of what was going on about her and sat with half closed eyes watching him. In the corners of her eyes lurked a gleam of amusement. She drew sketches of his huge mouth and nose on a pad of paper.

At McGregor's left [and] with his legs sprawled into the aisle sat a youth who was thinking of the yellow-haired girl and planning an attack on her. He was a typical American youth of the upper middle class and was in the University only because he was in no hurry to begin his life in the commercial world. His father was a manufacturer of berry boxes in a brick building on the West Side and he wished he were in school in another city so that it would not be necessary to live at home.[7] All day he thought of the evening meal [at home] and

6. Because Anderson attended Wittenberg Academy in 1899–1900, this episode at the University of Chicago may be based on his sister Stella's attendance there. See *Sherwood Anderson's Memoirs*, ed. White, pp. 135–39. John D. Rockefeller (1839–1937) in 1890 gave $35 million to the University of Chicago.

7. Both Anderson and the newspaperman Ben Hecht (1894–1964) later told identical stories of a Chicago box-factory owner. See the An-

of the coming of his father, nervous and tired, to quarrel with his mother about the management of the servants, [and] now he was trying to evolve a plan for getting money from his mother with which to enjoy a dinner at a down town restaurant. With delight he contemplated such an evening with a box of cigarettes on the table, and perhaps a woman sitting opposite him under red lights.

In front of McGregor sat another typical student, a pale, nervous young man who drummed with his fingers on the back of a book. He was very serious about acquiring learning and when the professor paused in his talk he threw up his hands and asked a question. When the professor smiled he laughed loudly. He was like an instrument on which the professor struck chords.

The professor, a short man with a bushy, black beard, heavy shoulders and large powerful eye glasses, spoke in a shrill voice, surcharged with excitement.

"The world is full of unrest," he said, "men are struggling like chicks in the shell. In the hinterland of every man's mind uneasy thoughts stir. I call your attention to what is going on in the Universities of Germany."

The professor paused and glared about. McGregor was so irritated by what he took to be the wordiness of the man that he could not restrain himself. He felt as he had felt when the socialist orator talked on the streets of Coal Creek. With an oath he arose and kicked out his foot, pushing his chair away. The pad of paper fell out of the large girl's lap and scattered its leaves about the floor. A light burned in McGregor's blue eyes. As he stood in the classroom before the startled class his head, big and red, had something of nobility about it like the head of a fine beast. His voice rumbled out of his throat. The girl looked at him, her mouth standing open.

"We go from room to room hearing talk," began McGregor. "On the street corners down town in the evening[*s] and in towns and villages men talk and talk. Books are written, jaws

derson *Memoirs*, ed. White, pp. 372–76; and Ben Hecht, *A Thousand and One Afternoons in Chicago* (Chicago: Covici-McGee, 1922), pp. 31–34.

wag. The jaws of men are loose. They wabble about saying nothing."

McGregor's excitement grew. "If there is all this unrest why does it not come to something?" he demanded. "Why do not you, who have trained brains, strive to find the secret of order in the midst of this disorder? Why is not something done?"

The professor ran up and down, on the platform. "I do not know what you mean," he cried nervously. McGregor turned slowly and stared at the class trying to explain. [All in the room had become silent, attentive.] "Why do not men lead their lives like men?" he asked. "They must be taught to march, hundreds of thousands of men. Do you not think so?"

McGregor's voice rose and his great fist was raised. "The world should become a great camp," he cried. "The brains of the world should be at the organization of mankind. Everywhere there is disorder and men chatter like monkeys in a cage. Why should some man not begin the organization of a new army? If there are men who do not understand what is meant let them be knocked down."

The professor leaned forward and peered through his spectacles at McGregor. "I understand your kind," he said and his voice trembled. "The class is dismissed. We deprecate violence here."

The professor hurried through a door and down a long hallway, [*with] the class chattering at his heels. McGregor sat in his chair in the empty class room, staring at the wall. As the professor hurried away he muttered to himself. "What's getting in here? What's getting into our schools?"

Late on the following afternoon McGregor sat in his room thinking of what had happened in the class. He had [just] decided that he would not spend any more time at the University but would devote himself entirely to the study of law [when] several young men came in.

Among the students at the University McGregor had seemed very old. Secretly he was much admired and had often been the subject of talk [and] those who had now come to see him

wanted [to invite] him to join a Greek Letter Fraternity. They
sat about his room, on the window sill and on a trunk by the
wall, smoking pipes, and were boyishly eager and enthusiastic.
A glow shone in the cheeks of the spokesman—a clean looking
youth with black curly hair and round, pink-and-white
cheeks, [*the] son of a Presbyterian minister from Iowa.

"You've been picked by our fellows to be one of us," said
the spokesman, "we want you to become an Alpha Beta Pi.
It's a grand fraternity with chapters in the best schools in the
country. Let me tell you."

He began reeling off a list of names of statesmen, college
professors, business men and [*well known] athletes who
belonged to the order [and was so excited he could not sit
quiet in his chair].

McGregor sat by the wall looking at his guests and wondering what he would say. He was a little amused and half hurt
and felt like a man who has had a Sunday School scholar stop
him on the street to ask him about the welfare of his soul.
He thought of Edith Carson waiting for him in her store on
Monroe Street; of the angry miners standing in the saloon in
Coal Creek plotting to break into the restaurant while he sat
with the hammer in his hand[*s] waiting for battle; of old
Mother Misery walking at the heels of the soldiers' horses
through the streets of the mining village; and last of all of the
terrible certainty that these bright-eyed boys would be destroyed, swallowed up by the huge commercial city in which
they were to live.

[The curly-haired youth continued his speech.] "It means
a lot to be one of us when a chap gets out into the world,"
[*the curly-haired youth] said. "It helps you get on, get in
with the right people. You can't go on without men, you know.
You ought to get in with the best fellows." He hesitated and
looked at the floor. "I don't mind telling you," he said, with an
outburst of frankness, "that one of our stronger men—
Whiteside, the mathematician—wanted us to have you. He
said you were worth while. He thought you ought to see us
and get to know us and that we ought to see and get to know
you."

McGregor got up and took his hat from a nail on the wall. He felt the utter futility of trying to express what was in his mind and walked down the stairs to the street with the file of boys in embarrassed silence, stumbling in the dark[*ness of the] hallway at his heels. At the street door he stopped and faced them, struggling to put the thoughts into words.

"I can't do what you ask," he said. "I like you and like your asking me to come in with you, [anyway] I am going to quit the University." His voice softened. "I should like to have you for friends," he added. "You say a man needs to know people after a while. Well, I should like to know you while you are what you are now. I don't want to know you after you become what you will become."

McGregor turned and ran down the remaining steps to the stone sidewalk and went rapidly up the street. A stern, hard look was in his face and he knew [that] he would spend a silent night thinking of what had happened. "I hate hitting boys," he thought as he hurried away to his evening's work at the restaurant.

CHAPTER III

WHEN McGregor was admitted to the bar and ready to take his place among the thousands of young lawyers scattered over the Chicago loop district he half drew back from beginning the practise of his profession. To spend his life quibbling [*over trifles] with other lawyers [in court rooms] was not what he wanted. To have his place in life fixed by his ability in quibbling seemed [*to him] hideous.

Night after night he walked alone in the streets thinking of the matter. He grew angry and swore. Sometimes he was so stirred by the meaninglessness of whatever way of life offered itself that he was tempted to leave the city and become a tramp, one of the hordes of adventurous, dissatisfied souls who [*spend their lives] drift[*ing] back and forth along the American railroads.

[In the meantime] he continued to work [as night cashier] in the South State Street restaurant that got its patronage from the underworld. In the evening[*s] from six until twelve trade was quiet and he sat reading books and watching the restless, thrashing crowds that passed the window. Sometimes he became so absorbed that one of the guests sidled past and escaped through the door without paying his bill. In State Street the people moved up and down wandering here and there going nervously [and] without purpose like cattle confined in a corral. Women, in cheap imitations of the gowns worn by their sisters two blocks away in Michigan Avenue and with painted faces, leered at the men. In gaudily lighted store rooms that housed cheap, suggestive shows pianos kept up a constant din.

In the eyes of the people who idled away the evenings in South State Street was the vacant, purposeless stare of modern life accentuated and made horrible. With the stare went the scuffling walk, the wagging jaw, the saying of words meaning nothing. On the wall of a building opposite the door of the restaurant hung a banner marked "Socialist Headquarters." There, where modern life had found well-nigh perfect expression, where [*there] was no discipline, [*and] no order, where men did not move, but drifted like sticks on a sea washed beach, hung the socialist banner with its promise of the co-operative commonwealth.

McGregor looked at the banner and at the moving people and was lost in meditation. Walking from behind the cashier's desk, he stood, in the street by the door, and stared about. A fire began to burn in his eyes and the fists that were thrust into his coat pockets were clenched. Again, as when he was a boy in Coal Creek, he hated the people. The fine love of mankind, that had its basis in a dream of mankind galvanized by some great passion into order and meaning, was lost.

In the restaurant after midnight trade briskened. Waiters and bartenders from fashionable restaurants of the loop district began to drop in to meet friends from among the women of the town. When a woman came in she walked up to one of these young men. "What kind of a night have you had?" they asked each other.

The visiting waiters standing about talked in low tones. As they talked they absentmindedly practised the art of withholding money from customers, a [dependable] source of income to them. They played with coins, pitched [*them] into the air, palmed them, made them appear and disappear with marvelous rapidity. Some of them sat on stools along the counter eating pie and drinking cups of hot coffee.

A cook, clad in a long dirty apron, came into the room from the kitchen and, putting a dish on the counter, stood eating its contents. He tried to win the admiration of the idlers by boasting. In a blustering voice he called familiarly to women seated at tables along the wall. At some time in his life the cook had worked for a traveling circus and he talked continually of his adventures on the road striving to make himself a hero in the eyes of his audience.

McGregor read the book that lay before him on the counter and tried to forget the squalid disorder of his surrounding[*s]. Again he read of the great figures of history, the soldiers and statesmen who have been leaders of men. When the cook asked him a question or made some remark intended for his ears he looked up, nodded and read again. When a disturbance started in the room he growled out a command and the disturbance subsided. From time to time well dressed, middle-aged men, half gone in drink, came [in], and leaning over the counter whispered to him. [*He] made a motion with his hand to one of the women sitting at the tables along the wall idly playing with toothpicks. When she came to him he pointed to the man and said, "He wants to buy you a dinner."

The women of the underworld sat at the tables and talked of McGregor each secretly wishing he might become her lover. They gossiped like suburban wives, filling their talk with vague reference[s] to things he had said. They commented upon his clothes and his reading. When he looked at them they smiled and stirred uneasily about like timid children.

One of the women of the underworld, a thin woman with hollow red cheeks, sat at a table talking with the other women of the raising of white leghorn chickens. She and her husband, a fat old man, a waiter in a loop restaurant, had bought a ten acre farm in the country and she was helping to pay for it with the money made in the streets in the evening. A small, black-eyed woman, sitting beside the chicken raiser, reached up to a raincoat hanging on the wall and, taking a piece of white cloth from the pocket, [*began] working out a design in pale blue flowers for the front of a shirt waist. A youth with unhealthy looking skin sat on a stool by the counter talking to a waiter.

"The reformers have raised Hell with business," [*the youth boasted], looking about to be sure of listeners. "I used to have four women working for me here in State Street in World's Fair year and now I only have one and she crying and sick half the time."

McGregor stopped reading the book. "In every city there is a vice spot, a place from which diseases go out to poison the people. The best legislative brains in the world have made no progress against this evil," it said.

He closed the book, threw it away from him, and looked at his big fist lying on the counter, and at the youth talking boastfully to the waiter. A smile played about the corners of his mouth. He opened and closed his fist reflectively. Then, taking a law book from a shelf below the counter, he began reading again, moving his lips and resting his head upon his hands.

McGregor's law office was upstairs over a second-hand clothing store in Van Buren Street. There he sat at his desk, reading and waiting, and at night he returned to the State Street restaurant [to work]. Now and then he went to the Harrison Street police station to hear a police court trial and, through the influence of [Tom] O'Toole, was occasionally given a case that netted him a few dollars. He tried to think that the years spent in Chicago were years of training. In his own mind he knew what he wanted to do but did not know how to begin. Instinctively he waited. He saw the march and countermarch of events in the lives of the people tramping on the sidewalks below his office window; saw in his mind the miners of the Pennsylvania village coming down from the hills to disappear below [*the] ground; looked at the girls hurrying through the swinging doors of department stores in the early morning, wondering which of them would presently sit idling with toothpicks in O'Toole's; and waited for the word or the stir on the surface of that sea of humanity that would be a sign to him. To an onlooker he might have seemed but another of the waste[*d] men of modern life, a drifter on the sea of things, but it was not so. The people, plunging through the streets afire with earnestness concerning nothing, had not succeeded in sucking him into the whirlpool of commercialism in which they struggled and into which year after year the best of America's youth was drawn.

In his mind the idea that had come [to him] as he sat on the hill above the mining town grew and grew. Day and night he dreamed of the actual physical phenomena of the men of labor marching their way into power and of the thunder of millions of feet rocking the world and driving the great song of order, purpose and discipline into the soul of Americans.

Sometimes it seemed to him that the dream would never be [anything] more than a dream. In the dusty little office he sat and tears came into his eyes. At such times he was convinced that mankind would go on forever along the old road, that youth would continue always to grow into manhood, become fat, decay and die with the great swing and rhythm of life an unthought of mystery to them. "They will see the seasons and the planets marching through space but they will not march," he muttered going to [*stand by] the window and staring down into the dirt and disorder of the street below.

CHAPTER IV

In the office McGregor occupied in Van Buren Street there was another desk beside[*s] his own. The desk was owned by a small man with an extraordinary long mustache and with grease spots on the lapel of his coat. In the morning he came in and sat in his chair with his feet on his desk, smoking long black stogies and reading the morning papers. On the glass panel of the door was the inscription, "Henry Hunt, Real Estate Broker." When he had finished with the morning papers he disappeared, returning tired and dejected in the late afternoon.

The real estate business of Henry Hunt was a myth. Although he bought and sold no property he insisted on the title and had in his desk a pile of letterheads setting forth the kind of property in which he specialized. He had a picture of his daughter, a graduate of the Hyde Park High School, in a glass frame on the wall. When he went out at the door in the morning he paused, looked at McGregor and said, "If anyone comes in about property, tend to them for me. I'll be gone for a while."

Henry Hunt was a collector of tithes for the political bosses of the First Ward. All day he went from place to place through the ward interviewing women, checking their names off a little red book he carried in his pocket, promising, demanding, making veiled threats. In the evening he sat in his flat, overlooking Jackson Park, and listened to his daughter playing on the piano. With all his heart he hated his place in life and as he rode back and forth to town on the Illinois Central train[*s] he stared at the lake and dreamed of owning a farm and living a free life in the country. In his mind he could see the merchants standing gossiping on the sidewalk before the stores in an Ohio village where he had lived as a boy and in fancy saw himself, again a boy, driving cows through the village street in the evening and making a delightful little slap, slap with his bare feet in the deep dust.[8]

It was Henry Hunt, in his secret office as collector and lieutenant to the "boss" of the First Ward, who shifted the scenes for McGregor's appearance as a public character in Chicago.

One night a young man—son of one of the city's plunging millionaire wheat speculators—was found dead in a little blind alley back of a resort known as Polk Street Mary's place. He lay crumpled up against a [worn] board fence, quite dead, [*and] with a bruise on the side of his head, [when] a policeman found him and dragged him to the street light at the corner of the alley.

For twenty minutes the policeman had been standing under the light, swinging his [night] stick. He had heard nothing. A young man, coming up, [had] touched him on the arm and whispered to him. When he turned to go down the alley the young man ran [*away] up the street.

The powers that rule the First Ward in Chicago were furious when the identity of the dead man became known. The "boss," a mild-looking, blue-eyed little man, in a neat grey suit and with a silky mustache, stood in his office opening and closing his fists convulsively. Then he called a young man and sent for Henry Hunt and a well known police official.

For some weeks the newspapers of Chicago had been conducting a campaign against vice. Swarms of reporters had overrun the ward. Daily they issued word pictures of life in the underworld. On the front page[*s] of the papers, with senators and governors and millionaires who had divorced their wives, appeared also the names of Ugly Brown, Chophouse Sam and Carolina Kate with descriptions of their places, their hours of closing and the class and quantity of their

8. As a boy in Clyde, Ohio, Anderson had driven cows as a part-time job. See *Sherwood Anderson's Memoirs*, ed. White, pp. 28, 63–64, 67.

patronage. A drunken man, rolled on the floor at the back of a Twenty-second Street saloon and [*robbed of] his pocket-book, had his picture on the front page of the morning papers.

Henry Hunt sat in his office on Van Buren Street trembling with fright. He expected to see his name in the paper and his occupation disclosed.

The powers that ruled the First—quiet, shrewd men who knew how to make and to take profits, the very flower of commercialism—were frightened. They saw in the prominence of the dead man a real opportunity for their momentary enemies—the press. For weeks they had been sitting quietly, weathering the storm of public disapproval. In their minds they thought of the ward as a kingdom in itself—something foreign and apart from the city. Among their followers were men who had not been across the Van Buren Street line into foreign territory for years.

Suddenly through the minds of these men floated a menace. Like the small, soft-speaking boss, the ward gripped its fist conclusively. Through [*the] streets and alleys ran a cry, a warning. Like birds of prey disturbed in their nesting places they fluttered, uttering cries. Throwing his stogie into the gutter Henry Hunt ran through the ward. From house to house he uttered his cry—"Lay low! Pull off nothing."

The little boss [sitting] in his office at the front of his saloon looked from Henry Hunt to the police official. "It's no time for hesitation," he said. "It will prove a boon if we act quickly. We've got to arrest and try that murderer and do it now. Who is our man? Quick. Let's have action."

Henry Hunt lighted a fresh stogie. He played nervously with the ends of his fingers and wished he were out of the ward and safely out of range of the prying eyes of the press. [*In fancy] he could [*hear] his daughter screaming with horror at the sight of his name spread in glaring letters before the world and thought of her with [*a] flush of abhorrence on her young face turning from him forever. In his terror his mind darted here and there. A name sprang to his lips. "It might have been Andy Brown," he said, puffing at the stogie.

The little [*boss] whirled his chair about. He began picking up [*the] papers scattered about his desk. When he spoke his voice was again soft and mild. "It was Andy Brown," he said. [He turned to the police official. "Make a stir," he said.] "Whisper the word about. Let a *Tribune* man locate Brown for you. Handle this right and you will save your own scalp and get the fool papers off the back of the First."

The arrest of Brown brought respite to the ward. The prediction of the shrewd little boss made good. The newspapers, dropping the clamorous cry for reform, began demanding instead the life of Andrew Brown. Newspaper artists, rushing into police headquarters, made hurried sketches to appear an hour later blazoned across the face of extras on the streets. Grave scientific men got their pictures printed at the heads of articles on "Criminal Characteristics of the Head and Face." An adept and imaginative writer for an afternoon paper spoke of Brown as a Jekyll and Hyde of the Tenderloin, and hinted [darkly] at other murders by the same hand. From the comparatively quiet life of a not markedly industrious yeggman, Brown came out of the upper floor of a State Street lodging house to stand stoically before the world of men—a storm center about which swirled and eddied the wrath of an aroused city.

The thought that had flashed into the mind of Henry Hunt, sitting in the office of the soft-voiced boss, was the making of [*an] opportunity for McGregor. For months he and Andrew Brown had been friends. The yeggman, a strongly built, slow talking man, looked like a skilled mechanic or a locomotive engineer. Coming into O'Toole's in the quiet hours between eight and twelve, he sat eating his evening meal and talking in a half bantering, humorous vein to the young lawyer. In his eyes lurked a kind of hard cruelty, tempered by indolence. It was he who gave McGregor the name that still clings to him in that strange savage land—"Judge Mac, the Big 'un."

When he was arrested Brown sent for McGregor and offered to give him charge of his case. When the young lawyer refused he was insistent. In a cell at the county jail they talked it over. By the door stood a guard watching them. McGregor peered into the half darkness and said what he thought should be said. "You're in a hole," he began. "You don't want me, you want a big name. They are all set to hang you over there." He waved his hand in the direction of the First. "They are going to hand you over as an answer to a stirred up city. It's a job for the biggest and best criminal lawyer in town. Name the man and I'll get him for you and help raise [*the] money to pay him."

Andrew Brown got up and walked to McGregor. Looking down at him he spoke, quickly and determinedly. "You do what I say," he growled. "You take this case. I didn't do the job. I was asleep in my room when it was pulled off. Now you take the case. You won't clear me. It ain't in the cards. But you get the job just the same."

He sat down again upon the iron cot at the corner of the cell. [Again] his voice became slow and had in it a touch of cynical humor. "Look here, Big 'un," he said, "the gang's picked my number out of the hat. I am going across. But there's good advertising in the job for someone, and you get it."

CHAPTER V

THE trial of Andrew Brown was both an opportunity and a test for McGregor. For a number of years he had lived a lonely life in Chicago. He had [*made] no friends and his mind had not been confused by the endless babble of small talk on which most of us subsist. Evening after evening he had walked alone through the streets and had stood at the door of the State Street restaurant a solitary figure aloof from life. Now he was to be drawn into the maelstrom. In the past he had been let alone by life. The great blessing of isolation had been his and in his isolation he had dreamed a big dream. Now the quality of the dream and the strength of its hold upon him was to be tested.

McGregor was not to escape the influence of the life of his day. Deep human passion lay asleep in his big body. Before the time of his Marching Men he had yet to stand the most confusing of all the modern tests of men, the beauty of meaningless women and the noisy clamor of success that is equally meaningless.

On the day of his conversation with Andrew Brown in the old Cook County jail on Chicago's North Side we are therefore to think of McGregor as facing these tests. After the talk with Brown he walked along the street and came to the bridge that led over the river into the loop district. In his heart he knew that he was facing a fight and the thought thrilled him. With a new lift to his shoulders he walked over the bridge looking at the people and again letting his heart be filled with contempt for them.

He wished that the fight for Brown were a fight with fists [and] boarding a West Side car [*he] sat looking out through the car window at the passing crowd and imagined himself among them, striking right and left, gripping throats, demanding the truth that would save Brown and set himself up before the eyes of men.

When McGregor got to the Monroe Street millinery store it was evening and Edith was preparing to go out to the evening meal. He stood looking at her. In his voice rang a note of triumph. Out of his contempt for the men and women of the underworld came boastfulness. "They've given me a job they think I can't do," he said. "I'm to be Brown's counsel in the big murder case." He put his hands on her frail shoulders, pulling her to the light. "I'm going to knock them over and show them," he boasted. "They think they are going to hang Brown—the oily snakes. Well, they didn't count on me. Brown doesn't count on me. I'm going to show them." He laughed noisily in the empty shop.

At a little restaurant McGregor and Edith talked of the test he was going through. As he talked she sat in silence looking at his red hair.

"Find out if your man Brown has a sweetheart," she said, thinking of herself.

America is the land of murders. Day after day in cities [*and] towns and on lonely country roads violent death creeps upon men. Undisciplined and disorderly in their [own] way of life the citizens can do nothing. After each murder they cry out for new laws which when they are written into the books of laws the very lawmaker himself breaks. Harried through life by clamoring demands their days leave them no time for the quietude in which thoughts grow. After days of meaningless hurry in the city they jump upon trains or street cars and hurry through their favorite paper to the ball game, the comic pictures and the market reports.

And then something happens. The [psychological] moment arrives. A murder, that might have got a single column on an inner page of yesterday's paper, today spreads its terrible details over everything.

Through the streets hurry the restless scurrying newsboys, stirring the crowds with their cries. The men, who [*have] passed impatiently the tales of a city's shame, snatching the papers, read eagerly and exhaustively the story of a crime.

And into the midst of such a maelstrom of rumors, hideous

impossible stories and well-laid plans to defeat the truth McGregor hurled himself. Day after day he wandered through the vice district south of Van Buren Street. Prostitutes, pimps, thieves and saloon hangers-on looked at him and smiled knowingly. As the days passed and he made no progress he became desperate. One day an idea came to him. "I will go to the good looking woman at the settlement house," he told himself. "She won't know who killed the boy but she can find out. I'll make her find out."

In Margaret Ormsby, McGregor was to know [*what was to him] a new kind of womanhood, something sure, reliant, hedged about and prepared as a good soldier is prepared to have the best of it in the struggle for existence. Something he had not known was yet to make its cry to the man.

[And] Margaret Ormsby like McGregor himself had not been defeated by life. She was the daughter of David Ormsby, head of the great plow trust with headquarters in Chicago, a man who because of a certain fine assurance in his attitude toward life had been called "Ormsby the Prince" by his associates. Her mother, Laura Ormsby, was small, nervous and intense.

With a self-conscious abandonment, lacking just a shade of utter security, Margaret Ormsby, beautiful in body and beautifully clad, went here and there among the outcasts of the First Ward. She like all women was waiting for an opportunity of which she did not talk even to herself. She was something for the single-minded and primitive McGregor to approach with caution.

Hurrying along a narrow street lined with cheap saloons McGregor went in at the door of the settlement house and sat in a chair at a desk facing Margaret Ormsby. He knew something of her work in the First [*Ward and] that she was [very] beautiful and self-possessed. He was determined that she should help him. Sitting in the chair and looking at her across the flat-top desk he choked back into her throat the [*terse] sentences with which she was wont to greet visitors.

"It's all very well for you to sit there dressed up and telling

me what women in your position can do and can't do," he
said, "but I have come here to tell you what you will do, if
you are of the kind that want to be useful."

The speech of McGregor was a challenge which Margaret,
the modern daughter of one of [*our] modern great men,
could not well let pass. Had she not brazened out her timidity
to go calmly among prostitutes and sordid muttering drunk-
ards, serene in her consciousness of business-like purpose?
"What is it you want?" she asked sharply.

"You have [*just] two things that will help me," said
McGregor, "your beauty and your virginity. These things are
a kind of magnet drawing the women of the street to you. I
know. I have heard them talk.

"There are women who come in here who know who it was
killed that boy in the passageway, and why it was done,"
McGregor went on. "You are a [kind of] fetish with these
women. They are children and [*they] come in here to look at
you, as children peep around curtains at guests sitting in the
parlor of their houses.

"Well, I want you to call these children into the room and
let them tell you family secrets. The whole ward here knows
the story of that killing. The air is filled with it. The men and
women keep trying to tell me, but they are afraid. The police
have [got] them scared and they half tell me and then
[they] run away like frightened animals.

"I want them to tell you. You don't count with the police
down here. They think you are too beautiful and too good to
touch the real life of the[*se] people. None of them—the
bosses or the police—are watching you. I'll keep kicking up
dust, and you get the information I want. You can do the
job if you are any good."

After McGregor's speech, the woman sat in silence looking at
him. For the first time, she had met a man who overwhelmed
her and was in no way diverted by her beauty nor her self-
possession. A hot wave, half anger, half admiration, swept
over her.

McGregor stared at the woman and waited. "I've got to
have facts," he said. "Give me the story and the names of

those who know the story and I'll make them tell. I've [got] some facts now—got them by bullying a girl and by choking a bartender in an alley. Now I want you, in your way, to put me in the way of getting more facts. You make the women talk and tell you and then you tell me."

When McGregor had gone Margaret Ormsby got up from her desk in the settlement house and walked across the city toward [*her father's office]. She was startled and frightened. In a moment, and by the speech and manner of this brutal young lawyer, she had been made to realize that she was but a child in the hands of the forces that played about her in the First Ward. Her self-possession was shaken. "If they are children—these women of the town—then I am a child, a child swimming with them in a sea of hate and ugliness."

A new thought came into her mind. "But he is no child— that McGregor. He is a child of nothing. He stands on a rock unshaken."

She tried to become indignant because of the blunt frankness of the man's speech. "He talked to me as he would have talked to a woman of the streets," she thought. "He wasn't afraid to assume that at bottom we are alike, just playthings in the hands of [*the] man who dares."

In the street she stop[*ped] and looked about. Her body trembled and she realized that the forces about her had become living things ready to pounce upon her. "Anyway I'll do what I can. I'll help him. I'll have to do that," she whispered to herself.

CHAPTER VI

THE clearing of Andrew Brown made a sensation in Chicago. At the trial McGregor was able to introduce one of those breath-taking, dramatic climaxes that catch the attention of the mob. At the tense, dramatic moment of the trial a frightened hush fell upon the court room [and the city] and that evening in their houses men turned instinctively from the reading of the papers to look at their beloved sitting about them. A chill of fear ran over the bodies of women. For a moment Beaut McGregor had given them a peep under the crust of civilization that awoke an age old trembling in their hearts. In his fervor and [his] impatience McGregor had cried out, not against the incidental enemies of Brown, but against all modern society and its formlessness. To the listeners it seemed that he shook mankind by the throat and that by the power and purposefulness of his own solitary figure he revealed the pitiful weakness of his fellows.

In the court room McGregor had sat, grim and silent, letting the State build up its case. In his face was a challenge. His eyes looked out from beneath swollen eyelids. For weeks he had been as tireless as a bloodhound running through the First Ward and building his case. Policemen had seen him emerge from alleyways at three in the morning. The soft spoken boss, hearing of his activities, had eagerly questioned Henry Hunt. A bartender in a dive on Polk Street had felt the grip of a hand at his throat and a trembling girl of the town had knelt before him in a little dark room begging protection from his wrath. In the court room he sat waiting and watching.

When the special counsel for the State, a man of great name in the courts, had finished his insistent persistent cry for the blood of the silent, unemotional Brown, McGregor acted. Springing to his feet, he shouted hoarsely across the silent court room to a large woman sitting among the witnesses. "They have tricked you, Mary," he roared. "The tale about the pardon after the excitement dies is a lie. They are stringing you. They are going to hang Andy Brown. Get up there and tell the naked truth or his blood be on your hands."

A furore arose in the crowded court room. Lawyers sprang to their feet, objecting, protesting. Above the noise arose [*a] hoarse accusing voice. "Keep Polk Street Mary and every woman from her place in here," he shouted. "They know who killed your man. Put them back there on the stand. They'll tell. Look at them. The truth is coming out of them."

The clamor in the room subsided. The silent red-haired attorney, the joke of the case, had scored. Walking in the streets at night the words of Edith Carson had come back into his brain and with the help of Margaret Ormsby he had been able to follow a clew given by her suggestion "Find out if your man Brown has a sweetheart."

In a moment he saw the message the women of the under-world, patrons of O'Toole's, had been trying to convey to him. Polk Street Mary was the sweetheart of [*Andy] Brown. Now in the silent court room, the voice of a woman arose, broken with sobs. To the listening crowd in the packed little room came the story of the tragedy in the darkened house before which stood the policeman idly swinging his night stick; the story of [*a] girl from [*an] Illinois village procured and sold to [*the] broker's son; of the desperate struggle in the little room between the eager, lustful man and the frightened brave-hearted girl; of the blow with the chair [*in the hands of the girl] that brought death to the man; of the women of the house trembling on the stairs; and [of] the body hastily pitched into the passageway.

"They told me they would get Andy off when this blew over," wailed the woman.

McGregor went out of the court room into the street. The glow of victory was on him and he strode along with his heart beating high. His way led over a bridge into the North Side and in his wanderings he passed the apple warehouse where he had made his start in the city and where he had fought with the German. When night came he walked in

North Clark Street and heard the newsboys shouting of his victory. Before him danced a new vision, a vision of himself as a big figure in the city. Within himself he felt the power to stand forth among men, to outwit them and outfight them, to get for himself power and place in the world.

The miner's son was half drunk with the new sense of achievement that [had] swept in on him. Out of Clark Street he went and walked east along a residence street to the lake. By the lake he saw a street of great houses surrounded by gardens and the thought came [to his mind] that at some time he might have such a house of his own. The disorderly clatter of modern life seemed very far away. When he came to the lake he stood in the darkness thinking of the useless rowdy of the mining town suddenly become a great lawyer in the city and the blood ran swiftly through his body. "I am to be one of the victors, one of the few who emerge," he whispered to himself and with a jump of the heart thought also of Margaret Ormsby[, the beautiful,] looking at him with her fine questioning eyes as he stood [up] before the men in the court[*room and by the force of his personality pushed his way through a fog of lies to victory and truth].

BOOK V

CHAPTER I

MARGARET ORMSBY was a natural product of her age and of American social life in our times. As an individual she was lovely. Although her father, David Ormsby the plow king, had come up to his position and his wealth out of obscurity and poverty and had known, during his early life, what it was to stand face to face with defeat, he had made it his business to see that his daughter had no such experience. The girl had been sent to Vassar; she had been taught to catch the fine distinction between clothes that are quietly and beautifully expensive and clothes that merely look expensive; she knew how to enter a room and how to leave a room and had also a strong, well trained body and an active mind. Added to these things she had, without the least knowledge of life, a vigorous and rather high handed confidence in her ability to meet life.

During the years spent in the eastern college Margaret had made up her mind that, whatever happened, she was not going to let her life be dull or uninteresting. Once when a girl friend from Chicago came to the college to visit her the two went for a day out of doors and sat down upon a hillside to talk things over. "We women have been fools," Margaret had declared. "If Father and Mother think [*that] I am [*going to come] [back] home and marry some stick of a man they are mistaken. I have learned to smoke cigarettes and have had my share of a bottle of wine. That may not mean anything to you. I don't think it amounts to much either but it expresses something. It fairly makes me ill when I think of how men have always patronized women. They want to keep evil things away from us——Bah! I'm sick of that idea and a lot of the other girls here feel the same way. What right have they? I suppose someday some little whiffit of a business man will set himself up to take care of me. He had better not. I'll tell you there is a new kind of women growing up and I'm going to be one of them. I'm going to adventure, to taste life strongly and deeply. Father and Mother might as well make up their minds to that."

The excited girl had walked up and down before her companion, a mild looking young woman with blue eyes, and had raised her hands above her head as though to strike a blow. Her body was like the body of a fine young animal standing alert to meet an enemy and her eyes reflected the intoxication of her [*mood]. "I want all of life," she cried, "I want the lust and the strength and the evil of it. I want to be one of the new women, the saviours of our sex."

Between David Ormsby and his daughter there was an unusual bond. Six foot three, blue-eyed, broad shouldered, his presence had a strength and dignity which marked him out among men and the daughter sensed his strength. She was right in that. In his way the man was inspired. Under his eye, the trivialities of plowmaking had become the details of a fine art. In the factory he never lost the air of command which inspires confidence. Foremen running into the office filled with excitement because of a break in the machinery, or an accident to a workman, returned to do his bidding quietly and efficiently. Salesmen going from village to village to sell plows became, under his influence, filled with the zeal of missionaries, carrying the gospel to the unenlightened. Stockholders of the plow company, rushing to him with rumors of coming business disaster, stayed to write checks for new assessments on their stock. He was a man who gave men back their faith in business and their faith in men.

To David plowmaking was an end in life. Like other men of his type he had other interests but they were secondary. In secret he thought of himself as capable of a broader culture than most of his daily associates and, without letting it interfere with his efficiency, [he] tried to keep in touch with the thought[*s] and movement[*s] of the world by reading. After the longest and hardest day in the office he sometimes spent half the night over a book in his room.

As Margaret Ormsby grew into womanhood she was a constant source of anxiety to her father. To him it seemed that she had passed from an awkward and rather jolly girlhood into a peculiarly determined new kind of womanhood over night. Her adventurous spirit worried him. One day he had sat in his office reading a letter announcing her homecoming. The letter seemed no more than a characteristic outburst from an impulsive girl who had but yesterday fallen asleep at evening in his arms. It confused him to think that an honest plowmaker should have a letter from his little girl talking of the kind of living that he believed could only lead a woman to destruction.

And then, the next day, there sat beside him at his table a new and commanding figure demanding [*his] attention. David got up from the table and hurried away to his room. He wanted to readjust his thoughts. On his desk [*was] a photograph brought home by the daughter from school. He had the common experience of being told by the photograph what he had been trying to grasp. Instead of a wife and child, there were two women in the house with him.

Margaret had come out of college a thing of beauty in face and figure. Her tall, straight, well-trained body, her coal-black hair, her soft brown eyes, the air she had of being prepared for life's challenge, caught and held the attention of men. There was in the girl something of her father's bigness, and not a little[, too,] of the secret blind desires of her mother. To an attentive household, on the night of her arrival, she announced her intention of living her life fully and vividly. "I am going to know things I can't get from books," she said. "I am going to touch life at many corners, getting the taste of things in my mouth. You thought me a child when I wrote home saying that I wouldn't be cooped up in the house and married to a tenor in the church choir or to an empty headed young business man but now you are going to see. I'm going to pay the price if necessary, but I am going to live."

In Chicago Margaret set about the business of living as though nothing were needed but strength and energy. In a characteristic American way she tried to hustle life. When the men in her own set looked confused and shocked by the opinions she expressed she got out of her set and made the common mistake of supposing that those who do not work and

148 MARCHING MEN

who talk rather glibly of art and of freedom are, by that
token, free men and artists.

Still she loved and respected her father. The strength in him
made an appeal to the native strong thing in her. To a young
socialist writer who lived in the settlement house, where she
presently went to live, and who sought her out to sit by her
desk berating men of wealth and position, she showed the
quality of her ideals by pointing to David Ormsby. "My father,
the leader of an industrial trust, is a better man than all of the
noisy reformers that ever lived," she declared. "He makes
plows, anyway—makes them well—millions of them. He
doesn't spend his time talking and running his fingers through
his hair. He works, and his work has lightened the labors of
millions while the talkers sit thinking noisy thoughts and
getting round-shouldered."

In truth Margaret Ormsby was puzzled. Had she been
allowed by a common fellowship in living to be a real sister
to all other women and to know the[*ir] common heritage of
defeat, had she, like her father, when he was a boy, but
known what it was to walk utterly broken and beaten in the
face of men and then to [a]rise again, and again to battle with
life, she would have been splendid.

She did not know. To her mind any kind of defeat had in
it a touch of something like immorality. When she saw all
about her only a vast mob of defeated and confused human
beings trying to make headway in the midst of a confused
social organization she was beside herself with impatience.

The distraught girl turned to her father [*and tried] to get
hold of the keynote of his life. "I want you to tell me things,"
she said but the father, not understanding, only shook his
head. It did not occur to him to talk to her as to a fine man
friend and a kind of bantering, half serious companionship
sprang up between them. The plowmaker was happy in the
thought that the jolly girl he had known before his daughter
went to college had come back to live with him.

After Margaret went to the settlement house she lunched
with her father almost every day. The hour together in the
midst of the din that filled their lives became for them both a

treasured privilege. Day after day they sat for an hour in a fashionable down town eating place renewing and strengthening their comradeship—laughing and talking amid the crowds —delightful in their intimacy. With each other they playfully took on the air of [*the] two men of affairs, each in turn treating the work of the other as something to be passed over lightly. Secretly neither believed as he talked.

In her effort to get hold of, and move, the sordid human wrecks floating in and out at the door of the settlement house, Margaret thought of her father at his desk directing the making of plows. "It is clean and important work," she thought. "He is a big and effective man."

At his desk in the office of the plow trust, David thought of his daughter in the settlement house at the edge of the First Ward. "She is a white thing shining amid dirt and ugliness," he thought. "Her whole life is like the life of her mother during the hours when she [*once] lay bravely facing death for the sake of a new life."

On the day of her meeting with McGregor father and daughter sat as usual in the restaurant. Men and women passed up and down the long carpeted aisles and looked at them admiringly. A waiter stood at [*Ormsby's shoulder], anxious for the generous tip. Into the air that hung over them, the little secret atmosphere of comradeship they cherished so carefully, was thrust the sense of a new personality. Floating in Margaret's mind, beside the quiet noble face of her father, with its stamp of ability and kindliness, was another face—the face of the man who had talked to her in the settlement house, not as Margaret Ormsby, daughter of David Ormsby of the plow trust, but as a woman who could serve his ends, and who he meant should serve. The vision in her mind haunted her, and she listened indifferently to the [*talk] of her father. She felt that the stern face of the young lawyer with its strong mouth and its air of command was as something impending, and tried to get back the feeling of dislike she had felt when first he thrust himself in at the settlement house door. She succeeded only in recalling certain firm lines of purpose that offset and tempered the brutality of [*his] face.

Sitting there in the restaurant, opposite her father, where day after day they had tried so hard to build a real partnership in existence, Margaret suddenly burst into tears.

"I have met a man who has compelled me to do what I did not want to do," she explained to the astonished man and then smiled at him through the tears that glistened in her eyes.

CHAPTER II

In Chicago the Ormsbys lived in a large stone house in Drexel Boulevard. The house had a history. It was owned by a banker who was a large stockholder and one of the directors of the plow trust. Like all men who knew him well the banker admired and respected the ability and integrity of David Ormsby [and] when the plowmaker came to the city from a town in Wisconsin to be the master of the plow trust he offered him the house to use.

The house had come to the banker from his father, a grim, determined old money making merchant of a past generation, who had died, hated by half [of] Chicago, after toiling sixteen hours daily for sixty years. In his old age the merchant had built the house to express the power wealth had given him. It had floors and woodwork cunningly wrought of expensive woods by workmen sent to Chicago by a firm in Brussels. In the long drawing room at the front of the house hung a chandelier that had cost the merchant ten thousand dollars. The stairway leading to the floor above was from the [*palace] of a prince in Venice and had been bought for the merchant and brought over seas to the house in Chicago.

The banker who inherited the house did not want to live in it. Even before the death of his father and after his own unsuccessful marriage he lived at a club down town. In his old age the merchant, retired from business, lived in the house with another old man, an inventor. He could not rest although he had given up business with that end in view. Digging a trench in the lawn at the back of the house he, with his friend, spent his days trying to reduce the refuse of one of his factories to something having commercial value. Fires burned in the trench and at night the grim old man sat in the house under the chandelier with hands covered with tar. After the death of the merchant the house stood empty, staring at passers[*by] in the street, its walks and paths overgrown with weeds and rank grass.[1]

David Ormsby fitted into his house. Walking through the long halls or sitting smoking his cigar in an easy chair on the wide lawn he looked arrayed and environed. The house became a part of him like a well-made and intelligently worn suit of clothes. Into the drawing room under the ten thousand dollar chandelier he moved a billiard table and the click of ivory balls banished the churchliness of the place.

Up and down the stairway[, brought over seas from Venice,] moved American girls, friends [*of] Margaret, their skirts rustling and their voices running through the huge rooms. In the evening after dinner David played billiards. The careful calculation of the angles and the English interested him. Playing in the evening with Margaret or with a man friend the fatigue of the day passed and his honest voice and reverberating laugh brought a smile to the lips of people [*passing] in the street. In the evening David brought his friends to sit in talk with him on the wide verandas. At times he went alone to his room at the top of the house and buried himself in books. On Saturday evenings he had a debauch and, with a group of friends from town, sat at a card table in the long parlor playing poker and drinking highballs.

Laura Ormsby, Margaret's mother, had never seemed a real part of the life about her. Even as a child the daughter had thought her hopelessly romantic. Life had treated her too well and from everyone about her she expected qualities and reactions which, in her own person, she would not have tried to achieve.

David had already begun to rise when he married her, the slender, brown-haired daughter of a village shoemaker. Even in those days the little plow company, with its ownership scattered among the merchants and farmers of the vicinity,

1. This inventor figure is comparable to the character Hugh McVey in Anderson's third novel, *Poor White* (1920). See the Introduction by Walter B. Rideout in *Poor White* (New York: Viking, [1966]), pp. ix–xx.

had started, under his hand, to make progress in the state. People already spoke of its master as a coming man and of Laura as the wife of a coming man.

To Laura this was, in some way, unsatisfactory. Sitting at home and doing nothing she had still a passionate wish to be known as a character, an individual, a woman of action. On the street, walking beside her husband, she beamed upon people but when the same people spoke, calling them a handsome couple, a flush rose to her cheeks and a flash of indignation ran through her brain.

Laura Ormsby lay awake in her bed at night thinking of her life. She had a world of fancies in which she at such times lived. In her dream world a thousand stirring adventures came to her. She imagined a letter, received through the mail, telling of an intrigue in which David's name was coupled with that of another woman and lay abed quietly hugging the thought. She looked at the face of the sleeping David tenderly. "Poor, hard-pressed boy," she muttered. "I shall be resigned and cheerful and lead him gently back to his old place in my heart."

In the morning after a night spent in this dream world Laura [sat at breakfast] looking at David, so cool and efficient, and was irritated by his efficiency. When he playfully dropped his hand upon her shoulder she drew away and sitting opposite him [°at breakfast] watched him read the morning paper all unconscious of the rebel thoughts in her mind.

Once, after she had moved to Chicago and after Margaret's return from college, Laura had the faint suggestion of an adventure. Although it turned out tamely it lingered in her mind and in some way sweetened her thoughts.

She was alone on a sleeping car coming from New York. A young man sat in a seat opposite her and the two fell into talk. As she talked Laura imagined herself eloping with the young man and under her lashes looked sharply at his weak and pleasant face. She kept the talk alive as others in the car crawled away for the night behind the green swaying curtains.

With the young man Laura discussed ideas she had got

from reading Ibsen and [Bernard] Shaw.² She grew bold and daring in the advancing of opinions, trying to stir the young man to some overt speech or action that might arouse her indignation.

The young man did not understand the middle-aged woman sitting beside him and talking so boldly. He knew of but one prominent man named Shaw and that man had been governor of Iowa and later a member of the cabinet of President McKinley.³ It startled him to think that a prominent member of the Republican party should have such thoughts or express such opinions. He talked of fishing in Canada and of a comic opera he had seen in New York, and at eleven o'clock yawned and disappeared behind the green curtains. As the young man lay in his berth he muttered to himself, "Now, what did that woman want?" A thought came into his mind and he reached up to where his trousers swung in a little hammock above the window and looked to see that his watch and pocketbook were still there.

At home Laura Ormsby nursed the thought of the talk with the strange [young] man on the train. In her mind he became something romantic and daring, a streak of light across what she was pleased to think of as her somber life.

Sitting at dinner she talked of him, describing his [*charms]. "He had a wonderful mind and we sat late into the night talking," she said, watching the face of David.

When she had spoken Margaret looked up and said laughingly, "Have a heart Dad. Here is romance. Don't be blind to it. Mother is trying to scare you about an alleged love affair."

2. Perhaps the idea for Margaret Ormsby came from "Shaw and Ibsen." Anderson refers to Bernard Shaw in *A Story Teller's Story*, ed. White, p. 80; and in *Sherwood Anderson's Memoirs*, ed. White, pp. 212, 215.

3. Anderson may refer to Leslie M. Shaw (1848–1932), Governor of Iowa from 1898 to 1902 and Secretary of the Treasury for President Theodore Roosevelt, 1902–7.

CHAPTER III

ONE evening three weeks after the great murder trial McGregor took a long walk [alone] in the streets of Chicago and tried to plan out his life. He was troubled and disconcerted by the event that had crowded in upon [him on] the heels of his dramatic success in the court room and more than troubled by the fact that his mind constantly played with the dream of having Margaret Ormsby as his wife. In the city he had become a power and instead of the names and the pictures of criminals and keepers of disorderly houses his name and his picture now appeared on the front pages of newspapers. Andrew Leffingwell, the political representative in Chicago of a rich and successful publisher of sensational newspapers, had visited him in his office and had proposed to make him a political figure in the city. Finley, a noted criminal lawyer, had offered him a partnership. The lawyer, a small smiling man with white teeth, had not asked McGregor for an immediate decision. In a way he had taken the decision for granted. Smiling genially and rolling a cigar across McGregor's desk he had spent an hour telling stories of famous court room triumphs. "One such triumph is enough to make a man," he [had] declared. "You have no idea how far such a success will carry you. The word of it keeps running through men's minds. A tradition is built up. The remembrance of it acts upon the minds of jurors. Cases are won for you by the mere connection of your name with the case."

McGregor walked slowly [*and heavily] through the streets without seeing the people. In Wabash Avenue near Twenty-third Street he stopped in a saloon and drank beer. The saloon was in a room below the level of the sidewalk and the floor was covered with sawdust. Two half drunken laborers stood by the bar quarreling. One of the laborers, who was a socialist, continually cursed the army and his words started McGregor to thinking of the dream he had so long held and that now seemed fading. "I was in the army and I know what I am talking about," declared the socialist. "There is nothing national about the army. It is a privately owned thing. Here it is secretly owned by the capitalists and in Europe by the aristocracy. Don't tell me. I know. The army is made up of bums. If I am a bum I became one then. You will see fast enough what [*fellows] are in the army if the country is ever caught and drawn into a great war."

Becoming excited the socialist raised his voice and pounded on the bar. "Hell, we don't know ourselves at all," he cried. "We have never been tested. We call ourselves a great nation because we are rich. We are like a fat boy who has had too much pie. Yes sir—that's what we are, here in America, and, as [*far] as our army [*goes], it is a fat boy's plaything. Keep away from it."

McGregor sat in the corner of the saloon looking about. Men came in and went out at the door. A child carried a pail down the short flight of steps from the street and ran across the sawdust floor. Her voice, thin and sharp, pierced through the babble of men's voices. "Ten cents' worth—give me plenty," she pleaded, raising the pail above her head and putting it on the bar.[4]

The confident smiling face of Finley the lawyer came back into McGregor's mind. Like David Ormsby the successful maker of plows [*the lawyer] looked upon men as pawns in a great game and like the plowmaker his intentions were honorable and his purpose clear. He was intent upon making much of his life, being successful. If he played the game on the side of the criminal that was but a chance. Things had fallen out so. In his mind was something else—the expression of his own purpose.

McGregor [a]rose and went out of the saloon. In the street

4. Compare this child's buying beer to a passage in Chapter 3 of *Maggie: A Girl of the Streets* (1893) by Stephen Crane: "Jimmy took a tendered tin pail and seven pennies and departed. He passed into the side door of a saloon and went to the bar. Straining up on his toes he raised the pail and pennies as high as his arms would let him. He saw two hands thrust down to take them. Directly the same hands let down the filled pail, and he left."

men stood about in groups. At Thirty-ninth Street a crowd of youths scuffling on the sidewalk pushed against the tall muttering man who passed with his hat in his hand. He began to feel that he was in the midst of something too vast to be moved by the efforts of any one man. The pitiful insignificance of the individual was apparent. As in a long procession the figures of [*the] individuals who had tried to rise out of the ruck of American life passed before him. With a shudder he realized that for the most part the men whose names filled the pages of American history meant nothing. The children who read of their deeds were unmoved. Perhaps they had only increased the disorder. Like the men passing in the street they went across the face of things and disappeared into the darkness.

"Perhaps Finley and Ormsby are right," he whispered [to himself]. "They get what they can, they have the good sense to know that life runs quickly like a flying bird passing an open window. They know that if a man thinks of anything else he is likely to become another sentimentalist and spend his life being hypnotized by the wagging of his own jaw."

In his wanderings McGregor came to an out-of-door[s] restaurant and garden far out on the South Side. The garden had been built for the amusement of the rich and successful. Upon a little platform a band played. Although the garden was walled about it was open to the sky and above the laughing people seated at the tables shone the stars.

McGregor sat alone at a little table [*on a balcony] beneath a shaded light. Below him along [*a] terrace were other tables occupied by men and women. On a platform in the center of the garden dancers appeared.

McGregor, who had ordered a dinner, left it untouched. [He was fascinated by the scene that lay before him.] A tall graceful girl, strongly suggestive of Margaret Ormsby, danced upon the platform. With infinite grace her body gave expression to the movements of the dance and like a thing blown by the wind she moved here and there in the arms of her partner, a slender youth with long black hair. In the figure of the dancing woman there was expressed much of the idealism man has sought to materialize in women and McGregor was thrilled by it. A sensualism so delicate that it did not appear to be sensualism began to invade him. With a new hunger he looked forward to the time when he should again see Margaret.

Upon the platform in the garden appeared other dancers. The lights at the tables were turned low. [The orchestra played with new zeal.] From the darkness laughter arose. McGregor stared about. The people seated at the tables on the terrace[s] caught and held his attention and he began looking sharply at the faces of the men. How cunning they were, these men who had been successful in life. Were they not, after all, the wise men? Behind the flesh that had grown so thick upon their bones what cunning eyes. There was a game of life and they had played it. The garden was a part of the game. It was beautiful and did not all that was beautiful in the world end by serving them? The arts of men, the thoughts of men, the impulses toward loveliness that came into the minds of men and women, did not all these things work solely to lighten the hours of the successful? The eyes of the men at the tables as they looked at the women who danced were not too greedy. They were filled with assurance. Was it not for them that the dancers turned here and there revealing their grace? If life was a struggle had they not been successful in the struggle? [5]

McGregor arose from the table leaving [his] food untouched. Near the entrance to the gardens he stopped and leaning against a pillar looked again at the scene before him. Upon the platform appeared a whole troup of women dancers. They were dressed in many-colored garments and danced a folk dance. As McGregor watched a light began to creep back into his eyes. The women who now danced were unlike her who had reminded him of Margaret Ormsby. They were short of stature and there was something rugged in their faces. Back and forth across the platform they moved in masses. By their

5. Such pragmatic use of Darwinian theory (uncommon in Sherwood Anderson) is discussed in Richard Hofstadter, *Social Darwinism in American Thought*, rev. ed. (New York: G. Braziller, 1959).

dancing they were striving to convey a message. [Was it their fault if the men with cunning eyes and the women with soft bodies could not understand?] A thought came to McGregor. "It is the dance of labor," he muttered. "Here in this garden it is corrupted but the note of labor is not lost. There is a hint of it left in these figures who toil even as they dance."

McGregor moved away from the shadows of the pillar and stood, hat in hand, beneath the garden lights waiting as though for a call out of the ranks of the dancers. How furiously they worked. How the bodies twisted and squirmed. Out of [a kind of] sympathy with their efforts sweat appeared on the face of the man who stood watching. "What a storm must be going on just below the surface of labor," he muttered. "Everywhere dumb, brutalized men and women must be waiting for something, not knowing what they want. I will stick to my purpose but I will not give up Margaret," he said aloud turning and half running out of the garden and into the street.

In his sleep that night McGregor dreamed of a new world, a world of soft phrases and gentle hands that stilled the rising brute in man. It was a world old dream, the dream out of which such women as Margaret Ormsby have been created. The long slender hands he had seen lying on the desk in the settlement house now touched his hands. Uneasily he rolled about in [the] bed and desire came to him so that he awakened. In the Boulevard people still passed up and down. McGregor arose and stood in the darkness by the window of his room watching. A theatre had just spat forth its portion of richly dressed men and women and when he had opened the window the voices of the women came clear[ly] and sharp[ly] to his ears.

The distracted man stared into the darkness and his blue eyes were troubled. The vision of the disordered and disorganized band of miners marching silently in the wake of his mother's funeral, into whose lives he by some supreme effort was to bring order, was disturbed and shattered by the more definite and lovely vision that had come to him.

CHAPTER IV

During the days since she had seen McGregor, Margaret had thought of him almost constantly. She weighed and balanced her own inclinations, and decided that, if the opportunity came, she would marry the man whose force and courage had so appealed to her, and was half disappointed that the opposition she had seen in her father's face, [*when] she had told him of McGregor and had betrayed herself by her tears, did not become more active. She wanted to fight, to defend the man she had secretly chosen. When nothing was said of the matter she went to her mother and tried to explain. "We will have him here," the mother said quickly. "I am giving a reception next week. I will make him the chief figure. Let me have his name and address and I will attend to the matter."

Laura arose and went into the house. A shrewd gleam came into her eye[*s]. "He will act like a fool before our people," she told herself. "He is a brute and will be made to look like a brute." She could not restrain her impatience and sought out David. "He is a man to fear," she said, "he would stop at nothing. You must think of some way to put an end to Margaret's interest in him. Do you know of a better plan than to have him here where he will look the fool?"

David took the cigar from his lips. He felt annoyed and irritated that an affair concerning Margaret [*had] been brought forward for discussion. In his heart he also feared McGregor. "Let it alone," he said sharply. "She is a woman grown and has more judgment and good sense than any other woman I know." He got up and threw the cigar over the veranda into the grass. "Women are not understandable," he half shouted. "They do inexplicable things, have inexplicable fancies. Why don't they go forward along straight lines like a sane man? I, years ago, gave up understanding you and now I am being [*compelled] to give up understanding Margaret."

At [*Mrs. Ormsby's] reception McGregor appeared arrayed
in the black suit he had purchased for his mother's funeral. His
flaming red hair and rude countenance arrested the attention
of all. About him on all sides crackled talk and laughter. As
Margaret had been alarmed and ill at ease in the crowded
court room [*where] a fight for life went on so he, among
these people who went about [*uttering] little [bits of] broken
sentences and laughing [*foolishly] at nothing, felt uncertain
and depressed. In the midst of the company he occupied much
the same position as a new and ferocious animal safely caught
and now on caged exhibition. They thought it clever of
[*Mrs. Ormsby] to have him and he was, in not quite the
accepted sense, the lion of the evening. The rumor that he
would be there had induced more than one woman to cut
other engagements and come to where she could take the hand
of, and talk with, this hero of the newspapers. The men, shaking his hand, looked at him sharply, wondering what power
and what cunning lay in him.

In the newspapers, after the murder trial, a cry had sprung
up about the person of McGregor. Fearing to print in full the
substance of his speech on vice, its ownership and its significance, they had filled their columns with talk of the man. The
huge Scotch lawyer of the Tenderloin was proclaimed as
something new and startling in the grey mass of the city's
population. Then, as in the brave days that followed, the man
caught irresistibly the imagination of writing men. Himself
dumb in written or spoken words, except in the heat of an inspired outburst, he expressed perfectly that pure brute force,
the lust for which sleeps in the souls of artists.

Unlike the men, the beautifully gowned women at the reception had no fear of McGregor. They saw in him something
to be tamed and conquered and [*they] gathered in groups to
engage him in talk and return the inquiring stare in his eyes.
They thought that with such an unconquered soul about life
might take on new fervor and interest, and like the women,
sitting playing with [the] toothpicks in O'Toole's restaurant,
more than one of the women at [*Mrs. Ormsby's] reception

had a half unconscious wish that such a man might be her lover.

One after another, Margaret brought forward the men and women of her world, coupling their names with McGregor's and trying to establish him in the atmosphere of assurance and ease that pervaded the house and the people. He stood by the wall, bowing and staring boldly about, and thought that the confusion and distraction of mind that had followed his first visit to Margaret at the settlement house was being increased immeasurably with every passing moment. He looked at the glittering chandelier on the ceiling and at the people moving about, the men at ease, comfortable—the women with wonderfully delicate, expressive hands and with their round white necks and shoulders showing above their gowns and a feeling of utter helplessness pervaded him. Never before had he been in a company so feminine. He thought of the beautiful women about him, seeing them in his direct, crude and forceful way merely as females at work among males, carrying forward some purpose. "With all [of] the softly suggestive sensuality of their dress and their persons they must in some way have sapped the strength and the purpose of these men who move among them so indifferently," he thought. Within himself he knew of nothing to set up as a defense against what he believed such beauty must become to the man who lived with it. [*Its] power, he thought, must be something monumental and he looked with admiration [*at] the quiet face of Margaret's father, moving among his guests.

McGregor went out of the house and stood in the half darkness on the veranda. When [*Mrs. Ormsby and Margaret] followed he looked at the older woman and sensed her antagonism. The old love of battle swept in on him and he turned and stood in silence looking at her. "The fine lady," he thought, "is no better than the women of the First Ward. She [*has] an idea I will surrender without a fight."

Out of his mind went the fear of the assurance and stability of Margaret's people that had almost overcome him in the house. The woman, who had, all her life, thought of herself as one waiting only the opportunity to appear as a commanding figure in affairs, made [*by her presence] a failure of the effort to submerge McGregor.

On the veranda stood the three people. McGregor the silent became the talkative. Seized with one of the inspirations that were a part of his nature, he threw talk about, sparring and returning thrust for thrust with Mrs. Ormsby. When he thought that the time [*had] come for him to get at the thing that was in his mind, he went into the house and presently came out carrying his hat. The quality of harshness, that crept into his voice when he was excited or determined, startled Laura Ormsby['s ears]. Looking down at her, he said, "I am going to take your daughter for a walk in the street. I want to talk with her."

Laura hesitated and smiled uncertainly. She determined to speak out, to be like the man, crude and direct. When she had her mind fixed and ready Margaret and McGregor were already half way down the gravel walk to the gate, and the opportunity to distinguish herself had passed.

McGregor walked beside Margaret, absorbed in thoughts of her. "I am engaged in a work here," he said waving his hand vaguely toward the city. "It is a big work and it takes a lot out of me. I have not come to see you, because I have been uncertain. I have been afraid you would overcome me and drive [the] thought[*s] of the work out of my head."

By the iron gate, at the end of the gravel walk, they turned and faced each other. McGregor leaned against the brick wall and looked at her. "I want you to marry me," he said. "I think of you constantly. Thinking of you I can only half do my work. I get to thinking that another man may come and take you and I waste hour after hour being afraid."

She put her hand upon his arm, and he, thinking to check an attempt at an answer before he had finished, hurried on.

"There are things to be said and understood between us before I can come to you as a suitor. I did not think I should feel toward a woman as I feel toward you and I have certain adjustments to make. I thought I should get along without your kind of woman. I thought [*you were not] for me with the work I have thought out to do in the world. If you won't marry me[, when I come,] I will be glad to know now, so that I can get my mind straightened out."

Margaret raised her hand and laid it on his shoulder. The act was a kind of acknowledgment of his right to talk to her so directly. She said nothing. Filled with a thousand messages of love and tenderness, she longed to pour into his ear, she stood [*in silence] [and with trembling knees] on the gravel path, [*with] her hand on his shoulder.

And then an absurd thing happened. The fear that Margaret might come to some quick decision that would affect all of their future together made McGregor frantic. He did not want her to speak and wished his own words unsaid. "Wait. Not now," he cried and threw up his hand intending to take her hand. His fist struck the arm that lay on his shoulder and it in turn knocked his hat flying into the road. McGregor started to run after it and then stopped. He put his hand to his head and appeared lost in thought. When he turned again to pursue the hat Margaret, unable longer to control herself, shouted with laughter.

Hatless, McGregor walked up Drexel Boulevard in the soft stillness of the summer night. He was annoyed at the outcome of the evening and in his heart half wished that Margaret had sent him away defeated. His arms ached to have her against his breast but his mind kept presenting one after another the objections to marriage with her. "Men are submerged by such women and forget their work," he told himself. "They sit looking into the soft brown eyes of their beloved, thinking of happiness. A man should go about his work thinking of that. The fire that runs through the veins of his body should light his mind. One wants to take the love of woman as an end in life, and the woman accepts that and is made happy by it." He thought with gratitude of Edith in her shop on Monroe Street. "I do not sit in my room at night dreaming of taking her in my arm[*s] and pouring kisses on her lips," he whispered.

. . . .

In the door of her house [*Mrs. Ormsby] had stood watching McGregor and Margaret. She had seen them stop at the end of the walk. The figure of the man was lost in shadows and that of Margaret stood alone, outlined against a distant light. She saw Margaret's hand thrust out—was she clutching his sleeve!—and heard [*the] murmur of voices. And then the man precipitating himself into the street, his hat catapulting ahead of him—and a quick outburst of half hysterical laughter broke the stillness. . . .

Laura [*Ormsby] was furious. Although she hated McGregor she could not bear the thought that laughter should break the spell of romance. "She is just like her father," she muttered. "At least she might show some spirit and not be like a wooden thing, ending her first talk with a lover with a laugh like that."

As for Margaret she stood in the darkness trembling with happiness. She imagined herself going up the dark stairway to McGregor's office in Van Buren Street, where once she had gone to take him news of the murder case, laying her hand upon his shoulder and saying, "Take me in your arms and kiss me. I am your woman. I want to live with you. I am ready to renounce my people and my world and to live your life for your sake." Margaret, standing in the darkness before the [*huge old] house [*in] Drexel Boulevard, imagined herself with Beaut McGregor, living with him as his wife in a small apartment over a fish market on a West Side street. Why a fish market she couldn't have said.

CHAPTER V

EDITH CARSON was six years older than McGregor and lived entirely within herself. Hers was one of those natures that do not express themselves in words. Although at his coming into the shop her heart beat high, no color came to her cheeks and her pale eyes did not flash back into his a message. Day after day she sat in her shop at work, quiet, strong in her own kind of faith, ready to give her money, her reputation, and, if need be, her life, to the working out of her own dream of womanhood. She did not see in McGregor the making of a man of genius as did Margaret and did not hope to express through him a secret desire for power. She was a working woman, and to her he represented all men. In her secret heart she thought of him merely as the man—her man.

And to McGregor Edith was companion and friend. He saw her sitting year after year in her shop, putting money into the savings bank, keeping a cheerful front before the world, never assertive, kindly, in her own way sure of herself. "We could go on forever as we are now and she be none the less pleased," he told himself.

One afternoon after a particularly hard week of work he went out to her place to sit in her little workroom and think out the matter of marrying Margaret Ormsby. It was a quiet season in Edith's trade and she was alone in the shop serving a customer. McGregor lay down upon the little couch in the workroom. For a week he had been speaking to gatherings of workmen night after night and later had sat in his own room thinking of Margaret. Now on the couch with the murmur of voices in his ears he fell asleep.

When he awoke it was late in the night, and on the floor by the side of the couch sat Edith with her fingers in his hair.[6]

6. In *Sherwood Anderson's Memoirs*, ed. White, pp. 162–63, the author recalls a similar episode from his Chicago days preceding the composition of *Marching Men*.

McGregor opened his eyes quietly and looked at her. He could see a tear running down her cheek. She was staring straight ahead at the wall of the room and by the dim light coming through a window he could see the drawn cords of her little neck and the knot of mouse colored hair on her head.

McGregor closed his eyes quickly. [Lying there] he felt like one who had been aroused out of sleep by a [*dash of cold] water across his breast. It came over him with a rush that Edith Carson had been expecting something from him—something he wasn't prepared to give.

She got up after a time and crept quietly away into the shop, and with a great clatter and bustle he arose also and began calling loudly, demanding the time and complaining about a missed appointment. Turning up the gas, Edith walked with him to the door. On her face sat the old placid smile. McGregor hurried away into the darkness and spent the rest of the night walking in the streets.

The next day he went to Margaret Ormsby at the settlement house. With her he used no art. Driving straight [*to the point], he told her of the undertaker's daughter sitting beside him on the eminence above Coal Creek, of the barber and his talk of women on the park bench, and how that had led him to that other woman kneeling on the floor in the little frame house [with] his fists in her hair, and of Edith Carson whose companionship had saved him from all of these.

"If you can't hear all of this and still want life with me," he said, "there is no future for us together. I want you. I am afraid of you and afraid of my love for you, [*but] still I want you. I have been seeing your face floating above the audiences in the halls where I have been at work. I have looked at babies in the arms of workingmen's wives and wanted to see my babe in your arms. I care more for what I am doing than I do for you, but I love you."

McGregor arose and stood over her. "I love you with my arms aching to close about you, with my brain planning the triumph of the workers, with all of [*the] old [*perplexing] human [sex] love that [*I had almost thought I would never want].

"I can't bear this waiting. I can't bear this not knowing so that I can tell Edith. I can't have my mind filled with the need of you just as men are beginning to catch the infection of an idea and are looking to me for clear headed leadership. Take me or let me go and live my life."

Margaret Ormsby looked at McGregor [standing before her in the settlement house]. When she spoke her voice was as quiet as the voice of her father, telling a workman in the shop what to do with a broken machine.

"I am going to marry you," she said simply. "I am full of the thought of it. I want you, want you so blindly that I think you can't understand."

She stood up facing him and looking into his eyes.

"You must wait," she said. "I must see Edith. I, myself, must do that. All [of] these years she has served you—she has had that privilege."

McGregor looked across the table into the beautiful eyes of the woman he loved.

"You belong to me even if I do belong to Edith," he said.

"I will see Edith," Margaret answered again.

CHAPTER VI

McGregor left the telling of the story of his love to [*Margaret]. Edith Carson who knew defeat so well and who had in her the courage of defeat was to meet defeat at his hands through the undefeated woman and he let himself forget the whole matter. For [*a month] he had been trying to get workingmen to take up the idea of the Marching Men without success and after the talk with Margaret he kept doggedly at the work.

And then one evening [*something] happened that aroused him. The Marching Men idea that had become more than half intellectualized became again a burning passion and the matter of his life with women got itself cleared up swiftly and finally.

It was night and McGregor stood upon the platform of the Elevated Railroad at State and Van Buren Streets. He had been feeling guilty concerning Edith and had been intending to go out to her place but the scene in the street below fascinated him and he remained standing [on the platform] looking along the lighted thoroughfare.

For a week there had been a strike of teamsters in the city and that afternoon there had been a riot. Windows had been smashed and several men injured. Now [in] the evening crowds gathered and speakers climbed upon boxes to talk. Everywhere there was a great wagging of jaws and waving of arms.

McGregor grew reminiscent. Into his mind came the little mining town and he saw himself again a boy sitting in the darkness on the steps before his mother's bake shop and trying to think. Again in fancy he saw the disorganized miners tumbling out of the saloon to stand on the street swearing and threatening and again he was filled with contempt for them.

And then in the heart of the great western city the same thing happened that had happened when he was a boy in

Pennsylvania. The officials of the city having decided to startle
the striking teamsters by a display of force sent a regiment of
state troops marching through the street[*s]. The soldiers
were dressed in brown uniforms. They were silent. With Mc-
Gregor looking down [at them] they turned out of Polk
Street and came with swinging, measured tread up State Street
past the disorderly mobs on the sidewalk and the equally
[*disorderly] speakers [*on] the curb. McGregor's heart beat
so that he [*nearly choked]. The men in the uniforms, each in
himself meaning nothing, had become by [*their] marching
together all alive with meaning. Again he wanted to shout, to
run down into the street and embrace them. The strength in
them seemed to kiss, as with the kiss of a lover, the strength
within him[*self] and when they had passed and the disorderly
jangle of voices broke out again he got on a car and went out
to Edith's with his heart afire with resolution.

Edith Carson's millinery shop was in the hands of a new
owner. She had sold out and fled. McGregor stood in the show
room looking about him at the cases filled with their feathery
finery and at the hats along the wall. The light from a street
lamp coming in at the window started millions of tiny motes
dancing before his eyes.

Out of the room at the back of the shop—the room where
he had seen the tears of suffering in Edith's eyes—came [*a]
woman who told him of Edith's having sold the business. She
was excited by the message she had to deliver and walked
past the waiting man, going to the screen door to stand with
her back to him and look up the street.

Out of the corners of her eyes the woman looked at him.
She was a small black-haired woman with two gleaming gold
teeth and with glasses on her nose. "There has been a lovers'
quarrel here," she told herself.

"I have bought the store," she said aloud. "She told me to
tell you that she had gone."

McGregor did not wait for more but hurried past the woman
into the street. In his heart was a feeling of dumb, aching loss.
On an impulse he turned and ran back.

Standing in the street by the screen door he shouted
hoarsely. "Where did she go?" he demanded.

The woman laughed merrily. She felt that she was getting
with the shop a flavor of romance and adventure very attrac-
tive to her. Then she walked to the [*door] [of the shop] and
smiled through the screen [door]. "She has only just left," she
said. "She went to the Burlington station. I think she has gone
West. I heard her tell the man about her trunk. She has been
around here for two days since I bought the shop. I think she
has been waiting for you to come. You didn't come and now
she has gone and perhaps you won't find her. She didn't look
like one who would quarrel with a lover."

The woman in the shop laughed softly as McGregor hurried
away. "Now who would think that quiet little woman would
have such a lover?" she asked herself.

Down the street ran McGregor and raising his hand stopped
a passing automobile. The woman saw him seated in the automobile talking to a grey-haired man at the wheel and [*then]
the machine turned and disappeared up the street at a law
breaking pace.

McGregor had again a new light on the character of Edith
Carson. "I can see her doing it," he told himself, "cheerfully
telling Margaret that it didn't matter, and all [of] the time
planning this in the back of her head. Here all of these years
she has been leading a life of her own. The secret longings, the
desires, and the old human hunger for love and happiness and
expression [*have] been going on under her placid exterior as
[*they have] under my own."

McGregor thought of the busy days behind him and realized
with shame how little Edith had seen of him. It was in the days
when his big movement [*of The Marching Men] was just
coming into the light and on the night before he had been in a
conference of labor men who had wanted him to make a public demonstration of the power he had been secretly building
up. [*Every] day his office [*was] filled with newspaper men
asking questions and demanding explanations. And in the

meantime Edith had been selling her shop to that woman and getting ready to disappear.

In the railroad station McGregor found Edith sitting in a corner, [*with] her face buried in the crook of her arm. [About her whole figure there was a look of utter fatigue.] Gone was the placid exterior. Her shoulders seemed narrower. Her hand hanging [loosely] over the back of the seat in front of her was white and lifeless.

McGregor said nothing but snatched up the brown leather bag that sat beside her on the floor and taking her by the arm led her up a flight of stone steps to the street.

CHAPTER VII

In the Ormsby household father and daughter sat in the darkness on the veranda. After Laura [*Ormsby's] encounter with McGregor there had been another talk between her and David. Now she had gone on a visit to [*her home-town in Wisconsin] and father and daughter sat together.

To his wife David had talked pointedly of Margaret's affair. "It isn't a matter of good sense," he had said, "one can't pretend there is a prospect of happiness in such an affair. The man is no fool, and may someday be a big man, but it won't be the kind of bigness that will bring either happiness or contentment to a woman like Margaret. He may end his life in jail."

McGregor and Edith walked up the [wide] gravel walk and stood by the front door of the Ormsby house. From the darkness on the veranda came the hearty voice of David. "Come and sit out here," he said.

McGregor stood silently waiting. To his arm clung Edith. Margaret got up and coming forward stood looking at them. With a jump at [*her] heart, she sensed the crisis suggested by the presence of these two people. Her voice trembled with alarm. "Come in [here]," she said, turning and leading the way into the house.

The man and woman followed Margaret. At the door McGregor stopped and called to David. "We want you in here with us," he said harshly.

In the drawing room the four people waited. The great chandelier threw its light down upon them. In her chair sat Edith looking at the floor.

"I have made a mistake," said McGregor. "I've been going on and on making a mistake." He turned to Margaret. "We didn't count on something here. There is Edith. She is not what we thought."

Edith said nothing. The weary stoop stayed in her shoulders. She felt that if McGregor had brought her to the house and to this woman he loved to seal their parting, she would sit quietly until that was over and then go on to the loneliness she believed [*must be her portion].

To Margaret the coming of the man and [the] woman was a portent of evil. She also was silent, expecting a shock. When her lover spoke, she also looked at the floor. To herself she was saying, "He is going to take himself away and marry this other woman. I must [*be prepared] to hear him say that."

In the doorway stood David. "He is going to give me back Margaret," he thought, and his heart danced with happiness.

McGregor walked across the room and stood looking at the two women. His blue eyes were cold and filled with intense curiosity concerning them and himself. He wanted to test them and to test himself. "If I am clear headed now I shall go on with the dream," he thought. "If I fail in this I shall fail in everything." Turning he took hold of the sleeve of David's coat and pulled him across the room so that the two men stood together. Then he looked hard at Margaret. As he talked to her he continued to stand thus with his hand on her father's arm. The action caught David's fancy and a thrill of admiration ran through him. "Here is a man," he told himself.

"You thought Edith was ready to see us get married. Well, she was. She is now and you see what it has done to her," said McGregor.

The daughter of the plowmaker started to speak. Her face was chalky white. McGregor threw up his hands.

"Wait," he said, "a man and woman can't live together for years and then part like two men friends. Something gets into them to prevent. They find they love each other. I have found [*out] that though I want you I love Edith. She loves me. Look at her."

Margaret half arose from her chair. McGregor went on. Into his voice came the harsh quality that made men fear and follow him. "Oh, we will be married, Margaret and I," he said, "her beauty has won me. I follow beauty. I want beautiful children. That is my right."

He turned to Edith [*and stood] staring at her.

"You and I could never have the feeling Margaret and I

had, looking into each other's eyes. We ached with it—each wanting the other. You are made to endure. You would get over [*anything] and be cheerful after a while. You know that, don't you?"

The eyes of Edith came up level with his own.

"Yes, I know," she said.

Margaret Ormsby jumped up from her chair, her eyes swimming.

"Stop," she [*cried]. "I don't want you. I would never marry you now. You belong to her. You are Edith's."

[*McGregor's voice] became soft and quiet.

"Oh, I know," he said, "I know! I know! But I want children. Look at Edith. Do you think she could bear children to me?"

A change came over Edith Carson. Her eyes hardened and her shoulders straightened.

"That is for me to say," she cried, springing forward and clutching his arm. "That is between me and God. If you intend to marry me come now and do it. I was not afraid to give you up and I am not afraid that I shall die bearing children."

Dropping McGregor's arm Edith ran across the room and stood before Margaret. "How do you know you are more beautiful or can bear more beautiful children?" she [*demanded]. "What do you mean by beauty anyway? I deny your beauty." She turned to McGregor. "Look," she cried, "she does not stand the test."

Pride swept over the woman that had come to life within the body of the little milliner. With calm eyes she stared at the people in the room and when she looked again toward Margaret there was a challenge in her voice.

"Beauty has to endure," she said swiftly. "It has to outlive long years of life and many defeats. It has [*to] be daring." [*A] hard look came [back] into her eyes as she challenged the daughter of wealth. "I had the courage to be defeated and I have the courage to take what I want," she said. "Have you that courage? If you have take this man. You want him and so do I. Take his arm and walk away with him. Do it now, here before my eyes."

Margaret shook her head. Her body trembled and her eyes looked wildly about. She turned to David Ormsby. "I did not know [*that] life could be like this," she said. "Why did you not tell me? She is right. I am afraid."

A light came into McGregor's eyes and he turned quickly about. "I see," he said looking sharply at Edith, "you have also your purpose." Turning again he looked into the eyes of David. "There is something to be decided here. It is perhaps the supreme test of a man's life. One struggles to keep [*a] thought in mind, to be impersonal, to see that life has a purpose outside his own purpose. You have perhaps made that struggle. You see I am making it now. I am going to take Edith and go back to work."

At the door McGregor stopped and put out his hand to David who took it, looking at the big lawyer respectfully.

"I am glad to see you go," said the plowmaker [*briefly].

"I am glad to be going," said McGregor, understanding that there was nothing but relief and honest antagonism in the voice and in the mind of David Ormsby.

BOOK VI

CHAPTER I

THE MARCHING MEN MOVEMENT was never a thing to intellectualize [about]. For years McGregor tried to get it under way by talking. He didn't succeed. The rhythm and swing that was at the heart of the movement hung fire. The man passed through long periods of depression and had to drive himself forward. And then, after the scene with Margaret and Edith in the Ormsby house, came action.

There was a man named Mosby about whose figure the action for a time revolved. He was bartender for Neil Hunt, a notorious character of South State Street, and had once been a lieutenant in the army. Mosby was what in modern society is called a rascal. After West Point and a few years at some isolated army post he began to drink and one night during a debauch and when half crazed by the dullness of his life he shot a private through the shoulder. He was arrested and put on his honor not to escape but did escape. For years he drifted about the world a [*haggard] cynical figure who got drunk whenever money came his way and who would do anything to break the monotony of existence.

Mosby was enthusiastic about the Marching Men idea. He saw in it an opportunity to worry and alarm his fellow men. He talked a union of bartenders and waiters, to which he belonged, into giving the idea a trial and in the morning they began to march up and down in the strip of park land that [*faced] the lake at the edge of the First Ward. "Keep your mouths shut," commanded Mosby. "We can worry the officials of this town like the devil if we work this right. When you are asked questions say nothing. If the police try to arrest us we will swear we are only doing it for the sake of exercise."

Mosby's plan worked. Within a week crowds began to gather in the morning to watch the Marching Men and the police started to make inquiry. Mosby was delighted. He threw up his job as bartender and recruited a motley company of young roughs whom he induced to practise the march step during the afternoons. When he was arrested and dragged into court McGregor acted as his lawyer and he was discharged. "I want to get these men out into the open," Mosby declared looking very innocent and guileless. "You can see for yourself that waiters and bartenders get pale and stoop[*shouldered] at their work and as for these young roughs isn't it better for society to have them out there marching about than idling in barrooms and planning God knows what mischief?"

A grin [*appeared] over the face of the First Ward. Mc-Gregor and Mosby organized another company of Marchers and a young man, who had been a sergeant in a company of regulars, was induced to help with the drilling. To the men themselves it was all a joke, a game that appealed to the mischievous boy in them. Everybody was curious and that gave the thing tang. They grinned as they marched up and down. For awhile they exchanged jibes with the spectators but McGregor put a stop to that. "Be silent," he said, going about among the men during the rest periods. "That's the best thing to do. Be silent and attend to business and your marching will be ten times as effective."

The Marching Men Movement grew. A young Jewish newspaper man, half rascal, half poet, wrote a scare-head story for one of the Sunday papers announcing the birth of the Republic of Labor. The story was illustrated by a drawing showing McGregor leading a vast horde of men across an open plain toward a city whose tall chimneys belched forth clouds of smoke. Beside McGregor in the picture, and arrayed in a gaudy uniform, was Mosby the ex-army officer. In the article he was called the war lord of "the secret republic growing up within a great capitalistic empire."

It had begun to take form—the movement of the Marching Men. Rumors began to run here and there. There was a question in men's eyes. Slowly at first it began to rumble through their minds. There was the tap of feet clicking sharply on pavements. Groups formed, men laughed, the groups disappeared only to again reappear. In the sun before factory doors men stood talking, half understanding, beginning to sense the fact that there was something big in the wind.

At first the movement didn't get anywhere with the ranks of labor. There would be a meeting, perhaps a series of meetings in one of the little halls where laborers gather to attend to the affairs of their union[*s]. McGregor would speak. His voice harsh and commanding could be heard in the streets below. Merchants came out of the stores and stood in the doorways listening. Young fellows who smoked cigarettes stopped looking at passing girls and gathered in crowds below the open windows. The slow working brain of labor was being aroused.

After a time a few young men, fellows who worked at the saws in a box factory and [*others who] ran machines in a factory where bicycles were made, volunteered to follow the lead of the men of the First Ward.[1] On summer evenings they gathered in vacant lots and marched back and forth, looking at their feet and laughing.

McGregor insisted upon the training. He never had any intention of letting his Marching Men [*Movement] become merely a disorganized band of walkers, such as we have all seen in many a labor parade. He meant that they should learn to march rhythmically, swinging along like veterans. He was determined that the thresh of feet should come finally to sing a great song, carrying the message of a powerful brotherhood into the hearts and brains of the marchers.

[In the vacant lots, after two or three evenings, the newly formed groups broke up. Someone laughed. Jeers arose. The men who had begun to march went sheepishly away.]

McGregor gave all of his time to the movement. He made a scant living by the practise of his profession but gave it no

---

1. Sherwood Anderson describes his work as a young man in a bicycle factory that came to Clyde, Ohio, in 1894, in *A Story Teller's Story*, ed. White, pp. 148–49; and in his *Memoirs*, ed. White, pp. 123–28. In *Tar*, ed. White, pp. 175, 176, 181, 214, Anderson describes his older brother Karl's work in this bicycle shop (although in fact Karl had permanently left Clyde in 1891).

thought. The murder case had brought him other cases and he had taken a partner, a ferret-eyed little man who worked out the details of what cases came to the firm and collected the fees, half of which he gave to the partner who was intent upon something else. Day after day, week after week, month after month McGregor went up and down the city, talking to workers, learning to talk, striving to make his idea understood.

One evening in September he stood in the shadow of a factory wall watching a group of men who marched in a vacant lot. The movement had become by that time really big. A flame burned in his heart at the thought of what it might become. It was growing dark and the clouds of dust raised by the feet of the men swept across the face of the departing sun. In the field before him marched some two hundred men, the largest company he had been able to get together. For a week they had stayed at the marching evening after evening and were a little beginning to understand the spirit of it. Their leader, on the field, a tall square shouldered man, had once been a captain in the State Militia and now worked as engineer in a factory where soap was made. His commands rang out sharp and crisp on the evening air. "Fours right into line," he cried. The words were barked forth. The men straightened their shoulders and swung out vigorously. They had begun to enjoy the marching.

In the shadow of the factory wall McGregor moved uneasily about. He felt that this was the beginning, the real birth of his movement, that these men had really come out of the ranks of labor and that in the breasts of the marching figures there in the open space understanding was growing.

He muttered and walked back and forth. A young man, a reporter on one of the city's great daily papers, leaped from a passing street car and came to stand near him. "What's up here? What's this going on? What's it all about? You better tell me," he said.

In the dim light McGregor raised his fists above his head and talked aloud. "It is creeping in among them," he said. "The thing that can't be put into words is getting itself expressed. Something is being done here in this field. A new force is coming into the world."

Half beside himself McGregor ran up and down swinging his arms. Again turning to the reporter who stood by a factory wall—a rather dandified figure he was with a tiny mustache—he shouted.

"Do you not see?" he cried. His voice was harsh. "See how they march. They are finding out what I mean. They have caught the spirit of it."

McGregor began to explain. He talked hurriedly, his words coming forth in short broken sentences. "For ages there has been talk of brotherhood. Always men have babbled of brotherhood. The words have meant nothing. The words and the talking have but bred a loose-jawed race. The jaws of men wabble about, but the legs of these men[, they] do not wabble."

He again walked up and down, dragging the half frightened man along the deepening shadow of the factory wall.

"You see it begins—now in this field it begins. The legs and the feet of men, hundreds of legs and feet make a kind of music. Presently there will be thousands, hundreds of thousands. For a time men will cease to be individuals. They will become a mass, a moving all-powerful mass. They will not put their thoughts into words but nevertheless there will be a thought growing up in them. They will of a sudden begin to realize that they are a part of something vast and mighty, a thing that moves, that is seeking new expression. They have been told of the power of labor but now, you see, they will become the power of labor."

Swept along by his own words and perhaps by something rhythmical in the moving mass of men McGregor became feverishly anxious that the dapper young man should understand. "Do you remember—when you were a boy—some man, who had been a soldier, telling you that the men who marched had to break step and go in a disorderly mob across a bridge because their orderly stride would have shaken the bridge to pieces?"

A shiver ran over the body of the young man. In his off hours he was a writer of plays and stories and his trained dramatic sense caught quickly the import of McGregor's words. Into his mind came a scene on a village street of his own place in

Ohio. In fancy he saw the village fife and drum corps marching past. His mind recalled the swing and the cadence of the
tune and again as when he was a boy his legs ached to run
out among the men and go marching away.[2]

Filled with excitement he began also to talk. "I see," he
cried, "you think there is a thought in that, a big thought that
men haven't understood?"

In the field the men, becoming bolder as they became less
self-conscious, came sweeping by their bodies falling into a
long swinging stride.

The young man pondered. "I see. I see. Everyone who stood
watching as I did when the fife and drum corps went past felt
what I felt. They were hiding behind a mask. Their legs also
tingled and the same wild militant thumping went on in
their hearts. You have found that out eh? You mean to lead
labor that way?"

With open mouth the young man stared at the field and at
the moving mass of men. He became oratorical in his thoughts.
"Here is a big man," he muttered. "Here is a Napoleon, a
Caesar of labor come to Chicago. He is not like the little leaders. His mind is not sicklied over with the pale cast of
thought. He doesn't think that the big natural impulses of men
are foolish and absurd. He has got hold of something here that
will work. The world had better watch this man."

Half beside himself he walked up and down at the edge of
the field, his body trembling.

Out of the ranks of the marching men came a workman.
In the field words arose. A petulant quality came into the voice
of the captain who gave commands. The newspaper man listened anxiously. "[*That's] what will spoil everything. The
men will begin to lose heart and will quit," he thought leaning
forward and waiting.

"I've worked all day and I can't march up and down [*here]
all night," complained the voice of [*the] workman.

Past the shoulder of the young man went a shadow. Before

2. Here the author again may present himself autobiographically,
remembering his Ohio boyhood.

his eyes on the field, fronting the waiting ranks of men, stood McGregor. His fist shot out and the complaining workman crumpled to the ground.

"[*This] is no time for words," said the harsh voice. "Get back in there. This is not a game. It is the beginning of men's realization of themselves. Get in there and say nothing. If you can't march with us get out. The movement we have started can pay no attention to [the] whimperer[*s]."

Among the ranks of men a cheer arose. By the factory wall the excited newspaper man danced up and down. At a word of command from the captain the line of marching men again swept down the field and he watched them with tears standing in his eyes. "It is going to work," he cried. "It is bound to work. At last a man has come to [*lead the men of labor]."

CHAPTER II

JOHN VAN MOORE, a young Chicago advertising man, went one afternoon to the offices of the Wheelright Bicycle Company.[3] The company had both its factory and offices far out on the West Side. The factory was a huge brick affair fronted by a broad cement sidewalk and a narrow green lawn spotted with flower beds. The building used for offices was smaller and had a veranda facing the street. Up the sides of the office building vines grew.

Like the reporter who had watched the Marching Men in the field by the factory wall John Van Moore was a dapper young man with a mustache. In his leisure hours he played a clarinet. "It gives a man something to cling to," he explained to his friends. "One sees life going past and feels that he is not a mere drifting log in the stream of things. Although as a musician I amount to nothing it at least makes me dream."

Among the men in the advertising office where he worked Van Moore was known as something of a fool, redeemed by his ability to string words together. He wore a heavy black braided watch chain and carried a cane and he had a wife, who after marriage had studied medicine and with whom he did not live. Sometimes on a Saturday evening the two met at some restaurant and sat for hours drinking and laughing. When the wife had gone to her own place, the advertising man continued the fun, going from saloon to saloon and making long speeches setting forth his philosophy of life. "I am an individualist," he declared strutting up and down and swinging the

3. The following episode is drawn from Anderson's own work in advertising writing in Chicago from 1900 to 1906, work he resumed in 1913. Anderson's recollections are in *A Story Teller's Story*, ed. White, pp. 190, 214–15, 227, 236, 241–48, 257, 269–70, 285–86, 296; and in *Sherwood Anderson's Memoirs*, ed. White, pp. 12–14, 17, 22, 24–25, 122, 199–234 ff. The standard history is William Alfred Sutton, "Sherwood Anderson: The Advertising Years, 1900–1906," *Northwest Ohio Quarterly*, XXII (Summer, 1950), 120–57.

cane about. "I am a dabbler, an experimenter—if you will. Before I die it is my dream that I will discover a new quality in existence."

For the bicycle company the advertising man was to write a booklet telling in romantic and readable form the history of the company. When finished the booklet would be sent out to those who had answered advertisements put into magazines and newspapers. The company had a process of manufacture peculiar to Wheelright bicycles and in the booklet this was to be much emphasized.

The manufacturing process in regard to which John Van Moore was to wax eloquent had been conceived in the brain of a workman and was responsible for the company's success. Now the workman was dead and the president of the company had decided that he would [himself] take credit for the idea. He had thought a good deal of the matter and had decided that in truth the notion must have been more than a little his own. "It must have been so," he told himself, "otherwise it would not have worked out so well."

In the offices of the bicycle company the president, a grey, gross man with tiny eyes, walked up and down a long room heavily carpeted. In reply to questions asked by the advertising man, who sat at a table with a pad of paper before him, he raised himself on his toes, put a thumb in the armhole of his vest and told a long rambling tale of which he was the hero.

The tale concerned a purely imaginary young workman who spent all of the earlier years of his life laboring terribly. At evening he ran quickly from the shop where he was employed and going without sleep toiled for long hours in a little garret. When the workman had discovered the secret that made successful the Wheelright bicycle he opened a shop and began to reap the reward of his efforts.

"That was me. I was that fellow," cried the fat man, who in reality had bought his interest in the bicycle company after the age of forty. Tapping himself on the breast he paused as though overcome with feeling. Tears came into his eyes. The young workman had become a reality [*to him]. "All day I ran about the little shop crying 'quality! quality!' I do that

now. It is a fetish with me. I do not make bicycles for money
but because I am a workman with pride in my work. You may
put that in the book. You may quote me as saying that. A big
point should be made of my pride in my work."

The advertising man nodded his head and scribbled upon
the pad of paper. Almost he could have written the story without the visit to the factory. When the fat man was not looking
he turned his face to one side and listened attentively. With a
whole heart he wished the president would go away and leave
him alone to wander in the factory.

On the evening before John Van Moore had taken part in
an adventure. With a companion, a fellow who drew cartoons
for the daily papers, he had gone into a saloon and there had
met another man of the newspapers.

In the saloon the three men had sat until late into the night
drinking and talking. The second newspaper man—that same
dapper fellow who had watched the marchers by the factory
wall—had told over and over the story of McGregor and his
Marchers. "I tell you there is something growing up here," he
had said. "I have seen this McGregor and I know. You may
believe me or not but the fact is that he has found out something. There is an element in men that up to now has not been
understood—there is a thought hidden away within the breast
of labor, a big unspoken thought—it is a part of men's bodies
as well as their minds. Suppose this fellow has figured that
out and understands it eh!"

Becoming more and more excited as he continued to drink
the newspaper man had been half wild in his conjectures as to
what was to happen in the world. Thumping with his fist upon
a table wet with beer he had addressed the writer of advertisements. "There are things that animals know that have not
been understood by men," he cried. "Consider the bees. Have
you thought that man has not tried to work out a collective
intellect? Why should man not try to work that out?"

The newspaper man's voice became low and tense. "When
you go into a factory I want you to keep your eyes and your
ears open," he said. "Go into one of the great rooms where

many men are at work. Stand perfectly still. Don't try to think. Wait."

Jumping out of his seat the excited man had walked up and down before his companions. A group of men standing before the bar listened, their glasses held half way to their lips.

"I tell you there is already a song of labor. It has not got itself expressed and understood but it is in every shop, in every field where men work. In a dim way the men who work are conscious of the song although if you talk of the matter they only laugh. The song is low, harsh, rhythmical. I tell you it comes out of the very soul of labor. It is akin to the thing that artists understand and that is called form. This McGregor understands something of that. He is the first leader of labor that has understood. The world shall hear from him. One of these days the world shall ring with his name."

In the bicycle factory John Van Moore looked at the pad of paper before him and thought of the words of the half drunken man in the saloon. In the great shop at his back there was the steady grinding roar of many machines. The fat man, hypnotized by his own words, continued to walk up and down telling of the hardship that had once confronted the imaginary young workman and above which he had risen triumphant. "We hear much of the power of labor but there has been a mistake made," he said. "Such men as myself—we are the power. Do you see we have come out of the mass? We stand forth."

Stopping before the advertising man and looking down the fat man winked. "You do not need to say that in the book. There is no need of quoting me there. Our bicycles are being bought by workingmen and it would be foolish to offend them, but what I say is nevertheless true. Do not such men as [*I], with our cunning brains and our power of patience, build these great modern organizations?"

The fat man waved his arm toward the shops from which the roar of machinery came. The advertising man absent-minded[*ly] nodded his head. He was trying to hear the song of labor talked of by the drunken man. It was quitting time and there was the sound of many feet moving about the floor of the factory. The roar of the machinery stopped.

Again the fat man walked up and down talking of the career of the laborer who had come forth from the ranks of labor. From the factory the men began filing out into the open. There was the sound of feet scuffling along the wide cement sidewalk past the flowerbeds.

Of a sudden the fat man stopped. The advertising man sat with pencil suspended above the paper. From the walk below sharp commands rang out. Again the sound of men moving about came in through the windows.

The president of the bicycle company and the advertising man ran to the window. There on the cement sidewalk stood the men of the company formed into columns of fours and separated into companies. At the head of each company stood a captain. The captains swung the men about. "Forward! March!" they shouted.

The fat man stood with his mouth open looking at the men. "What's going on down there? What do you mean? Quit that!" he bawled.

A derisive laugh floated up through the window.

"Attention! Forward, guide right!" shouted [*a captain].

The men went swinging down the broad cement sidewalk, past the window and the advertising man. In their faces was something determined and grim. A sickly smile flitted across the face of the grey-haired man and then faded. The advertising man, without knowing just what was going on, felt that the older man was afraid. He sensed the terror in his face. In his heart he was glad to see it.

The manufacturer began to talk excitedly. "Now what's this?" he demanded, "what's going on? What kind of a volcano are we men of affairs walking over? Haven't we had enough trouble with labor? What are they doing now?" Again he walked up and down past the table where the advertising man sat looking at him. "We will let the book go," he said. "Come tomorrow. Come any time. I want to look into this. I want to find out what is going on."

Leaving the office of the bicycle company John Van Moore

ran along the street past stores and houses. He did not try to
follow the Marching Men but ran forward blindly filled with
excitement. He remembered the words of the newspaper man
about the song of labor and was drunk with the thought that
he had caught the swing of it. A hundred times he had seen
men pouring out of factory doors at the end of the day. Always
before they had been just a mass of individuals. Each had been
thinking of his own affairs and each man had shuffled off into
his own street and had been lost in the dim alleyways between
the tall grimy buildings. Now all of this was changed. The men
did not shuffle off alone but marched along the street shoulder
to shoulder.

A lump came also into the throat of this man and he like that
other by the factory wall began to say words. "The song of
labor is here. It has begun to get itself sung," he cried.

John Van Moore was beside himself. The face of the fat
man, [*pale] with terror, came back into his mind. On the
sidewalk before a grocery store he stopped and shouted with
delight. Then he began dancing wildly about, startling a group
of children who with fingers in their mouths stood with staring
eyes watching.

CHAPTER III

ALL through the early months of that year in Chicago rumors of a new and not understandable movement among laborers ran about among men of affairs. In a way the laborers understood the undercurrent of terror their marching together had inspired and like the advertising man, dancing on the sidewalk before the grocery, were made happy by it. Grim satisfaction dwelt in their hearts. Remembering their [own] boyhoods and the creeping terror that invaded their fathers' houses in times of depression they were glad to spread terror among the homes of the rich and the well-to-do. For years they had been going through life blindly, striving to forget age and poverty. Now they felt that life had a purpose, that they were marching toward some end. When in the past they had been told that power dwelt in them they had not believed. "He is not to be trusted," thought the man at the machine looking at the man at work at the next machine. "I have heard him talk and at bottom he is a fool."

Now the man at the machine did not think of his brother at the next machine. In his dreams at night he was beginning to have a new vision. Power had breathed its message into his brain. Of a sudden he saw himself as a part of a giant walking in the world. "I am like a drop of blood running through the veins of labor," he whispered to himself. "In my own way I am adding strength to the heart and the brain of labor. I have become a part of this thing that has begun to move. I will not talk but will wait. If this marching is the thing then I will march. Though I am weary at the end of the day that shall not stop me. Many times I have been weary and was alone. Now I am a part of something vast. This I know, that a consciousness of power has crept into my brain and [*al]though I be persecuted I shall not surrender what I have gained."

In the offices of the plow trust a meeting of men of affairs was called. The purpose of the meeting was to discuss the movement going on among the workers. At the plow works it had broken out. No more at evening did the men shuffle along, [*like] a disorderly mob, but marched in companies along the brick-paved street that ran by the factory door.

At the meeting David Ormsby had been, as always, quiet and self-possessed. A halo of kindly intent hung over him and when a banker, one of the directors of the company, had finished a speech he arose and walked up and down, his hands thrust into his trousers pockets. The banker was a fat man with thin brown hair and delicate hands. As he talked he held a pair of yellow gloves and beat with them on a long table at the center of the room. The soft thump of the gloves upon the table made a chorus to the things he had to say. David motioned for him to be seated. "I will myself go to see this McGregor," he said walking across the room and putting an arm about the shoulder of the banker. "Perhaps there is, as you say, a new and terrible danger here but I do not think so. For thousands, no doubt for millions of years, the world has gone on its way and I do not think it is to be stopped now.

"It has been my fortune to see and to know this McGregor," added David, smiling at the others in the room. "He is a man and not a Joshua to make the sun stand still."

In the office in Van Buren Street David, the grey and confident, stood before the desk at which sat McGregor. "We will get out of here if you do not mind," he said. "I want to talk to you and I would not like being interrupted. I have a fancy that we talk out of doors."

The two men went in a street car to Jackson Park and forgetting to dine walked for an hour along the paths under the trees. The wind from the lake had chilled the air and the park was deserted.

They went to stand on a pier that ran out into the lake. On the pier David tried to begin the talk that was the object of their being together but felt that the wind and the water that beat against the piling of the pier made talk too difficult. Although he could not have told why, he was relieved by the necessity of delay. Into the park they went again and found a seat upon a bench facing a lagoon.

In the presence of the silent McGregor David felt suddenly embarrassed and awkward. "By what right do I question him?" he asked himself and in his mind could find no answer. A half dozen times he started to say what he had come to say but stopped and his talk ran off into trivialities. "There are men in the world you have not taken into consideration," he said finally, forcing himself to begin. With a laugh he went on, relieved that the silence had been broken. "You see the very inner secret of strong men has been missed, by you and others."

David Ormsby looked sharply at McGregor. "I do not believe that you believe we are after money [*, we men of affairs]. I trust you see beyond that. We have our purpose and we keep to our purpose quietly and doggedly."

Again David looked at the silent figure sitting in the dim light and again his mind ran out striving to penetrate the silence. "I am not a fool and perhaps I know that the movement you have started among the workers is something new. There is power in it as in all great ideas. Perhaps I think there is power in you. Why else should I be here?"

Again David laughed uncertainly. "In a way I am in sympathy with you," he said. "Although all through my life I have served money I have not been owned by it. You are not to suppose that men like me have not something beyond money in mind."

The old plowmaker looked away, over McGregor's shoulder to where the leaves of the trees shook in the wind from the lake. "There have been men and great leaders who have understood the silent, competent servants of wealth," he said, half petulantly. "I want you to understand these men. I should like to see you become such a one yourself—not for the wealth it would bring but because in the end you would thus serve all men. You would get at truth thus. The power that is in you would be conserved and used more intelligently.

"To be sure, history has taken little or no account of the men of whom I speak. They have passed through life unnoticed, doing great work quietly."

The plowmaker paused. Although McGregor had said nothing the older man felt that the interview was not going as it

should. "I should like to know what you have in mind, what in
the end you hope to gain for yourself or for these men," he said
somewhat sharply. "There is after all no point to our beating
about the bush."

McGregor said nothing. Arising from the bench he began
again to walk along the path, [*with] Ormsby [*at] his side.

"The real[*ly] strong men of the world have had no place
in history," declared Ormsby bitterly. "They have not asked
that. They were in Rome and in Germany in the time of Martin
Luther but nothing is said of them. Although they do not
mind the silence of history they would like other strong men to
understand. The march of the world is a greater thing than the
dust raised by the heels of some few workers walking through
the streets and these men are responsible for the march of the
world. You are making a mistake. I invite you to become
one of us. If you plan to upset things you may get yourself into
history but you will not really count. What you are trying to
do will not work. You will come to a bad end."

When the two men emerged from the park the older man
had again the feeling that the interview had not been a success. He was sorry. The evening he felt had marked for him
a failure and he was not accustomed to failures. "There is a
wall here that I cannot penetrate," he thought.

Along the front of the park beneath a grove of trees they
walked in silence. McGregor seemed not to have heard the
words addressed to him. When they came to where a long row
of vacant lots faced the park he stopped and stood leaning
against a tree and looked away into the park lost in thought.

David Ormsby also became silent. He thought of his youth
in the little village plow factory, of his efforts to get on in the
world, of the long evenings spent reading books and trying
to understand the movements of men.

"Is there an element in nature and in youth that we do
not understand or that we lose sight of?" he asked. "Are the
efforts of the patient workers of the world always to be abortive? Can some new phase of life arise suddenly upsetting
all of our plans? Do you, can you, think of men like me as
but part of a vast whole? Do you deny to us individuality,

the right to stand forth, the right to work things out and
to control?"

The plowmaker looked at the huge figure standing beside
the tree. Again he was irritated and kept lighting cigars which
after two or three puffs he threw away. In the bushes at the
back of the bench insects began to sing. The wind, coming
now in gentle gusts, swayed slowly the branches of the trees
overhead.

"Is there an eternal youth in the world, a state out of
which men pass unknowingly, a youth that forever destroys,
tearing down what has been built?" he asked. "Are the mature
lives of strong men of so little account? Have you, like the
empty fields that bask in the sun in the summer, the right to
remain silent in the presence of men who have had thoughts
and have tried to put their thoughts into deeds?"

Still saying nothing, McGregor pointed with his finger along
the road that faced the park. From a side street a body of
men swung about a corner, coming with long strides toward
the two. As they passed beneath a street lamp, that swung
gently in the wind, their faces, flashing in and out of the
light, seemed to be mocking David Ormsby. For a moment
anger burned in him and then something, perhaps the rhythm
of the moving mass of men, brought a gentler mood. The men,
swinging past, turned another corner and disappeared beneath
the structure of an elevated railroad.

The plowmaker walked away from McGregor. Something in
the interview, terminating thus with the presence of the marching figures, had he felt unmanned him. "After all there is youth
and the hope [*of youth. What he has in mind may work],"
he thought climbing aboard a street car.

In the car David put his head out at the window and looked
at the long line of apartment buildings that lined the streets.
He thought again of his [*own] youth and of the evenings in
the Wisconsin village when, himself a youth, he went with
other young men singing and marching in the moonlight. In
a vacant lot he again saw a body of the Marching Men, moving
back and forth, [*and] responding quickly to [*the] com-

mands given by a slender young man who stood on the sidewalk beneath a street lamp and held a stick in his hand.

In the car the grey-haired man of affairs put his head down upon the back of the seat in front. Half unconscious of his own thoughts his mind began to dwell upon the figure of his daughter. "Had I been Margaret I should not have let him go. No matter what the cost I should have clung to the man," he muttered.

CHAPTER IV

It is difficult not to be of two minds about the manifestation now called, and perhaps rightly, "The madness of the Marching Men." In one mood it comes back to the mind as something unspeakably big and inspiring. We go, each of us, through the treadmill of our lives, caught and caged like little animals in some vast menagerie. In turn we love, marry, breed children, have our moments of blind futile passion and then something happens. All [*un]consciously a change creeps over us. Youth passes. We become shrewd, careful, submerged in little things. Life, art, great passions, dreams, all of these pass. Under the night sky the suburbanite stands in the moonlight. He is hoeing his radishes and worrying because the laundry has torn one of his white collars. The railroad is to put on an extra morning train. He remembers that fact, heard at the store. For him the night becomes more beautiful. For ten minutes longer he can stay with the radishes each morning. There is much of man's life in the figure of the suburbanite, standing absorbed in his own thought[*s] in the midst of his radishes.

And so about the business of our lives we go and then of a sudden there comes again the feeling that crept over us all in the year of the Marching Men. In a moment we are again a part of the moving mass. The old religious exaltation, strange emanation from the man McGregor, returns. In fancy we feel the earth tremble under the feet of the men—the marchers. With a conscious straining of the mind we strive to grasp the processes of the mind of the leader during that year when men sensed his meaning, when they saw as he saw the workers —saw them massed and moving through the world.

My own mind, striving feebly to follow that greater and simpler mind, gropes about. I remember sharply the words of a writer who said that men [*make] their own gods and [*realize] that I myself saw something of the birth of such

a god. For he was near to being a god then—our McGregor.
The thing he did rumbles in the minds of men yet. His long
shadow will fall across men's thoughts for ages. The tantalizing
effort to understand his meaning will tempt us always into
endless speculation.

Only last week I met a man—he was a steward in a club
and lingered talking to me by a cigar case in an empty billiard-
room—who suddenly turned away to conceal from me two
large tears that had jumped into his eyes because of a kind
of tenderness in my voice at the mention of the Marching
Men.

Another mood comes. It may be the right mood. I see spar-
rows jumping about in an ordinary roadway as I walk to my
office. From the maple trees the little winged seeds come flut-
tering down before my eyes. A boy goes past sitting in a
grocery wagon and over-driving a rather bony horse. As I walk
I overtake two workmen shuffling along. They remind me of
those other workers and I say to myself that thus men have
always shuffled, that never did they swing forward into that
world-wide rhythmical march of the workers.

"You were drunk with youth and a kind of world madness," says my normal self as I go forward again striving to
think things out.

Chicago is still here—Chicago after McGregor and the
Marching Men. The elevated trains still clatter over the frogs
at the turning into Wabash Avenue; the surface cars clang
their bells; the crowds pour up in the morning from the runway leading to the Illinois Central trains; life goes on. And
men in their offices sit in their chairs and say that the thing
that happened was abortive, a brain storm, a wild outbreak
of the rebellious [and] [*the] disorderly and the hunger in
the minds of men.

What begging of the question. The very soul of the Marching Men was a sense of order. That was the message of it,
the thing that the world hasn't come up to yet. Men haven't
learned that we must come to understand the impulse toward
order, have that burned into our consciousness, before we
move on to other things. There is in us this madness for in-

dividual expression. For each of us the little moment of running forward and lifting our thin childish voice[*s] in the midst of the great silence. We haven't learned that out of us all, walking shoulder to shoulder, there might arise a greater voice, something to make the waters of the very seas to tremble.

McGregor knew. He had a mind not sick with much thinking of trifles. When he had a great idea he thought it would work and he meant to see that it did work.

Mightily was he equipped. I have seen the man in halls talking, his huge body swaying back and forth, his great fists in the air, his voice harsh, persistent, insistent—with something of the quality of the drums in it—beating down into the upturned faces of the men crowded into the stuffy little places.

I remember that newspaper men used to sit in their little holes and write, saying of him that the times [had] made McGregor. I don't know about that. The city caught fire from the man at the time of that terrible speech of his in the court room when Polk Street Mary grew afraid and told the truth. There he stood, the raw, untried, red-haired miner from the mines and the Tenderloin, facing an angry court and a swarm of protesting lawyers and uttering that city-shaking philippic against the old rotten First Ward and the creeping cowardice in men that lets vice and disease go on and pervade all modern life. It was in a way another ["*J'Accuse!"] from the lips of another Zola.[4] Men who heard it have told me that when he had finished in the whole court no man spoke and no man dared feel guiltless. "For [*the] moment something—a section, a cell, a figment, of men's brains opened—and in that terrible illuminating instant they saw themselves as they were and what they had let life become."

They saw something else, or thought they did, saw McGregor a new force for Chicago to reckon with. After the trial one young newspaper man, returned to his office and running from desk to desk, yelled in the faces of his brother reporters. "Hell's out for noon. We've got a big red-haired

4. Émile Zola opened his defense of Albert Dreyfus, unjustly accused Jewish French officer, with "J'accuse," *Aurore*, January 13, 1898.

Scotch lawyer up here on Van Buren Street that is a kind of a new scourge of the world. Watch the First Ward get it."

But McGregor never looked at the First Ward. That wasn't bothering him. From the court room he went to march with men in a new field.

Followed the time of waiting and of patient quiet work. In the evenings McGregor worked at the law cases in the bare room in Van Buren Street. That queer bird, Henry Hunt, still stayed with him, collecting tithes for the gang, [*and] going to his respectable home at night, a strange triumph of the small that had escaped the tongue of McGregor on that day in court when so many men had their names bruited to the world in McGregor's roll call—the roll call of the men who were but merchants, brothers of vice, the men who should have been masters in the city.

And then the movement of the Marching Men began to come to the surface. It got into the blood of men. That harsh, drumming voice began to shake their hearts and their legs.

Everywhere men began to see and hear of the Marchers. From lip to lip ran the question, "What's going on?"

"What's going on?" How that cry ran over Chicago. Every newspaper man in town got assignments on the story. The papers were loaded with it every day. All over the city they appeared, everywhere—the Marching Men.

There were leaders enough! The Cuban War and the State Militia had taught too many men the swing of the march step for there not to be at least two or three competent drill masters in every little company of men.

And there was the marching song the Russian wrote for McGregor. Who could forget it? Its high pitched, harsh, feminine strain rang in the brain. How it went pitching and tumbling along in that wailing, calling, endless high note. It had strange breaks and intervals in the rendering. The men did not sing it. They chanted it. There was in it just the weird, haunting something the Russians know how to put into their songs and into the books they write. It isn't the quality of the soil. Some of our own music has that. But in this Russian song there was something else, something world-wide and religious—a soul, a spirit. Perhaps it is just the spirit that broods over that strange land and people. There was something of Russia in McGregor himself.

Anyway the marching song was the most persistently penetrating thing Americans [*had] ever heard. It was in the streets, the shops, the offices, the alleys and in the air overhead —the wail—half shout. No noise could drown it. It swung and pitched and rioted through the air.

And there was the fellow who wrote it for McGregor. He was the real thing and [*he] bore the marks of the shackles on his legs. He had remembered the march from hearing the men sing [*it] as they went over the Steppes to Siberia, the men who were going up out of misery to more misery. "It would come out of the air," he explained. "The guards would run down the line of men shouting and striking out with their short whips. 'Stop it!' they cried. And still it went on for hours, defying everything, there on the cold, cheerless plains."

And he had brought it to America and [had] put it to music for McGregor's Marchers.

Of course the police tried to stop the marchers. Into a street they would run, crying, "Disperse!" The men did disperse only to appear again on some vacant lot working away at the perfection of the marching. Once an excited squad of police captured a [*company] of them. The same men were back in line the next evening. The police could not arrest a hundred thousand men because they marched shoulder to shoulder along the streets and chanted a weird march song as they went.

The whole thing was not an outbreak of labor, it was something different from anything that had come into the world before. The unions were in it but besides the unions there were the Poles, the Russian Jews, the Hunks from the stock yards and the steel works in South Chicago. They had their own leaders, speaking their own language[*s], and how they could throw their legs into the march. The armies of the old world had for years been training men for the strange demonstration that had broken out in Chicago.

The thing was hypnotic. It was big. It is absurd to sit writing of it now in such majestic terms but you have to go back to the newspapers of that day to realize how the imagination of men was caught and held.

Every train brought writers tumbling into Chicago. In the evening fifty of them would gather in the back room at Weingardner's restaurant where such men congregate.

And then the thing broke out all over the country, in steel towns like Pittsburgh and Johnstown and Lorain and McKeesport; [*and] men, working in little independent factories in towns down in Indiana, began drilling and chanting the march song on summer evenings on the village baseball ground.

How the people, the comfortable, well-fed middle class people, were afraid. It swept over the country like a religious revival, the creeping dread.

The writing men got to McGregor, the brain back of it all, fast enough. Everywhere his influence appeared. In the afternoon there would be a hundred newspaper men standing on the stairway leading up to the big, bare office in Van Buren Street. At his desk he sat, big and red and silent. He looked like a man half asleep. I suppose the thing that was in their minds had something to do with the way men looked at him but in any case the crowd in Weingardner's agreed that there was in the man something of the same fear-inspiring bigness [that] there was in the movement he had started and was guiding.

It seems absurdly simple now. There he sat at his desk. The police might have walked in and arrested him. But if you begin figuring that way the whole thing was absurd. What differs it if men march coming from work, swinging along shoulder to shoulder, or shuffle aimlessly along—and what harm can come out of the singing of a song?

You see McGregor understood something that all of us hadn't counted on. He knew that everyone [*has] an imagination. He was at war with men's minds. He challenged something in us that we hardly realized was there. He had been

sitting there for years thinking it out. He had watched
Dr. Dowie and Mrs. Eddy.[5] He knew what he was doing.

A crowd of newspaper men went one night to hear
McGregor at a big, outdoor meeting up on the North Side.
Dr. Cowell was with them—the big English statesman and
writer, who later was drowned on the *Titanic*.[6] He was a big
man, physically and mentally, and was in Chicago to see
McGregor and try to understand what he was doing.

And McGregor got him as he had all men. Out [*there]
under the sky the men stood silent, Cowell's head sticking up
above the sea of faces, and McGregor talked. The newspaper
men declared he couldn't talk. They were wrong about that.
McGregor had a way of throwing up his arms and straining
and shouting out his sentences that got to the souls of men.

He was a kind of crude artist, drawing pictures on the
mind.

That night he talked about labor as always—labor personified—huge crude Old Labor. How he made the men before him see and feel the blind giant who [*has] lived in
the world since time began and who still [*goes] stumbling
blindly about rubbing his eyes and lying down to sleep away
centuries in the dust of the fields and the factories.

A man arose in the audience and climbed upon the platform beside McGregor. It was a daring thing to do and men's
knees trembled. While the man was crawling up to the
platform shouts arose. One has in mind a picture of a bustling
little fellow going into the house and into the upper room
where Jesus and his followers were having the last supper
together, going in there to wrangle about the price to be
paid for the wine.

The man who got on the platform with McGregor was a
socialist. He wanted to argue.

But McGregor did not argue with him. He sprang forward,

5. Anderson refers to John Alexander Dowie (1847–1907), Scots
"spiritual leader" active in the United States; and to Mary Baker Eddy
(1821–1910), founder of the Church of Christ, Scientist, in 1879 and
author of *Science and Health with Key to the Scriptures* (1875).
6. "Dr. Cowell" is apparently a fictitious name.

it was a quick tiger-like movement, and spun the socialist about making him stand small and blinking and comical before the crowd.

Then McGregor began to talk. He made of the little stuttering, arguing socialist a figure representing all labor, made him the personification of the old weary struggle of the world. And the socialist who went to argue stood with tears in his eyes, proud of his position in men's eyes.

All over the city McGregor talked of Old Labor and how he was to be built up and put before men's eyes by the movement of the Marching Men. How our legs tingled to fall in step and go marching away with him.

Out of the crowds there came the note of that wailing march. Someone always started that.

That night on the North Side Doctor Cowell got hold of the shoulder of a newspaper man and led him to a car. He who knew Bismarck [7] and who had [*sat] in council with kings went walking and babbling half the night through the empty streets.

It is amusing now to think of the things men said under the influence of McGregor. Like old Doctor Johnson and his friend Savage they walked half drunk through the streets swearing that whatever happened they would stick to the movement.[8] Doctor Cowell himself said things just as absurd as that.

And all over the country men were getting the idea—The Marching Men—Old Labor in one mass marching before the eyes of men—Old Labor that was going to make the world see—see and feel its bigness at last. Men were to come to the end of strife—men united—marching! Marching! Marching!

7. Otto Eduard Leopold von Bismarck (1815–98), Chancellor of the German Empire from 1871 to 1890.

8. Dr. Samuel Johnson (1709–84) published his story of the impoverished poet Richard Savage (1697?–1743), *Life of Savage,* in 1744.

CHAPTER V

In all of the time of The Marching Men there was [*but] one bit of written matter from the leader McGregor. It had a circulation running into the millions and was printed in every tongue spoken in America. A copy of the little circular lies before me now.

THE MARCHERS

"They ask us what we mean.

Well, here is our answer.

We mean to go on marching.

We mean to march in the morning and in the evening when the sun goes down.

On Sundays they may sit on their porches or shout at men playing ball in a field

But we will march.

On the hard cobble stones of the city streets and through the dust of country roads we will march.

Our legs may be weary and our throats hot and dry,

But still we will march, shoulder to shoulder.

We will march until the ground shakes and tall buildings tremble.

Shoulder to shoulder we will go—all of us—

On and on forever.

We will not talk nor listen to talk.

We will march and we will teach our sons and our daughters to march.

Their minds are troubled. Our minds are clear.

We do not think and banter words.

We march.

Our faces are coarse and there is dust in our hair and beards.

See, the inner parts of our hands are rough.

And still we march—we the workers."

CHAPTER VI

WHO will ever forget that Labor Day in Chicago? How they marched!—thousands and thousands and more thousands! They filled the streets. The cars stopped. Men trembled with the import of the impending hour.

Here they come! How the ground trembles! The chant, chant, chant of that song! It must have been thus that Grant felt at the great review of the veterans in Washington when all day long they marched past him, the men of the Civil War, the whites of their eyes showing in the tan of their faces.[9]

McGregor stood on the stone coping above the tracks in Grant Park. As the men marched they massed in there about him, thousands of them, steel workers and iron workers and great red-necked butchers and teamsters.

And in the air wailed the marching song of the workers.

All of the world that was not marching jammed into the buildings facing Michigan Boulevard and waited. Margaret Ormsby was there. She sat with her father in a carriage near where Van Buren Street ends at the boulevard. As the men kept crowding in about [*them] she clutched nervously at the sleeve of David Ormsby's coat. "He is going to speak," she whispered and pointed. Her tense air of expectancy expressed much of the feeling of the crowd. "See, listen, he is going to speak out."

It must have been five in the afternoon when the men got through marching. They [*were] massed [*in there] clear [*down] to the Twelfth-street Station of the Illinois Central.

9.   Anderson may refer to the huge reception given General Grant, on his return from a world tour, in San Francisco in late September, 1879; but more likely Anderson refers to a larger reception given Grant November 12, 1879, in Chicago, where perhaps twelve thousand militia and citizens marched. See L. T. Remlap (*pseud.* L. T. Palmer), *The Life of General U. S. Grant* (St. Louis: Hebert and Cole, 1885), pp. 624–67.

McGregor lifted his hands. In the hush his harsh voice carried far. "We are at the beginning," he shouted and silence fell upon the people. In the stillness one standing near her might have heard Margaret Ormsby weeping softly. There was the gentle murmur that always prevails where many people stand at attention. The weeping of the woman was scarcely audible but it persisted like the sound of little waves on a beach at the end of the day.

BOOK VII

CHAPTER I

THE idea prevalent among men that the woman to be beautiful must be hedged about and protected from the facts of life has done something more than produce a race of women not physically vigorous. It has made them deficient in strength of soul also. After the evening when she stood facing Edith and when she had been unable to arise to the challenge flung at her by the little milliner, Margaret Ormsby was forced to stand facing her own soul and there was no strength in her for the test. Her mind insisted on justifying her failure. A woman of the people placed in such a position would have been able to face it calmly. She would have gone soberly and steadily about her work and after a few months of pulling weeds in a field, trimming hats in a shop or instructing children in a schoolroom would have been ready to thrust out again making another trial at life. Having met many defeats she would have been armed and ready for defeat. Like a little animal in a forest inhabited by other and larger animals she would have known the effectiveness of lying perfectly still for a long period making her patience a part of her equipment for living.

Margaret had decided that she hated McGregor. After the scene in her house she gave up her work in the settlement [*house] and for a long time went about nursing her hatred. In the street as she walked about her mind kept bringing accusations against him and in her room at night she sat by the window looking at the stars and said strong words. "He is a brute," she declared hotly, "a mere animal untouched by the culture that makes for gentleness. There is something animal-like and horrible in my nature that has made me care for him. I shall pluck it out. In the future I shall make it my business to forget the man and all of the dreadful lower strata of life that he represents."

Filled with this idea Margaret went about among her own

people and tried to become interested in the [*men and women] she met at dinners and receptions. It did not work and when after a few evenings spent in the company of men absorbed in the getting of money she found them only dull creatures whose mouths were filled with meaningless words her irritation grew and she blamed McGregor for that also. "He had no right to come into my consciousness and then take himself off," she declared bitterly. "The man is more of a brute than I thought. He no doubt preys upon everyone as he has preyed upon me. He is without tenderness, knows nothing of the meaning of tenderness. The colorless creature he has married will serve his body. That is what he wants. He does not want beauty. He is a coward who dares not stand up to beauty and is afraid of me."

When the Marching Men Movement began to make a stir in Chicago Margaret went on a visit to New York. For a month she lived, with two women friends, at a big hotel near the sea and then hurried home. "I will see the man and hear him talk," she told herself. "I cannot cure myself of the consciousness of him by running away. Perhaps I am myself a coward. I shall go into his presence. When I hear his brutal words and see again the hard gleam that sometimes comes into his eyes I shall be cured."

Margaret went to hear McGregor talk to a gathering of workingmen in a West Side hall and came away more alive to him than ever. In the hall she sat concealed in deep shadows by the door and waited with trembling eagerness.

On all sides of her were men crowded together. Their faces were washed but the grime of the shops was not quite effaced. Men from the steel mills with the cooked look that follows long exposure to intense artificial heat, men of the building trade[*s] with their broad hands, big men and small men, misshapen and straight, laboring men, all sat at attention waiting.

Margaret noticed that as McGregor talked the lips of the working men moved. Fists were clenched. Applause came quick and sharp like the report of guns.

In the shadows at the further side of the hall the black coats of the workers made a blot, out of which intense faces looked and across which the flickering gas jets in the center of the hall threw dancing lights.

The words of the speaker were shot forth. The sentences seemed broken and disconnected. As he talked giant pictures flashed through the minds of the hearers. Men felt themselves big and exalted. A little steel worker sitting near Margaret who, earlier in the evening, had been abused by his wife because he wanted to come to the meeting instead of helping with the dishes at home, stared fiercely about. He thought [that] he would like to fight hand in hand with a wild animal in a forest.

Standing on the narrow stage McGregor seemed a giant seeking expression. His mouth worked. The sweat stood upon his forehead and he moved restlessly up and down. At times, with his hands advanced and with the eager forward crouch of his body, he was like a wrestler waiting to grapple with an opponent.

Margaret was deeply moved. Her years of training and of refinement were [*stripped] off and she felt that, like the women of the French Revolution, she should like to go out into the streets and march screaming and fighting in feminine rage for the things of this man's mind.

[On the stage] McGregor had scarcely begun to talk. His personality, the big, eager something in him, had caught and held this audience as it had caught and held other audiences in other halls night after night for months.

McGregor was something the men to whom he talked understood. He was themselves become expressive and he moved them as no other leader had ever moved them before. His very lack of glibness, the things in him wanting expression and not getting expressed, made him seem like one of them. He did not confuse their minds but drew for them great scrawling pictures and to them he cried, "March!" and for marching he promised them realization of themselves.

"I have heard men in colleges and speakers in halls talking of the brotherhood of man," he cried. "They do not want such a brotherhood. They would flee before it. But we will make, by our marching, such a brotherhood [for them] that they will tremble and say to one another, 'See, Old Labor is awake. He has found his strength.' They will hide themselves and eat their words of brotherhood.

"A clamor of voices will arise, many voices, crying out, 'Disperse! Cease marching! I am afraid!'

"This talk of brotherhood. The words mean nothing. Man can not love man. We do not know what they mean by such love. They hurt us and underpay us. Sometimes one of us gets an arm torn off. Are we to lie in our beds loving the man who gets rich from the iron machine that ripped the arm from the shoulder?

"On our knees and in our arms we have borne their children. On the streets we see them—the petted children of our madness. See, we have let them run about, misbehaving. We have given them automobiles and wives with soft, clinging dresses. When they have cried we have cared for them.

"And they, being children with the minds of children, are confused. The noise of affairs alarms them. They run about shaking their fingers and commanding. They speak with pity of us—Labor—their father.

"And now we will show them their father in his might. The little machines they have in their factories are toys we have given them and that for the time we leave in their hands. We do not think of the toys nor the soft bodied women. We make of ourselves a mighty army, a marching army going along shoulder to shoulder. We can love that.

"When they see us, hundreds of thousands of us, marching into their minds and into their consciousness then will they be afraid. And at the little meetings they have when three or four of them sit talking, daring to decide what things we shall have from life, there will be in their minds a picture. We will stamp it there.

"They have forgotten our power. Let us reawaken it. See, I shake Old Labor by the shoulder. He arouses. He sits up. He thrusts his huge form up from where he was asleep in the dust and the smoke of the mills. They look at him and are afraid. See, they tremble and run away, falling over each other. They did not know Old Labor was so big.

"But you workers are not afraid. You are the arms and the

legs and the hands and the eyes of Labor. You have thought
yourself small. You have not got yourself into one mass so
that I could shake and arouse you.

"You must get that way. You must march shoulder to shoulder. You must march so that you yourselves shall come to
know what a giant you are. If one of your number whines or
complains or stands upon a box throwing words about, knock
him down and keep marching.

"When you have marched until you are one giant body then
will happen a miracle. A brain will grow in the giant you have
made.

"Will you march with me?"

Like a volley from a battery of guns came the sharp reply
from the eager, upturned faces of the audience, "we will! Let
us march!" they shouted.

Margaret Ormsby went out at the door and into the crowds
on Madison Street. As she walked in the press she lifted her
head in pride that a man possessed of such a brain and of
the simple courage to try to express such magnificent ideas
through human beings had ever shown favor toward her.
Humbleness swept over her and she blamed herself for the
petty thoughts concerning him that had been in her mind.
"It does not matter," she whispered to herself. "Now I know
that nothing matters, nothing but his success. He must do
this thing he has set out to do. He must not be denied. I
would give the blood out of my body or expose my body to
shame if that would bring him success."

Margaret became exalted in her humbleness. When her
carriage had taken her to her house she ran quickly upstairs
to her own room and knelt by her bed. She started to pray
but presently stopped and sprang to her feet. Running to the
window she looked off across the city. "He must succeed,"
she cried again. "I shall myself be one of his marchers. I will
do anything for him. He is tearing the veil from my eyes,
from all men's eyes. We are children in the hands of this giant
and he must not meet defeat at the hands of children."

CHAPTER II

On the day of the great demonstration, when McGregor's power over the minds and the bodies of the men of labor sent hundreds of thousands marching and singing in the streets, there was one man who was untouched by the song of labor expressed in the threshing of feet. David Ormsby had, in his quiet way, thought things out. He expected that the new impetus given to solidarity in the ranks of labor would make trouble for him and his kind, that it would express itself finally in strikes and in wide-spread industrial disturbance. He was not worried. In the end he thought that the silent, patient power of money would bring his people the victory. On that day he did not go to his office but in the morning stayed in his own room thinking of McGregor and of his daughter. Laura Ormsby was out of the city but Margaret was at home. David believed he had measured accurately the power of McGregor over her mind but occasional doubts came to him. "Well, the time has come to have it out with her," he decided. "I must reassert my ascendency over her mind. The thing that is going on here is really a struggle of minds. McGregor differs from other leaders of labor as I differ from most leaders of the forces of money. He has brains. Very well I shall meet him on that level. Then, when I have made Margaret think as I think, she will return to me."

When he was still a small manufacturer in the Wisconsin town David had been in the habit of driving out in the evening with his daughter. During the drives he had been almost a lover in his attentions to the child and now when he thought of the forces at work within her he was convinced that she was still a child. Early in the afternoon he had a carriage brought to the door and drove off with her to the city. "She will want to see the man in the height of his power. If I am right in thinking that she is still under the influence of his personality there will be a romantic desire for that.

"I will give her the chance," he thought proudly. "In this struggle I ask no quarter from him and shall not make the common mistake of parents in such cases. She is fascinated by the figure he has made of himself. Showy men, who stand out from the crowd, have that power. She is still under his influence. Why else her constant distraction and her want of interest in other things? Now I will be with her when the man is most powerful, when he shows to the greatest advantage, and then I will make my fight for her. I will point out to her another road, the road along which the real victors in life must learn to travel."

Together David the quiet efficient representative of wealth and his woman child sat in the carriage on the day of McGregor's triumph. For the moment an impassable gulf seemed to separate them and with intense eyes each watched the hordes of men who massed themselves about the labor leader. At the moment McGregor seemed to have caught all men in the sweep of his movement. Business men had closed their desks, labor was exultant, writers and men given to speculation in thought walked about dreaming of the realization of the brotherhood of man. In the long narrow, treeless park the music made by the steady, never-ending thresh of feet arose to something vast and rhythmical. It was like a mighty chorus come up out of the hearts of men. David was unmoved. Occasionally he spoke to the horses and looked from the faces of the men massed about him to his daughter's face. In the coarse faces of the men he thought he saw only a crude sort of intoxication, the result of a new kind of emotionalism. "It will not outlast thirty days of ordinary living in their squalid surroundings," he thought grimly. "It is not the kind of exaltation for Margaret. I can sing her a more wonderful song. I must get myself ready for that."

When McGregor arose to speak Margaret was overcome with emotions. Dropping to her knees in the carriage she put her head down upon her father's arm. For days she had been telling herself that in the future of the man she loved there was no place for failure. Now again she whispered to herself that this great sturdy figure must not be denied the fulfillment of its purpose. When in the hush that followed the massing of the laborers about him the harsh booming voice floated over the heads of the people her body shook as with a chill. Extravagant fancies invaded her mind and she wished it were possible for her to do something heroic, something that would make her live again in the mind of McGregor. She wanted to serve him, to give him something out of herself, and thought wildly that there might yet come a time and a way by which the beauty of her body could be laid like a gift before him. The half mythical figure of Mary, the lover of Jesus, came into her mind and she aspired to be such another. With her body shaken with emotions she pulled at the sleeve of her father's coat. "Listen! It is going to come now," she murmured. "The brain of labor is going to express the dream of labor. An impulse sweet and lasting is going to come into the world."

David Ormsby said nothing. When McGregor had begun to speak he touched the horses with the whip and drove slowly along Van Buren Street, past the silent, attentive ranks of men. When he had got into one of the streets near the river a vast cheer arose. It seemed to shake the city and the horses reared and leaped forward over the rough cobblestones. With one hand David quieted them while with the other he gripped the hand of his daughter. They drove over a bridge and into the West Side and as they went the marching song of the workers, [*rising] up out of thousands of throats, rang in their ears. For a time the air seemed to pulsate with it but as they went westward it grew continually less and less distinct. At last, when they had turned into a street lined by tall factories, it died out altogether. "That is the end of him for me and mine," thought David and again set himself for the task he had to perform.

Through street after street David let the horses wander while he clung to his daughter's hand and thought of what he wanted to say. Not all of the streets were lined with factories. Some, and these, in the evening light, were the most hideous, were bordered by the homes of workers. The houses of the workers, jammed closely together and black with grime, were filled with noisy life. Women sat in the doorways and children ran screaming and shouting in the road. Dogs barked and howled. Everywhere was dirt and disorder, the terrible evidence of men's failure in the difficult and delicate art of living. In one of the streets a little girl child, who sat on the post of a fence, made a ludicrous figure. As David and Margaret drove past she beat with her heels against the sides of the post and screamed. Tears ran down her cheeks and her disheveled hair was black with dirt. "I want a banana. I want a banana," she howled, staring at the blank walls of one of the houses. In spite of herself Margaret was touched and her mind left the figure of McGregor. By an odd chance the child on the post was the daughter of that socialist orator who one night on the North Side had climbed upon a platform to confront McGregor with the propaganda of the Socialist Party.

David turned the horses into a wide boulevard that ran south through the factory district of the west. As they came out into the boulevard they saw, sitting on the sidewalk before a saloon, a drunkard with a drum in his hand. The drunkard beat upon the drum and tried to sing the marching song of the workers but succeeded only in making a queer grunting noise like a distressed animal. The sight brought a smile to David's lips. "Already it has begun to disintegrate," he muttered. "I brought you into this part of town on purpose," he said to Margaret. "I wanted you to see with your own eyes how much the world needs the thing he is trying to do. The man is [*terribly] right about the need for discipline and order. He is a big man, doing a big thing, and I admire his courage. He would be a really big man had he the greater courage."

On the boulevard into which they had turned all was quiet. The summer sun was setting and over the roofs of buildings the West was ablaze with light. They passed a factory surrounded by little patches of garden. Some employer of labor had tried thus [*feebly] to bring beauty into the neighborhood of the place where his men worked. David pointed with the whip. "Life is a husk," he said, "and we men of affairs

who take ourselves so seriously because the fates have been
good to us have odd silly little fancies. See what this fellow
has been at, patching away, striving to create beauty on the
shell of things. He is like McGregor, you see. I wonder if the
man has made himself beautiful, if either he or McGregor
has seen to it that there is something lovely inside the husk he
wears around and that he calls his body, if he has seen through
life to the spirit of life. I do not believe in patching nor do I
believe in disturbing the shell of things as McGregor has dared
to do. I have my own beliefs and they are the beliefs of my
kind. This man here, this maker of little gardens, [*is] like
McGregor[*. He] might better let men find their own beauty.
That is my way. I have, I want to think, kept myself for the
sweeter and more daring effort."

David turned and looked hard at Margaret, who had begun
to be influenced by his mood. She waited looking with averted
face at the sky over the roofs of buildings. David began to talk
of himself in relation to her and her mother. A note of impatience came into his voice.

"How far you have been carried away, haven't you?" he said
sharply. "Listen. I am not talking to you now as your father
nor as Laura's daughter. Let us be clear about that. I love you
and am in a contest to win your love. I am McGregor's rival.
I accept the handicap of fatherhood. I love you. You see I
have let something within myself alight upon you. McGregor
has not done that. He refused what you had to offer but I do
not. I have centered my life upon you and have done it quite
knowingly and after much thought. The feeling I have is
something quite special. I am an individualist but believe in
the oneness of man and woman. I would dare venture into
but one other life beyond my own and that the life of a woman.
I have chosen to ask you to let me venture so into your life.
We will talk of it."

Margaret turned and looked at her father. Later she thought
that some strange phenomena must have happened at the
moment. Something like a film was torn from her eyes and she
saw the man David not as a shrewd and calculating man of
affairs but as something magnificently young. Not only was he

strong and solid but in his face there was at the moment the deep lines of thought and suffering she had seen on the countenance of McGregor. "It is strange," she thought. "They are so unlike and yet the two men are both beautiful."

"I married your mother when I was a child as you are a child now," David went on. "To be sure I had a passion for her and she had one for me. It passed but it was beautiful enough while it lasted. It did not have depth or meaning. I want to tell you why. Then I am going to make you understand McGregor, so that you may take your measure of the man. I am coming to that. I have to begin at the beginning.

"My factory began to grow and as an employer of labor I became concerned in the lives of a good many men."

His voice again became sharp. "I have been impatient with you," he said. "Do you think this McGregor is the only man who has seen and thought of other men in the mass? I have done that and have been tempted [as he has been tempted]. I also might have become sentimental and destroyed myself. I didn't. Loving a woman saved me. Laura did that for me although when it came to the real test of our love, understanding, she failed. I am nevertheless grateful to her that she was once the object of my love. I believe in the beauty of that."

Again David paused and began to tell his story in a new way. The figure of McGregor came back into Margaret's mind and her father began to feel that to take it entirely away would be an accomplishment full of significance. "If I can take her from him I and my kind can take the world from him also," he thought. "It will be another victory for the aristocracy in the never-ending battle with the mob."

"I came to a turning point," he said aloud. "All men come to that point. To be sure the great mass of people drift quite stupidly but we are not now talking of people in general. There is you and me, and there is the thing McGregor might be. We are each in our way something special. We come, people like us, to a place where there are two roads to take. I took one and McGregor has taken another. I know why and perhaps he knows why. I concede to him knowledge of what he has done. But now it is time for you to decide which road you will take.

You have seen the crowds moving along the broad way [that] he has chosen and now you will set out on your own way. I want you to look down my road with me."

They came to a bridge over a canal and David stopped the horses. A body of McGregor's Marchers passed and Margaret's pulse began to beat high again. When she looked at her father however he was unmoved and she was a little ashamed of her emotions. For a moment David waited, as though for inspiration, and when the horses started on again he began [again] to talk. "A labor leader came to my factory, a miniature McGregor with a crooked twist to him. He was a rascal but the things he said to my men were all true enough. I was making money for my investors, a lot of it. They might have won in a fight with me. One evening I went out into the country to walk alone under the trees and think it over."

David's voice became harsh and Margaret thought it had become strangely like the voice of McGregor talking to working-men. "I bought the man [*off]," David said. "I used the cruel weapon men like me have to use. I gave him [the] money and told him to get out, to let me alone. I did it because I had to win. My kind of men always have to win. During the walk I took alone I got hold of my dream, my belief. I have the same dream now. It means more to me than the welfare of a million men. For it I would crush whatever opposed me. I am going to tell you of the dream.

"It is too bad one has to talk. Talk kills dreams and talk will also kill all such men as McGregor. Now that he has begun to talk we will get the best of him. I do not worry about McGregor. Time and talk will bring about his destruction."

David's mind ran off in a new direction. "I do not think a man's life is of much importance," he said. "No man is big enough to grasp all of life. That is the foolish fancy of children. The grown man knows he cannot see life at one great sweep. It cannot be comprehended so. One has to realize that he lives in a patchwork of many lives and many impulses.

"The man must strike at beauty. That is the realization maturity brings and that is where the woman comes in. That is what McGregor was not wise enough to understand. He is a child you see in a land of excitable children."

The quality of David's voice changed. Putting his arm about his daughter he drew her face down beside his own. Night descended upon them. The woman who was tired from much thinking began to feel grateful for the touch of the strong hand on her shoulder. David had accomplished his purpose. He had for the moment made his daughter forget that she was his daughter. There was something hypnotic in the quiet strength of his mood.

"I come now to women, to your part," he said. "We will talk of the thing I want to make you understand. Laura failed as the woman. She never saw the point. As I grew she did not grow with me. Because I did not talk of love she did not understand me as a lover, did not know what I wanted, what I demanded of her.

"I wanted to fit my love down upon her figure as one puts a glove on his hand. You see I was the adventurer, the man mussed and moiled by life and its problems. The struggle to exist, to get money, could not be avoided. I had to make that struggle. She did not. Why could she not understand that I did not want to come into her presence to rest or to say empty words? I wanted her to help me create beauty. We should have been partners in that. Together we should have undertaken the most delicate and difficult of all struggles, the struggle for living beauty in our everyday affairs."

Bitterness swept over the old plowmaker and he used strong words. "The whole point is in what I am now saying. That was my cry to the woman. It came out of my soul. It was the only cry to another I have ever made. Laura was a little fool. Her mind flitted away to little things. I do not know what she wanted me to be and now I do not care. Perhaps she wanted me to be a poet, a stringer together of words, one to write shrill little songs about her eyes and lips. It does not matter now what she wanted.

"But you matter."

David's voice cut through the fog of new thoughts that were

confusing his daughter's mind and she could feel his body stiffen. A thrill ran through her own body and she forgot McGregor. With all the strength of her spirit she was absorbed in what David was saying. In the challenge that was coming from the lips of her father she began to feel there would be born in her own life a definite purpose.

"Women want to push out into life, to share with men the disorder and mussiness of little things. What a desire. Let them try it if they wish. They will sicken of the attempt. They lose sight of something bigger they might undertake. They have forgotten the old things, Ruth in the corn and Mary with the jar of precious ointment, they have forgotten the beauty they were meant to help men create.

"Let them share only in man's attempt to create beauty. That is the big, the delicate task to which they should consecrate themselves. Why attempt instead the cheaper, the secondary task? They are like this McGregor."

The plowmaker became silent. Taking up the whip he drove the horses rapidly along. He thought that his point was made and was satisfied to let the imagination of his daughter do the rest. They turned off the boulevard and passed through a street of small stores. Before a saloon a troop of street urchins, led by a drunken man without a hat, gave a grotesque imitation of McGregor's Marchers before a crowd of laughing idlers. With a sinking heart Margaret realized that even at the height of his power the forces that would eventually destroy the impulses back of McGregor's Marchers were at work. She crept closer to David. "I love you," she said. "Someday I may have a lover but always I shall love you. I shall try to be what you want of me."

It was past two o'clock that night when David arose from the chair where he had been for several hours quietly reading. With a smile on his face he went to a window facing north toward the city. All through the evening groups of men had been passing the house. Some had gone scuffling along, a mere disorderly mob, some had gone shoulder to shoulder chanting the marching song of the workers and a few, under the in-

fluence of drink, had stopped before the house to roar out
threats. Now all was quiet. David lighted a cigar and stood for
a long time looking out over the city. He was thinking of
McGregor and wondering what excited dream of power the
day had brought into the man's head. Then he thought of his
daughter and of her escape. A soft [°light] came into his eyes.
He was happy but when he had partially undressed a new
mood came and he turned out the lights in the room and
went again to the window. In the room above Margaret had
been unable to sleep and had also crept to the window. She
was thinking again of McGregor and was ashamed of her
thoughts. By chance both father and daughter began at the
same moment to doubt the truth of what David had said
during the drive along the boulevard. Margaret could not express her doubts in words but tears came into her eyes.

As for David he put his hand on the sill of the window and
for just a moment his body trembled as with age and weariness.
"I wonder," he muttered. "If I had youth. Perhaps McGregor
knew he would fail and yet had the courage of failure. I
wonder if both Margaret and myself lack the greater courage,
if that evening long ago when I walked under the trees I made
a mistake? What if after all this McGregor and his woman
knew both roads? What if they, after looking deliberately
along the road toward [beauty and] success [°in life], went,
without regret, along the road to failure? [°What if McGregor
and not myself knew the road to beauty?"]

APPENDIXES
AND
BIBLIOGRAPHY

SELECTED ESSAYS
1902–1914

[In the summer of 1900, Sherwood Anderson became an advertising solicitor in the Chicago office of the Crowell Publishing Company. The following year he joined Crowell as an advertising copywriter. Later in 1901 he began writing copy for the Frank B. White Company, which in 1903 became the Long-Critchfield Company. Anderson published his first writing as monthly columns on business in *Agricultural Advertising*, the company's trade journal. After leaving his Ohio business in 1913, Anderson returned to Chicago and published again in *Agricultural Advertising*. By 1914, he had published over thirty articles, of which the following twelve are selected to show his developing literary acumen, leading up to the appearance in 1914 of Anderson's first professionally published short story, "The Rabbit-pen." The essays reprinted here from *Agricultural Advertising* omit illustrative drawings and groups of "gnomic" sayings often appended to Sherwood Anderson's columns. The drawings are not by Anderson; the "sayings" may not be his. *The Reader* was a literary magazine published by the Bobbs-Merrill Company in Indianapolis.]

THE FARMER WEARS CLOTHES
Agricultural Advertising, IX (February, 1902), 6.

Some of the big, general advertisers seem to be grasping the fact that the agricultural press is tucked up close to the hardest reading, best living class of people in the world, the American farmer. Still, there are, as one of our friends remarked a year ago at Milwaukee, "acres of diamonds that have never been worked." [1]

1. Anderson refers to *Acres of Diamonds* (1888) by Russell H. Conwell (1843–1925), the founder of Temple University, who justified capitalism through Christian doctrine.

Here on the desk is one of our best 25-cent magazines. A glance through its advertising pages shows several full-page advertisements of ready-made clothing. Now, is it not fair to say that at least one-third of the readers of a magazine of this character are women? I would venture the assertion that one-half of the men who are on their list have all of their clothing made by a tailor, and that there is only a small proportion of the possible buyers remaining that do not live in the country, and could not be reached through the agricultural press.

On the other hand, the farm paper goes to the man who always buys his clothes in the clothing store. Its pages are filled with matter of vital importance to him and his success. It is read by every member of the family, and the hired man. If there are any young fellows about the place, and there always is at least one, he has a girl. On Sunday afternoon he hitches up the best horse in the barn, carefully groomed for the occasion, and drives off down the road in a spotlessly clean buggy. That fellow has dollars in his pocket—very likely a bank account—and down in his heart there is a longing to be just as well dressed when he goes forth to town, or on his weekly mating tours, as any other man.

If a manufacturer can convince this fellow, or his father either, for that matter, that his particular line of clothing is the proper and right thing to wear, it is going to open up a veritable gold mine for that manufacturer. There is one way, and only one way, to do it. That is, by talking to him in the right way, in the best paying advertising mediums on earth—the high-class farm papers.

ROT AND REASON

Agricultural Advertising, X (April, 1903), 12, 14.

Doing Stunts

Back in the small towns of Ohio and Kentucky twenty years ago they had a class of horses called "quarter horses." They used to get them out on Saturday afternoons and literally tear up the ground between Perkins' corner and the grocery store. Everybody turned out and whooped things up, and sometimes the tavern-keeper would bet as much as three dollars against Bill Enright's sorrel—(first having a quiet talk with Bill).

It is said that these horses could beat anything living for the distance, but no one owned a stop watch then, and the horses never lasted long or did a decent whole mile, so this is doubtful.

My, but it was exciting though! Slamming down through between the farm buildings and the row of farm wagons; and a race won made the winner the village hero and got him talked about for at least a month at every livery stable.

I often wonder how many of us are "quarter horses" and are doing stunts among the store boxes. And whether, if turned square about, we could do one good long heart-breaking mile. 'Tis satisfying, I will admit. Have done a few myself and then bought fellows' lunches so I could tell about it. But it won't put our man high up among advertising men like facing the game and working hard day and night through the years. It's cheap, too. For never was there a quarter horse, a doer of stunts, who couldn't be bought by an inn-keeper for one dollar and fifty cents.

Packingham

In the village of Omaha, on the trail of the tourist, there lived and worked one Packingham, a short, broad-shouldered man with a merry eye and a foolish fondness for his work and his firm.

Now, it's all right to be loyal, but Packingham was more than loyal. He was a fool. He did all the work that anyone wanted him to do and then went back and did some more just for fun. The stenographers grew wroth with him and the night-watch, who wanted to lock up and go down and tell the engineer how the Gray Eagle ran in the third, positively hated him. He used to refuse to dance after midnight because he wanted to have a steady eye in his head when he talked to Prowler, of the Union Pacific, in the morning. He was good to Mrs. Packingham, but, as people often said, she was almost as big a fool as he.

Packingham had a beautiful theory about his work and his attitude toward his firm and it went something like this:

"Because my work is more to me than anything else in the world, I will make it my religion. When I am tempted to be full of sin and unclean, I will remember that such a course would make my work full of sin and unclean. When I am tempted to lie and cheat, I shall expect the book-keeper to lie and cheat. When I'm lonely and sad on moonlight nights, I'll just come down here and this old job and I will have a good long social evening together, then perhaps, when I die I will go to some place where a fellow will not have to waste so much time sleeping."

In the fullness of time Packingham became known in the land, and men said that although the poor chump knew nothing but work, he certainly did know that. He developed a scheme for turning a lot of pig iron into a machine used in the families of the humble, and this machine, which worked just like Packingham, enabled his firm to capture the market and sell something for two dollars that had formerly cost six or eight. He did about everything but talk about himself and then the thing happened that gained him his title of "fool."

A trust lawyer took the morning train over into New Jersey one morning and came back some time later with the charter for The American Amalgamated Labor Saving Wringer Co. in his pocket and a beautiful and devilish plan for disposing of the stock, in his head.

Because the name of Packingham was big in the wringer line he took another train for Omaha that night. At Omaha he was joined by one Wescott, a very dear friend and earnest adviser of Packingham, and together they descended on the silent man of work.

Now, all the talk and all the advice of New Jersey and Wescott would take much space, so we will simply say that they offered Packingham thirty-five thousand a year and a two hundred thousand dollar bonus if he would desert his firm and come into the Amalgamated. Not only offered it, but arranged to put the entire amount into the hands of whomever Packingham might name. And Packingham's salary was just five thousand a year. And Packingham laughed and went home and told Mrs. Packingham and she laughed. Wasn't he a fool?
. . . .

There was an old fellow at home that hoed corn. He was grim, grey and silent, but because he pleased my boyish heart I was glad to hoe beside him for the dignity of his presence. One hot day when we had hoed to the end of a particularly long and weedy row and were resting in the shade by the fence he put his big hand on my shoulder and said, "Don't the corn make you ashamed, Sherwood, it's so straight?"

Of No Value

A system in the hands of an unsystematic man.

A friend who demands no manhood in you.

A wife who inspires you to no better work.

Money you have not fairly earned.

Fame got by trickery or a pose.

Advertising that you are going to do when you have got more money than you know what to do with.

Mr. Special Representative, Mr. Agency Man, Mr. Advertising Manager, you look like a fool when you strut, and you really haven't begun to do your work well yet.

Chicago Inspirations

The morning sun shining on the Field Columbian museum.

The lake front at night with the lights of the trains and the lake ahead, and the roar of the city behind.

The front platform of an elevated train going around the Union Loop.

The view on Upper State Street at night.

The new offices of Agricultural Advertising, in the Powers Building.

ROT AND REASON

Agricultural Advertising, X (May, 1903), 20, 22.

Unfinished

The life of every busy man who really gets into the game is one everlasting, unceasing effort to catch up the broken strings of things, tie the ends and feel at last that there is something finished, something done. In this as in everything else worth while, no man really succeeds. A few clever, clocklike men appear to succeed, but they don't. And the great mass of us never even make a showing of success. Enthusiasm follows enthusiasm in hot succession; dream follows dream; and the life's ambition of to-day is left broken and torn on the Jericho road while we with eager eyes are tearing and scraping at the obstacles on some ever endless path.

Morning finds the advertising man full of the spirit of "get things done," but alas, what a sorry mess it is when the rattling machines cease their rattling and the office boy has gone for the night, Smith's letter unanswered, Colver's copy unfinished, issues missed. An endless, heart-breaking mess it is, lapping always into the next day, the next month and the next year.

In the first waking sickness of it, how many the good men who have felt like dropping the whole thing and going out to find a healthy, reasonable job as end man on a sewer contract. A most hopeful, cheerful beggar he is, the advertising man, seeing his hardest licks go smash, his cleverest lines muddled and his finest talk interrupted. And how decent he is about it in the end. Day after day, week after week, year after year, he faces his own failures and yet believes down in the heart of him that he is in the greatest business on earth and that next year will set all straight and turn all his penny marbles into diamonds.

It seems to advertising men that their work is particularly unfinishable and it is true that ever and ever the new is taking the place of the old, but who among them would change it? Gray old veterans will shake their old heads and with withered finger under your nose talk of the days to come when advertising shall come into its own just as though they too had all the work ahead.

It makes a man glad he is alive and young now and it makes him doubly glad that he is in even such an unfinishable business as advertising.

Finding Our Work

We all hear more or less talk about the good fortune of the man who has found his work. It is a thing much discussed by school teachers and mothers with sons out of a job, but not much heard of in the man talk of the office and the shop.

Of course not every man can sell goods. Not every man can run a lathe. And very few men can successfully run a business. But I think it true in the great majority of cases, it isn't so much a question of finding your work as it is of finding yourself, your faith, your courage.

Your really successful man is he who runs the lathe well, who in some way manages to make sales, who does well with a set of books, and who in good time makes himself felt as the director of all these. He does these things well because he believes the work at hand is his work and believing gives it his love and throws about it all of that glamour that comes to any place where a strong man works.

The average man looking for work to love is much like a certain acquaintance of mine (only that this was an honest chap) who used to stretch himself and lazily say that he would like to be in a place where a man could roll down to work about 11:30, look over his correspondence and then about 1:30 roll back home.

We are all chasing shadows no doubt, shadows of love, shadows of art, shadows of death, but there is no need chasing the shadow of my work.

God intended us to be a cracking good office boy, a wide-awake, careful clerk, an earnest, conscientious salesman, and finally, perhaps, an understanding, fearless boss. But he didn't intend us to go pining through the day and moaning through the night because we could find no work to love.

Let's save our pining and our moaning for our love affairs and be brave and cheerful about the work. It takes so much time out of our lives, and then perhaps if we are brave and clean and true, our work will appear there in the midst of the work at hand.

A BUSINESS MAN'S READING
The Reader, II (October, 1903), 503–4.

I meet often enough such as you—bright, quick-minded fellows who, in a clash of wordy wits or a plunge into philosophy on a country road, are opponents worthy enough for any man. You go to the bottom of every truth; you catch every fleeting thought; you run swiftly ahead while we talk and build a breastwork of truth and logic, from behind which you rake us fore and aft when we come abreast. And then when we seek the storehouse from which you have so well filled your mental magazine, you promptly tell us that you are not readers; that you find Stevenson dull and Browning a bore; that you are business men and acquire your knowledge in the great human grind of the work, or in society if you happen to be of the petticoat faction.

Now, I have no quarrel with the statement that there is all the knowledge of a Solomon used in a wheat deal, nor that many writers are unspeakably dull. Neither do I expect Johnson or Williams to like what gives me joy. But I do quarrel with the way you approach reading and the end you think men seek.

To what purpose do you come to my room with your pipe when the lights are lit? You don't love me, surely, and I have no wife. Then, I conclude, because you storm up and down and look into my eyes and dig neck-breaking holes for me in the wilderness of argument, that you are here to whet your wit, to swing mental dumb-bells, and when the last pipe is lit and we are stripped for a finishing round, to knock me down and out with a storm of your best and strongest thoughts. And you had thought you could not fight with Stevenson nor take issue with Socrates? That Shakespeare spoke only the truth and Johnson was invincible? Where all that bravado with which you strutted away after your conquest of me? Where all that fire and logic? Here are fellows to shake you. Why not rush at Carlyle's conclusions as you did at mine? Lay a trap for Browning's unshaken faith. Say for me the things that Shakespeare neglected. Leave me at peace with my pipe and my book. The bookshelf is there.

I am told that the Woman's Club of Ypsilanti, Michigan, will study Tennyson's "In Memoriam" this winter, and I suppose that all Ypsilanti women not in the club will have an uncomfortable time ere spring and golf, unless they, too, read hard of the English bard. Of course they won't all read and discuss to the end that they may quote, but many will, and those that do will sicken the heart of our clear-headed fellow of the street. They will quote to him over the cereal, and cut the morning orange with a sentence recommended in the critical introduction.

But you? Of course you will not be so absurd. You are a business man. You care not what Smith said when he had succeeded in merging the coffee-roasting interests. You wanted to know his plan, whether this or that move was good or bad; how he overcame this difficulty and how he avoided that sink-hole. You want the heart of the thing. Yes, but Tennyson was greater than Smith, and Emerson shrewder and clearer-headed than Jay Gould.

Go to them on the shelf there, and, forgetting the woman's club and the school oration, read. If they convince you against your own judgment you had better look to your next deal in corn, or your late shipment to Argentine. You were not so invincible then, were you? If you find there your own truths expressed better, ah, much better, than you or I can ever express them, read them, spend more time there and less time keeping me from my work. You will be a better man in the market place, and we shall smoke our pipes in peace.

THE MAN AND THE BOOK
Reader, III (December, 1903), 71–73.

We are told by the learned and wise that the great mass of people who read at all, read only for the charm of the un-ravelled tale, and that the story with its little shivers of fear, its complications, and its heroine who goes bravely out into that boggy ground called matrimony, and thus out of the story, with her head tucked safely away on the broad shoulder of Sir Harold of Castlewood Hall, is the sort of thing most likely to run into the hundred thousands and build a country house for its author. "You must stop thinking and put your arms round William's neck," said a certain man of the world to a love-weary maiden, and to stop thinking and drag poor

William down with the white arms of a woman is, we may suppose, the easiest way to the end and a certain name in the world.

These things may well be left to the authors, however, and surely they who feed us so generously should know what is best. At any rate, we may let the critics fight out their battles and turn to another fellow.

The man in the street,—he who knows the unravelled tale in the sound of music from lighted houses at night, from lovers walking arm in arm in the park, and from wan, tired faces in the drift of the sidewalks,—the man, in short, who, having much work to do in a short time, has learned the value of the hours given to reading and how to apply the good gleaned to the militant game of life as he plays it,—this man, believing that the salvation of his soul can be worked out in the shoe business or the meat business or the hardware business, is apt to demand the kind of reading that will make him a better man in his work, and often falls into a habit of depending upon a few close friends among books.

I know a salesman for a wholesale grocery house who carried a volume of Macaulay's Essays in his hand-bag for years because he thought the reading of it on the trains and in the hotels at night helped him to sell soft sugar to Ohio grocerymen; and, as one who keeps faith with a friend and is rewarded by finding the friend strong where he himself is weak, and hopeful where he is cast down, so I can imagine this fellow of sugar and side-meat turning in his hours of weakness to the strong logical mind of the lordly Macaulay for support. I'll warrant he found his Lordship sadly lacking many times; but where is he who has found a friend in the flesh who always feeds his hunger? And what a store of rich meaty sentences he had ever at hand, sentences that came back and said themselves over in his mind in the night time.

Take the case of young Billy Collins, the commercial artist. His friend and room-mate, Aldrich, guessed that knowing a few good books would awaken the sleeping ambition in Collins and make him produce better work. It began with leaving open books on the table and stopping a moment to cry their praises as Aldrich went out for the evening. This did not seem to work, and so Aldrich took to staying home of an evening and reading aloud. Collins was mightily bored, I'll tell you. He wanted to go and talk to the landlady's daughter. He didn't, though. He walked up and down, smoking his pipe and saying, "Hang the beastly old crew in your books." Aldrich went grimly on night after night, trying stories of adventure, Greek philosophers, biographies, everything, in fact, but stories with landlady's daughters in them. And then one night he found the thing that caught and held the heart of his friend and made him a reader of books, and finally an artist full of earnest love of his work. "The night Billy got the glory," Aldrich would say, lingering over the memory of it, "I wasn't trying for him at all. I just sat there reading alone. I'd lost hope in the dog, and didn't pay any attention when he came in and sat by the fire filling his pipe. It was Robert Louis [*sic*] and 'Will o' the Mill,' and you know how a fellow loves to linger over the sentences and say them aloud.² It's like kissing a sweetheart. 'Why don't you read and not mumble that way?' he said, when he had filled his pipe. So I began and went through for him. When I had finished he asked me for the book, put it in his pocket and went out, and that night, after I had been abed for hours, I turned over and saw him sitting there by the fire, his face all lighted up and a look in his eye I hadn't seen before. I didn't say anything. I just rolled over and left him with Robert to watch the fish hanging in the current by the bridge and the people always going downward to the valley."

I might tell you of another case, of a friend of my own. A hot, strong-headed, silent man, from a family whose men had for generations burned the oil of life at a fierce blaze and gone to their deaths loved of women and with the names of bad men upon them. I can remember my own father telling of them and how they went their hot, handsome ways, careless and unafraid. This friend of mine was the son of one of the worst

2. Robert Louis Stevenson, "Will o' the Mill," *Cornhill Magazine*, XXXVII (January, 1878), 41–60; and in *The Merry Men and Other Tales and Fables* (London: Chatto and Windus, 1887), pp. 71–108.

of these, but lived a quiet, sober, and useful life in the face of much head-shaking and wait-and-see talk among the wisest and best of our home folks. How grimly went the fight, and how in desperation he cast about for an outlet for the fierceness inside him, I knew. One day he came begging to go home for the evening, and when we had dined at a little place in Fourteenth Street we started home in the rain. I grumbled when he asked me to walk the two miles home, but finally consented, and we went off at a round pace. I was troubled about a piece of work on hand, and thought little of the man at my side, only to wonder at the way he covered ground, until as we turned for the last half mile the rain struck us in a wild flood and a fierce glad cry burst from the lips of him striding along, hat in hand, his big face thrust eagerly forward into the storm, the water dripping from his hair, and his eyes under the lights dancing with the excitement of it. Full of the old blood, I thought to myself and shuddered—a shudder that became a glow of admiration when at home over the fire he told me of the fight he had fought and how the battle went with him. Showed me his scars, poor devil, and then mended his battered armor with the man talk till morning. This is not a discussion of what is right or wrong for such a man. He had made a game fight, that is all we need to know, and when the lust of his fathers was strong on him and he was near to the sin he fought against, he would go into his room alone, and over and over repeat King Henry's cry to the English at Harfleur, "Once more unto the breach, dear friends!" He told me that at such times he forgot even the meaning of the words on his lips, but that the rolling music of them soothed him and at last made him sleep unbeaten. And unbeaten he died, let me add for your curiosity's sake.

It is no difficult thing to find these instances of the way in which men call upon their friends among books in their hour of need. These few my eyes have seen, and only last week a young Chicagoan told me that the combination of words in the title "The Drums of the Fore and Aft"[3] had come into his

3. Rudyard Kipling's "The Drums of the Fore and Aft," which appeared in his *Wee Willie Winkie and Other Stories* (London: Sampson Low, Marston, Searle, and Rivington, 1890).

mind when he stood trembling outside an office where he had been sent with an important commission, and that they braced him and helped him to carry his plans through. "And," he laughingly told me, "I never have read the story." Americans go naturally to their work like boys going to a foot-ball game, and, although they sometimes give their lives to the making of money, there is much of the music of words in them. Perhaps it is safe to say that in many instances their best work is done under the inspiration drawn from books, whose very titles are lost in the hurry and hubbub of their lives.

BUSINESS TYPES

Agricultural Advertising, XI (January, 1904), 36.

The Good Fellow

He is probably a fat man and it is sure he sleeps at night. He doesn't always give you a contract and many, many times he sends you away without even a promise, but there is something more than contracts and promises in this advertising business, and sometimes an hour spent with the good fellow will net you a dozen contracts in other places. The real good fellow, like the real poet, is born, not made. His the pleasant, ringing laugh, his the cheerful belief in other men's honesty and good intent. Peace be to him and may his lines forever fall in pleasant places.

He is interested in you and your lot. He has a few helpful suggestions to smooth the road for you. He wants to make you as happy, as good natured and as hopeful as himself, and he usually succeeds.

Ben Yeager is a young fellow, just out of school, who becomes an advertising solicitor. Being quick, earnest and not afraid of work, he is given a place in the western office of an eastern farm paper. Just to break him in, and incidentally to get a lot of disagreeable work off his own hands, the boss sends him against the toughest games in the field. For weeks young Yeager beats the bushes, and starts no game. He hears rumors of business going out and daily he is told that there is business in the line he is working for a good man. "Stick to it, my boy. It will do you good, and don't be afraid to kick yourself. You probably need it." This is the half cynical advice of the boss. As though he wasn't sticking to it and fairly sweating blood in his effort to make good. He begins to lose faith in himself, to feel like a homeless little yellow dog. A grunted refusal is his lot in most places, and he has got so used to these refusals that he grows to expect them and can't for the life of him make a fight for business. And then he stumbles in on the good fellow.

The good fellow asks him to have a chair; he talks to him of crops and results; he makes the boy's heart jump by asking his advice about some matter of business policy. Young Yeager begins to feel like a man again. His knees go back into their places with a snap. He straightens his back. He begins to breathe again, the color comes back into his cheeks, his eyes glow, and he talks of that paper of his as he never had talked of it before. He talks as he used to talk up in the old college dormitory. He realizes that he is a man on the earth with other men; that he has a right to breathing room; to an opinion; to a place to work. He may get the good fellow's order or he may not, but he goes from the room a new man; a fellow to reckon with; a fellow who has proved himself.

Off with your hats then to this genial soul, he of the smile and the words of cheer, and may the advertising game yearly find in its ranks more of this good breed who are called good fellows, and are in reality only true born gentlemen after all.

BUSINESS TYPES

Agricultural Advertising, XI (March, 1904), 36–38.

The Man of Affairs

Peter Macveagh was an Indiana boy who came up to Chicago to make his fortune. A clear-eyed, rosy-cheeked, country boy, Peter was so healthy both in body and in mind that the whole world was a bright and cheerful place to him, and the winds that blew over the old farm had left in his soul no creepy dread or distrust of other humans to chill or dampen his fine ardor.

Down in Indiana on the farm Peter used to get out of bed every morning at daylight and go singing across the fields to the creek to wash the drowsiness all out of his body by a good plunge into the cold water. Then he would go back across the fields to the barn, clean the horses, milk the cows and eat his breakfast. After this, it was a straight stretch right through until night, plowing, seeding, hoeing, or some such work out in the open fields under the clear sky. Peter used to get covered with mud and he smelled rather badly of the stables at times, but under his rough clothes he was clean, right down through to his heart. It shone through the mud of the fields and the dust of the stables. It was in his fine eyes and his clear, red skin. He was like the fields and the woods, sort of kept clean by God and the seasons.

One day Peter packed up his little bundle of clothes and came to Chicago to live. He came because he wanted to mix with men, and stretch his mental muscles. He rented a little back room on West Monroe street and went to work in a down town coal office.

Now in this house on West Monroe street where Peter had come to live there lived, also, the usual assortment of Chicago boarding house people: Green, an assistant bookkeeper at the Corn Exchange; Miss Humphrey, a stenographer in the Fisher Building; Tomlinson, a shoe clerk; two medical students and a dentist with an office on Madison street, and Peter's coming was woe to all of these.

Before coming to Chicago, Peter had had a talk with the old family minister down at home and as a result of that talk he had brought with him a box of good books, and being wide-awake and determined to advance, he intended to read those books. But work at the office was new to him and sitting at a desk very wearying to his active body, so that he found himself at night so tired and stupid that he couldn't read with an interest or beneficial result. "Well," said Peter, "then I'll read in the mornings."

So next morning when the shoe clerk and medical students and Miss Humphrey were deep in their morning slumber, they were awakened by a great splashing in the common bathroom in the center of the house. It was Peter washing his body awake for his morning hours of reading.

We will pass lightly over the events of the next three months. Peter was a human animal that washed himself, got up on Sunday morning, whistled in the halls, read Keats and Shakespeare aloud in a voice trained to call the cows, and truth is that Peter so shook up the dry bones in that boarding house that sad-eyed little Mrs. Thomas, the landlady, had to ask him to find another place. She didn't want to do it because she liked the boy, and his habit of coming down into the kitchen and reading to her the while she cooked the breakfast. Then Peter had a way of making his own bed, and he swept and tidied his own room, and was very neat and careful about picking up his clothes; so that it was but little work for her to take care of him. But Mrs. Thomas was helplessly in the hands of the angry multitude, and Peter had to go.

Not that Peter cared. For his part he had been learning things these three months. First, he learned that the stories of financial influence, told at Mrs. Thomas' table by the assistant bookkeeper, were mostly lies; that the medical students, who went off so fine in the morning with books under their arms, were not scholars and that they spent most of their evenings in Madison street dance halls; and that for a fellow like himself, who really wanted to do good work, it was infinitely better to dine alone even at a cheap restaurant and enjoy the peace and comfort of silence, than to sit on Sundays and evenings in the gloomy silence among Mrs. Thomas' sleepy-faced boarders.

Of course, Peter was not settled in his mind about these people, but he went whistling about his work and thought of it only at odd moments. Slowly, however, the conviction began to creep in on him that in this world there are many people who are stupid and incompetent, and many more that are unclean pretenders. He wondered the more about this because of the miracles in the life about him and the great forces that seemed to be always at work, moving the life of the city forward. As he went about his work on the street, and sometimes at his desk in the office at nights, he would pause and take in a quick breath at the wonder of it: the great, useful, massive buildings standing clean against the sky; the elevated trains with their loads of passengers; the great ships, unloading their cargoes in the man-made river. Everywhere was work getting itself done. Somewhere back of it all was another kind of man; his kind; clean, stout of heart, clear of mind, square and vigorous. When he passed a big office building, hurrying about his work as a solicitor (for Peter had been promoted), he would stop for a moment to feast his eye and say (with a little chuckle in his throat, as he passed on), "I wonder if that bookkeeper fellow built that." One evening, as he sat at his desk after the day's work, he decided to write to his friend, the old family minister down in Indiana, about it all. So he told him about the shoe clerk and the bank fellow and Miss Humphrey and the two medical students; of the drainage canal and of the buildings that sprang up in a night, and then he asked him the question: "Where are these other men; the men that do these things?"

The letter from his old friend was fine and fair and tempered with wisdom and much love for Peter. "Be fair with yourself, Peter," it said, "and don't worry about Mrs. Thomas' boarders. You are on the right track. Just keep on taking those 4:30 baths and reading your books; and when you can't understand a thing, whistle and wait. The men who made and are making Chicago were just the sort of boys you are, Peter, and after a time when you deserve to know these men, you will."

So Peter kept on at his work, and he grew; and he went forward; and he made money; and, by wisely investing it, became rich and in time was a very powerful man; but he was not the sort of man the Indiana minister intended; and, for that matter, he was not the sort of man that young Peter had dreamed of when he was a solicitor for a coal office and walked the streets of Chicago. It were of little use to tell the story of Peter Macveagh and his affairs and end it here. To do so is only to repeat what has been said by dozens of men, and well said. Articles have been written, and are being written every month, on the careers of such men as Peter. Their shrewdness, boldness and success have been bruited forth until our ears are filled with the din of it. But all of them go just as far with their man as I have gone with my Peter Macveagh, and then they drop him. He is clean, he is frugal, his morals are right, he has made money and, having made money, has succeeded; is about the tone usually assumed by the scribe who tackles the problem.

To us Americans this much seems to be taken for granted and the thought that Peter Macveagh, (strong, rich and powerful), may be a failure, never seems to occur to us. We never dream of the possibility of his old friend and well-wisher (the family minister down in Indiana) having another sort of man in mind when he wrote his letter to Peter Macveagh. We lose sight of the fact that in buckling down to his work and building factories and getting away from Mrs. Thomas' boarders and forming trusts, Peter was doing about the simplest task there is to do: that is to say, about the simplest task for men like Peter. Here was a fellow of unusual vigor, and moral cleanliness, cast down among the hopeless ruck of folk who don't bathe more than once a week and are not thoroughly awake once in a year. How could he help getting rich? Or, for that matter, getting about anything else he might chance to want?

America is the sort of country that breeds strong men. It is rich with wonderful opportunities—opportunities that we, who walk in our sleep, don't see; and yet, in spite of the fact that it is a country for strong men, a really powerful man only appears in about the proportion of one to one hundred thousand of us common folks; and it is not to the glory of us who look up to such men, and who, by our praises, influence them in their desires that these men bend all of their powerful energies to the acquisition of a few millions of dollars. In extenuation of such men and their lives, it is common for us to say that the strong men don't care for the money; that it is the power they seek; but, for my part, I am not able to see the distinction. The result to the man is exactly the same. Peter, grown in power, is not the Peter of old days; no more the good books nor the letters to his friend, the minister. He has learned the weaknesses of humanity now and is busy playing upon these weaknesses, and the blood that hurries through his brain draws warmth from his once big heart. Because he despises and sees the weaknesses of all men, all men hate and fear him, and he goes on his way, envied by no man except it be Green, the assistant bookkeeper, or the dentist on Madison street. Peter Macveagh is a product of the times and the opportunities. His lust for power is satisfied because most of us are asleep. Mere living is so simple a matter for a man of average energy and intelligence that Peter, with no more effort comparatively, becomes rich and works his own ruin, for if we pay for our stupidity and drowsiness, Peter also pays for his title, Man of Affairs.

BUSINESS TYPES

Agricultural Advertising, XI (May, 1904), 31–32.

The Undeveloped Man

The advertising man sat upon his upturned grip at a railroad junction. It was midnight, a drizzle of rain was in the air and close about him lay the unbroken blackness of a cloudy night.

Down the tracks in the railroad yards a freight engine was making up a train. The banging of the cars, the rumbling of the wheels, the swinging lanterns and the voices of the trainmen lent interest to a long, dull wait. Suddenly up the track there came a rippling string of oaths, and for the next ten minutes the air was filled with them. In the words of Mark Twain, there was "swearing in that railroad yard, swearing that just laid over any swearing ever heard before."

The engineer swore and he wasn't half bad; the conductor deftly caught up the refrain and embellished it, and then from far down in the yards the voice of a brakeman cut into the game.

It was all about a box car and a coupling pin that wouldn't catch, and it was nothing less than genius the way that brakeman handled his subject. He swore scientifically. He worked over the ground already covered by the engineer and conductor and from it harvested another crop, and then he caught his breath, waved his lantern and started into the dense forest of untried oaths. The best part of it all was the way he clung to that box car, he went far enough afield for words but when he used them they were pat, they were all descriptive of the car and its peculiar and general uselessness.

"He is a sort of genius in his way, ain't he?" said a weak, piping little voice at the advertising man's elbow. "He ought to be down in Texas punching cows. Take a feller with that kind of natural talent and he's simply being wasted working on a freight train. Why, the first thing he knows some mean, consumptive, little town marshal'll come along and arrest him, and then where'll he be? Now take it down in Texas where there's a lot of room and breathing space and where it gets all still at night and a feller like that could do some fine work. I guess you don't know what I'm talking about. I seen you settin' here, and you seemed kind-a interested, so I thought I'd come over and see you. I got a bunch of steers back here. Takin' 'em in. I'm a cow man, what you might call a cow man; not a rancher. I ain't none of these new business-man kind of a cow man that's cuttin' out all of the old ways. I'm just a little one doin' most of my own work and I guess that's why I'm so interested in that fellow down there. He don't mean no harm by that cussin', course he don't. It's kind a like singin' to him and eases him off like. I've known hundreds of that kind in my day, the country down where I live used to be full of them. Trouble is they get so interested in their little old swearing that they ain't no good for anything else,—they get so they do it for a stunt. It's like a feller I knew once in Arizona. He could imitate a jewsharp by puttin' his finger along side his nose and blowing. He got so interested in it he couldn't hold a job. I guess it's so most anywhere. A feller gets so he can do some little fool thing pretty well and he becomes sort a satisfied. Take that feller down there in the yards. I'll bet he wouldn't have that blamed proud ring in his voice that-a-way if he'd a been where now and then he could hear some real swearin'.

"Say, young feller, you're different. What you so interested in that feller for?"

"Well, I'll tell you," said the advertising man. "I was just thinking what a good man he would be in the advertising business. He knows the value of words, that fellow does. Did you hear the way he made that conductor and that engineer look faded out like a scorched shirt front? He knows how to use words and that's why I think he'd make an advertising man. How to use words, and say, Mr. Cowman, that's what advertising is, just using words; just picking them out like that fellow picked out his swear words and then dropping them down in just the right place so they seem to mean something. I don't want you to be making fun of that brakeman. You'll find he's a long ways different man than that Arizona chap you tell of imitating a jewsharp. He's a word man, that brakeman is, and words are the greatest things ever invented.

"There's a lot of men can talk and talk, but that fellow didn't waste a bit of his. He used just about two inches single column on that box car, and you noticed she went where he wanted her to go, didn't you? Of course, you don't know what I'm talking about. But see here. You and I didn't see that brakeman at all, did we? No, we just heard him swear and here we are, you and I, quarreling about him. You want him to go down into Texas to punch cows, but you're wrong. Down in that country there won't anybody ever hear him except maybe a few scared steers. Up in this country it's different. Why, there're millions of people just waiting for some one to come along and develop that brakeman. Say, I'll bet I could take him for six months and have him making people believe I could pull their teeth by mail. He's just pure waste now. He's an undeveloped advertising man, that's what that brakeman is.

"Well, here comes my train. Good night, Mr. Cowman. And say, you leave that brakeman alone. Maybe he'll reform, go into the advertising business, and quit wasting his talent on cuss words."

BUSINESS TYPES

Agricultural Advertising, XI (June, 1904), 27–29.

The Liar—a Vacation Story

They had met by chance at the lake: the fish were not biting: the hotels were being filled rapidly with what the younger man called "a lot of Howard Chandler Christy people": [4] and their vacation wasn't more than half ended. And so they bought them each a heavy blanket, to bear in a roll across the back, and, comforted by a vague belief that towns and occasional farm houses would provide them food and shelter on rainy nights, they started forth on a walking tour through Wisconsin.

There were six men in the party: a tall, lank, heavy jawed man, from his mannerisms, evidently a lawyer; a dapper, nervous little man, with a red nose; a quiet bearded man; a minister, who had put away his broadcloth and his sermon for a month of freedom; a youth; and the liar.

When the party was making up, the liar had not been counted in. He was a new arrival at the lake and had no acquaintance among the five. He seemed, though, to give each individual the impression that he was in some way very intimately acquainted with all of the other five. And so it came about that he was counted in.

It was agreed in the beginning, no man should reveal his identity or talk of business.

"We'll tramp, have some fun, say and do what we please, and then go on about our business," said the youth. "I hate this idea of making a little vacation together the excuse for reunions and all that sort of thing. If we don't happen to like each other over much at the end of the week, we can just drop each other, and there you are."

The thing worked beautifully the first day. They left the hotel at the day's beginning, and, laughing and talking, went in pairs along a shady road that wound in and out among the hills. At noon the little man, with the red nose, who had been walking with the liar, shifted to the minister. He didn't say anything to betray his dissatisfaction at the result of his morning's walk, but during the long afternoon he occasionally looked back with something very like glee on his face to where the liar walked beside the man of law, who seemed oblivious to the glories of the afternoon, and only looked miserable

4. Howard Chandler Christy (1873–1952), American painter and illustrator.

toward the setting sun. After supper at a farm house, they went to a convenient hay loft for the night.

"We should have asked that fellow about the road for tomorrow," said the lawyer, as they stretched their legs upon the straw. "I think it would be as well to know at least the general directions: where the rivers are and things like that, you know."

"Oh! Never mind that!" said the liar. "I know this country like a book."

The party looked at him with a show of surprise. The lawyer and the man with the red nose went to the top of the loft to sleep together.

It was the minister's turn the next day and he hung on like a dog till night. Truth is, he could do nothing else. At times there were none of the others in sight, and, when late in the afternoon they came upon red nose sitting under a tree, he refused to join them and hurried off after the bearded one.

The bearded man caught it the next morning, and the youth came in for his punishment in the afternoon.

That night in a little clump of trees above the river, five men sat about a camp fire. The liar had gone to the river for water. The young man got to his feet and said, with some show of warmth, "See, here! We've got to down that fellow. He's a public pest. Anybody got a plan?"

"Yes," said the minister, "we've got to nail him down on something we know down to the ground. He won't talk about anything he thinks we're likely to know. I tried that. Why, say! he told me he was with Grant when he wrote his memoirs, and that he knew Teddy Roosevelt at Harvard." "It was Blaine with me," said the lawyer. "The way he laid out Blaine's private life was something horrible." [5]

"It was the inner secrets of Spanish politics, he told me," said the red nosed one. "I never have wanted to fight with any one so badly in my life. I'm going to do something if he isn't choked off."

5. James G. Blaine (1830–93), Republican presidential candidate defeated in 1884.

"Let's get down to business," said the youngster, "he'll be back in a minute."

"Look here," said the bearded man. "I know about bicycles. I manufacture them. Let's see if we can land him there."

"All right," said the youngster, "that's a go. Here he comes."

When the liar got up to the fire he found the youngster, the red nose and the bearded man deep in a discussion of bicycles.

"I'll tell you it can't be done," said the bearded one. "There isn't a machine made that could spread the paint out over all those little joints as smooth as that. No, sir, it can't be done."

"Well, a fellow told me," said the youth, "said he knew, said he worked in a bicycle factory once."

"I think it's done with some kind of a squirt gun," said the minister; "seems like I heard a story like that once. I've never been in a bicycle factory, however."

"What you fellows talking about?" cut in the liar.

"Oh! about bicycles: how they're made, and how the paint is put on," said the bearded man. "We were wondering if automobiles would ever be reduced in price as bicycles have been. The boy here says he talked to a fellow who worked in a shop where they were made. Says it's nearly all done by machinery. Says even the paint is put on by machinery. We don't happen to want to believe that, it's done so smooth and nice, you know."

"Oh, well," said the lawyer, "I don't suppose he knows anything about it."

"Let him tell what he knows. He may be able to set us all straight in the matter," said red nose.

"I guess you're about right there," said the liar; "I ought to know something about the business; I worked in a bicycle factory for three years. I guess I've done about everything there is to do about making bicycles. Why, say, look here, you fellows know who Col. Pope is, don't you? You don't? That's funny, why he's the biggest man in the bicycle business. What's that got to do with it? I'm coming to that. Don't be in such an all-fired hurry. This Col. Pope's a friend of mine. No, he don't paint bicycles. Are you fellows all fools? You see, this Col. Pope and I started in business together and when it comes

to the painting of bicycles I can tell you mighty quickly that
you are all pretty wide of the mark. They aren't painted at
all, you see. No, sir! it's enamel."

The four looked knowingly at each other and then settled
down to take the full brunt of it. And they got it. The liar began
with a long story of how he became interested in the bicycle
business; he told of his father, and of his father's station in
life; he recalled the days when bicycles were unknown, and
touched on the old high wheels of his early manhood; and then
dropping the autobiographic end of his little study, he con-
ducted the party through a bicycle factory. He told of how the
forgings entered the works, and wandered off into a little
dissertation on tubing and the making of rubber tires. Then
coming back to the work at hand, and surveying the party
with the cock-sure glitter in his eye that had so upset them on
the road, he dived boldly into the inner workings of the bicycle
business. He told of the filers and the polishers, of the black-
smiths and the assemblers, of the truers and the machinists,
of gear and of crank hangers, of bearings and of handle bars,
and then, after fifteen busy minutes in the enameling room, he
closed with a short sermonette on prices and selling methods,
yawned, knocked out his pipe, and with a proud look at the
wondering faces of the five, he went off to the barn to sleep.

Four men sat silent before the dying fire. "Something tells
me we've got it in the neck," said the youth.

"Can't you say something?" groaned the minister, looking at
the bearded man.

"Oh! there's nothing to say," growled the manufacturer of
bicycles. "He didn't leave one opening. He put every spoke in
that wheel just where it belonged."

"What are we going to do?" asked the lawyer. "We'll have to
believe every blamed lie he tells now."

"I know what I'm going to do," said red nose, "that fellow
where we stopped for supper told me about a town five miles
straight ahead down this road. I'm going there. Maybe I
can catch a train to Chicago."

"Don't make so much noise," said the minister a few minutes
later to the youth. "You can whistle when we get around that

bend, not before. You don't want him to hear you now, with liberty just in sight, do you?"

In the barn the liar rolled over in the straw and went to sleep, with a satisfied grin upon his lips.

BUSINESS TYPES

Agricultural Advertising, XI (August, 1904), 21–24.

The Solicitor

The publisher of the paper had often been heard to say that he didn't want an advertiser to keep on paying money to the *Farmer's Blast,* who did not find that his advertising in that worthy organ paid. "However," he remarked, looking knowingly at his Western representative, "we'll go on the principle of believing the *Blast* to be innocent until it's convicted and we'll let the advertiser hand down the judgment against us. We won't do it ourselves. It's like this in business," he went on. "We can't tell when an advertiser is going to strike oil. Why, when I was a bit younger, I used to be mighty proud when I told a man to stay out of my paper because it wouldn't pay him. Felt almost as good as I might have felt with his order in my pocket. You see I considered it sort of a moral victory, like paying a street car conductor when he has overlooked you, or returning an umbrella you've accidentally picked up in church. Well, as I was going to say, it went along until I found out that some of the fellows whom I had kind of looked down on as being robbers, because they took copy I had turned down, were around with testimonials telling how their paper had paid this same advertiser. Mind you, maybe the paper they had used wasn't any better medium for that particular advertiser than mine. Of course, I don't want you fellows to think I am looking for the earth, but I think you are badly mistaken about that Curtis-Crosby business and I don't think you need stay away from Curtis because of any qualms you may have on the score of the paper not paying him."

"Well, I don't know as we could get it any way," said Bradley, the Western Manager. "The truth is, I've been over there and tried."

"Well now, that is something like," said the publisher, with a grin. "Why didn't you say that at first and not come in here with all that high-moral-plane talk? Of course, if you can't land him, you can't, I suppose, and there's an end of it. Just the same, I'm going over there to try it myself. You won't care, will you?"

"Care! No, I'll be delighted. Why, I talked three mortal hours to that fellow and never moved him. Then I made up my mind we didn't want it. I thought maybe I would sleep better if I looked at it that way."

A week later the publisher strolled into the Western Office of the paper:

"Say, Bradley," he remarked, lighting a cigar, "I've been down there to see Curtis. No, never mind about that, I can't stay. I'm just passing through, going back home, you see. Of course I'll tell you about it. I guess I've been thinking enough of it coming up on the train. Most of all, I've been thinking of how Curtis looked up and said 'goodbye' in that surly way of his. I guess, after all, you are right. We don't want that copy for the *Blast*. It might be wrong, morally wrong, you know, to take it. I wonder how you and I would feel if we saw a news item in the paper some morning that Curtis had murdered some one and was going to be hung. Say, I'll tell you what we'll do. We'll send the boy down there and let him tackle that fellow. He needs breaking in. I don't know any place where he can get more of it in fifteen minutes than by going down there and putting in that much time with Curtis after you and I have had it out with him."

The boy was a new comer in the advertising field, a bright, young fellow, fresh from school, who was trying hard to break into the business. He had been dashing about for three months. It was hot summer and things were dull and the boy was discouraged.

"I don't seem to be able to line them up," he remarked to the Western Manager a few mornings later. "I guess I must be overlooking something."

"Oh, well! you needn't be discouraged," said the head of the office. "You've been after a lot of dead ones any way. It's summer now and things are a bit dull. I suppose you'd better take a few days off and sort of take treatment for your nerve. But, say, look here. Here's something for you to do. Get on the train and go down here to Springfield. See Curtis, of the Curtis-Crosby Company. Get a thousand lines for the *Blast* from him. I don't know whether I ought to tell you, but this Curtis isn't a pleasant fellow. Fact is, he's sort of a terror. Look here, you go down there and land him. It means a raise in salary for you."

It was two days later and the boy was on the train bound for Springfield. He wasn't a bit deceived by the game to send him up against Curtis, though he hadn't said anything about it. In fact he had been watching the effort to capture that bit of business with no little interest and on the train that night as he lay in his berth, looking out at the fields, he was nervous, so nervous he couldn't sleep, and the worst part of it was he couldn't see any way out of it for him.[6]

At Springfield the boy got up early and sat around the hotel, trying to think up some good plan. Then he went for a walk; walked around past the Curtis-Crosby plant; went back and got his breakfast; walked around past the plant again; went back and bought a cigar; and walked around again.

"Well," he said to himself, "this won't do. It's ten o'clock and I guess I better tackle it," so back he came again to the door of the Curtis-Crosby Company. "I'm getting acquainted on this street," he said to himself, with a nervous smile, as he went in at the door. "I reckon people along here are getting so they know me. I wonder if they think I'm in training."

Inside the office the boy received the message that he was to step right in with something like a shock: he hadn't expected that: he had expected to be kept waiting for at least an hour: he almost always had been even with what Bradley called the "dead ones." For all that he stepped bravely enough up to the desk.

"I am the boy," he said. "I am from the *Blast*. I am sent down here to try and get that thousand line order the other

6. The following episode is autobiographical, as told by Anderson in his *Memoirs*, ed. White, p. 200.

fellows couldn't get. I don't know what I'm going to say to you. I guess there isn't anything to say, but any way, I would like to have the order."

Curtis looked up at him in a surprised manner a moment, then laughed and said, "You're a modest boy any way, only asking for a thousand lines. Why, see here, I've got the order made out for five thousand. Here it is."

When the boy got back to the office, he started in to tell Bradley all about it, but Bradley only laughed and said, "You're altogether too modest, my boy," and so he got his salary raised and he got the name of being a good solicitor, which perhaps he was. At any rate, he is now, and that's all the story.

BUSINESS TYPES

Agricultural Advertising, XI (September, 1904), 24–26.

The Hot Young 'Un and the Cold Old 'Un

There were two of them concerned in the matter, an old man, grown body-worn and watery about the eyes from hard service, and a young man not long out of the schools. The young man had the very best of chances for the place. He was a forceful young fellow with something clean and clear cut about him, and there wasn't a flaw in his business record. Bunker's big *Monthly* wanted a representative. The place offered a good salary and unusual chances for more in the future. Now, Bunker was not the kind of a man to take ahold of a thing and then let it go, and he had it figured out that this new *Monthly* was going to be the best thing he had ever floated.

"It seems to take ahold with its teeth, don't it?" he said to the advertising manager. "If we can only get the right man for the West, now, we are fixed." This question of the right man for the Western end had been hanging fire for three months, and Bunker felt that something ought to be done at once.

Young Cartwright's friends—and he had a lot of them—bold, clear-headed men of affairs—were ready to go far to back him. These friends were pulling every wire to land him in the place, and it was about settled in Bunker's mind that he should have it when a letter came in from the old man. It was a simple straight-forward document, that letter from the old man, and it was something more than a business letter. "It's literature, that's what it is," said Wright, the editor. "You see he don't stick to dollars and cents and he don't tell what he has done, but he touches a fellow's heart, don't he? Better have him come up here, don't you think so?" "Have him up here? Well, I rather think so," said Bunker. "Tell you what I'll do: I'll have both of them up here next Saturday afternoon. We'll go down to that back room over the Mailing Department, and sit around the table. There'll be Wright, here, and Sutherland and myself, and I'll rig in two dummies just to add to the general impression of ponderous thought. I hate to say it, but you fellows don't give much of an impression of weight. You are both so thin about the legs and you haven't any place in particular where the bosom of a man's size shirt would lay flat, but I have got the boys in mind. One is a barber over on Fifteenth street, and the other runs a tobacco store out in our suburb. I'll have them both put on their best black clothes and a strong, dignified expression, and then I'll lead these two men in and let them work out their own salvation. You fellows can do the talking, but I'll make them think the two broad-chested boys are the ones they must convince. I haven't told you, have I, that the tobacconist out in our suburb is as deaf as a post."

It was Saturday afternoon, and five men sat by the table in the back room. Across from them sat the old man and young Cartwright. Wright, the editor, was talking, the old man apparently all unconscious of the weightiness of his words, was looking off across the housetops to where the lake lay, cool and green, with the cloud shadows fleeting across it. Cartwright sat up very straight and business-like in his chair. "You may consider it a bit unfair but this is rather an important thing to us—this choosing a Western representative," said Wright. "The West is getting the business, just now, and we want a man out there who can go in and nail down a contract on the spot. We figure that the man who can come in here, this afternoon, and land this job, can go into other offices on other afternoons, and sell pages for *The Herald*. Mr. Cartwright, will you kindly arise and tell the gentlemen why you think you are the man for the place."

"And please speak right out, I'm a trifle deaf," said the tobacconist, who, born for director's duties, and compelled by fate to sell five-cent cigars to clerks having to catch morning trains, was feeling the importance of his newly acquired dignity. His silk hat lay before him on the table. His broad chest swelled with the importance of his mission. "Look at him," whispered Bunker to Wright. "He believes it himself. Looks a bit like the pictures of Napoleon at Austerlitz."

The young man's voice, rising to a feverish pitch, cut the afternoon stillness of the building. It floated out on the afternoon breeze and some boys, playing at baseball in a vacant lot near-by, dropped their game and climbed upon a convenient fence to hear the speech. "I am not going to waste words," he began; "I am here for business, and I know you are. I have had four papers since I broke into the game out in the West, and I have smashed a record every time." (Here he looked over at the old man.) "I am young too," he went on, "young enough to say to you gentlemen that I can bring the best years of my life to you and to your proposition. I will work for it; I will lay awake nights for it; I will give my brains and my strength and my love to it; and I will make it go. I know I will make it go. I won't think of any other possible result. I believe I am the man for the place, and if you hire me I want you to know that I will be your man, body and soul."

He really said a lot more than this, but you have the meat of it. He grew excited, as he talked; he rose on his toes and pumped his arms up and down; he leaned far over the table toward the tobacconist, and looked deeply into his eyes. He was very much in earnest, was young Cartwright, and, as he talked, a smile played about the corners of the old man's mouth, but he kept his head resolutely turned to the open window.

"I am indeed sorry that one of you gentlemen cannot hear," said he in his turn. "But I am afraid I am a bit old to shout,

and anyway I just rise to second this young gentleman's
nomination. He says he will give his every pulse-beat to you
and to your interests and you see I am a bit old to be so
generous with my own blood and muscle. It's a good, long
ways back to the time when I was a young man like that and
hadn't made any failures and now you know I have made a
lot of them, indeed I have, gentlemen. Nearly everything I
have ever touched has slipped like water through my fingers,
and then I couldn't possibly keep awake nights to think of you
men and your business success. You're a very decent looking
lot of men, but I don't know you and I hardly think I would
ever get to know you so well but that I would want to forget
you were alive in the evening when I got home and was sitting
by my fireside. I wouldn't even want to realize that I had to
work for you at all. When I wrote that letter I really thought
I wanted this place and I came up here determined to go far
to get it, but as I have been sitting here listening to this young
man and thinking of the times when I have talked that way to
men who were about to trust me with good places, something
old and worn touched me on the arm, and out there and
through the window and away over there by the lake I saw an
empty bench by the park. I guess that is the place for me. But
now I'm here and this young man has told you about himself,
and what he is going to do for *The Herald.* I'm going to go
over to the other side of the fence and tell you some things. I
ought to be there, anyway. I ought to be sitting up there
looking dignified and important and helping to hire a man
for the place instead of standing over here on this side, an old
man, asking for a chance to try again."

The tobacconist pushed his silk hat over to the side of his
head, and caught his thumb in the arm-hole of his vest. Bunker
leaned over the table and looked at the floor. Everyone else in
the room was looking at the old man. "So here is my advice to
you," he went on. "Hire this young man. You see that set
look about the jaws, don't you? His hands you see grip the
back of the chair." Young Cartwright arose and, ramming his
hands deep into his pockets, walked to the window. "He is
ready to do all he says he will do for you. He has a wife,
possibly, but he will walk the floor at night thinking of schemes

to advance your business. He has memories of the quiet days when he was a fellow in school, and wandered out in the woods in the summer afternoons and feasted his soul on a good book, but he has heard of other American hustlers who forewent everything pleasant and quiet and hammered through a long hot life on the trail of dollars and he is ready to do that for you. Gentlemen, it would be very foolish of you not to take him on."

The old man turned and went quietly out of the room. Young Cartwright followed as though he would speak to him. The barber and the tobacconist arose and put on their hats. "Here, you fellows stay and see this out," demanded Bunker, but they only shook their heads and went out without speaking.

"Well, what are you going to do?" asked Wright. "Which man gets the place?" "Neither of those two," growled Bunker, "one is too hot, and the other is too blame cold."

THE RABBIT-PEN

Harper's Magazine, CXXIX (July, 1914), 207–10.

In a wire pen beside the gravel path, Fordyce, walking in the garden of his friend Harkness and imagining marriage, came upon a tragedy. A litter of new-born rabbits lay upon the straw scattered about the pen. They were blind; they were hairless; they were blue-black of body; they oscillated their heads in mute appeal. In the center of the pen lay one of the tiny things, dead. Above the little dead body a struggle went on. The mother rabbit fought the father furiously. A wild fire was in her eyes. She rushed at the huge fellow again and again.

The man who had written two successful novels stood trembling in the path. He saw the father rabbit and the furious little mother struggling in the midst of the new life scattered about the pen, and his hands shook and his lips grew white. He was afraid that the mother of the litter would be killed in the struggle. A cry of sympathy broke from his lips. "Help here! Help! There is murder being done!" he shouted.

Out at the back door of the house came Gretchen, the housekeeper. She ran rapidly down the gravel path. Seeing the struggle going on in the wire pen, she knelt, and, tearing open a little door, dragged the father rabbit out of the pen. In her strong grasp the father rabbit hung by his ears, huge and grotesque. He kicked out with his heels. Turning, she flung him through an open window into a child's play-house standing amid the shrubbery beside the path.

Fordyce stood in the path, looking at the little dead rabbit in the center of the pen. He thought that it should be taken away, and wondered how it might be done. He tried to think of himself reaching through the little door into the cage and taking the little blue-black dead thing into his hand; but the housekeeper, coming from the child's play-house with a child's shovel in her hand, reached into the pen and threw the body over the shrubbery into the vegetable-garden beyond.

Fordyce followed her—the free-walking, straight-backed Gretchen—into the stable at the end of the gravel path. He heard her talking, in her bold, quick way, to Hans, the stableman. He wondered what she was saying that made Hans smile. He sat on a chair by the stable door, watching her as she walked back to the house.

Hans, the stableman, finished the righting of things in the home of the rabbits. The tragedy was effaced; the dead rabbit buried among the cabbages in the garden. Into the wire pen Hans put fresh, new straw. Fordyce wondered what Gretchen had said to Hans in that language. He was overcome by her efficiency. "She knew what to do, and yet, no doubt, like me, she knew nothing of rabbits," he thought, lost in wonder.

Hans came back into the stable and began again polishing the trimmings of a harness hanging on the wall. "He was trying to kill the young males," he explained in broken English.

Fordyce told Harkness of the affair of the rabbit-pen. "She was magnificent," he said. "She saved all of that new life while I stood by, trembling and impotent. I went up to my room and sat thinking of her. She should be spending her days caring for new life, making it fine and purposeful, and not be counting sheets and wrangling with the iceman for an old, worn-out newspaper hack like you."

Joe Harkness had laughed. "Same old sentimental, susceptible Frank," he had shouted, joyously. "Romancing about every woman you see, but keeping well clear of them, just the same."

Sitting on the wide veranda in the late afternoon, Fordyce read a book. He was alone, so it was his own book. As he read, he wondered that so many thousands of people had failed to buy and appreciate it. Between paragraphs he became entangled in one of his own fancies—the charming fancies that never became realities. He imagined himself the proud husband of Gretchen, the housekeeper.

Fordyce was always being a proud husband. Scarcely a week passed without the experience. It was satisfying and complete. He felt now that he had never been prouder husband to a more beautiful or more capable woman than Gretchen. Gretchen was complete. She was a Brünnhilde. Her fine face, crowned by thick, smooth hair, and her quiet, efficient manner, brought a thrill of pride. He saw himself getting off the train in the evening at some Chicago suburb and walking through the shady streets to the frame house where Gretchen waited at the door.

Glancing up, his eyes rested on the wide emerald lawn. In the shrubbery, Hans, the stableman, worked with a pair of pruning-shears. Fordyce began thinking of the master of the house and its mistress, Ruth—the brown-eyed, soft-voiced Ruth with the boyish freckles. Joe, comrade of the struggling newspaper days, was married to pretty Ruth and her fortune, and went off to meetings of directors in the city, as he had done this afternoon. "Good old Joe," thought Fordyce, with a wave of tenderness. "For him no more uncertainties, no more heartaches."

From the nursery at the top of the house came the petulant voices of the children. They were refusing to be off to bed at the command of their mother, refusing to be quiet, as they had been refusing her commands all afternoon. They romped and shouted in the nursery, throwing things about. Fordyce could hear the clear, argumentative voice of the older boy.

"Don't be obstinate, mother," said the boy; "we will be quiet after a while."

The man sitting on the veranda could picture the gentle mother. She would be standing in the doorway of the nursery —the beautiful children's room with the pictures of ships on the walls—and there would be the vague, baffled, uncertain look in her eyes. She would be trying to make herself severe and commanding, and the children would be defying her. The listening man closed his book with a bang. A shiver of impatience ran through him. "Damn!" he said, swiftly. "Damn!"

From below-stairs came the sharp, clicking sound of footsteps. A voice, firm and purposeful, called up to the nursery. "*Schweig!*" commanded the voice of Gretchen, the housekeeper.

Above-stairs all became quiet. The mother, coming slowly

down, joined Fordyce on the veranda. They sat together discussing books. They talked of the work of educators among children.

"I can do nothing with my own children," said Ruth Harkness. "They look to that Gretchen for everything."

In the house Fordyce could hear the housekeeper moving about, up and down the stairs, and in and out of the living-room; he could see her through the windows and the open doors. She went about silently, putting the house in order. Above in the nursery all was peace and quiet.

Fordyce stayed on as a guest at Cottesbrooke, finishing his third book. With him stayed Gretchen, putting the house in order for the winter; Harkness, with Ruth, the two boys and the servants, had gone to the city home. It was autumn, and the brown leaves went dancing through the bare shrubbery on the lawn. In his overcoat Frank now sat on the veranda and looked at the hurrying leaves. He was being one of the leaves.

"I am dead and brown and without care, and that is I now being blown by the wind across the dead grass," he told himself.

At the end of the veranda, near the carriage entrance, stood his trunk. His brown bag was by his feet.

Out through the door of the house came Gretchen. She stood by the railing at the edge of the veranda, talking. "I am not satisfied with this family," she said. "I shall be leaving them. There is too much money."

She turned, waving her hand and talking vehemently. "It is of no account to save," she declared. "I am best at the saving. In this house all summer I have made the butter for the table from cream that has spoiled. Things were wasted in the kitchen and I have stopped that. It has passed unnoticed. I know every sheet, every towel. Is it appreciated? Master Harkness and mistress—they do not know that I know, and do not care. The sour cream they would see thrown to the pig. Uh!—It is of no use to be saving here."

Fordyce thought that he was near to being a real husband.

It came into his mind to spring from his chair and beseech this frugal woman to come and save the soured cream in a frame house in a Chicago suburb. While he hesitated, she turned and disappeared into the house. *"Auf Wiedersehen!"* she called to him over her shoulder.

He went along the veranda and climbed into the carriage. He went slowly, looking back at the door through which she had disappeared. He was thinking of the day in the green summer when he had stood in the gravel path by the wire rabbit-pen, watching her straighten out the affair in the family of the rabbits. As on that day, he now felt strangely impotent and incapable. "I should be taking things into my own hands," he reflected, while Hans drove the carriage along the road under the bare trees.

Now it was February, with the snow lying piled along the edges of the city streets. Sitting in the office of his friend Harkness, Fordyce, looking through the window, could see the lake, blue and cold and lonely.

Fordyce turned from the window to his friend, at work among the letters on the desk. "It is of no avail to look sternly and forbiddingly at me," he said. "I will not go away. I have sold the book I wrote at your house, and have money in my pocket. Now I will take you to dine with me, and after dinner I will get on a train and start on a trip to Germany. There is a reason why I should learn to speak the German language. I hear housekeepers talking to stablemen about the doings of rabbits in pens, and it gets into my mind that I don't know what they say. They may whisper secrets of life in that language. I have a wish to know everything, and I shall begin by knowing the German language. Perhaps I shall get me a wife over there and come home a proud and serious husband. It would be policy for you to drop letter-signing and come to dine with me while yet I am a free man."

In the restaurant they had come to the cigars, and Harkness was talking of life in his house. He was talking intimately, as a man talks only to one who is near and dear to him.

"I have been unhappy," said Harkness. "A struggle has gone on in which I have lost."

His friend said nothing. Putting down his cigar, he fingered the thin stem of the glass that sat before him.

"In Germany I engaged Gretchen," said Harkness, talking rapidly. "I got her for the management of our house and for the boys. They were unruly, and Ruth could do nothing with them. Also we thought it would be well for them to know the German language.

"In our house, after we got Gretchen, peace came. The boys stayed diligently at their lessons. When in the school-room at the top of the house they were unruly, Gretchen came to the foot of the stairs, '*Schweig!*' she shouted, and they were intent upon their lessons.

"In the house Gretchen went about quietly. She did the work of the house thoroughly. When I came home in the evening the toys of the children no longer were scattered about underfoot. They were gathered into the boxes put into the nursery for the purpose.

"Our two boys sat quietly with us at the evening meal. When they had been well-mannered they looked for approval to Gretchen, who talked to them in German. Ruth did not speak German. She sat at the table, looking at the boys and at Gretchen. She was unhappy in her own home, but I did not know why.

"One evening when the boys had gone up-stairs with Gretchen she turned to me, saying intensely, 'I *hate* German!' I thought her over-tired. 'You should see a physician for the nerves,' I said.

"And then came Christmas. It was a German Christmas with German cakes and a tree for each of the boys. Gretchen and I had planned it one evening when Ruth was in bed with a headache.

"The gifts on our Christmas trees were magnificent. They were a surprise to me. Ruth and I had not believed in costly gifts, and now Ruth had loaded the trees with them. The trees were filled with toys, costly mechanical toys for each of our two boys. With them she had planned to win the boys.

"The boys were beside themselves with joy. They ran about the room shouting. They played with the elaborate toys upon the floor.

"Ruth took the gifts from the trees. In the shadow by the door stood Gretchen. She was silent. When the boys got the packages from the trees they ran to her, shouting, *'Mach' es auf! Mach' es auf! Tante Gretchen!'*

"I was happy. I thought we were having a beautiful Christmas. The annoyance I had felt at the magnificence of Ruth's gifts passed away.

"And then, in one moment, the struggle that had smoldered under the surface of the lives of the two women in my house burst forth. Ruth, my gentle Ruth, ran out into the middle of the floor, shouting in a shrill, high voice, 'Who is mother here? Whose children are these?'

"The two boys clung to the dress of Gretchen. They were frightened and cried. Gretchen went out of the room, taking them with her. I could hear her quick, firm footsteps on the stairs.

"Gretchen put the two boys into their white beds in the nursery. At her word they ceased weeping.

"In the center of the room they had left, lighted only by the little electric bulbs in the branches of the Christmas trees, stood Ruth. She stood in silence, looking at the floor, and trembling.

"I looked at the door through which our boys had gone at the command of Gretchen. I did not look at Ruth. A flame of indignation burned in me. I felt that I should like to take her by the shoulders and shake her."

Fordyce had never seen his friend so moved. Since his visit to Cottesbrooke he had been thinking of his old comrade as a man in a safe harbor—one peacefully becalmed behind the breakwater of Ruth and her fortune, passing his days untroubled, secure in his happiness.

"My Ruth is wonderful," declared Harkness, breaking in on these reflections. "She is all love and truth. To me she had been more dear than life. We have been married all these years, and still like a lover I dream of her at night. Sometimes I get out of bed and creep into her room, and, kneeling there in the darkness, I kiss the strands of her hair that lie loose upon the pillow.

"I do not understand why it is not with our boys as it is with me," he said, simply. "To myself I say, 'Her love should conquer all.'"

Before the mind of Fordyce was a different picture—the picture of a strong, straight-backed woman running down a gravel path to a wire rabbit-pen. He saw her reach through the door, and, taking the father rabbit by the ears, throw him through the window of the child's play-house. "She could settle the trouble in the rabbit's pen," he thought; "but this was another problem."

Harkness talked again. "I went to where Ruth stood trembling and took her in my arms," he said. "I made up my mind that I would send Gretchen back to Germany. It was my love for Ruth that had made my life. In a flash I saw how she had been crowded out of her place in her own home by that able, quiet, efficient woman."

Harkness turned his face away from the eyes of his friend. "She lay in my arms and I ran my hand over her hot little head," he said. "'I couldn't keep it back any longer, Joe; I couldn't help saying it,' she cried. 'I have been a child, and I have lost a fight. If you will let me, I will try now to be a woman and a mother.'"

Fordyce took his eyes from the face of his friend. For relief he had been feeding an old fancy. He saw himself walking up a gravel path to the door of a German house. The house would be in a village, and there would be formal flower-plots by the side of the gravel path.

"To what place in Germany did she go, this Gretchen?" he demanded.

Harkness shook his head. "She married Hans, the stableman, and they went away together," he said. "In my house the mechanical toys from the Christmas tree lie about underfoot. We are planning to send our boys to a private school. They are pretty hard to control."

SUBSTANTIVE DELETIONS FROM THE TYPESCRIPT AND UNINCORPORATED TYPESCRIPT READINGS

9.1–
.5   It was Uncle Charlie Wheeler who gave a name to
        Cracked McGregor's tall son and fixed upon him the
        attention of Coal Creek. Standing before the counter
        in Nance McGregor's bake shop, Uncle Charlie
        laughed

9.4   pleased Uncle Charlie and

9.14   as though in deep

9.26   shook the minister.

9.28   One guessed that

10.13   The minister was preening

11.28   do it and

12.17–
.18   By the art of Uncle Charlie Wheeler he had become

12.19–
.20   before the reader.

14.8   for confirmation.

14.17–
.18   deformed the shoulder   clouded

14.24   day lit up by

15.11–
.12   eyes, filling his soul with the

15.23   on the eminence

15.25   their native songs.

15.33–
.34   bed that night

16.31   A sort of panic

17.34   the boy saw

18.8	the puzzled look of the perplexed
19.1	For some years
22.2–.3	boy with black hair and rings
22.22	would come out.
22.24	away from the town," she
22.27	and began climbing over
23.8–.9	nothing of the ring.
23.25	woman. He thought that in leaving the two boys on the log and coming away with her he had completed a day. Without
23.27	he said, "I
24.11	believe now that the
24.31	Beaut began talking
24.33	on his mind
25.25	he burst out. "They
25.35–.36	down, you red man," she said, "and
26.36–.37	ovens lit up the
26.38–27.1	hatred blazed up in him.
27.17	been making love. I
27.25	thought preening himself on the encounter.
28.3	looked out at
29.5–.6	on the top of the hill.
29.15–.16	joined the strikers.
30.6	strikers destroyed the garden
30.18–.22	lodging. Rumors of significant movements . . . began to come to him.
31.17	on dumb with sympathy.
31.20–.21	dandified man of
32.13–.14	He began to talk in the French language and

33.13   from their homes she
34.20   in a chair trembling.

34.23   walked at the tail of the horses
35.36–   boy sitting silently before
·37

36.8   the depot down the street.
36.11–   soldiers, their guns
.12

36.16–   street and disappeared into
.17

37.26   nervously. He slid
38.12   of McGregor, the red one.
38.25–   on reflecting, wondering
.26

38.35–   he sat thus looking at the town and thinking of
·37   himself.
40.32–   is a kind of genius at . . . things he doesn't like,"
.34   said
42.5   looking out at their
42.24   of that town had
45.1   summer of 1903 when
45.6–   know how to handle the growth
·7

45.8–   financial depression that
·9

46.27–   desperation, by misery and losing all sense of living,
.28   went
46.5   of Chicago University, addressing
46.15–   who, in another time and place might
.16

46.19–   graceful of body,
.20

46.27   to be bluffed with
47.21–   as good an impulse
.22

47.30   a wonderfully clear and lucid

47.33– .34	rich men lying abed in . . . have rolled uneasily in their sleep as
48.12	short, fat
48.25	made braves of
49.1	in 1903 and
49.17– .18	not consult the want
49.29	on the west side
50.5	who struggled with
50.13	began preparing to
50.31– .32	sharp, restless eyes
50.35	the Germans. "Tell
51.1	out at the door and turned
51.26– .27	challenge which he . . . and which he
51.34	Struggling terrible
52.3	Weeks in Coal
52.13– .14	down a passageway
52.26– .27	waiting before them.
53.17	said, handing out
53.26	win that. Of the other he was immensely proud. The
53.27	he knew, had intended to patronize
54.9– .10	McGregor came was
54.22	man's minds so
55.15	the ROOMS FOR RENT sign
56.21– .22	rented lodging houses and
56.33– .34	by the wind and
58.20	with the tall girl, he
59.1	With this young man the
59.21	wife and two children
60.5	book of the

60.19   Cars, coming to the park filled and went away.

61.22   A young story writer walking past with his sweet-
         heart and swinging a cane in his hand paused and
         stood with eyes and mouth open staring at the figure
         on the bench. "There is something that frightens me
         about that fellow," he said nudging the woman who
         walked with him. "He is strangely like the personifi-
         cation of that terrible new force that is coming into
         the world, the thing of which I once told you, and
         that I myself might be if I weren't afraid."

62.5   do about woman, about getting

62.23–   town before a blacksmith shop.
.24

64.23   do you know about

65.12   don't want it."

65.16   about Socialism.

65.26   that are growing up.

66.3   afraid of woman. It

69.21   of hardship and defeat. It's no worse for a woman to
         sell herself on the street than it is for men to sell
         themselves in a place like the stockyards, or in the
         mines where you came from."

69.25–   pensions and real independence and anything
.27

70.16   barber, and thought it fine that one who had started
         on the long and dangerous journey through life
         should have met such a friend on the way. He felt

71.22   sit at cheap

71.24–   old world states is
.25

72.1–   confused in the matter
.2

72.16   him with her hand.

73.20–   and waiting, trembling
.21

76.30   him fight, fight, fight.

77.20   mind. The thing that was growing in him and that
was to make him so huge a figure in the world would
not let him sit quietly at work. He

77.28   work. They cost him one dollar each." The

77.37   out the two dollars

78.6   barber began urging McGregor

78.12   and began pulling his

78.19   been another failure.

80.16   so frail that

80.18   had had a lover—a fat,

80.28–   with a kind of grim satisfaction.
.29

80.30   opened the shop of

81.24   economy not only in her personal habits but also in

81.29   friends," who were generous.

82.11   door to her shop. The

82.26–   in the glass. "I'll
.27

82.23   room about tables

83.17   again began talking of

83.26–   me," he said gruffly.
.27

84.15   before the glass in

84.17   decided to go to

84.19   fear ran through

84.28   smoke. She noticed that his hand did not tremble.
He had

86.6–   to Edith's place and sat by a little table in the back
.8   room

86.21–   she was happy
.22

87.18   in ourselves. On

87.20–   we continually say
.21

89.11   McGregor, who had become foreman in the warehouse, had a conversation with the shipping clerk.
They stood

89.14   cattle have children," said

89.36   delight. He thought of himself as one inspired as he went eagerly here and there and saw more work being done, even while the length of the payroll was shortened.

89.38   want to become the father

90.8   or orderly intents. It

90.10   by this insect here. The

90.11–
.12   flies, their coming feeds

90.19   came. Here men live and think as they live and think in Coal Creek," he said aloud going again among the passages his mind resuming the planning of order in the place where he worked.

90.28   "it don't need

92.2   hearts of man lay

92.20   do their own part.

92.24   figure. And all over the city the little parts of the machine ran crazily.

95.7–
.8   common among laboring

96.26   he said jeeringly.

98.3   From the depot he

98.31–
.32   as he had done

99.1–
.2   woman might yet come

99.20   hole he had dug and with the pick and shovel again slung over his shoulder. McGregor strode

100.7   critically at woman than

101.11   and upon the box climbed

101.36   Arouse yourself. Join

101.37   You yourself can be the master

103.29–
.30   a tailor-made black suit. He

104.9–
.10   son and the minister.

105.11   behind other hills to

105.36   upon the log

106.31	he began trying to
108.13	began climbing the hill.
114.2	city. Poets have not sung of the corn. They are busy singing of themselves. Even the poets have forgotten that a tired out world expected a new song from America. In striving to realize the American dream of gain, of prosperity, the poets and the writers have forgotten that the great singer makes all men sing. They have forgotten all but the shrill cry for gain that
114.8	arose and found its voice in Twain, Crain [*sic*] and Norris.
114.16–.17	the band plays in the park. In
114.31	playing at a piano.
115.15	business at hand."
115.27–.28	The walker stands in the shadow of a building and sees a tall, red-haired man striding along in the silent street. He sees
115.30–.31	face turned up to the lamplight.
115.37	fancy his two sons
116.18–.19	wishes for something lovely to come
117.13–.16	felt that the talk he had once had with McGregor on the corner before the saloon had unmanned him. "A
120.4	country's great business men,
120.11	how he should get
121.31	head of a lion. His
122.11	attentive. There have been big figures in the world," he said loudly. Napoleon and Caesar, did they not move men about. In the corps there was a vast order. Men had one purpose. When they arose and went along roads and fields nothing could stop them.
122.18–.19	a new army, an army that had been organized not to fight but to live?
123.12	and great athletes
123.14	village; of the barber, talking of women on the bench in the park, and of the woman kneeling on the floor

in the little squalid room on Lake Street pleading and putting money into his hand.

125.14 railroads, half stupid with inactivity and wholly without color in this character because of the lack of any dash of purpose to their lives.

127.7   him. McGregor made

127.26 pocket, begins working

127.30– business," said the youth boastfully, looking
.31

132.2   and his pocketbook taken, had

132.6   disclosed. Men sitting in the street cars hurried past the vice tales on the front page of the paper, turning to the baseball news. Their wives read the startling stories and, dressing themselves carefully, went in the afternoon or evening to public meetings in the churches or clubs to be scolded at by other women and by earnest, stern-faced men, crying out for a clean city.

132.32 could see his daughter

132.34 with the flush

132.38 The little man whirled

133.24– of the opportunity for
.25

135.12 tested.

In Chicago in McGregor's time there were perhaps hundreds of men and women who had realized the disorder and ineffectiveness of modern life. Not all Americans believe in the blatant talk of taking our national greatness for granted or listen to the words poured into our ears

136.33– who had passed
.34

137.14 man.

Margaret Ormsby was of the type of modern womanhood to whom justice is not done by artists writing of women. The writers who have put her into books have, in their writing, retained something of the stupidity out of which she has come. A madness

has destroyed their clearness of vision. They have
their eyes upon another kind of woman. The woman
of whom they talk is the woman that has been defeated in the world-old game of womanhood.

137.29–   lined with tall warehouses McGregor went
.30

137.35–   the epigrammatic sentences with
.36

138.5   one of the modern

139.8   toward the office of her father. She

140.32   to the sweetheart of Andrew Brown.

141.5   arose the hoarse

141.22–   story of the girl
.23

141.23–   sold to a broker's son; of
.24

141.31   the woman.
           After the trial McGregor walked again in the
           streets of Chicago and on all sides of him

145.21–   am coming back home
.22

146.8   of her mind. "I want

147.13   desk sat a

148.28   father, striving to get

149.22   at the shoulder of Ormsby,

149.32   to the bantering of her father

149.38   of the face!

151.16   long parlor at

151.18–   from the house of
.19

152.11   girls, friends to Margaret, their

154.23–   his beauty. "He
.24

155.27   people and going heavily along. In

156.7   what bums are in

156.13–   and, as for our army, it
.14

156.25   plows he looked upon

160.6   face, at the luncheon where she

160.9   chosen. Instead she sat silent at the luncheon with her father and found herself strangely inattentive and uninterested in her work at the settlement house. The men and women who came to the house on Drexel Boulevard seemed, after McGregor, unspeakably futile and puerile.

Margaret had not expected McGregor to come to her again. In thinking it out she

160.23–   Margaret should have been brought forward
.24

160.32   being forced to give up

161.1   At Laura's reception

161.6   room when a fight

161.7   about shouting little

161.8   laughing, joyously, at nothing, felt

161.9   depressed. Like her on that other occasion he had in mind a picture. He was trying to imagine the black-haired boy, who racked balls in the pool room in Coal Creek, standing as he stood under the ten thousand dollar chandelier and having questions and remarks flung at him by gorgeously arrayed women.

161.11–   of Laura to have
.12

161.37   at Laura's reception

162.25–   it. Their power, he . . . admiration on the
.26

162.30–   When Laura, accompanied by her daughter, followed
.31

162.34–   She had an idea
.35

163.8   time has come for

164.2   thought it wasn't for me

164.10   stood silent and

165.1   house Laura had

165.23–   the great house on Drexel
.24

166.1   Carson was ten years

167.7–   by a cold bath of water across
   .8
167.19–   straight at the mark, he
   .20
167.28   you, and still I
167.36–   of that old misunderstood human sex love that colors
   .38   the life and the actions of all people everywhere.
169.1–   love to the other woman. Edith
   .2
169.5   For months he
169.9   evening a thing happened
170.7–   equally disordered speakers at the
   .8
170.9   so that he was near choking. The
170.24–   came the woman who
   .25
171.5   to the front of the shop
171.27–   expression has been going . . . as it has
   .28
171.35   up. During the day . . . had been filled
173.4–   visit to the Wisconsin town and
   .5
173.18   jump at the heart
174.4   believed had been reckoned out for her.
174.9   must have myself ready to hear
174.22   himself.
          McGregor stood beside David talking to his daugh-
          ter Margaret.
          "You
174.37   to Edith staring at her.
175.3   over everything and
175.9   she said.
175.11   The voice of McGregor became
175.23–   she said earnestly. "What
   .24
175.32–   daring." The hard look
   .33
176.16   plowmaker quietly.

179.17   world a ragged cynical
179.24–   that faces the lake
    .25
180.6   and stoop shoulders at
180.10   grin appeared
183.5   see?" he demanded. His
183.35   The young man from the newspaper—he had a slen-
           der, graceful body and wore his hat on the side of his
           head—became also excited. A
184.19   muttered, shaking himself loose from the hand that
           gripped his shoulder.
184.30   "This is what
184.34   of a workman.
185.4   "It is no
185.14   come to Chicago."
186.1   On an evening in the early spring on the year of the
           Marching Men, John
186.11–   he also wrote plays and stories. It
    .12
189.31–   men as me, with
    .32
190.22   shouted the captains.
191.3   with excitement. "It has come," he muttered. "The
           song of labor is here and it has found a voice." The
           face of the fat man, palled [sic] with terror, came
           back into his mind. On the sidewalk before a grocery
           store he stopped and shouting with delight began
           dancing wildly among a group of children who with
           fingers in their mouths stood with staring eyes watch-
           ing.
191.17   pallid with terror
193.28   McGregor and Ormsby walked in the gravelled paths
           to Jackson Park.
195.6   path, Ormsby by his side.
196.29   hope in it," he thought.
198.11   the surburbanites stands
198.32–   men make their own Gods and realized that
    .33

200.25   another "I accuse" from

200.28   For one moment something

201.4   court room he had said, "I leave you to cleanse your
          stables while I go to march with men in a new field.
          I leave you with your comfortable homes and your
          salaries and customers from the country with whom
          you get half-drunk and wander pop eyed through
          this sewer. I leave you sitting all day rejoicing and
          worrying over trivialities. When I come again I will
          come at the head of men marching and menacing."

201.15   the city.

          There is a story that McGregor began the move-
          ment of the Marching Men in a union of waiters and
          bartenders to which he belonged. I know nothing of
          that. In all the quiet months he went talking from
          hall to hall organizing, pleading, working, building
          up his organization—the marchers.

201.24   the Marching Men.

          And then appeared the guns, the wooden guns
          painted black. Men must have been whittling them
          out and painting them in a hundred thousand homes
          before they appeared on the shoulders of men march-
          ing in vacant lots and in little side streets all over the
          city.

202.24   a squad of them. The

202.25   evening with their guns. The

203.35   everyone had an

204.12   talk. Whitey Fauver said he could write a better
          speech than McGregor ever delivered. They

204.19   who had lived in

204.21   still went stumbling

205.17   had set in

206.1–   was only one bit
  .2

212.1–   in the people she
  .2

213.19   were sloughed off and

218.26   workers, roaring up

219.29   is terrible right
219.36   tried thus feeble to bring
220.11–   gardens, like McGregor, might
  .12
222.18   man out," David
225.6   soft look came

A SELECTED
BIBLIOGRAPHY

I. BOOKS BY SHERWOOD ANDERSON

Windy McPherson's Son. New York: John Lane Company, 1916; New York: B. W. Huebsch, 1922 (revised); Chicago: University of Chicago Press, 1965, Introduction by Wright Morris.

Marching Men. New York: John Lane Company, 1917; New York: B. W. Huebsch, [1921].

Mid-American Chants. New York: John Lane Company, 1918; New York: B. W. Huebsch, [1921].

Winesburg, Ohio. New York: B. W. Huebsch, 1919; New York: Viking Press, 1960, Introduction by Malcolm Cowley [with critical essays, edited by John Ferres, 1966].

Poor White. New York: B. W. Huebsch, 1920; New York: Viking Press, [1966], Introduction by Walter B. Rideout.

The Triumph of the Egg. New York: B. W. Huebsch, 1921.

Horses and Men. New York: B. W. Huebsch, 1923; New York: Peter Smith, [1933].

Many Marriages. New York: B. W. Huebsch, 1923; New York: Grosset and Dunlap, [1929].

A Story Teller's Story. New York: B. W. Huebsch, 1924; New York: Grove Press, [1958]; New York: Viking Press, [1969], Introduction by Walter B. Rideout.

Dark Laughter. New York: Boni and Liveright, 1925; New York: Liveright Publishing Corporation, [1960], Introduction by Howard Mumford Jones.

The Modern Writer. San Francisco: Lantern Press, 1925.

Sherwood Anderson's Notebook. New York: Boni and Liveright, 1926; Mamaroneck, N. Y.: Paul P. Appel, [1970].

Tar: A Midwest Childhood. New York: Boni and Liveright, 1926, [1931].

A New Testament. New York: Boni and Liveright, 1927.

Alice and the Lost Novel. London: Elkin Mathews and Marrot, 1929.

Hello Towns! New York: Horace Liveright, 1929; Mamaroneck, N. Y.: Paul P. Appel, [1970].

Nearer the Grass Roots. San Francisco: Westgate Press, 1929.

The American County Fair. New York: Random House, 1930.

Perhaps Women. New York: Horace Liveright, 1931; Mamaroneck, N. Y.: Paul P. Appel, [1970].

Beyond Desire. New York: Liveright, Inc., 1932; New York: Liveright Publishing Corporation, [1961], Introduction by Walter B. Rideout.

Death in the Woods. New York: Liveright, Inc., 1933.

No Swank. Philadelphia: Centaur Press, 1934; Mamaroneck, N. Y.: Paul P. Appel, [1970].

Puzzled America. New York: Charles Scribner's Sons, 1935. Mamaroneck, N. Y.: Paul P. Appel, [1970].

Kit Brandon. New York: Charles Scribner's Sons, 1936.

Plays, Winesburg and Others. New York: Charles Scribner's Sons, 1937.

Five Poems. San Mateo, Calif.: Quercus Press, 1939.

A Writer's Conception of Realism. Olivet, Mich.: Olivet College, 1939.

Home Town. New York: Alliance Book Corporation, 1940.

Sherwood Anderson's Memoirs. New York: Harcourt, Brace and Company, 1942.

The Sherwood Anderson Reader. Edited by Paul Rosenfeld. Boston: Houghton Mifflin Company, 1947.

The Portable Sherwood Anderson. Edited by Horace Gregory. New York: Viking Press, 1949.

Letters of Sherwood Anderson. Edited by Howard Mumford Jones and Walter B. Rideout. Boston: Little, Brown and Company, 1953; New York: Kraus Reprint Corporation, [1969].

Sherwood Anderson: Short Stories. Edited by Maxwell
Geismar. New York: Hill and Wang, 1962.

*Mid-American Chants, 6 Mid-American Chants by Sher-
wood Anderson/11 Midwest Photographs by Art Sinsa-
baugh.* Highlands, N. C.: Nantahala Foundation, 1964,
Introduction by Edward Dahlberg.

*Return to Winesburg: Selections from Four Years of Writ-
ing for a Country Newspaper.* Edited by Ray Lewis
White. Chapel Hill: University of North Carolina Press,
1967.

A Story Teller's Story: A Critical Text. Edited by Ray
Lewis White. Cleveland: Press of Case Western Reserve
University, 1968.

Sherwood Anderson's Memoirs: A Critical Edition. Edited
by Ray Lewis White. Chapel Hill: University of North
Carolina Press, 1969.

Tar: A Midwest Childhood, A Critical Text. Edited by
Ray Lewis White. Cleveland: Press of Case Western
Reserve University, 1969.

II. BOOKS ABOUT SHERWOOD ANDERSON

Anderson, David D. *Sherwood Anderson.* New York: Holt,
Rinehart and Winston, 1967.

Burbank, Rex. *Sherwood Anderson.* New York: Twayne
Publishers, 1964.

Chase, Cleveland B. *Sherwood Anderson.* New York: R. M.
McBride, 1927.

Fagin, Nathan Bryllion. *The Phenomenon of Sherwood
Anderson: A Study in American Life and Letters.* Balti-
more: Rossi-Bryn, 1927.

Howe, Irving. *Sherwood Anderson.* New York: William
Sloane, 1951; Stanford: Stanford University Press,
[1966].

The Newberry Library Bulletin, 2d Ser., No. 2 (December,
1948). The Sherwood Anderson Memorial Number.

La Revue des Lettres Modernes, Nos. 78–80 (1963). *Con-
figuration Critique de Sherwood Anderson.* Edited by
Roger Asselineau.

Schevill, James. *Sherwood Anderson: His Life and Work.* Denver: University of Denver Press, 1951.

Sheehy, Eugene P. and Kenneth A. Lohf. *Sherwood Anderson: A Bibliography.* Los Gatos, Calif.: Talisman Press, 1960; New York: Kraus Reprint Corporation, [1968].

Shenandoah, XIII (Spring, 1962). The Sherwood Anderson Number.

Story, XIX (September–October, 1941). The Sherwood Anderson Memorial Number.

Sutton, William A. *Exit to Elsinore.* Muncie, Ind.: Ball State University, 1967.

Weber, Brom. *Sherwood Anderson.* Minneapolis: University of Minnesota Press, 1964.

White, Ray Lewis, ed. *The Achievement of Sherwood Anderson: Essays in Criticism.* Chapel Hill: University of North Carolina Press, 1966.

———. *Checklist of Sherwood Anderson.* Columbus, Ohio: Charles E. Merrill, 1969.

III. Translation of *MARCHING MEN*

V Nogu! Leningrad: Mysl, 1927. Translated by Mark Volosov; foreword by V. Lavretski.

IV. Reviews of *MARCHING MEN*

Bookman, XLXI (November, 1917), 338—H. W. Boynton.

Dial, LXIII (September 27, 1917), 274–75—George B. Donlin.

Manuscripts Number Five, March, 1923, p. 3.

Nation, CV (October 11, 1917), 403.

New Republic, XII (September 29, 1917), 249–50—Francis Hackett.

New York Call, November 11, 1917, p. 14—J. N. Beffel.

New York Times Book Review, October 28, 1917, p. 442.

New York Tribune, October 27, 1917, p. 9.

Pittsburgh Monthly Bulletin, XXII (November, 1917), 748.

Publishers' Weekly, XCII (October 20, 1917), 1372—Doris Webb.

Smart Set, LIII (December, 1917), 143—H. L. Mencken.

This book was set in eleven-point Caledonia.
It was composed, printed, and bound by
Kingsport Press, Inc., Kingsport, Tennessee.
The paper is Warren's Olde Style,
manufactured by the S. D. Warren Company, Boston.
The design is by Edgar J. Frank.